DEADLY SECRET

O'HALLERAN SECURITY INTERNATIONAL, VOLUME 1

TJ LOGAN

DEADLY SECRET by TJ Logan

Published by TJL Creative Works LLC, 2019

tjloganauthor.com

First edition: August 21, 2019

Paperback ISBN: 9781095920169

Cover Art: Wicked Smart Designs

Editors: Hanna Rhys Barnes, Chris Kridler

I would like to dedicate Deadly Secret, my very first book, to the most important people in my life— my family.

First, to my sons, Softball Guy and Helo Boy, you two are proof that, at least twice, I got it right! I love you both infinitely and am so proud of you and the lives you are building. Molly and Jordan, I love you for bringing light and joy into my sons' lives— and for your patience in doing so. Theodore and Brenley, my absolutely perfect grandchildren. The love in my heart grew immeasurably the moment I looked into your eyes. I am so excited to see where your journeys will take you.

To my husband, Joel. You're my rock, my biggest fan, and my voice of reason. You truly believe I can do anything and you have this magical way of making me believe it, too. Your ability to get me to step outside my well-established comfort zone would be eerie if I didn't trust you so completely. In so many ways, Deadly Secret and all the other books in the O'Halleran Security International series never would've happened without you. I love you for loving me.

ACKNOWLEDGMENTS

I would like to acknowledge some very special people who have walked this amazingly rewarding, sometimes arduous, seven-year-long journey with me. There are many and I'm sure I will miss a few, for that, I apologize in advance.

A special thank you to Hanna Rhys Barnes, my editor, mentor, and friend. Hanna, had you not been so tough on me at the very beginning, I am certain my writing would've floundered and this book never would've seen the light of day. You taught me so much, nudged me when I needed it (literally), and you never ever gave up on me. You may have started as my Evil Editor, but you became my dear friend and my life is richer for having you in it.

To all my friends in the Evergreen RWA and Greater Seattle RWA, especially Carmen Cook, Holly Cortelyou, Samantha Saxon, and LE Wilson. You have all been so open and generous with your time, talents and knowledge. Your willingness to answer my bazillion questions helped make this book a reality. You all mean so much to me, and I am so grateful to have found you.

To my amazing Beta readers, Jennifer Farmer and Sally Kalarovich. Thank you for your willingness to slog through my many versions and for providing me with invaluable feedback. You guys rock!

PROLOGUE

In a dark room on the thirteenth floor of a nondescript federal building, FBI Special Agent Beckett O'Halleran stared into the soulless eyes of a monster. Nikolai Radoslav couldn't see through the two-way mirror, but he would know Beck was there.

Thanks to a complaint from Radoslav's attorney—some bullshit about "disrespectful treatment of his client by members of the task force"—Beck was stuck observing while his commander got to sit face to face with the psychopath. After what the sick son of a bitch did, he was lucky to be alive.

Black eyes peered out from beneath the Russian mob boss's thick, bushy white brows. A conspicuous road map of very fine red veins spread across his bulbous nose, an unsightly side effect of a life spent dumping rotgut vodka into his system. Too bad it hadn't killed him. He dipped his shoulder sideways for his attorney to whisper in his ear. He threw back his head, and his fat neck bobbled with laughter. His attention returned to the mirror, and a slow smile slithered across his bloated face.

The douchebag's defense attorney dug into his expensive, hand-stitched briefcase and pulled out a tin of mints then offered one to his client.

Beck's hands fisted at his sides, and he ground his molars until his jaw hurt.

Something was wrong with this picture. Radoslav was staring down the barrel of being charged with the murder of a federal agent. A capital offense, punishable by death. Yet, here they were, relaxed and shooting the shit like they were hanging out at a bar.

Commander Samuel Simmons walked in the door, dropped a folder on the table, unbuttoned his jacket, then sat across from the two men. A consummate professional, he gave away none of the repressed rage churning just beneath the surface. Beck knew it was there because he was feeling it too.

Beck reached over and flipped on the speaker.

Without saying a word, Sam opened the folder and, one by one, laid out a series of grisly crime scene photos, each one more horrific than the one before.

Sweat beaded across the lawyer's brow, and all the color —and arrogance—drained from his face. His throat bobbed up and down, and he quickly covered his mouth and nose with his handkerchief, as if he could actually smell the blood.

His client, on the other hand, looked bored as he sucked his teeth and looked at his perfectly manicured nails. The overhead fluorescents flashed off the blood-red ruby in his ring.

For the next forty-five minutes, jaw tight, muscles tensed, Beck watched and listened to Radoslav's lawyer do all the talking.

"No, the warehouse does not belong to my client."

"No, Mr. Radoslav was nowhere near the warehouse

where the body was found. He was having dinner with friends."

"No, my client has never seen that knife before."

"No, my client does not recognize the body in these photographs."

The "body" he so callously referred to was that of Jodi Andrews, a young agent on her first undercover assignment. She was part of the Organized Crime Task Force—until Radoslav kidnapped, raped and tortured her.

Beck reached for the doorknob, ready to charge into the interrogation room and beat the truth out of the Russian bastard, just as Sam's cellphone vibrated on the table.

"Simmons." He listened for a moment. His shoulders stiffened, and his spine visibly straightened as he looked across the table at Radoslav. "But sir, we ... Yes, sir."

Beck's boss stood. The chair screeched across the floor, and Sam shoved his phone in his breast pocket.

"Thank you for your time, Mr. Radoslav." He gathered the photos and slipped them back in the folder. "The agent on the other side of the door will show you out."

The Russian smirked.

What. The. Hell?

Radoslav stood, smoothed his silk tie and buttoned his three-thousand-dollar Armani jacket over his large belly. He smiled as he shook his scumbag lawyer's hand, then turned to Sam.

His commander glanced down at the extended hand, back up at Radoslav's smug grin. Then Sam turned and walked away without so much as a "kiss my ass."

Was that ... ?

Beck stepped close to the window, his nose almost touching the glass. Yeah, that was a twitch in the Russian's left eye. Seems the old man wasn't used to getting the brush-off and didn't like it much.

He hung back long enough to ensure Radoslav and his lawyer had left the building before he charged into his boss's office.

"What the hell was that?" Beck pointed his thumb over his shoulder toward the interrogation room.

Sam stood, and his shoes scuffed across the old carpet as he crossed his office to shut the door.

"Have a seat, O'Halleran." He pointed to a chair in front of his desk.

"Have a seat? You have got to be fucking kidding me." Beck jammed his hands on his hips, exposing the gold shield and weapon clipped on either side of his waist.

"Fine, stay standing. I can do this either way." The old chair Sam had been using since he started with the bureau creaked when he dropped into it with a heavy sigh. The only personal item in the cramped space, an outdated picture of his wife and two daughters, sat hidden behind a stack of files teetering on the corner of his gray, government-issued desk.

"Why'd you cut him loose?" Beck was confident they'd nailed the old psychopath this time.

"The call I got was from someone providing an alibi for Radoslav." His boss's jaw jumped, and his eyes blazed with anger. "Said they were at dinner together during the time of death."

"Let me guess ... " Beck hesitated. "Barlow?"

Simmons gave one quick nod.

"Come on, Sam." He threw his hands up in frustration. "We both know that's bullshit."

"Maybe." Resignation settled into Sam's shoulders. He yanked off his reading glasses and tossed them on the desk. "But I was given a direct order to cut him loose."

Beck shook his head, then stared at the hand-carved bureau emblem mounted on the wall behind his boss, a gift from his team when he hit his twenty-year mark. It pissed him off that the deputy director was dirty. Even the rank and file within the bureau—the men and women in the field doing the real work—knew he was, but proving it was the challenge. The guy was Teflon.

"Looks like I need to add the deputy director to my investigation." Beck scrubbed his hand down the scruff on his face, started pacing back and forth.

"You know how this works, O'Halleran. You're out."

Beck stopped midstep and turned to his boss ... his friend.

Sam's hand went up to cut off any protest. He leaned forward, his elbows on his desk. The dark circles under his eyes suddenly made him look twenty years older. Shit like this did that to you.

"You're too close to this thing—you've lost your objectivity—not to mention you're burned out. I'm moving you to another case." Sam pointed at Beck. "And I'm ordering you to stay clear of Radoslav and especially Barlow."

"I have been tracking this deranged piece of shit for three years. *Three years*, Sam. And Jodi was *my* responsibility." Beck shook his head, his voice steady, resolute. "No, you can't pull me off this now. Radoslav is mine."

"That's where you're wrong. As of right now"—Simmons rose from behind his desk and got in Beck's face— "you are off this task force. If I find out you've disobeyed my order, I will yank your shield, your creds, and your weapon, *before* I notify the Office of Professional Responsibility. Are we understood, Special Agent O'Halleran?"

Beck didn't flinch at the stern edge in his old friend's voice. He knew it came from a place of concern. And being reported to the OPR no longer mattered to him. His course had been set the minute he'd found Jodi lying dead in that filthy warehouse.

He pulled his creds from his pocket, unclipped his shield and gun from his belt, then leaned over and carefully placed them in the middle of the cluttered desk.

"No need, Sam. I'm done."

CHAPTER ONE

Gwen Tamberley stood on the top step and stared up at the old building. Feelings of sorrow and loneliness wrestled with her excitement. She tried not to feel intimidated by the task ahead. Easier said than done.

She turned, scanned the length of the street and sighed. There were a lot of risks involved in her plan. After all, most people had given up on this part of San Francisco. Considered it nothing more than a stain on an otherwise pristine city.

"Maggie's Embrace" would be a community center and shelter named in honor of her mother. It would serve the homeless as well as the good, honest, hardworking families who had lived here for multiple generations. People just trying to eke out a life in the neighborhood they loved. You could see signs of optimism everywhere. In the flowers and plants growing from window boxes here and there. In the shop owners committing their hearts and souls to their businesses.

You could hear it in the sounds of children laughing as they played jump rope or wrote with chalk on the sidewalk. You could feel it in the two old neighbor ladies leaning out and talking to each other from their front windows, their hands flying as they told their stories. In so many other ways, this area proved it was worth saving.

The center would offer a reprieve from the drug dealers, prostitutes and pimps brazenly conducting business on every corner.

"This is for you, Momma," she whispered as she admired the boundless hopefulness, "and them."

Six months, two days, nineteen hours and—she glanced at her watch—twenty-seven minutes. That's how long it had been since her mother died in her arms. The result of a still unsolved hit-and-run. The shelter was Gwen's way of helping others improve their lives and to give them something her mother never seemed to have—a sense of safety.

She took a deep breath and released it, casting off the lingering guilt and melancholy that tried to sabotage her happiness.

Chin high, she hiked her tote onto her shoulder and turned to the front door of the dilapidated corner building. She jiggled the key in the beat-up lock and, using her shoulder, like a pint-size offensive lineman, managed to partially shove open one of the large wooden doors. She picked up the broom and bucket of cleaning supplies and squeezed through the narrow opening into what would become the fulfillment of a dream.

She set down the supplies, flipped on the overhead light and pulled out her legal pad. *Call locksmith* and *Repair door* were added to her growing list of things to do. She'd been inside the building several times, but standing here now, holding the keys, it felt different—more real.

The dream was real, all right ... and it reeked. The stench of backed-up plumbing, rotting garbage, and years-worth of plain old neglect wrinkled her nose. She shivered when she saw all the cobwebs—*lots* of them. She desperately tried to convince herself those webs were absolutely uninhabited. Anything else was unacceptable and would have to be dealt with immediately.

Glad she'd worn her work boots, she shoved aside a pile of garbage with her foot and headed down the long hallway. At the far end, sunlight spilled through the doorway of the bright, airy kitchen. Gwen could imagine the family who must've lived here in the past. She was proud to play a part in filling this old place with life again.

Over the sink was a large window. She stood on her tippy-toes to peek through the grime at a small, fenced-in backyard. "*Yard cleanup*" was added to her list of things to do. Maybe she could pay a couple of the kids from the neighborhood to help.

Across the hall, she stepped into a room she hoped would be big enough for her double bed and dresser. There were larger spaces within the building, but this one adjoined her office. Someone had even left behind a massive oak desk. She was pretty sure the only reason it hadn't been taken was because it was too darn big to move. A little TLC and some wood cleaner, and it would be as good as new.

In addition to the beautiful crown molding and built-in bookcases, one of her favorite features of the room was the generous brick-faced fireplace with a large stone mantle. Stepping over and around garbage, she tentatively approached it. As she got closer, a strange scratching sound stopped her dead in her tracks. She gulped as she strained to hear. The noise would seem to indicate there was at least one family of birds or—heaven forbid—some other less friendly creature currently in residence. She cursed her vivid imagination as a shudder ran through her.

Thinking about doing battle with spiders already had her on edge; add this latest unseen foe, and she had to fight the urge to run screaming from the room. Introducing herself to her new neighbors by running into the street like a crazy woman was probably not such a great idea.

"You're being ridiculous, Gwen. It's just a cute little bird." As if saying it out loud would make it so. Without taking her eyes off the fireplace—convinced the creature currently living there was just waiting to sneak up on her—she backed away.

Her heel caught in a tear in the carpet.

She shrieked, and her arms cartwheeled through the air.

As if in slow motion, her notepad and pen went airborne and her big bag slipped from her shoulder and fell to the floor just before she landed in a less than delicate heap on her butt.

The dust settled. She did a mental inventory of her body. Other than bruising her pride, she'd escaped injury, thanks to a ratty old cushion.

Gwen reached for her scattered belongings just as a very large, very hairy spider crawled across her wallet before disappearing into the floor vent. She let loose another scream as she scooped up her stuff and ran behind the desk. Because, you know, the spider would never think to look for her there. She rolled her eyes and shook her head at her silliness, then hastily added "*HIRE CHIMNEY SWEEP & EXTERMINATOR*" to the *top* of her list.

Her head tilted at the sound of someone struggling to open the front door. *Shoot!* Her hands had been full and she'd forgotten to lock it. She peeked around the doorjamb and saw Joseph Chadwick standing just inside. He looked around the large foyer, disgust obvious on his face. Dread raised goosebumps across her arms. The urge to flee out the back door was powerful.

Those feelings snuck up on her sometimes, the result of her unorthodox childhood. She'd been raised by a mother who spoke to no one and expected the same of her daughter. A mother who kept them isolated, practically living off the grid. Heck, Gwen had even been homeschooled, when all she'd ever wanted was to be around other kids. Often, she'd felt cheated, had wanted to rebel. The desperation and fear that lived in her mother's eyes had always stopped her. Gwen was left with an ingrained inability to trust, especially a guy like Chadwick.

He represented the large faceless corporation who owned the building before her. As the sale progressed, he'd begun showing up at fundraisers she attended. She hadn't paid him much attention until he began standing unnervingly close, giving the impression they were together. Using any excuse to touch her, a lot. Taking advantage of the fact she wouldn't dare make a scene in front of so many potential investors.

Repeatedly deflecting his efforts and tactfully letting him know she wasn't even interested in a platonic friendship had become exhausting. She'd stopped attending fundraisers weeks ago ... and it really ticked her off. She needed to be out there, raising money. Hiding herself away to avoid an egocentric lothario was reminiscent of her mother's behavior. Gwen vowed she would not live her life that way ever again.

Still, he was the last person she wanted to see today ... or any other day.

"Okay, you're being ridiculous." She mumbled and focused on calming her nerves. "He's just here to make sure I didn't have any issues getting into the building. That's all."

Just in case she was wrong, she hustled to stand behind the big desk. Crazy as it sounded, the old, solidly built piece of furniture made her feel safer, less exposed.

He muttered derogatory remarks as he passed piles of garbage and debris. Stuck-up jerk didn't realize sound carried down the hall like a funnel.

Her shoulders stiffened, and she felt indignation on behalf of the old building.

Chadwick stepped into the room and looked around. In the past, every time she saw him, he looked like he spent a great deal of time on his appearance. Clean-shaven, never a hair out of place. With his high-priced tailored suits and shirts with engraved cufflinks, he exuded wealth. She was pretty sure she could run the shelter for a month with the money he paid for the expensive Italian shoes on his feet. The man was downright obsessive in his fastidiousness.

As he approached the desk, he looked mussy and wrinkled, like he'd slept in his clothes. The bead of sweat running down his temple was out of place, considering it was a typical cool San Francisco day. Strangely restless, he frantically wrung his hands together. His eyes continually darted around the room, never stopping to focus on any one thing.

Gwen had seen this type of behavior many times in her job as a social worker. She'd never noticed anything before to indicate he might have a drug problem. Which, of course, meant nothing. People got really good at hiding things when they were high, and their behavior could radically change in the blink of an eye.

That happy thought now cluttering her brain, the idea of having a giant wooden barrier between them no longer seemed quite so crazy, especially when he stopped directly in front of her, leaned down and put his hands in the middle of the desk. He was close enough she could smell alcohol on his breath. Troubling, considering it was barely 11 a.m. His pungent cologne mixed with his strong body odor was enough to gag her, and she stuck a surreptitious finger under her nose to diffuse the odor.

Tension radiated from him.

As if the lecherous smirk on his face wasn't creepy enough, his eyes slowly wandered to her chest and lingered. Unwilling to give him the satisfaction of seeing her discomfort, she resisted the urge to squirm or to shift the tote on her shoulder to cover herself.

As his eyes slowly drifted to her face, he said, "Hey there,

Gwen-do-lyn? You're looking awful"—his tongue dragged across his bottom lip— "tasty today."

Seriously? *Ew*. This went beyond the not-so-subtle passes he usually tried on her. And the way he'd said her name was new ... and disturbing ... and super annoying.

Stubborn pride wouldn't allow her to cower. Disregarding his crude comment, she forced herself to look directly at him and noticed his dilated pupils and runny nose. These indicators, combined with his general fidgetiness, gave her cause for concern. Experience and training taught her the important thing was not to agitate him but to keep him calm.

She plastered on her most believable smile.

"Good afternoon, Mr. Chadwick. This is certainly a surprise." Not a pleasant one, either. "What can I do for you today?"

"Always so formal." He pulled a handkerchief from his breast pocket, scrubbed it under his nose, then jammed it back in his jacket. "Don't you think it's about time we move on to something more ... personal? I'm bored by this little game of yours."

Gwen had dealt with clients in this condition many times, even a few who mistook her professional concern for personal interest. She'd always been able to transfer them to another social worker. With him, that wasn't an option.

Shoulders back, jaw set, she moved around the desk, stopping just out of his reach.

Determined to be as honest with him as possible, she said, "Joseph, I appreciate all you did during the sale of the building, but I'm just not interested in—"

He lunged at her, jerked her into his body and trapped her arms against her sides. Lifting her off her feet, he shoved her against the desk hard, and pain shot across the backs of her thighs. She thrashed and fought. Old rags and newspapers scattered everywhere. An abandoned, half-empty bottle of soda tipped over and poured onto the floor. Her resistance seemed to encourage him. He managed to clamp one hand around her wrists and held them behind her back. With his free hand, he grabbed her jaw in a punishing grip to hold her head still and slammed his mouth over hers. She whimpered and attempted to pull against his hold. Her lips pressed tightly together against the assault of his tongue.

Gwen kicked and twisted until he lost his balance, giving her an opening to push him away and break free. He fell backward and tripped over the same cushion she'd tumbled over earlier, then crashed to the floor.

Gasping for breath, chest heaving, she used the back of her hand to wipe her mouth, leaving a trace of blood from where her tooth cut the inside of her lip. No longer worried about losing any supposed donors he could bring to the shelter, she looked him straight in the eye and said, "You're wasted out of your mind, Chadwick. I want you out. Now. You are no longer welcome here."

"Yeah, right. Kick me out?" he scoffed. "You need me, you pathetic twit." He laughed as he stood, wiped his forearm across his face, then brushed off the butt of his pants. "You really should think about what you're doing, Gwen-do-lyn." He snapped the front of his jacket to straighten it and speared his fingers through his hair to slick it back into place.

When she didn't back down, his condescending laughter suddenly stopped. His temper exploded, sent spittle flying. "I know all sorts of people, and with one phone call, ONE"—he held up his index finger—"I can destroy you and this pathetic little shelter of yours!"

He reminded her of a spoiled, petulant child who didn't get what he wanted for Christmas.

Gwen wasn't foolish enough to turn her back on him as she moved to put the desk between them. She felt around in her bag for her phone, grabbed it and dialed 9-1-1. Her finger hovering over the "call" button, she stiffened her spine and looked directly at him.

"Get. Out. Now. Or I *will* call the police."

His entire body tight, he took a menacing step forward.

She stood her ground.

The twitch in his eye made her nervous enough to lay her hand over a broken piece of glass on the desk.

Chadwick clenched his jaw, opening and closing his fists several times, then rolled his neck and ran his hand down his tie. With a sneer, he turned and stomped out of her office.

Gwen didn't move. She waited. Listened. Waited some more. Hearing nothing but the blood pounding in her ears, she rushed to shut the doors and flipped the old locks into place. She turned, and her head fell back against the door with a *thunk*. The sturdy surface of the wood supported her until her knees gave way and, like a lifeless rag doll, she melted to the floor. The old, rough wood barely registered as it scraped along the backs of her bare arms. Her insides felt like they would shatter into a million pieces. She hugged her knees to her chest, closed her eyes and waited for the adrenaline rush to subside.

After a few minutes, she opened her eyes, took a deep breath and let it out, then picked herself up off the floor. There was too much work to be done, and she didn't have the luxury of sitting around, feeling sorry for herself.

CHAPTER TWO

Beck stood in the walk-in closet of his guest room staring at the large gun safe he'd bought for himself the day he closed on this house. His favorite pistol, the Glock 21 .45, was already comfortably clipped to his belt. He spun the dial, turned the lever and swung open the four-inch-thick steel door. His eyes scanned over the Mossberg shotgun and the AR-15 rifle and landed on the Walther PPQ 9 mil. He picked it up. "Hello, old friend."

He grabbed the loaded magazines for the Glock, empty ones for the PPQ, and a couple of boxes of ammunition. The door swung shut, he dropped the lever, and the one-inch diameter steel deadbolts slipped into place with a muffled *clank*.

With a bounce, the ammo, mags and Walther landed on the bed next to his duffle. Like he'd been doing since the first time his dad showed him how in the big field behind their house, he slipped his gun from his holster, popped out the magazine to ensure it was fully loaded and that there was a round in the chamber. The butt of his hand slammed the magazine back in place, and he tucked it into its custom-fit

Kydex holster. The 9mm was next. Beck pulled back the slide, ensured the chamber was clear. He released the slide —*ca-chunk*. The powerful spring slammed it back into place. After zipping it into a gun pouch, he stowed it under the rest of his gear with the extra ammunition. He hefted it over his shoulder, headed to the kitchen and set it on the floor next to the back door.

Beck leaned against the counter, mentally going over his next move as he scarfed down a sandwich and chugged a bottle of water. He yanked the full garbage bag from under the sink, then swung his duffle onto his shoulder. After a last look around the kitchen, he punched in the alarm code, shut the door and waited for the beep and the digital voice to confirm, "System armed."

He chucked the garbage in the can out front, then loaded his gear into the back of his SUV and slid his six-foot-four frame behind the wheel.

Beck checked his watch. Radoslav would be settling in for the night.

The hour it took to get to Little Russia gave him too much time to think of all the things that could go wrong with this plan. Good thing he had several backups.

He pulled into a spot a couple of blocks away from the Mt. Elbrus Restaurant. Last thing he needed was to be seen anywhere near the old man's favorite hangout.

At the back of the SUV, he popped the hatch. Inside his go bag was the box of *toys* one of his brother had sent him. Real cutting-edge stuff, the little listening devices hadn't even hit the market yet. Not only were they critical to his surveillance, but it was an excellent way to test them in a real-world scenario.

He zipped the box into the pocket of his dark jacket, lowered the SUV door and pressed it shut with a quiet *click*. Boots silent, he made his way down the dark alley, ducked into the shadows concealing the back door of the restaurant and listened. A quick scan of the area confirmed he was alone, and he pulled out his lock picks. Lucky for him, there were no cameras or alarms to hassle with. His earlier surveillance had uncovered a surprising lack of security in the old place. No one would be fool enough to break in to a place as mobbed up as this one. Or so they thought. It took very little effort to unlock the back door.

A last look around, and he let himself in.

The restaurant was quiet. The only sounds were the low *hum* from the industrial refrigerator and the *ca-clunk-ca-clunk* of ice dropping into the bin of a large icemaker.

Steps silent on the old linoleum, Beck got to the main room and looked around. Placement was critical in order to gain the full benefit of his brother's gadgets. The front of the room was cast in a muted gold glow from the streetlight shining through two large windows.

Shit. Anyone walking by would see him moving around inside.

Belly-crawl was the only way to get to the hostess's podium without being seen. He dropped to the floor. *Here goes nothin'*. After maneuvering around tables and chairs, he reached up and stuck one to the underside of the second shelf.

He crawled back and wedged one on the underside of Radoslav's favorite table. The third would go in the men's room. Back in the darkness of the hallway, he stepped into the cramped space and scanned his options. A cheap utility sink had been shoved against one wall. He managed to slip one of the devices behind it.

Beck flipped off the light and, just as he was leaving the bathroom, heard muffled Russian and keys rattling in the front door, then bells jangled. *Shit.* He quietly pushed the door shut. Other than the sink, there was only one stall and a urinal. Moonlight eked through a dirty window high up. *No help there.* His shoulders would never squeeze through the narrow opening. He ducked into the stall and locked the door, lowered the flimsy lid on the john and stepped up onto it. He really hoped he didn't have to knock this guy out, but he couldn't afford to get caught.

He strained to hear what the man was saying. The voice became louder the closer it got. Sounded like the owner. He was on the phone with someone.

If Beck's Russian wasn't failing him, the guy was getting his ass chewed for not bringing home a roast for dinner. Apparently, the dumbass was halfway home when his wife called to remind him. He was pissed about having to come all the way back.

The latch clanked open on the large fridge, and a hinge squealed. A minute later, the big door slammed shut with a *thud.* Fading footsteps accompanied a few choice words muttered in Russian. Bells *jangled.* Once when the door opened, again when it closed. The keys rattled in the lock, then silence.

Beck waited ten full minutes before stepping down off the john. He left the stall and slowly cracked open the door. Hearing nothing, he pulled it open, turned right and walked toward the back door.

He reached up, slipped the cover off the exit sign above the door and stuck the last device in the frame. The old man liked to sneak in the back sometimes. The cover back in place, he walked out the door and relocked the deadbolt.

Only thing left to do now was wait.

He made it to his car without any trouble, climbed in and tossed the empty box onto the passenger seat. The low rumble of the big V8 engine joined the sounds of a dog barking in the distance, an argument trailing down from an apartment high above. Beck started toward his next destination, an auto-repair shop about ten minutes away. Radoslav's limo had mysteriously ended up with a couple of flat tires. In less than an hour, the final device hidden inside the dome light, Beck was headed to his final destination for the night.

Headlights off, he turned onto a street lined with very large, very pricey homes. Radoslav's was nestled among them. An animal surrounded by humans.

Beck parked down the block, shut off the engine and lowered his window. He pinched a rock into the sling of his old wrist rocket, pulled back and let it fly. *Bull's-eye.* The streetlight shattered, and small pieces of glass sprinkled to the ground.

There was only one way in or out of the estate, and Beck now had eyes on it. He hunkered down in his seat and settled in for the long, hopefully boring night ahead of him.

CHAPTER THREE

Two months had passed since Beck found Jodi's body. A month later, he'd walked away from the task force. His entire focus had been on Radoslav since. For the past few weeks, he'd shadowed his every move and, thanks to a few well-placed bugs, listened in on a significant number of the man's conversations.

Determined to bring Radoslav down on his own—unwilling to drag anyone into this battle—he'd cut himself off from everyone, especially his family. But his investigation had reached a point where he had no choice but to call in help, and the only people he trusted were his family.

Crouched down in the front seat of his rig, he watched the front of the restaurant. Radoslav was feeding his face, so Beck decided to take advantage of the lull in conversation. He yanked out the earpiece, grabbed his phone from the cupholder and hit the speed dial for his brother Caleb, who was on the tail end of recovering from a serious injury. Not quite two years younger, he knew Beck better than anyone. His brother might not like it, but he would understand Beck's need to finish this himself, even if it meant working outside the system.

He would've called another brother, Jonathan, a Navy SEAL, but he was on an assignment with his team to an undisclosed location, for an undisclosed purpose, for an undisclosed length of time. In other words—no one knew a damn thing.

The phone rang once before Caleb answered, "What's up, brother man? Enjoying your time off?"

Sometimes his brother's laid-back cheerfulness annoyed the shit out of Beck. Now, he welcomed the momentary reprieve it offered from the hollowness he'd been feeling.

He got straight to the point. "I'm outside Radoslav's favorite place, the Mt. Elbrus Restaurant. You know the one —in the middle of Little Russia?"

"Shit." Caleb grumbled. "Thought you were told to stay away from Radoslav. If you screw this up and get in the way of the *real* investigation, you *do* know it could end your career with the bureau, right? Or worse, get you killed."

"I'm done with the bureau." His response was simple and direct. "This is where I have to be. It ends with me—one way or another."

"Come on, man. I'm your brother—I know you. You've wanted to be an agent for as long as I can remember."

"Not anymore." He was done with the red tape, bureaucracy and corruption at the top.

"Beck, I was there when the internal review board determined Jodi got caught in the wrong place at the wrong time. She never had a chance to give anyone a heads-up."

His brother had said the same thing the last time they'd seen each other—immediately after the board announced their findings.

"In conclusion, it is the finding of this board that Special Agent

Beckett O'Halleran is hereby cleared of any and all responsibility in the death of Agent Jodi Andrews." The speaker then looked up from his report, peered over the top of his glasses. *"This board would like to thank you for your cooperation in this investigation, Special Agent O'Halleran. You're free to go."*

"Mom and Dad are worried about you. You haven't been in touch with them since Jodi's funeral."

His gut twisted hearing about their parents. He couldn't think about how he was hurting them right now, nor did he need his brother reminding him of the review board—even if he was trying to help.

"The only reason I'm pulling you into this is because I can't be in two places at once and I trust you. I know you're on medical leave, but what are the chances you can help me out on this?"

Caleb sighed. "Where and when do you need me?"

Beck closed his eyes. His shoulders relaxed. For the first time in weeks, he felt like he might finally find his way back to some kind of normal. "I know it's short notice, but can you get here in the next day or two? If it's a problem—"

"Say no more. I'm on my way."

"Thanks, man." Beck didn't even try to hide his relief. "I owe you one."

"You would do the same for anyone else in the family. Oh, hey, how are my little toys working out for you?"

"They're all working well. Not one glitch." Caleb's gadgets were invaluable. Keeping track of Radoslav would've been impossible without them.

"Good, glad to hear it," Caleb said. "Take it easy and watch your back. And Beck ... think about giving mom and dad a call, will ya? I'll see you soon, bro." He hung up before Beck could respond.

Beck wedged his phone into his pocket. Thought about

his parents, thankful to have a family he could always count on—especially during times like this—when he really didn't deserve them.

CHAPTER FOUR

Joseph Chadwick was still fuming as he sat in a booth at the back of the Mt. Elbrus Restaurant. He stifled a cough, and his eyes watered from the heavy smoke hanging in the air. It pissed him off knowing his favorite Bruno Cucinelli suit was going to stink when he left here. *Damned Russians and their obsession with cigarettes.*

Gwendolyn Tamberley acted like she was too good for him. *What a joke.* He was the one with all the power. All it would take is one well-placed rumor of mismanagement of funds, and he could bring an end to her stupid little shelter. There was a time he'd found her constant rebuffs to be a turn-on—the thrill of the chase and all—but it had become tiresome. He would make her regret turning him down, would make her life a living hell. It was the only reason he was sitting in a smoke-filled restaurant across from Nikolai Radoslav, a man who scared the hell out of him.

He'd started working with the Russian a few years ago, handling the sale of several of his commercial real estate holdings. Since then, he'd branched out and become a sales agent for a different kind of property—high-grade cocaine, still the drug of choice among his circle of wealthy friends, as well as some high-end clients. Due to their rising popularity, he'd also begun dealing in Rohypnol and oxycodone as well. Radoslav supplied the drugs and, for a percentage of the profits, Joseph supplied the customers and transported the merchandise.

Decent money was coming to him from the drugs side of the business, but the real money started rolling in when he began introducing women to Radoslov. The old perv had a specific appetite for a particular "type" of female, and Joseph did his best to locate one when requested. He knew better than to ask for details—total deniability and all that crap. Kept him above the sordid ugliness of it all.

It had been a sweet deal, right up until he'd started sampling the merchandise. The drugs, not the women. Only a fool would mess with a woman intended for Nikolai Radoslav. Before long, Joseph was enjoying the product a bit too much and suddenly found himself in the hole for two hundred grand. A guaranteed one-way trip to the bottom of the bay. Not because the Russian gave a shit about the money, a pittance to a man like him. It was about sending a clear message to anyone else who might think they could steal from him.

Joseph had requested this meeting with the old man under the guise of talking about some choice commercial real estate. In reality, he hoped to kill two birds with one stone. He could settle his debt to Radoslav and get payback against little Miss High-and-Mighty at the same time.

He choked down a spoonful of the putrid ukha he'd ordered. *How the hell was I supposed to know it was cold fish soup?* He'd been disinclined to ask someone to interpret the Russian menu. He rinsed his mouth with a swallow of water. "Like I said, there is a prop—"

Radoslav lifted his hand. "We both know even you are not dumb enough to ask for meeting—during my lunchtime—

with something this unimportant. Get to point of why you are *really* here before you ruin my meal."

Word on the street was Radoslav immigrated from Russia years ago, a cocky, street-smart teenager. In all that time, he'd made no effort to shake his intimidating, gutter-rat accent. No doubt, he enjoyed the reaction it garnered from people. Like the cold finger of death sliding down your spine.

Joseph glanced around, lowered his voice. "Nikolai, I've got a very high quality, sweet piece of merchandise I think you'll love. Someone I think you'll find irresistible and who could bring you a great deal of pleasure."

Joseph took another swig of water, hoped no one noticed how his hand shook. "If for some reason she doesn't interest you ... " He swallowed and wiped his mouth unnecessarily. "I'm sure you'll have at least one buyer who would be happy to take her off your hands."

Radoslav's bulky body leaned over his borscht soup. His eyes never left his bowl as he spoke. "*You* are to call me Mr. Radoslav." *Slurp.* "Do not presume to be so familiar. We are not friends, Chadwick." *Slurp.* "You would be smart to remember this. Da?"

Joseph gulped loudly enough he was sure everyone nearby could hear. "Um, okay, sorry, Mr. Radoslav." He hated kowtowing to anyone, but this man was an evil narcissist who would accept nothing less.

Desperation could lead a man to do things others would find unimaginable. Offering Gwen up for sale to a man like Nikolai Radoslav for his sick sexual games ranked right at the top of the list. Yet Joseph didn't give it a second thought. He was in deep preservation mode and had a deal to make. More importantly, he had a score to settle. The little bitch would learn soon enough she'd made a big mistake when she rejected him.

Anxious to get the hell away from here, he looked around

the restaurant again, then leaned closer to Radoslav and whispered, "As I was saying, I know of a fine young lady you'd have some real fun with. If not, I'm sure you could get a premium for her."

Time to play his hand. He took a deep breath and wiped the sweat from his upper lip. "Here's the deal—I'm willing to point her in your direction in exchange for clearing all my debt to you."

Radoslav didn't respond, just kept eating as if he hadn't spoken.

Joseph nervously cleared his throat. "She has a very unique look about her and could pass for a teenager. From the way she acts, I'd bet good money she's still a virgin. I'm guessing that's worth a little something extra to you, right?"

Whether it was true or not, he had no idea, but it might help sweeten the pot if Radoslav thought she was.

He fidgeted, waited for something, anything, from the old man. Joseph rushed to fill the silence. "She's this frigid do-gooder setting up a homeless shelter in one of your most productive neighborhoods. I think she could be a refreshing challenge. I'm confident I can convince her to meet with you. I'll just make up something about you being interested in becoming a long-term donor to the shelter." There was no hiding his loathing as he said, "It's the only damn thing she cares about, so I'm sure she'll take the bait. You can check her out, see I'm not exaggerating when I say she is a fine piece of ass."

For the longest time, the Russian seemed to ignore him. Just sat there—a big, doughy lump, slurping his foul soup.

Joseph gnawed the inside of his cheek. His knee bobbed up and down under the table. He tried to ignore the bead of sweat trickling down his back under his tailored dress shirt.

He'd just about given up on getting a response when Radoslav grumbled, "She will come here tonight at seven o'clock. *If* I like what I see, I will make arrangements to have her picked up, and your debt, it will be cleared." For the first time, he turned and looked at Joseph. "Hear me well, Chadwick. If I do *not* like what I am seeing, I will collect my payment from you in my own way. Do you understand what I am telling to you?"

Joseph's blood froze as the man's black eyes seemed to pierce his skin. Mouth suddenly dry, all he could manage was a nod of his head. He reached into his jacket pocket, grabbed his pen and a business card. After writing Gwen's name on the back, he slid it across the table.

"Now go away. You have already ruined my meal." Radoslav dismissed him with a flick of his wrist, then turned back to his soup.

Joseph said nothing at being shooed away like an annoying fly. Just wiped his mouth and sweaty palms on his napkin, set it on the table and slithered out of the booth. He pulled his phone from his pocket as he wound his way around tables and out the door. Once outside, he dialed Gwen's number.

THANKS TO YOUTUBE and a tight budget, Gwen had completed a lot more on her own than she thought possible, and for that she was pretty darn proud. It was finally time to call in a professional. As excited as she was to move to the next phase, she was a bit sad, too. Every paint color selected and bag of garbage she'd manhandled to the container in the alley, each broken nail and ache she'd tried to soothe in a hot bath, left her feeling a special connection to the old place. Silly as it might sound, she wasn't sure she was ready to share it with a stranger just yet.

She'd enjoyed moments of pure joy and had been so busy, whole lengths of time passed without thoughts of her mother intruding on her happiness. Even if she'd known the ache in her back and neck would become a constant, that she'd forget what her hair looked like without paint in it, or that she would fall into bed each night unbelievably exhausted from all the strenuous work ... she still would have done it herself.

Her phone rang in her pocket, and her euphoria burst like a bubble when Chadwick's name appeared on the screen. *Shoot.* After what happened, she'd meant to block his number, then she'd gotten busy and completely forgot.

What could he possibly want?

She waged an internal debate about whether to answer or not. He was on the phone and couldn't hurt her, and she was curious about the reason for his call.

Gwen tapped the screen.

"Gwendolyn Tamberley." She kept her voice professional, aloof.

"Gwendolyn, it's Joseph, Joseph Chadwick. I'm calling to apologize for what happened earlier." He cleared his throat before continuing, "Just before coming to see you, I found out a big deal I'd been working on for months had fallen through. Like an idiot, I tried to drown my disappointment in a few too many ill-timed martinis."

Gwen rolled her eyes. There had been more than alcohol responsible for his behavior.

"It's no excuse for what I did, but ... " he stammered, "I'm hoping you will at least *try* to forgive me."

Not being able to see his eyes made it difficult for Gwen to gauge his sincerity. Knowing him, she doubted his apology was genuine.

"I'd like to try to make it up to you." He sounded desperate enough, but she just couldn't be sure.

She remained silent, waited for him to continue. After all, he'd called her.

"There's this wealthy businessman I'm working with who

is looking for a charitable cause he can make a sizable donation to." He sniffled. "I'm guessing it's for tax purposes. Anyway," another sniffle, "of course I told him about the great things you hope to accomplish there, and he's interested in meeting with you to hear more. There are no strings attached, Gwen. Honestly." He had to suspect her lack of trust, but it didn't stop him from forging ahead. "I'm hoping to show you how sorry I am and how much I care about what you're doing there."

Gwen rolled her eyes again. Chadwick never gave a fig about her mission with the community center and shelter.

"Don't let my stupid mistake keep you from taking advantage of what could be a wonderful opportunity for the shelter."

His motivation might not be wholly pure, but at least he was presenting her with an opportunity to seek out another donation. After a moment of consideration, she decided she had nothing to lose.

"All right, Mr. Chadwick, I'll meet with him."

"Thank you, Gwen." The words rushed out of his mouth, as if he'd been worried she might say no.

"Just because I agreed to meet with him doesn't mean I've forgiven you for what you did." It was important she made that crystal clear, because she could still remember what it felt like to have his hands on her, to feel his foul breath on her face.

"I understand and, again, I'm very sorry about what happened." His attempt at sounding contrite fell short. "His name is Nikolai Radoslav, and"—he cleared his throat—"he'd like to meet with you at seven o'clock this evening. He'll be at the Mt. Elbrus Restaurant in Little Russia for an earlier meeting and was hoping you could just meet him there."

"I've never heard of him, and even if I had, I can't possibly meet with him on such short notice." She looked down at her filthy work clothes and knew her hair was a nightmare. Even if she ignored the niggling doubt, going to an unfamiliar place alone, at night, to meet with a complete stranger—prominent businessman or not—was probably not the smartest idea. The mere thought of it would've horrified her mother. "If you'll give me his number, I'll give him a call and reschedule for a more mutually convenient time."

He didn't respond right away, and she looked at the screen, found herself *hoping* their connection had been lost.

No such luck. A beat later, he blurted, "He's leaving the country tomorrow for an extended period of time and wants to take care of this before he goes. You know how eccentric rich people can be," he scoffed, as if sharing a private joke.

Gwen chewed her bottom lip. "You've known for some time I've been soliciting donors. Why are you just now introducing me to him?" This whole thing just didn't feel right to her.

"Quite frankly, it never entered my mind he would be interested in making any kind of donation since he already gives to so many other charities."

She cringed as he blew his nose in her ear.

"Sorry, I'm fighting a terrible cold."

A cold. Right. Sure, let's go with that.

"I only know about it now because, during our meeting at lunch today, he happened to mention his interest in finding a good cause to support." There was a momentary silence before Chadwick said, "I will admit, it was partly selfishness on my part. I'd hoped this would convince you to forgive me. But if you're not interested, I'll let Mr. Radoslav know so he can seek out another charity."

Gwen hesitated, weighing her concern against the importance of every single donation.

"Well, I wish I had a bit more time to prepare." Who was she kidding? She'd given the pitch so many times, she could do it in her sleep. "But since he's going out of town ... I guess I have no choice but to meet with him this evening." She walked toward her office and grabbed her day planner. To be on the safe side, she would tell one of her former co-workers about the meeting.

"Oh, that's great, Gwen." He heaved a sigh, and she got the strangest feeling it wasn't because he felt repentant. "Thank you."

She shook off her suspicions and said, "Please let Mr. Radoslav know I'll see him at seven o'clock this evening."

CHAPTER FIVE

Concealed in shadows across the street from the restaurant, Beck was seething. Through his high-powered binoculars, he watched the guy make a phone call, then climb into his expensive sedan and speed off down the street. Getting the license plate number was a bust —the angle sucked. No help there in finding out more about him.

The late afternoon sun had moved behind the building and his view through the restaurant window was perfect. Thanks to Caleb's gadgets, he'd listened through his earpiece and watched as the guy he knew only as Chadwick laid out his proposition. First name or last name, he wasn't sure, but he *really* wanted to know more about him.

Sizing him up had been quick and easy. Late thirties, slick, maybe five nine, five ten, thinning, dirty-blond hair, a little too well-groomed. He'd primped like a peacock before walking into the restaurant. Self-importance poured off him. Beck had instantly disliked the guy. Looked like his instincts were right.

Radoslav had been all but ignoring him until things took a

decidedly dark and disturbing turn when the ass-wipe bartered a young woman in exchange for clearing his debt.

He knew better than most the world was swarming with sick, depraved bastards, but hearing that creep offer up an innocent woman made him want to grab the worthless piece of dog shit by the neck and choke the life out of him.

If he could somehow get his hands on that damn business card, he could warn her. But it wasn't going to happen. The best he could do was keep watch over her when she showed up for her meeting. If she was truly an innocent, he'd find a way to keep her away from the old man.

It would be nice to be able to save at least one person in this whole goddamn nightmare.

A few hours later, a gloomy fog had settled in, blanketing everything and choking out the radiance of the full moon. Just another fall night in San Francisco. On night's like this, Beck felt every one of his thirty-three years. The cold of the dank wall he leaned against seeped into his bones, and the old knee injury he'd suffered rappelling from a helicopter ached like a bitch.

Radoslav had stuck around, holding court from his table. He did that some days, just parked his fat ass in the booth and swapped stories about the *old country* with the owner.

They always spoke Russian, which wasn't a problem. Thanks to Uncle Sam, he had a working knowledge of the language.

He eased back into the darkness when the headlights from an old Honda skimmed past the alley. Usually wasn't much traffic in this area; most people knew to avoid it, especially after dark. He looked at his watch, and his gut told him he was about to see the woman Chadwick set up.

He raised his binoculars and watched the car park near the door of the restaurant. A woman climbed out and looked his way over the roof of the car.

Holy hell. She was absolutely stunning.

In the glow of the streetlight, she looked like a damn angel. A stark contrast to the neighborhood and dreary night surrounding her.

God, he hoped he was wrong about her reason for being here. Maybe she was just another person coming to enjoy the food.

Why did it matter so much to him?

For months, since Jodi's murder, his every thought, every action had been driven by his need to avenge her death. Now he was worrying about a woman he'd never met?

He shoved thoughts of her aside. She was a distraction he couldn't afford right now.

Cautiously, she checked out the area, hesitating when she came to the alley where he stood hidden. After a moment, she mumbled, and Beck would give just about anything to know what it was she'd said to herself.

Eyes closed, she took a deep breath and shook out her hands. By the time her eyes opened, she looked like a woman on a mission.

A little bitty thing, she circled around the front of the car, pulled the passenger door open and bent to wrestle a large messenger bag from the floor. It blessed him with an excellent view of a supremely fine backside.

Bag gripped in one hand, she straightened her shapeless suit with the other. The skirt fell to just above her knees and the sky-high heels she wore did incredible things for her legs. Rebellious strands of amazing golden-red hair had slipped from her long ponytail. He narrowed his eyes and noticed how her fingers shook as she tucked it behind her ears. It left Beck feeling oddly protective.

"Who are you, honey? And why are you here?" The damp air muted his murmured words.

Another tug and she straightened her jacket ... again.

Then, chin up, she pushed the strap to her bag over her shoulder and marched toward the front door. Beck applauded her efforts to look calm and composed, but a guy like Radoslav never missed a thing.

He stood, powerless, as she walked right into the viper's nest. Too vulnerable, too innocent, a wide-eyed cherub about to be cast among hellish beasts.

Sure, there was a chance she worked for the very man he was trying to destroy. But after witnessing her uneasiness and forced bravado, Beck was less inclined to believe it. If he found out she was a part of his organization, she would go down with Radoslav and to hell with his unexpected attraction to her.

Back ramrod straight, she pulled open the door and confidently walked up to the hostess.

"Good evening. I'm meeting with Mr. Radoslav." Her smooth voice filtered through his earpiece. The device at the podium worked perfectly.

Christ, she is *the one*. Beck closed his eyes and sighed.

"Yes, miss. You are right on time. Right this way, please."

Binoculars up, he watched her move to Radoslav's table.

Stomach tight, he flashed back several years to a cliff face overlooking an Afghan village. He'd watched a young child chase an old soccer ball into a live mine field. The inevitable had happened.

For a second, he was back there all over again, helpless. Unable to step in and get her out of there without blowing his cover and destroying months' worth of work.

He stuffed his apprehensions in a box and shoved it to the back of his brain. Then he adjusted his earpiece and listened carefully.

CHAPTER SIX

Gwen followed the hostess, and they wound their way around the close-set tables toward a semicircular booth all the way at the back. As she approached the table, she got a partial look at the man she assumed she was meeting.

He turned his head and spoke to the person sitting on his left. His large, wrinkled forehead loomed over a pair of deep-set, too-close-together dark eyes. Actually, *dark* wasn't a strong enough word to describe them—they were black as coal. His build reminded her of Santa, minus the beard or any signs of jolliness.

Hunched over, a napkin tucked into his collar, he slurped something from a bowl. The crude sound traveled across the restaurant, went ignored by the men sitting with him.

The hostess announced her with a shaky voice, then scurried away as if her presence was urgently needed back at the podium, even though there was no one else in the place.

Gwen waited for Radoslav to acknowledge her presence. After a moment or two, she cleared her throat.

He finally looked up at her with cold, sharklike eyes, and

his spoon fell, clanking loudly into the porcelain bowl. The contents splashed across the tablecloth, its dark red color ghoulish and stark against the white fabric. Mouth open, he continued to stare.

Ignoring the overwhelming impulse to turn and run from the room, she reached out to shake his hand. Still, his mouth gaped and his eyes crawled over her face.

She felt ridiculous standing there with her hand hanging out. Maybe he was one of those people with a weird fetish about shaking hands.

Days later ... okay, maybe not *days,* although it certainly felt like it, he reached out and wrapped his thick hand around hers. She stifled a shiver when cold traveled from their joined hands, flashed up her arm, and shot through her like a splash of ice water. Eyes squinted, he slowly leaned closer as he scanned her face, his grip tightening. He held on to her for an uncomfortably long time, and she decided enough was enough.

With three quick pumps, she took charge of the handshake. "Good evening, Mr. Radoslav. I'm Gwendolyn Tamberley. I appreciate you making time in your busy schedule to discuss the community center and shelter with me."

When he didn't respond, she began to wonder if he might be having some sort of medical episode.

"Mr. Radoslav?" She looked at the men in his booth, then back at him. "Are you okay?"

He blinked a few times but continued to stare as he whispered something in Russian.

"Excuse me?" Gwen was having serious doubts about agreeing to this meeting.

He cleared his throat with a quick shake of his head.

"Oh, yes, I ... " His voice was harsh, almost mean-sounding. "It is just ... " He looked her over from head to toe. "You remind me of someone I knew many years ago."

She forced herself not to fidget under his intense scrutiny. "Oh ... well, that's ... interesting."

His odd behavior made her anxious, and she wanted to move things along.

"I am sorry, please to forgive me." The sudden smile on his bloated face seemed contrived and in no way softened him. And he still held her hand captive in his. "I was mistaken. It was very long time ago."

She glanced down at their joined hands, and he slowly dragged his palm free. Gwen curled her fingers tight to keep from wiping her hand on the back of her skirt.

"Please. Join me." He growled something in Russian, and his tablemates clumsily rushed to gather up their plates, utensils and napkins and scurried off to another table.

She perched on the end of the leather bench, putting as much space between them as possible without falling on the floor. Something in the way he continued to look at her creeped her out and made her skin crawl.

He raised his hand and, with the slightest flick of two fingers, summoned the hostess. The young woman rushed over and set a place for Gwen.

"Thank you," Gwen said. Head down, the girl gave her a quick nod and scurried away, never making eye contact.

"Have you ever tried ptichye moloko?"

"I don't care for it, but my mother loved it." The soufflé-like cake had always been too rich for Gwen. "A cup of tea would be lovely, however."

She didn't want to offend him, but her sole objective was to get this meeting over with and get the heck out of there.

He snapped his fingers to get the server's attention, then barked something in Russian across the restaurant. The poor thing dashed to the back like she'd received an electric shock.

When her tea arrived, Gwen broke the awkward silence and started talking about the community center and shelter and its mission. She pulled the business plan from her bag and launched into the sales pitch she'd given countless times before.

"I'm not sure how much Joseph Chadwick told you about the shelter, but it has been a dream of mine for several years."

Throughout the next several minutes, she fell into her groove. Explained how her professional background and social services connections would help ensure the shelter's success. Her passion for the project made it easy to convey her excitement.

She finished her speech and looked over at him.

Bushy brows furrowed, he looked at her in the same discomfiting way. It was obvious he hadn't heard a word she'd said. She could've been trying to sell him a timeshare on Mars and he wouldn't have noticed.

The server arrived and quietly cleared his dishes.

Gwen looked up and glanced at her nametag. She could've sworn she detected a plea for help in the girl's tired eyes. "Thank you, Marissa."

A moment later, the young girl returned and placed a small glass of vodka in front of Radoslav.

She smiled up at her. "Marissa, are you—"

Radoslav cleared his throat. The young girl stiffened, the color drained from her face, and he waved her away without so much as a word. Shoulders hunched, focused on the floor, she quickened her pace and headed toward the kitchen.

How odd.

Gwen pulled her eyes away from the retreating girl. Spiel complete, she sipped her tea, determined to wait him out.

Two can play this game, Mr. Radoslav.

"What did you say was your mother's name?"

"I beg your pardon?" She placed her cup in the saucer.

What an odd first question.

"Your mother." Impatience tinged his words. "You said she liked ptichye moloko cake. What. Is. Her. Name?" He enunciated each word, whether to compensate for his stilted English or because he thought she might be a bit slow, she wasn't quite sure.

"Her name was Maggie. The shelter was something I've been passionate about for years. Naming it after her is my way of honoring her memory."

Gwen believed her mother could've benefited from a shelter like the one she was creating, but that was none of his business.

"And your father, what is his name?"

"Mr. Radoslav, I don't understand why you—" Gwen jumped when he pounded his fist on the table. Her teacup rattled in the saucer, and the small bud vase teetered, then fell over, its contents dripping onto the table.

"His name, what is it?" His words came out in a snarl.

"I'm not sure why it's relevant, but his name was Richard Tamberley."

"Was?" Eyes squinted, he pressed further.

"Yes, *was*. He died shortly before I was born." Gwen began gathering her paperwork. "Mr. Radoslav, this is in no way relevant to the shelter." She was beyond uncomfortable and wanted to get out of there.

"What happened to your mother?" With no apparent concern for propriety, he continued to pry, as if he had every right to know.

"Again—" Gwen hesitated. "I'm not sure what any of this has to do with the shelter."

Before speaking of her mother, she still found it necessary to bolster herself against the onslaught of lingering pain. A stranger's idle curiosity was not a strong enough motivation to dredge up all those feelings.

He scrubbed his thick hand over his face. She sensed it

was an attempt to calm himself. When he spoke again, he affected a more considerate tone.

"I only ask you this because you look so familiar to me. I thought perhaps I've met your mother."

Considering her mother spent her life avoiding most people, the chances she'd met this man were slim to none.

"I don't know about that, but my mother died a few months ago."

Something like shock raced across his features before he deftly masked it behind a look of indifference. She got the impression Radoslav was no novice at hiding things.

"I am so sorry for your loss. How did she die?" His words were shallow, lacked sincerity.

"She was killed by a hit-and-run driver." Gwen turned to slip her pen into her bag, ready to end this meeting now.

He coughed and sputtered. She turned back to him just as his glass of vodka dumped over on the table. The man certainly was making a mess of things.

"Mr. Radoslav, are you okay?"

She hesitated then leaned over and awkwardly thumped on his broad back. His coughing subsided, and he cleared his throat. He flicked his wrist, and she looked over her shoulder just as two large men settled back into their seats.

"Thank you for meeting with me, Ms. Tamberley. I will be in touch." And with that, he dismissed her.

Fine and dandy with me.

After an excruciatingly long hour, during which she'd done most of the talking, she was happy to be leaving. Who was she kidding? She'd been ready to leave before she ever walked into this dark, creepy place.

Gwen wiped the corners of her mouth, folded her napkin as if perfection mattered, and placed it carefully on the table. She gave extra care to gathering up the rest of her papers and tucked them into her bag before rising from the booth.

No surprise he didn't stand. Radoslav didn't seem like the kind of man who stood for anyone.

"Thank you for considering a donation to the shelter, Mr. Radoslav." She steeled herself, then reached out and gave his hand a quick shake. Her skin crawled and this time, she gave in to the impulse and wiped her hand down the side of her skirt.

Without another word, she weaved her way back to the front of the restaurant, feeling his eyes on her back the entire time. She pushed open the door and, even though everything in her wanted to run, she forced herself to walk to her car.

Her hand shook. Her keys rattled against the door. After multiple attempts, she managed to unlock it. Once inside, she tossed her bag to the other seat and twisted around to lock the door. Borderline frantic, she grabbed the little bottle of antibacterial liquid from the center console and squeezed it into her hands.

A half-bottle later, satisfied she'd washed all trace of Nikolai Radoslav from her skin, she took her first deep breath since sitting down at his table.

Looking back at the restaurant, Gwen shivered, fully expecting to see his jet-black eyes staring out at her.

Another deep breath, and she shook her head and chided herself for her foolishness. She pulled her seat belt over her shoulder, clicked it in place. Eyes closed, she sent a silent prayer up to the God of Old Cars and turned the key. After two tries, the old engine fired to life. Gwen smiled and looked up.

"Glad to know *someone* is listening to me tonight."

Hand on the gear shift, she hesitated, her gaze drawn to the shadows across the street. An odd warmth settled over her, and the bone-deep chill she'd felt all day dissipated. She squinted into the darkness, strained to see what had garnered her attention, oddly disappointed to find nothing there.

"Okay, Gwen, it's official." She rolled her eyes and muttered. "You're losing it."

Anxious to get back to the relative safety of the shelter, she flipped on the headlights.

"There is no boogie man waiting to jump from the shadows." She sighed. "Unfortunately, there is no knight in shining armor hanging out over there either."

HER NAME WAS GWENDOLYN TAMBERLEY. Beck knew she was okay, had heard the entire conversation. Yet he was still relieved when she walked out the door.

He watched her do another visual sweep of the area, uneasiness tightening her shoulders. After being near a man like Radoslav, it was to be expected.

What *had* been unusual was Radoslav's disturbing reaction to her. And what was with all those questions about her parents? The whole thing was one big red flag.

He snapped a picture of her with his cell phone, then sent a quick text to Caleb with the slightly grainy image, her name, and her parents' names. His brother could work some of his computer magic to pull together as much information on her as possible. Depending upon what they found, maybe he could use her to get closer to the Russian.

He slowly straightened from the wall and lowered his binoculars. She stared his way, couldn't see him, yet he felt an odd sense of connection.

She shook her head, put the car in gear and pulled away from the curb.

Instinct screamed at him to keep an eye on her. As he walked back down the alley to where he'd parked, his phone vibrated.

He slipped it from his pocket as he unlocked his car. "Hey, Caleb. You get my text?"

"So you feel you just *have* to follow the gorgeous woman, right?"

Yep, he got the text.

"Purely as part of this investigation you're running, right?" Caleb continued.

Smart-ass. Heaven forbid one of his siblings miss an opportunity to give him a hard time.

"It couldn't possibly have anything to do with the fact she's smokin' hot, could it?" Caleb could be such a pain in the ass sometimes.

As he fired up the engine and pulled onto the quiet street, Beck told his brother, in not-so-gentlemanly terms, *exactly* what he could do with his questions. Then he filled him in on what he knew about Gwendolyn Tamberley.

"I want you to dig up everything you can on a guy named Joseph Chadwick. If he's ever jaywalked or gotten so much as a parking ticket, I want to know about it."

"Roger that. I just landed. As soon as I pick up my rental car, I'll head to your place."

"How the hell did you get here so fast?" His brother lived in Virginia. He was a Tactical K9 Specialist on the FBI's elite Hostage Rescue Team, headquartered out of Quantico.

"I was up at mom and dad's and was able to get a last-minute flight out of Seattle. By the way, they said to tell you 'hello,' and they want to see you whenever you're ready."

Their parents were the two most important people in Beck's life. He missed them—their affection, warmth, and acceptance. He would love to surrender to their understanding and compassion but kept his distance, unwilling to risk bringing them to Radoslav's attention. Isolating himself from his family was the only way to keep them all safe.

"How are they?"

"Instead of asking me, why don't you call them and find out for yourself? You know they would love to hear from you." Caleb's voice lacked its usual carefree lilt.

Beck rubbed his fingers across his forehead. "You know that's not possible right now."

"Yeah, you think you're keeping them safe or some dumbass thing, but they wouldn't agree with your method. When we were growing up, what did they always tell us? *Family is everything*. I just want you to try to remember that, is all."

The gloom of the city at night matched Beck's mood. His mission to destroy Radoslav had become the center of his world. There were only a few good things left in his life, and he wouldn't risk them.

"This is different, and I have to handle it my way. I promise, I'll get in touch with them when I can."

"If you say so. Anyway, I'll see you back at your place." His brother hung up.

The whole way back to his townhouse, he thought about how many opportunities he'd had to take out Radoslav. To rid the world of at least one source of evil. Tempting as it was, cutting off the head of the snake would not be enough. He had to be patient and do this right—for Jodi, and to prove to himself a small piece of his humanity still remained intact.

CHAPTER SEVEN

Nikolai watched Gwendolyn Tamberley walk out the door. He scrubbed his hand down his face and tried to regain some of the composure he was feared for.

When he'd looked into those unique eyes, he'd been hammered by memories. They were the same teal color he'd been unable to purge from his mind for twenty-five years. From her golden strawberry hair to the way her body moved, even the sound of her voice. Everything about her was unnervingly similar to a girl he'd known years ago.

He'd come upon Alice Madison in an alley—filthy, bruised and beaten, hiding from her drunk stepfather. She'd stared up at Nikolai with her large hypnotic eyes and managed to do something no other woman before or since had ever done. She'd bedeviled him, as if she'd cast some type of sorceress spell over him. From that day forward, Nikolai harbored an insatiable, blinding obsession for her.

He'd taken her in, cleaned her up and given her things she'd never had. He'd denied his innate animal urge to take what he wanted, choosing instead to be patient and treat her like a princess. Then one day she'd disappeared, taking cash and two of his business ledgers with her.

Nikolai had spent hundreds of thousands of dollars tracking her down, worried she would turn the information over to the feds.

Alice's death had given him the retribution he'd long been denied and ensured he was protected from the secrets she'd stolen from him years ago. He'd thought the threat to his empire had been eliminated. Then he'd gazed into the eyes of Gwendolyn Tamberley.

Could the woman he'd just spent an hour sitting close enough to touch be Alice's daughter? If so, it meant Talbot missed her during his investigation.

His teeth ground together.

For years, certain factions within the FBI had been relentless in their efforts to bring him down. Could she be working with them as part of some elaborate scheme to entrap him?

He tossed his napkin on the table and lumbered his way out of the booth. He charged toward the door, knocking aside chairs in his path, his security detail hurrying to catch up.

Before the chauffeur could open the car door for him, Nikolai yanked it open and hefted his bulk into the backseat. He slammed the door, leaving his driver, Gregor and his other bodyguard outside to scan the street.

Alone in the car, he tugged from his pocket a burner phone with a single number programmed into it.

On the fifth ring, Radoslav cursed in Russian. He was about to toss the phone when Talbot answered.

"Yeah," Talbot grumbled in a voice thickened by sleep, alcohol or both.

The disgraced former P.I. was a disgusting, boorish man, but he had connections that had proven beneficial from time to time. It seemed this time, they'd failed him. Radoslav wanted to reach through the phone and strangle the incompetent imbecile.

"Get me everything you can find on a woman by the name of Gwendolyn Tamberley. Father's name is Richard Tamberley; mother's name is Maggie Tamberley."

He could hear shuffling through the phone.

"Do any of those names sound familiar to you, Talbot?"

"Sure. Maggie Tamberley rings a bell." He hesitated. "Oh, yeah, she's the gal I tracked down for you a few months back. The one from the diner. Why?"

Radoslav exploded. "Why did you not tell me she had a daughter? Did you think this was not important information for me to have?"

Gregor directed his men to move away from the car, giving Radoslav added privacy.

"A ... what? A daughter? What the ... ? There wasn't ... I'm telling you, there was no daughter." The idiot stammered and stuttered.

The man's weakness disgusted Nikolai.

"You incompetent piece of drunken gutter trash. I just spent the last hour with a woman who could be her younger twin."

CLUTCHING THE PHONE, Talbot threw off the sheets and swung his legs over the side of the bed. His stockinged feet hit the floor. Half-asleep, still drunk, he rubbed his hand back and forth over his head and grabbed the pen from the nightstand.

"That's not possible." He hacked to clear his voice. "Give me the name again." He looked around, leaned over and picked up a liquor store receipt from the floor.

"Gwen-do-lyn Tam-ber-ley." Radoslav's English was uncharacteristically spot on.

"I'm telling you, I never saw her with anyone outside of work." He scribbled the name on the small slip of paper.

The venom in Radoslav's voice made Talbot regret having taken shortcuts with his investigation. The woman hadn't seemed like much of a threat.

"She is setting up some kind of shelter down in the Tenderloin district." Radoslav barked out the address. "Find out everything you can about her and report back to me."

Talbot struggled to fit everything on the small piece of paper, a task made more difficult by his shaking hand.

He scratched out a few more notes on his forearm, then wedged the phone between his shoulder and ear. He ground the heels of his hands into his eyes. The rubbing did nothing to clear the hazy feeling left over from too much booze and too little sleep.

"What difference does it make if she had a daughter?"

"It is none of your fucking business!" Radoslav lost it.

Talbot fumbled his phone and wrestled it back to his ear, surprised by the outburst. It was atypical of a man who had proven time and again, in the harshest possible ways, he was void of all emotion.

"I do not pay you for questions. I pay you for answers." Like a screaming teakettle removed from a flame, the Russian's tirade ceased. "You have failed me once." His voice was controlled, interwoven with menace. "Trust me when I tell you this—another failure will not be tolerated."

The threat hung heavy in the air as the line went dead. Talbot tossed his phone on the nightstand, then the pen and piece of paper.

Why the hell does the old man care if there's a daughter?

Talbot shrugged it off. The less he knew, the better.

He took in the room around him. It was bathed in an

intermittent red glow from the blinking *Vacancy* sign on the wall just outside the window. *Off* ... *On* ... *Off* ... *On* ... The rank combination of cheap perfume and body odor, fried food and sex, hung in the air. He shook his head. What a goddamn cliché.

Looking over his shoulder, he checked out the naked woman passed out facedown on the bed next to him. What the hell was her name?

Whatever. Doesn't matter.

Not like he'd ever see her again. All he'd cared about was her willingness and ability to give one hell of a blow job, among a few other carnal skills. A slow smile crept across his face as fuzzy memories of the past few hours came to him.

His bare ass stuck in the air, he crawled around on the floor, feeling around in the dark for the whiskey bottle he knew was there somewhere. He swept his hand across the ratty carpet until his fingertips brushed against the bottle under the bed. He wrapped his fingers around it, stood, and leaned back to stretch as he scratched his ass. Not wanting them to feel left out, he moved his hand around front to give his balls equal time.

Have to show the boys some love, too.

He chuckled at his own joke as he twisted off the cap, tipped back the bottle and downed the last of the whisky.

A wave of dizziness hit him when he bent to pick up his pants. He fell, slammed his shoulder against the cheap dresser. He ended up spread-eagle, naked, cheek smashed to the floor. The bottle bounced on the carpet just shy of his nose, and he released a deep breath.

Eventually, the room stopped spinning and he used the edge of the dresser to heave himself up. He shuffled around, gathering his clothes strewn about the room.

Talbot got dressed and stuffed his feet into his scuffed loafers. He yanked his wallet from his back pocket and dug out a fifty, dropping the wrinkled bill on the nightstand. After a last look around, he opened the door, pulled it shut, and walked away from the rundown room. He left nothing behind but the stranger passed out on the bed.

NIKOLAI STEPPED out of the car and straightened his suit.

"Put someone on Talbot immediately." He pushed up the knot of his tie as he walked past Gregor.

His most loyal employee pulled his phone from his pocket. "Find Talbot and follow him. Watch him. Do nothing without speaking to me first." He stuffed his phone back in his pocket. "It is done." Ever diligent, the bodyguard scanned the area.

Radoslav nodded, smoothed back his thinning white hair, and headed back into the restaurant.

CHAPTER EIGHT

Gwen pulled into the one and only parking space next to the shelter. She turned off the ignition, and her hand dropped to her lap with a sigh. Her head fell back against the headrest, and she closed her eyes. And to think, this day had started out so well.

One minute she'd been reveling in her progress at the shelter, then her day steadily declined into weirdness, starting with Chadwick's phone call and ending with her bizarre ... *encounter* with Radoslav.

She lifted her head and looked around. Sitting outside, at night, alone in this neighborhood was not the smartest thing to do. She reached over and grabbed her messenger bag, then shoved the door open.

The second her feet hit the ground, she grimaced. Pain shot through the balls of her feet. A not-so-friendly reminder of her ridiculously high heels. Unfortunately, the added height seemed to make people take her more seriously.

She bent to lock the car door and instantly felt eyes on her. A troubling thought at this time of night, in this part of town. Tamping down her nerves, she lifted her bag onto her shoulder, gripped the small canister of pepper spray on her keychain and, doing her best to look casual, stepped to the sidewalk. She scanned the area out of the corners of her eyes. Her mother's obsessive instructions filtered through her subconscious.

Always be aware of your surroundings, Gwen.

Never let your guard down, Gwen.

Trust no one, Gwen.

Burnt-out streetlights and oppressively thick fog made it difficult to see anything other than the old car left abandoned across the street several days ago. If she didn't call someone to take care of it, it would sit there forever, stripped of everything of value, a hollowed-out symbol of everything wrong with this neighborhood.

She walked toward the building and felt a strange kind of energy, like a low electrical vibration around her. She shook her head.

Probably just residual uneasiness from her meeting with Nikolai Radoslav. It might also be fatigue caused by all her hard work.

Lacking the energy to think about it, she made her way up the steps and unlocked the door. She shoved against it once, twice, and, on the third try, it pushed open. Inside, she took a deep breath and wedged her shoulder against the door to shut it. The new locks she'd installed after Joseph's first unexpected visit were great, but it still took effort to open and close the big, solid wood doors. Rubbing her shoulder, she made a mental note: *Fix doors ASAP*. Either that, or she'd have to invest in some heavy-duty shoulder pads. She'd watched a You-Tube video that showed how to plane a door. No way she could handle such a big job. Definitely time to hire a contractor.

She flipped on the light and kicked off her shoes. *Instant relief.* She wiggled her toes and looked around. The quiet of the building surrounded her.

Would the pride in what she was accomplishing here one day be enough to fill the emptiness she carried inside?

A worry for another day. Standing around having her little pity party wasn't going to accomplish anything. If she intended to keep to her schedule, she had paperwork to finish before going to bed.

Shoes in hand, she padded to her small room at the end of the hall. Her sanctuary away from all the construction mess, and where she kept her few personal items.

Gwen crossed to the small table next to the bed and picked up the framed picture. About a month ago, while looking for a picture of the building on her phone, she'd come across this one. She'd forgotten all about it. It was of her mother sitting on their old loveseat, staring out the window with such longing. As if she desperately wanted what was on the other side, but was too afraid to go after it.

Her mother had gone to great lengths to avoid having her picture taken, so it was one of Gwen's most prized possessions.

She stroked her thumb over her mother's delicate cheek then set the frame down and walked to the closet. *Clunk-clunk*, her shoes dropped to the floor and she took off her suit and hung it with the others. Her fingers dragged over the row of hangers and, for the first time, she noticed her mother's influence. All subdued colors and unflattering styles. Nothing that would make her stand out or gain anyone's attention. Why had she never noticed before? And why was she noticing now?

Okay, enough.

She was going to blame these arbitrary thoughts, as well as all the other weird stuff about this evening, on mental exhaustion.

Aiming for comfort, she removed her bra. Not that it made much difference if she wore one or not. Like her height, the size of her breasts was unimpressive. After putting on her large Giants t-shirt, comfy pajama pants and warm wooly socks, she headed across the dark hall to the kitchen. Sensing food nearby, her stomach chose that moment to growl, reminding her she hadn't eaten since lunch.

Gwen snapped on the overhead light and put water on to boil. She rummaged through the canister on the counter and pulled out her favorite herbal tea.

She opened the new industrial-sized fridge she'd just had installed and scanned her options. The meager contents—a bowl of pasta salad, half dozen eggs, pint of milk, sliced cheese and head of romaine lettuce—looked pitifully lonely in the large space. *I really need to find time to get to the grocery store.* She pulled out the pasta salad and set it on the counter.

On her tiptoes, she reached for a plate and the Giants mug she got when she was ten. After a firm yank on the stiff wooden drawer, she pulled out a fork and spoon.

Crossing to the whistling kettle, she flipped off the burner and poured water over the tea bag. Nose hovered over the steam, she inhaled a deep, fragrant breath and could instantly feel her nerves settling.

Plate in one hand, she blew across the top of the mug in the other and strolled to her office. She sat down and the squeal of the springs beneath the old desk chair broke the silence in the quiet room. She took a careful sip of tea, then set the large mug on a coaster. After a few bites of pasta salad, she set the plate off to the side, ready to tackle the pile of paperwork in front of her.

BECK SAT in his Tahoe and scanned the neighborhood. The

Tenderloin District was one of the most dangerous parts of San Francisco. Back in the early thirties, it had been rampant with vice, corruption, graft. It was considered the "soft underbelly" of the city, like the cut of meat. Hence the nickname. Legend has it cops who worked the area "back in the day" got hazard pay and could afford the more expensive tenderloin instead of chuck steak. Not much had changed.

Gwendolyn had parked in a spot next to an old building. The address matched the one Radoslav had given to a guy named Talbot. Whoever the hell he was. Beck got pissed thinking about someone snooping into the pretty young woman's life, intruding on her privacy. Considering his own hope of using her, that made him a first-class hypocrite.

The range on Caleb's electronics was pretty impressive, allowing Beck to keep a keen ear on Radoslav as he followed her across town. Just in case he lost her, he'd managed to sneak one of his brother's nearly undetectable tracking devices under Gwendolyn's bumper.

Shortly after leaving the restaurant, the microphone he'd planted in the limo had crackled to life with an explosion of Russian expletives. Whoever Talbot was, it sounded like he'd screwed the pooch.

Beck had perked up at the mention of Gwendolyn's name. God, he hated hearing it uttered by that sick fuck, especially when the bastard sounded close to coming unhinged. Radoslav was a stone-cold, merciless killer. His tirade was uncharacteristic and punctuated the bizarre behavior that started the moment he'd laid eyes on her and continued throughout their meeting. Hell, Beck had spent enough time listening to the old man's voice to recognize the slight hesitance and odd quiver as he questioned her. And then to find out he'd had someone trying to track down Maggie Tamberley before he'd ever even met her daughter?

Yeah, something definitely wasn't right about this situation, and Gwendolyn was stuck right smack in the middle of the whole mess.

He felt a twinge of guilt. Using Gwendolyn could thrust her directly into Radoslav's crosshairs. It felt too much like what had happened to Jodi. He was beginning to question whether he wanted to take the risk.

Suddenly, a swath of golden light poured into the dark alley outside one of the main floor windows. A small silhouette moved back and forth.

Beck quietly rolled forward until he had a clear view of the entire building, then shut off his car.

An hour later, the light still shone from the window. He checked in with Caleb, who'd taken his place outside the restaurant.

"Hey, Beck."

"What's happening there?" He asked.

"Radoslav was definitely out of sorts. Guy was tossing back vodka like it was water."

To a guy with his background, vodka was *like water.*

"About an hour or so into his little booze-fest, he started loosening up and he ... " Caleb hesitated, his voice tense.

"He what?"

"He was bragging, slurring his words, but I'm sure he said something about outsmarting a bunch of Feds who tried to interfere with one of his arms deals a few months ago." He could hear his brother's rage building.

"No fuckin' way. Are you telling me—"

"Remember when I was shot?" Caleb chuckled, but there was no humor behind it. "Never mind. Don't answer that—of course you do. Anyway, I never told you this, but we were set to meet someone from The Farm."

"The religious cult up in Montana, right?" His brother had been working the investigation for months before he was shot.

"Yeah," Caleb continued. "Anyway, the guy said he had some damning evidence. Weapons being stockpiled, young girls being offered up to VIPs, and a growing meth operation funding the whole damn nightmare. The timing, along with other circumstantial evidence, led us to believe one of the cult leaders is getting his weapons from none other than Nikolai Radoslav."

Beck cursed. Goddamn Russian's fingerprints were everywhere.

"Son of a bitch laughed," Caleb said. "Said he could give a shit about some dog getting killed. All he cared about was making sure he could still deliver his merchandise."

"Look, if you need to head back to Quantico to deal with this, I totally understand." Beck had to cut him loose.

The pain of losing Power was still a raw wound and would take a lot longer to heal than the one to Caleb's shoulder. What an amazing testament to his brother's control—being able to sit by and do nothing as Radoslav callously dismissed his canine's murder.

"The investigation has hit a wall. You know how it is. Without solid evidence, the bureau can't do a damn thing." Caleb blew out a deep breath. "Right now, my time is better spent here, helping you."

"And I appreciate that, more than I can say. Any time you want to leave, just say the word. Got it?"

"Yeah. I got it." He cleared his throat and continued, "So, what's shakin' with the hottie?"

Beck rolled his eyes. "You mean, Gwendolyn?"

"Gwendolyn, huh? Not Ms. Tamberley?" Caleb teased.

"I know you're dying to say something." He sighed. "Might as well go ahead and spit it out."

"It's just ... Well, your voice is ... different whenever you talk about her."

Ridiculous.

"You don't know what you're talking about. She's just ... Ya know what, never mind."

Caleb chuckled. "Fine, have it your way. What's shakin' with Gwendolyn?"

"I followed her to a decrepit old building in the Tenderloin District." He glanced over at the window.

"The Tenderloin District. Jesus. What the hell is she doing down there this time of night?" Confusion and concern rippled through Caleb's voice.

"She's setting up a community center and homeless shelter." Beck scanned the street. A sense of apathy and despair hung over everything around him. The old neighborhood really did need a boost. He wasn't sure how wise it was for her to be the one providing it. "Christ, she has a *lot* of work ahead of her." He leaned forward, gave the building a critical once-over. "I'm shocked she's actually staying in it."

"You mean to tell me she's *living* down there?"

Yeah, Beck wasn't real keen on the idea either.

He filled his brother in on the conversation between Radoslav and Talbot, about how Talbot had tracked down Maggie Tamberley months before meeting Gwendolyn. "Do me a favor and find out everything you can about this Talbot guy."

"Shouldn't be too difficult."

Beck could almost hear the wheels turning in his brother's huge brain.

"The way Radoslav reacted to her tonight had nothing to do with the deal he made with Chadwick." Talking about Gwendolyn as part of some fucked-up trade sent renewed fury slicing through Beck. "The old man was stunned to the point of speechless. It was ... troubling. Then I find out he had some guy trying to find her mother months ago?"

"Whatever the reason for any of it, we both know it can't be good," Caleb said.

"People have no clue the kind of animal he really is." Over the years, the Russian had perfected his conservative, benevolent businessman persona. What a joke. The old man was pure evil.

Jodi's brutalized body flashed through his mind, assaulted his senses.

"Beck? You there?"

He shook his head, pushing the horrific images back to the far recesses of his mind where they'd been shoved months before.

"Yeah, sorry." Beck cleared his throat. "Stick with him but be careful. After what went down tonight, I don't want us to get caught with our pants down around our ankles."

"Roger that. As soon as I have anything, I'll let you know."

"Thanks, man." He hung up, shoved his phone in his pocket and settled in for what would likely be a long, boring night of surveillance. Until the pesky hairs at the back of his neck—the ones he'd learned not to ignore—demanded his attention.

His eyes skimmed the alley adjacent to Gwendolyn's building. A subtle movement in the shadows caught his attention. Gaze steady, he reached for his binoculars. A moment later, someone lumbered from the shadows and dragged themselves through her window.

CHAPTER NINE

Talbot barely missed knocking over a garbage can as he snuck down the alley. *Christ, what I wouldn't give for a drink*. The back door was a no-go. The damned motion-sensor light would give him away. If he couldn't get in through one of the windows in the alley, he was screwed. His knees crackled and popped as he crouched behind a dumpster and checked for activity in the building.

What the hell is the deal with the light inside? Was it meant to be a deterrent, or was someone really in there? He wasn't squeamish about roughing someone up. He just didn't feel like dealing with the hassle.

He scrubbed his hand over his face, the rough sound of his whiskers against his palm loud in the dark space. Things had gotten too damn hot in his world, and this job would give him enough cash to finally set himself up in style in Mexico.

"To hell with it." He pulled on his gloves and tugged down his dark ski mask. He wanted this over with.

Hefting himself up from behind the dumpster with a groan, he rubbed his hands up and down his tingling legs to restore some circulation and looked around. Coast clear, he skulked across the dark, sloppy alley as fast as his now-soggy loafers could carry him. The shadows were his friends, and he was careful to avoid the beam of light pouring from the window. He stopped and leaned against the wall and tried to catch his breath. The back of his sweater snagged on the rough brick as he craned his neck up for a quick look.

A woman faced away from him, head down, arms folded on the desk. Could he be so lucky that this was the little gal who had old Radoslav's panties in a bunch? Maybe he'd just get some answers from her.

He worked his way over to the next window. A quick peek, and he could see this room was empty. Talbot stretched up, wedged the crowbar under the frame and jimmied it open a few inches. Old buildings made it so damn easy.

He laid the crowbar on the windowsill, hauled himself halfway up, then fell back to the ground with a grunt. Things went better on his second attempt. He rested his elbows on the windowsill to catch his breath again. One hand wedged under the opening, he puffed and chuffed until the window shoved up. About a third of the way, it let out a loud *SCREECH.*

He froze.

Heart pounding, sweat building, he waited, looked around. His arms quivered and he almost lost a shoe as his feet scrabbled for purchase on the rough brick. He managed to reach in and quietly set the crowbar on the floor. A burning sensation shot across his back and belly when he scraped between the sill and the bottom edge of the frame. He wriggled to get his ass unstuck. The floor rushed up, and he landed face-first on the rug. Wheezing, sweat burning his eyes, he rolled over and stared up at the ceiling.

Jesus, I'm too damn old for this shit.

He rolled to his hands and knees and listened. Nothing.

He hiked his pants up when he stood and limped his way toward the open door.

Talbot watched her sleep. A twisted smile curved up beneath his mask. With all the stealth his broken-down body could muster, he approached the desk.

A few feet from her, close enough to smell her perfume, the old floorboards *creaked* loud enough to wake the dead. And the sleeping beauty in front of him.

GWEN'S HEAD shot up off the desk. Unfocused from sleep, she scanned the room until she connected with a set of dark eyes glaring from behind a mask. Floating in a sleep-induced muzziness, she remained rooted in place. She frowned, unsure if it was real or a too-vivid dream.

He took a step forward. When he bumped into the chair in front of her desk, she was jerked from the fog of sleep. This was no dream.

Gwen screamed, jumped from her chair and sent it crashing into the shelf behind her. Her eyes fell to the crowbar in his hands, and she flew into action. She grabbed the closest thing available and flung it at him as hard as possible. Caught by surprise, he grunted when the heavy stapler hit his shoulder. The next thing to go was her half-full mug of tepid tea. He ducked and the mug shattered against the wall behind him. Clear brown liquid spotted the floor and ran down the wall.

She continued a steady flow of screaming, grabbing, and tossing.

Using her plate like a Frisbee, she whipped it at him, sending the uneaten pasta flying everywhere. His arm came up to shield his face and the edge ricocheted off his forearm.

"You bitch," he cursed, and continued to close the space between them.

Gwen chucked the cup of pens and pencils, its contents scattered everywhere like shrapnel. She heaved her heavy planner, the desk lamp—anything she could get her hands on, she threw at him.

THE LAMP TOSS had been a bull's-eye, hitting him in the head and knocking him down. A flash on the floor caught her eye —the letter opener. *Shoot!* Too far away to be of any help. Her fight or flight instinct kicked in, and she shoved the chair at him and bolted for the door.

Just as she was about to make her escape, his hand wrapped around her ankle, and she fell forward and landed hard. Air exploded from her lungs. Unable to catch her breath, she flailed her other leg to keep him from pinning both ankles. Her heel caught him in the cheek.

"Motherfucker," he roared.

He recovered quickly and overpowered her. Scrambling up, he straddled her back and squeezed his knees together. Gwen cried out when he twisted her arms behind her.

"Stop moving, or I'll kill you."

She froze at the utter conviction of the words hissed close to her ear.

A SCREAM RIPPED through the night. Beck bolted from the car and ran across the street.

He took the steps in one leap. The door was locked. He tried to shoulder his way through with no luck. He yanked a pouch from his pocket, slipped out his lock picks. A series of clicks and success. He shoved his way through the door, ran toward the sound of a scuffle.

A man dressed all in black sat on top of Gwendolyn.

White-hot rage with the intensity of a thousand suns exploded through Beck.

He attacked.

One arm wrapped around the front of the guy's neck, the other across the back. He squeezed. The chokehold made it easy to yank him off her. Pulling his gun wasn't an option—he couldn't risk hitting her.

Beck turned him, drew back his arm and smashed a monstrous right cross into the man's face. A devastating left jab followed before the asshole could regain his composure. The guy's arms swung limp around his sides. His head snapped side to side with each violent blow.

Bones crunched and blood sprayed through the nose hole in his mask. A solid uppercut sent the intruder reeling backward, and he crashed to the floor.

Beck's breaths sawed in and out, his chest heaving, shoulders rising and falling. Fury pumped through his system. Clenching and unclenching his fists, Beck watched the man on the floor, hoping he'd make a move.

A distressed whimper jerked him from his rage. He rushed to crouch next to Gwendolyn.

"Hey, hey ... " He kept his voice low and helped her sit up. "Take it easy."

Her brow furrowed. She grabbed her head and closed her eyes.

He took a chance and gently rested his hand on shoulder. It trembled beneath his touch and she felt so small and fragile.

Her eyes slowly opened. She blinked a few times before they seemed to focus on his.

"Are you okay?"

Eyes wide, she raised a shaky finger and pointed behind him.

He looked over his shoulder. Her attacker swayed on his feet, mask crooked, blood smeared down his neck, he held the crowbar high, ready to strike.

Fluid as water flowing over smooth rocks, Beck ducked in front of Gwendolyn, drew the gun from his holster, spun and fired. A deafening *boom* rang out and sparks exploded from the end of the barrel. The bullet slammed into the guy. He staggered back a step, arms flailing, and crashed through the unopened window.

Beck draped himself over Gwendolyn, felt the sting of shards and splinters of exploding glass against his back. The tinkling of glass ceased, and an eerie quiet blanketed the room. The acrid smell of gunpowder hung in the air.

He unwrapped himself from her and rushed to stand to the side of the broken window. Weapon raised, he risked a quick look into the alley. At the far end, a man shuffled away, left arm hanging limp at his side. The darkness swallowed him, and he was out of sight.

Unwilling to leave Gwendolyn alone, he'd leave it to the locals to track the shithead down. The satisfaction of knowing he'd inflicted a painful gunshot wound did little to quell the disappointment of his escape.

The overhead light flipped on, and Beck turned around. Gwendolyn stood near the open door, brandishing a broken lamp in front of her. Wavy strands of her golden-red hair fell from the loose knot at the top of her head. Broken glass sparkled like gems on the floor all around her. In spite of her outward show of bravado, her large, beautiful eyes, the ones he'd hungered to see up close, reflected nothing but terror.

Hands shaking, she raised the lamp higher. "D-don't m-move any c-closer."

He held up his hands, the tremor in her voice flaying him.

Her eyes leapt back and forth from his face to the weapon gripped in his hand. She stiffened when he moved to tuck it back in his holster.

He froze. "It's okay, honey." Voice quiet, he made no sudden moves. "I'm just going to put this away." He slowly secured the big gun.

She swallowed hard but didn't protest.

Beck picked up the pieces of the cordless phone, popped the battery in and snapped it together. Eyes never leaving hers, he hit the "ON" button, and it came to life. He dialed 9-1-1, rattled off the address to the shelter and gave a brief description of what happened. He hung up and laid the handset on the desk.

He had never hesitated to use his intimidating size to his advantage. Unfortunately, this time, the adrenaline and battle-ready tension surging through his system worked against him. He took a deep breath, released it slowly, rolled his shoulders, tilted his head side-to-side.

A shout from the front of the building interrupted his chance to reassure her.

"San Francisco Police Department. We're responding to a 9-1-1 call."

To be on scene so quickly, in this area, someone must've heard her scream and called it in. Unprecedented. Perhaps her efforts to improve the neighborhood hadn't gone unnoticed. Or unappreciated.

"We're back here," Beck called as they stared at each other.

Two police officers cautiously peeked around the doorway. An older officer entered, followed by what looked like a wide-eyed rookie. Their eyes darted around the room, taking in the mess.

Doing a double-take when he got to Gwendolyn, the

younger cop gawked at her like a love-struck teenager. His mouth dropped open, and Beck half-expected to see his tongue roll out.

He stifled a growl. He understood the kid's reaction. Didn't mean he liked it.

"Officer, I have a concealed carry permit and am in possession of a weapon." Voice modulated, he held his hands up and away from his body.

In a situation like this, there were two important things to remember. Always give them a heads-up if you're carrying, and *never* use the word "gun." It set everyone's nerves on edge, and you never knew how they'd react.

As if to prove his point, the young cop's body language tightened. He unsnapped his holster, hovered his hand over his weapon and moved closer to Gwendolyn. Nervousness poured off him. Beck respected the kid's willingness to protect her, but the proximity of his shaky gun hand to her body was seriously pissing him off.

The veteran officer stepped up to Beck and removed his gun from the holster. With skill borne of years on the job, he released the magazine into one hand, ejected the round from the chamber and brought the gun to his nose with the other.

The whole time, Gwendolyn's eyes never strayed from Beck's.

"Has this gun been fired recently?" He tucked the magazine into his shirt pocket and pulled Beck's hands behind his back to cuff him.

Gwendolyn made a move toward him, and the young cop grabbed her arm.

"Take your hand off her," Beck growled.

The kid released her like he'd been burned.

"Everyone just ... relax." The older officer waved the kid back. "Ma'am, please step back."

Beck took a deep breath. "Yes, I fired a shot at the intruder, hit him in the left shoulder."

"Why are you handcuffing him?" Gwendolyn's hands were on her hips, fire in her eyes. She was magnificent.

"It's okay. It's protocol." He was heartened by her defense of him, but he didn't want her putting herself at risk.

"We need to make sure everything's copasetic. Then we'll release him." The older cop's unflappable calm was impressive.

"Well, if you ask me, it seems kind of ridiculous." She *harrumphed* and grudgingly stepped back.

Beck ducked his head, hiding his grin.

"My name is Officer Marden, and this is Officer Packard. Do you have any other weapons on you?"

"There's a knife in my right boot." Beck never went anywhere without one.

Marden slid the eight-inch KA-BAR from Beck's boot and set it on the desk.

Gwen leaned in to get a closer look.

The officer patted him down and pulled out his wallet. It was no coincidence one of his leftover bureau-issued business cards sat right next to his driver's license. It wasn't the same as having his gold shield, but it could prove helpful.

A sense of loss struck him mid-chest. Obtaining his gold shield and credentials had been one of the happiest days of his life, the achievement of a goal he'd set for himself when he was twelve years old. Then it had all turned to crap.

The cop studied the card and gave Beck a sideways glance.

He gave a slight shake of his head and a kind of *I'll explain later* look. The veteran cop picked up on it, didn't say anything.

"Ma'am, I'll accompany Mr. O'Halleran to the other room

for questioning. Officer Packard will take your statement in here."

Packard's face lit up like a kid in a candy store, and he flashed her a big, toothy grin. She'd just been through hell, and he was looking at her like a guy picking up his prom date.

Beck stepped in front of her, effectively blocking the young cop from her view. He wanted to check her for injuries, make her sit down, bring her a glass of water ... something ... *anything*. Mostly, he wanted to wrap his arms around her, protect her from everything.

Stupid, O'Halleran. What the hell was wrong with him?

"Tell Officer Packard everything that happened, okay?" He ducked to her eye level. "I'll just be in the other room."

Gwendolyn looked at him, and Beck's breath caught in his throat. He slowly straightened to his full height.

This close, she was quite simply the most stunning creature he had ever seen. In the center of her heart-shaped face perched a small, slightly upturned nose with a hint of freckles sprinkled across it. They enhanced her peaches-and-cream complexion. Her luminous eyes dominated her delicate features. Their unique combination of blue and green was the purest representation of teal he'd ever seen. The loneliness in them called to him on an almost primal level.

"Mr. O'Halleran, if you'll just come with me." Marden's voice broke their connection.

"Will you be okay here?" He hated leaving her to be grilled by an overeager young cop.

"I'll be fine." Her nose went up, and she drew back her shoulders.

"Good. I'll be back in a couple minutes." His fingers itched to touch her, but the handcuffs—and his better judgment—prevented him from doing so.

He turned to Packard. "Try to remember *she's* the victim."

The young cop sputtered as Beck turned and walked away.

"Okay ma'am, there's nothing to be afraid of. I'll take care of everything."

Beck shook his head at the young cop's naiveté. *If you only knew, kid.*

CHAPTER TEN

Marden removed the handcuffs after Beck convinced him he was working deep undercover. Just in case the veteran officer was hit by a latent burst of motivation to dig deeper, Beck gave him Caleb's name as a point of contact at the bureau. Lucky for him, his younger brother could sling enough bullshit to provide him with the cover story he needed.

"We'll check out the side and back alley." Marden flipped his notebook shut, tucked it into his chest pocket. "Do a walk-around of the building, see what we can find."

Beck nodded, and Marden returned his weapon and magazine to him.

They walked into the foyer.

"Packard, head out to the back alley and start the search there," Marden called out to the other officer, then turned to Beck. "I'm assuming you want to stick around?"

"I'm not going anywhere."

The cop nodded. "Yeah, I sorta figured."

Packard came out of the office, tucking his own notepad

away. He puffed out his chest and stood to his full height when he walked past Beck.

Marden rolled his eyes and shook his head before following his *very* young partner out the door.

Beck made a quick call to update Caleb and let him know he might be getting a call from SFPD. They agreed to talk later, after things settled down at the shelter.

He rounded the corner into the office and got his first good look at the room. Paper and assorted office supplies littered the floor, an old wooden chair sat upside down, something was splattered on the wall, and the broken lamp she'd brandished earlier lay atop the desk, the crushed shade on the floor nearby.

His blood heated. He wanted to destroy the man who'd done this.

On her hands and knees, Gwendolyn picked up papers, trying to straighten them. She kept starting over because her hands shook so badly.

Without thought, Beck crossed to her, his only thought to soothe her.

She was alerted to his presence when his boots crunched over the glass. Startled, she jumped up and backed away from him, papers clutched to her chest like a shield.

He stopped, raised his hands. "It's okay ... I won't come any closer."

Her delicate throat moved up and down. Small stockinged feet peeked out from the bottom of her long pajama pants.

"Don't move." He held out his hand.

A crease formed between her brows as her chin drew back. "Why can't I—"

He pointed to the floor. "There's glass all over the place. I don't want you to cut yourself."

She looked down at the glass twinkling up from the large, old rug.

He cursed under his breath. Why the hell hadn't that idiot cop gotten her something to put on her feet? Too busy flirting, would be Beck's guess.

"If you tell me where your shoes are, I'll get them for you." The innocent suggestion seemed to make her very uncomfortable.

"Is that really necessary? I mean, can't you just get the broom from the kitchen?"

Okay, so she obviously didn't want him rummaging around her things. Why? Was she hiding something? The thought disturbed him more than it should.

"No, I don't think that's a good idea. It's going to take more than a broom to get this all up."

She gnawed her bottom lip, looking at the devastation around her. Her shoulders sagged, and she sighed.

"Fine. My room is through there." She pointed at a doorway between the office and another room. "I have a pair of tennis shoes in the closet."

Before he made it to the door, she called out, "Wait!"

Beck stopped and looked back over his shoulder.

"Please ... " She nibbled her thumbnail. "Um ... just get my shoes and come right back. Okay?"

"Sure. Straight to your closet. Get your shoes. Come right back. Got it." Hell, he would be more than happy to pick her up and carry her there but didn't think she'd be on board with that idea.

Picking his way through the broken glass, he walked into her bedroom. The scent of lilac lingered in the air. He crossed to her closet and opened the door, surprised by what he saw. Or more, what he *didn't* see. She had very little hanging in there and, unlike most women he knew, had only a few pairs of shoes lined up in a neat row. Next to the stiletto heels she'd worn earlier sat a pair of well-worn, paint-splattered work boots. The contrast between the two reflected the contrasts within their owner. Delicate and fragile-looking on the outside while possessing a core of strength and toughness.

As he reached for her tennis shoes, he noticed some boxes stacked in the dark behind the clothes and wondered if they were the reason she didn't want him in her space.

Shoes in hand, he turned and gave the sparsely furnished room a quick once-over before moving back into her office. He stepped over a pile of papers and handed the shoes to her. She bent to put them on, and Beck noticed something dark seeping through her shirt near her waist.

He gently touched her shoulder, pleased when she didn't flinch. "What's that?"

"What's what?" She straightened and followed his eyes to a spot about the size of a nickel and spreading. She twisted her body away from him before lifting the bottom edge of her shirt. Blood seeped from a one-inch gash in her side. Adrenaline must have kept her from feeling any discomfort.

Beck snarled, wanting to shoot the guy all over again. "You're hurt."

He looked around the room, stalked over to a crushed box of Kleenex and picked it up. He popped a couple free and handed them to her.

She hissed when she dabbed it on the wound. A quiet "ouch," and she mumbled under her breath, "Little bugger stings."

Before he could ask about a first aid kit, Gwendolyn dropped the bottom of her shirt at the sound of footsteps in the hall.

Marden held a plastic evidence bag containing the crowbar.

"Well, we found this in the alley." He lifted the bag. "But since you said he was wearing gloves, I doubt we'll pull any prints off of it, but we'll give it a shot. Found a blood trail, but it ended down the street. The perp probably hopped in a car and took off."

They recited the standard spiel about changing locks and getting an alarm system.

"This isn't the best neighborhood, so I'd make that happen sooner rather than later. Once it's installed, you'll need to be vigilant about using it."

Marden followed up with an assurance they'd do what they could. Considering the area, Beck figured the attack would be written off as a random act of violence. Just something that happened in a neighborhood like this.

His gut told him otherwise.

"I'm sorry, Gwendolyn." Packard slowly approached her. "I wish there was more we could do." He reached into his pocket and pulled out a business card. "If you have any other problems, just give me a call."

"Thanks." Beck clenched his jaw, stepped between them again and took the card. "I'll hang on to this for her."

The kid's mouth opened and closed as he if he wanted to say something. In the end, he merely turned to leave.

Sorry, kid. From now on, Gwendolyn has me. He didn't want her leaning on anyone else.

The two officers said their farewells and headed for the door.

Beck turned to Gwendolyn. "I'll be right back."

He shook their hands, then closed and locked the doors. He leaned with one hand flat against the scarred surface and dropped his head forward. Adrenaline from his wrestling match still surged through his system. A few deep breaths later, he straightened, dropped his hand and walked back to the office.

Shoulders sagging, she looked small standing there holding a wad of tissue to her side, staring at the destruction around her. She might look lost, defenseless even, but the state of the room was a testament to her fighting spirit.

Her shoulders drew back when she heard him enter. Heaven forbid she show any weakness.

An old upholstered chair remained upright in the corner, having escaped the carnage. He grabbed the soft afghan hanging over the back and held it open behind her.

"Gwendolyn—" Beck cursed himself when she flinched. Back to that again.

"I'm sorry, I didn't mean to startle you. Let's put this around your shoulders."

She looked at the afghan, and he carefully draped it around her.

She was starting to trust him. Beck shoved aside his regret and the guilty twinge nagging at his conscience, keeping his focus on this moment.

Her tension, a light trembling, could be felt through the thickness of the old afghan. Delayed shock kicking in. With one hand, he held the blanket together in front of her; the other swept her silky hair over her shoulder.

"Gwendolyn, we need to take care of that cut on your side." His fingertip glided down her temple and skimmed some hair away from her face. Like the petal of a flower, her skin was soft and supple beneath his touch and just as delicate.

Beck felt responsible for her, had a driving need to care for her. He couldn't live with another woman's blood on his hands.

"Where's your first aid kit?" He focused on keeping his voice low, calm. Difficult to do, since he was still trying to regain the control shattered when he saw her being held down and struggling.

The heat pouring off him calmed Gwen's frayed nerves, and the deep rumbling of his voice comforted her. His softly spoken words contradicted his powerful, very large body. The fanciful notion of wanting him to wrap his big arms around her, to make her feel safe and secure, flashed through her mind. Curious, since she'd spent her entire life trusting no one, letting no one get too close.

She looked up ... way, *way* up into eyes the purest shade of sapphire. They stared back at her, reached into a place deep inside where she kept her mistrust and loneliness tucked safely away. Gwen stared deeply into their azure depths, sensing she wasn't the only one hiding something.

At the light caress of his finger, an unfamiliar awareness had suffused her. Like warmed oil pouring through her veins, heat spread, chasing away the cold grip of fear.

She dragged her eyes from his and took in the rest of him. And there was a lot of him to take in. She openly surveyed his handsome face, noticing the look of concern there.

A few locks of dark hair had fallen across his forehead. Without thinking, she reached to brush it aside and stopped herself. Curled her fingers into her palm.

His tight black T-shirt stretched across shoulders so broad, she wondered if he struggled to pass through a doorway.

Strength exuded from every part of him.

"Gwendolyn?" His deep voice drew her from her perusal.

She gave her head a shake and looked up at him.

"Please, call me Gwen." Why did she tell him to do that? Her mother was the only person she'd ever let call her Gwen.

"Gwen." He seemed to roll it around in his head. "It suits you."

"Thanks."

"My name is Beck. Well, Beckett, really, but only my

mother calls me that, and only when she's mad." His deep voice mesmerized her. "Do you have a first aid kit?"

She gave herself an internal slap to the forehead. *Of course. A first aid kit.* She'd been so busy blatantly checking him out, she'd forgotten what he asked.

"I keep it in the walk-in pantry in the kitchen." She started to move.

He stopped her with his hand on her forearm.

"Why don't you sit down and let me get it for you?" He steered her toward the old tufted club chair she'd scored at a garage sale then waited until she sat down. As if he expected her to collapse at his feet or some such nonsense.

"I'll be right back."

She opened her mouth to object, but he'd already turned and walked away. She shamelessly took advantage and checked him out, discovering his backside was as impressive as his front. He rolled his shoulders as if to relax himself. The muscles across his back rippled and bulged, forming a "V" to his narrow hips. She almost fell from the chair as she leaned sideways to watch him as his long legs ate up the distance across the hall to the kitchen. For a guy his size, he moved with an amazing amount of grace and efficiency. Not to mention stealth.

The distinctive squeak of the pantry door sounded across the hall, followed by footsteps a moment later. She sat bolt upright just before he walked into the office, the same purposeful strides eating up the space between them.

He squatted down in front of her, set the kit on the floor and rummaged through it. She looked at the top of his head. His thick hair had a slight wave to it. What she wouldn't give to run her fingers through it.

He grabbed some gauze pads, the antiseptic spray, and a Band-Aid way too big for the puny cut on her side. As odd as it felt to have someone fussing over her, she had to admit it was ... kind of nice. But for heaven's sakes, she'd suffered worse injuries working around the shelter.

"Gwen, can you lift your shirt for me?"

She lowered the afghan from her shoulder and scrunched up the shirt to expose the tiny cut.

Feeling his eyes on her, she looked at him, and everything stopped. The air around them stilled. The wreck surrounding them faded. The only things in focus were the striations of blue flashing in his eyes. Her eyes drifted shut, and she swayed toward him, inhaling deeply, taking in his intoxicating scent. Something more than cologne, it was dark, primal male.

Gwen opened her eyes at what sounded like a low growl and discovered she'd moved to within inches of his face.

His pupils dilated, and the deep blue iris became nearly nonexistent. He looked at her ... No, it was more than that. He looked *into* her, seemed to touch a part of her she hadn't known existed. She couldn't decide if he was too close or not close enough.

"I'm just going to—" He cleared the roughness from his voice. "I'm going to clean it. It might sting a little." He soaked a gauze pad in antiseptic and reached out to touch it to her side, hesitating.

"Don't be ridiculous." She rolled her eyes. "It's just a little cut." She smiled at him. "Here, give it to me and I'll do it." She reached out, and he drew back his hand.

"No, I need to do it."

He needs *to? Why in the world would he say that?*

His fingers quivered, and she hid her grin, amused by the fact this big, strong guy was having such a difficult time with such a tiny little cut.

He lightly dabbed the medicine to the wound. She *hissed,* and he drew back like he'd received a shock.

"I told you it was going to hurt." He ran his fingers

through his hair. The pained look on his face was sweet but unnecessary.

"Oh, for pity's sake. Just finish, would you? Sheesh." Gwen wasn't used to being treated like some sort of fragile flower, and she wasn't sure how she felt about it.

He took a deep breath and, with the speed of a triage medic, finished cleaning the cut and slathered some antibiotic gel on it. He used his teeth to rip open a Band-Aid about the size of half a football field and gently pressed it on.

Overkill much?

She wondered where he'd learned to treat a wound with such skillful efficiency.

His fingertips gently brushed over the edge of the bandage, sending a riot of goosebumps skittering across her flesh. She allowed herself a moment to enjoy the sensation. When was the last time anyone touched her with any kind of gentleness or caring? His touch soothed an ache she had kept suppressed deep inside. A loss she'd refused to acknowledge since her mother's death.

"You okay, honey?" The rumble of his voice and the endearment heightened her bliss. She practically melted into the chair when he wrapped his big hand over her knee.

What the heck was going on with her? She'd never responded this way to anyone in her life. Why this man? Why now? Maybe it was a simple case of hero-worship.

Heat flared across her cheeks, and she averted her gaze. Thanks to the curse of being a redhead, he surely noticed.

"Oh my gosh, Beck." Her words came out in a rush. "I am a terrible person. I haven't even thanked you for coming to my rescue. You came charging out of nowhere and took that guy on, and all I did was lay there like a helpless ninny. But he was so heavy, and I couldn't catch my breath, and ... " She was babbling. She knew it but couldn't seem make herself stop.

"Shhh." He saved her from herself by putting his finger over her lips. "It's okay. I'm just glad I was here to help you."

Suddenly reminded he was a complete stranger, Gwen shifted away from his touch.

"Why *were* you here?" The question blurted straight from her mind to her mouth. "I don't mean to sound ungrateful." After all, he had just saved her life. "It's just ... how did you know I needed help?"

What possible reason could he have for being in this neighborhood in the middle of the night?

CHAPTER ELEVEN

Doubt crept into Gwen's expression. *Shit*. Beck's only concern had been getting to her. There'd been no time to consider the ramifications.

Over her shoulder, peeling wallpaper and a poorly patched hole in the wall drew his eye. An idea came to him.

"I'm in construction and heard through the grapevine you might be looking for someone to help with the renovations here." He sent a silent shout-out to his dad. When most kids were spending their summer riding their bikes or swimming in the bay, he and his brothers were working for his dad's construction company. They'd learned to use just about every piece of construction equipment ever invented.

"I decided to check the place out on my way home. Quite frankly, I didn't expect anyone to be here." More lies to heap on the pile. Beck picked up the first aid kit, turned to set it on the desk and busied himself straightening the contents. "I'd just parked across the street when I saw someone climb through the window in there." He tipped his chin toward the other room. "I take it you live here?"

She practically jumped from the chair. Delicate shoulders

back, umbrage level turned up to high, she stepped close to him. All *damn the torpedoes and full speed ahead.*

"Is there a problem with that?" Hands fisted on her hips, she challenged him to question her judgment.

"Whoa." He held up his hands. "Relax, killer. I'm just surprised, is all." Apparently, he'd hit a nerve.

"Oh." Her posture relaxed—slightly. Her hands dropped to her sides. "Sorry."

"Without risk of injury, am I allowed to ask *why* you live here? This isn't exactly the safest neighborhood for a wo—"

She crossed her arms, cocked her hip and squinted at him.

"—for *anyone* to live alone."

Indignation crackled off the little dynamo. Beck guessed her good manners were the only thing stopping her from telling him to mind his own damn business.

Certain she wouldn't appreciate it, he held back a grin. She was so friggin' cute. He wedged his hands into his pockets to keep from reaching out and touching her.

The second she became aware of their closeness, her eyes dropped and a warm blush suffused her beautiful face. She turned and started folding the afghan like it was the most important task in the world.

"I can't imagine your family is comfortable with you being here all alone."

A brief flash of sadness crossed her features. Just as quickly, it disappeared. *How did she get so good at hiding her feelings?*

"Never mind." He backed off. "It really is none of my business."

"No." Blanket hugged close to her chest, she sighed and turned back to him. "I apologize. You were kind enough to jump in to help me, and I'm being rude." Gwen draped the quilt over the back of the chair. "I know it's hard to imagine anyone wanting to stay in this big, old, drafty building all alone." Her hand smoothed over the old bookshelves. "Especially in its current condition."

She turned to him. A sad smile and shadows under her eyes telegraphed exhaustion. "But I feel ... " She lifted a shoulder. "I don't know ... somehow connected to my mother here."

GWEN TURNED AROUND. Started straightening things on the shelf. *Why did I just tell him that?*

"Gwen?" She flinched when he leaned around to look at her face.

How does he move so silently?

"Are you okay?"

"My mother was the only family I ever had." The words just sort of tumbled out. "I mean, she was the only family I ever *knew*. My father died before I was born."

"Was?"

Oh God. Can I really do this?

She looked up at him. The compassion and understanding pouring from his eyes encouraged her to continue.

"About seven months ago, my mother was killed by a hit-and-run driver in front of our apartment." Her hand went to her chest, as if to rub away the ache of loss.

"I'm so sorry, Gwen." Sympathy imbued his words.

She quickly wrapped herself in the emotional armor she'd kept close at hand since childhood.

The friction of his calloused hand stroking up and down her arm soothed her more than she was comfortable admitting.

"You don't have to talk about this right now."

Relief flooded her. She didn't think she had the energy to deal with a bunch of crazy emotions.

"Thank you." She brushed her hands together and stepped around him. "Well, I'd better get this place cleaned up."

Gwen puffed out a breath and fluttered her bangs from her eyes. She walked into the kitchen and grabbed the broom and dustpan from the pantry.

By the time she got back to the office, Beck was picking up the broken pieces of her favorite mug.

"Um, what are you doing?" Surely, he had somewhere else to be tonight.

"I'm helping you clean up." There was a definite hint of *duh* in his voice. He righted the garbage can and tossed the shards away.

"But ... why?" She cocked her head.

"Why not?" He shrugged one big shoulder.

"I can manage it by myself." She rushed to get around him. "Besides, I'm sure you've got someplace you need to be."

A girlfriend or wife waiting for you somewhere? She scowled at the thought. *Ridiculous.*

"No, there's nowhere I need to be." Beck grinned. "No girlfriend or wife waiting for me tonight either."

She stumbled. *Holy crap. It's like he can see inside my head.*

"Do you mind if I ask you a question?" He bent and picked up the chair.

"Huh? I'm sorry, what did you say?" She needed to stop staring at the way his jeans pulled tight over his backside.

"Are you sure you're okay?" He reached out.

"Really, I'm fine." Gwen waved him away before he made contact. If he touched her again, she wasn't sure she could handle it.

He gave her an appraising look, then turned and started picking things up from the floor.

Gwen leaned over and picked up a large piece of the broken glass. Her reflection bounced back at her, and she cringed.

Here she was, in the same room with the most handsome man she'd ever seen—in her life—and she was a wreck. Her outfit was far from flattering. Strands of hair had escaped her bun and were hanging all over her face. Not to mention, a glob of pasta salad was smashed on the front of her shirt.

Great.

She set down the piece of glass and tugged the scrunchie from the unruly mass and wrapped it around her wrist. Her hair fell free to her waist, and she ran her fingers through it to get it off her face.

Gwen turned and found Beck's eyes following her hair as it shifted around her. They slowly traveled back to her face and, if she wasn't mistaken, he looked ... hungry. And not in an *I could really go for a sandwich* kind of way either. Their eyes locked and held. No man had ever looked at her like that before.

Before she could say anything, he blinked, and the in-charge, controlled man was back. Had she imagined what had passed between them?

"How old are you?" His eyes searched her face, as if he'd find the answers to some great mystery there.

She dropped her hand to her hip and said, "Why, Mr. O'Halleran, don't you know a man should never ask a woman her age?"

"A modern woman such as yourself can't possibly subscribe to such an antiquated philosophy." He crossed his arms.

"Fine." She heaved a dramatic sigh as she pulled her hair into a ponytail. "If you *must* know, I'm twenty-six. But I'll be twenty-seven in a couple months."

The fact she looked younger than her age could be a bit of a hot-button issue. Not for her, but other peopled often wondered whether she was mature enough for the task ahead of her. She loved seeing their expressions when she told them she'd earned her post-graduate school degree by the time she was twenty. All while working as a social worker.

"Don't you have a boyfriend or husband?" He tossed the question out there like he had every right to know.

"Why do you ask?" She couldn't keep suspicion from seeping into her voice.

"Because if you were mine, there is no way in hell I'd leave you here alone."

If I was yours? In spite of the fact his sexist tone should grate against her modern female sensibilities, her body responded to his deep and gravelly voice. She gulped, her lips parted, and she shivered.

He tilted his head and looked at her as if she were some great mystery.

"Beck?"

He blinked and, with a quick shake of his head, his eyes shuttered. But not before something dark passed over his features. Without a word, he took the broom from her, stepped back and began sweeping.

CHAPTER TWELVE

Disguised in the shadows deep within the bowels of the large, empty parking structure, Talbot sat in his car. The only light was a sickly, yellowish glow cast from an old overhead fixture that buzzed nearby. Far-off sounds from the city bled down through the concrete stairwells, mixed with the random clicks and pops coming from the cooling engine.

"Where the hell had that guy come from?" he mumbled. Considering the man's size and the way he'd fought, Talbot was lucky he wasn't laid out on a slab at the morgue right now.

Pain shot through him when he swiped his arm across his forehead. *Fuck!* He hissed a breath through his teeth, squeezed his eyes tight, panted until the sharp pain dulled. Every beat of his heart pounded through the wound in his shoulder. He twisted the rear-view mirror to get a look at his nose. Damn thing was broken and he could taste blood trickling down the back of his throat.

He exhaled. His head fell back against the headrest. He couldn't stop shivering, yet sweat poured off him. The noxious smells of old motor oil, dank cement and urine, combined with the distinctive coppery tang of his own blood, made his stomach roil.

Everything was going to shit because of that damned Tamberley broad. *How the hell was I supposed to know she had a daughter?* He would've been better off if he had never found her.

His failure tonight meant his options were dwindling. The walls were already closing in on him. There was no place he could hide where Radoslav wouldn't find him. The only alternative would be going to the Feds. Maybe he could work out some kind of deal. Who was he kidding? Even if he ended up in a cushy federal prison, Radoslav would still get to him.

A tire squealed in the distance. Talbot hunkered down in the seat, watched and waited, half expecting to see one of the old man's big black cars.

Relax. No one knows where you are.

Blood still seeped from the wound, though not as quickly. From what he could tell, it was a through-and-through. That was good, all things considered. The absolute last goddamned thing he needed was to have a bullet lodged inside him doing shit only knows what to his system. He couldn't do anything until he dealt with this fucking gunshot wound. Emergency rooms were out—too many damn questions.

Just my fucking luck the asshole was carrying.

This was going to suck, but it had to be done. He took a deep breath and, with one hand, reached over his head and wrestled off his shirt and sweater, dropped them in his lap.

The parking lot spun and everything dimmed to a pinpoint. Gritty eyes closed tight, he gave his head a quick shake, then reached over to yank open the glove box. Buried under some candy wrappers, a crushed pack of cigarettes, miscellaneous paperwork, and a half-empty pint of whiskey—

which he tossed on the passenger seat—was a small plastic container.

Talbot dumped everything from the container onto the seat next to him. He swiped his shirt over his face and rummaged through the pile. Half the contents fell to the floor. Before it rolled off the seat, he snagged the small bottle of hydrogen peroxide and gave it a shake.

Almost full. Good. He'd need every drop.

He wedged it between his knees, wrapped the trembling fingers of his good hand around the top and twisted. His bloody fingers slipped. An intense burning sensation sliced across his chest and back.

He wiped his hand down his pant leg, leaving behind a swath of blood to soak into the polyester. Teeth gritted, he heaved a sigh as the cap finally came off, dropped out of his hand and rolled to a stop near his foot.

Talbot shoved open the door, leaned out and quickly poured the entire contents of the bottle over the bullet hole. Fire lanced across his chest, over his shoulder and down his arm like a blowtorch against his flesh. He squeezed his eyes shut while it bubbled and fizzed. Dark pink liquid dripped to the concrete, forming a narrow stream that snaked across the filthy ground.

He let loose an involuntary, gut-wrenching growl, amplified by the concrete walls of the cavernous parking lot. A cat screeched nearby, and his eyes popped open. He squinted into the dark corners, certain to find a Russian lurking there.

Shit. I gotta get the hell outta here.

A sweaty hand on the steering wheel, he hauled himself back into the car and dragged the door shut. He pressed a large gauze pad over the wound and used his teeth to open the whiskey. He flipped off the cap of the near-empty bottle of ibuprofen, dumped the remaining pills into his mouth and choked them down with one long swallow.

Talbot's eyes drooped shut, and his head dipped to the side. The bottle slipped from his hands and fell to the floor.

He wasn't sure how long he'd been out when the distinctive reek of a Russian brand cigarette crept through the open window and up his nostrils. A shoe scuffed across the pavement.

Weak, struggling between conscious and unconscious, he fought to open his eyes.

Smoke blew across his face. He coughed, and pain lanced through him. Too late, he felt the cold muzzle of a gun pressed against his left temple.

So much for Mexico.

A SOFT KNOCK sounded on Nikolai Radoslav's hand-carved office door.

"Enter." In his silk pajamas and robe, Nikolai relaxed back into his large leather chair, a snifter of rare hundred-year-old Louis XIII Cognac cradled in one hand. A sun-grown Maduro Robusto smoldered in the other.

Gregor stepped in and quietly closed the door. "It is done."

"What about the other matter?" Talbot's incompetence was the least of his problems.

"Things are in motion. As soon as you give the word, she can be retrieved."

"Good. Good." A deep drag, and the end of his cigar sizzled and burned an angry red. The smoke circled above his head. "What do you know about the other man?"

"Evgeni could only say he was big, so I have instructed him to watch the shelter. If he becomes a problem, he will be dealt with." There was no conceit in Gregor's words. Only the confidence of a man who knew how to do his job.

“And the shipment?” Nikolai leaned forward and tapped the edge of the ashtray with his cigar. A one-inch chunk of ash dropped off.

“Payment was verified and Teague’s man picked up the shipment an hour ago.”

Nikolai nodded, then settled back. “As you know, I will be out of the country for a few days.” The soft leather creaked beneath his shifting weight. “You will stay and oversee this ... situation while I am gone. Da?”

“Da,” Gregor responded.

Nikolai dismissed him with a wave of his pudgy hand. The door clicked shut.

He swirled the amber liquid, glazing the inside of the crystal glass. He brought it to his nose, closed his eyes and inhaled the rich, woodsy aroma before tipping it back for a smooth mouthful. Heat curled around his tongue, down his throat, and coated his stomach. What was left of his cigar teetered on the edge of the ashtray, and a slow smile crept across his face.

CHAPTER THIRTEEN

Beck gathered his oversize duffle and his tool belt from the backseat. He locked his rig and shoved the key fob in his pocket. As he walked across the street, the hairs on the back of his neck tingled. His pace steady, he surreptitiously scanned his surroundings.

The sun's rays had just begun to peek over the top of the haggard rooftops, reflecting off the top-floor windows on the opposite side of the street. Everything below, including the shelter, was soaked in an amber glow. The hope of a new day, even in this forgotten corner of the city.

Folks who'd sought shelter for the night in darkened doorways of row houses or businesses were gathering up their meager belongings, moving out of sight before the old neighborhood fully awakened. Down the street, the clank of an accordion gate dragging open broke through the silence. His mouth watered as the rich scent of meat already smoking at the local BBQ joint wafted through the air. Across the street from it, the small family-owned bakery pumped out its own soothing aromas.

Just because he couldn't see anyone watching the shelter didn't mean they weren't. Radoslav's people knew how to be invisible. Which was exactly why he hadn't wanted to leave Gwen last night. Unfortunately, the stubborn woman had given him no choice.

As they'd cleaned up the mess, he'd come up with an idea of how to stick close to her.

The first step, convincing her to hire him to do the renovations, had been relatively easy. After he'd boarded up the broken window with a piece of scrap plywood he'd found out back and fixed a few other things, she'd said, "You're hired."

The second step, however, had taken a bit more persuasion.

Gwen had balked hard when he suggested he crash in a room upstairs as payment for a portion of his work. She'd stood firm until he said it would be more convenient if he didn't have to make the long trip to and from his place every day. Gwen being Gwen, she was too nice to say no.

To seal the deal, he'd reminded her that his presence would be an effective deterrent against a repeat of what had happened to her. It had bordered on emotional blackmail, but he would do whatever was necessary to get close to her.

Once he'd made sure she was locked up tight, he'd grabbed a business card from his pocket and made a quick call as he walked back to his vehicle. Ten minutes later, Marden's black and white had rolled up alongside his SUV. He'd assured Beck they'd cruise past the shelter periodically until their shift ended, by which time Beck would be there.

Marden had called him earlier this morning and let him know everything had been quiet. Beck was anxious to see for himself. He climbed the steps and, when he pushed the old button next to the door, nothing happened.

Looks like fixing the buzzer is my first job.

He knocked, waited a few minutes, then knocked again. She still didn't answer. Beck became concerned, pounding on the door as he called her name.

"I'm coming. I'm coming. Hold your horses."

Relief washed over him at her grumbled words.

The deadbolt clunked, and the knob turned. Both hands around the knob, she struggled to drag it open.

He grabbed the edge of the door.

"Hang on. Let me get it." Beck set down his gear and looped his toolbelt over his shoulder.

"Back up a little bit." When she didn't move, he added, "Please."

Her hands dropped. She turned and shuffled out of the way.

He pushed the door open, grabbed up his duffle, shoved the door shut and locked it. He turned to find her glaring daggers up at him. Beck had personal experience with grumpy, sleepy women. His baby sister, Emily, wasn't even close to being human until she'd had at least two cups of strong tea and a glazed donut. Unfortunately, he hadn't thought to pick up either in his haste to get here. Huge tactical error on his part.

Wonder if the bakery down the street has doughnuts?

She opened her mouth, most likely to give him hell for waking her, and he held up his hand.

"I'm sorry it's so early, but I figured you'd want to get your window replaced as soon as possible."

Truth was, he'd been a little crazed thinking about her here alone.

Her mouth snapped shut and she looked down, noticing his duffle bag for the first time. She sighed, as if just remembering their agreement—and regretting it.

Too bad, sweetheart. You're stuck with me now.

In spite of her scowl, she was adorable with her messy braid trailing down her back. The big T-shirt she wore had slipped, exposing a graceful shoulder. She was sleepy and looked soft and warm and sexy as hell. Like a woman who'd spent the night rolling in the sheets with someone. A thought he quickly shoved aside.

"Please tell me you're not one of those annoyingly chipper early morning people." She turned away and started walking without waiting for his answer. "Because if you are, we're going to have to rethink this whole arrangement."

She stopped, turned back to him. "Are you just going to stand there or what?"

Beck set his stuff at the base of the stairs and followed her into the big kitchen.

Gwen shuffled to the counter, yawned and started dumping scoops of coffee into a filter. As she was about to add the seventh scoop, he spoke up.

"Are you planning to use that to peel wallpaper?" He wrinkled his nose and jerked his chin to the near-overflowing filter.

She looked down, then her head fell back on a sigh. "This is your fault for waking me up so early."

"Are you hurt anywhere else?" He pointed to the bruises beginning to show on her small wrists. Beck wanted to destroy the man who'd put them there.

She held them up and turned them, as if noticing the marks for the first time.

"Here, let me." He took the scoop from her and guided her to the table.

She pulled out a chair and plopped down onto it. Her head landed with a *thunk* on top of her folded arms.

"You do realize how late it was when you left, don't you? Late? HA! I should've said *early.*" Though her voice was muffled, it was clear she was not happy he'd shown up this early. It was also obvious she wasn't going to discuss her injuries.

He dumped the coffee grounds back into the canister and started over. Assured the coffee wouldn't kill them, he pressed *brew*, turned and leaned back against the counter, arms crossed over his chest, legs crossed at the ankles.

"Yes, it was two thirty. But don't worry, I managed a few hours of sleep."

She lifted her head. "I am *such* a jerk." Crankiness had been replaced by guilt. "Here you are, being so nice to me after basically saving my life last night, not to mention helping me clean up that awful mess, and I'm treating you so horribly."

Her forehead *thud, thud, thudded* against the table.

"Hey, hey." Beck squatted next to her chair and put his hand between her head and the hard surface. "I was only kidding."

"Please don't be nice to me." She lifted her head and whispered, "I don't deserve it."

"Now you're just pissing me off." He cupped her cheek. "How much sleep did you get anyway?"

"Probably more than you, since you had to drive home." Elbow on the table, she leaned her head in her hand and looked at him.

He swept a rebellious strand of golden-red hair from her face. His fingers massaged into the back of her neck. She hummed, and her eyes drifted shut.

The coffee sputtered. She opened drowsy eyes and looked at him. A warm pink brightened her face just before she cleared her throat and scooted out the other side of the chair. For a few magical moments, she'd relaxed at his touch. And he'd liked it. A lot.

What the hell am I doing? It was going to be ugly enough

when she found out he had lied to her. The last thing he needed was to encourage any kind of physical relationship.

It probably would've been a better idea for Caleb to stay with her. After all, Beck had felt the sparks between him and Gwen last night. But the idea of his charming, man-whore of a brother being anywhere near her aggravated the hell out of him.

Oh well. Too late to change things now. He was just going to have to redouble his focus to keep this small woman from wreaking havoc with his hard-earned control.

GWEN MADE BREAKFAST FOR THEM. It was the least she could do after being such a hag to him. She usually preferred tea, but she'd enjoyed multiple cups of his exceptionally good coffee and watched in awe as he managed to polish off a ridiculously tall stack of pancakes.

It's no wonder. *For heaven's sake, look at him.*

Against her protests, Beck helped clean the kitchen, then she showed him to his room.

"There's not much to it right now, but it's big and has its own bathroom." Gwen looked from him to the bed.

"Um ... I'm afraid you'll have to make do with the queen-size bed. Unless you'd prefer to bring your own."

"It'll be fine." Beck chuckled, the sound rusty, like it was something he didn't do often.

He dumped his stuff on the bed and went straight to work. The buzzer at the front door had been his first project. He'd offered to replace it with a traditional doorbell, but she'd declined. The shrill sound of the original buzzer reminded her of a simpler time. And you could hear it all over the building.

Two hours later, she leaned against the bottom banister

and watched him reinstall the big front doors. Gwen took advantage of the opportunity to really look at him.

My. Oh. My.

The muscles across his back strained and bulged under his T-shirt. His tool belt hung low, emphasizing his narrow hips and those crazy-wide shoulders she seemed enamored with. She figured his ripped physique was the byproduct of his years working construction.

Her eyes trailed from his big weathered boots up his very long legs, where they lingered on his tight butt. Funny, she'd never given much thought to men's backsides before. Though she was far from an expert on the subject, her own personal ranking of his would be *spectacular*.

Her perusal continued up his broad back to the back of his head. His dark brown hair was kept short, except where it lay slightly longer at the top, creating waves that grazed his forehead. Several times today, she'd resisted the urge to reach up and slip her fingers through it, to stroke it back from his face.

Beck was just so incredibly ... male. And she couldn't take her eyes off him.

He easily shut the doors, he slid the new lock in place, flipped two aggressive-looking deadbolts, turned and smiled. "All right. Good as new."

"I'd like to keep them unlocked during the day," Gwen said.

He looked at her like she was crazy. "Well, I'd like to keep them locked. At all times."

"I want the people from the neighborhood to feel welcome. Which isn't going to happen if they show up and the door's locked." She crossed her arms and tapped her foot.

He threw his hands up and stomped toward the back door, grumbling something about *stubborn women*.

In his wake, she strolled up, opened the myriad locks and went back to work.

Being around him all morning had been ... oddly comfortable. Gwen had never shared a space with anyone but her mother. Let alone a tall, dark, intense stranger who made her feel things she never had before. Things she didn't understand and wasn't quite sure she could handle. Now that he was here, she could admit, if only to herself, she was happy about it.

He'd asked a lot of questions about her, her work as a social worker, her mother. She still couldn't believe she'd told him last night how her mother died.

She'd been surprised how easy it was to open up to him again today. "I haven't heard from the detective working my mom's case since he basically said, 'Don't call us, we'll call you.' I understand the police are busy, but this is my mother. She was my only family. It's like they don't even care."

"Gwen, I wish there was something I could say, but I don't know what I would do if something like that happened to my mom."

He didn't realize just being able to talk to him about it made her feel better.

It didn't escape her attention that was the closest he'd come to talking about himself or his family. Any time she asked for details about his life, he would divert attention back to her or the shelter. She already knew he was a contractor, loved her pancakes and made awesome coffee. The only other things she'd learned—he was thirty-three and single.

A couple of times she got the distinct feeling he was hiding something, and her mother's voice whispered through her memory. *Don't trust anyone, Gwen. Keep people at a distance, and they can't hurt you.*

She refused to live the rest of her life that way. Afraid of everything, of everyone.

You're wrong this time, Momma.

Gwen kept reminding herself Beck's personal life was really none of her business. His job at the shelter didn't require him to divulge all his deep, dark secrets. No matter how much she wished he would.

BECK OPENED THE BACK DOOR. Closed it. Opened it again. The new hinges were smooth and quiet. Worth every penny.

Before he closed it, he got a good look at the back yard. All the tall weeds and junk were a security nightmare.

He shut the door and locked it. The neighbors would all have to come through the main doors.

Beck headed to Gwen's office. He rounded the doorway and said, "Gwen, do you happen to have a lawnmower?"

She looked up at him. Distress wrinkled the space between her brows.

He set his tools down and crossed to her desk. "What's the matter?"

"What do you mean?" She shuffled papers on her desk. "Nothing's the matter. I was just about to come ask you if you're ready for some lunch."

He crossed his arms and, one eyebrow lifted, looked down at her. Maybe if he waited long enough, she would tell him the truth. Because she'd definitely been troubled by something.

She stepped around the desk. Head tipped back, she mirrored his stance.

They stared at each other until one corner of his mouth lifted.

"Okay, honey, you win." He relaxed. "This time," he said under his breath as he turned and walked away.

"Why do you call me that?"

Beck slowed his pace when he heard her work boots rushing up behind him.

"Call you what?" He turned, and she was so close, he got a whiff of her lilac shampoo. "Honey?"

Gwen stepped back, and her gulp could be heard around the open space. She whispered, "Yeah."

"I don't know." He wedged his hands in his pockets, drew his shoulders up. "I guess it just slips out. Does it bother you?"

"I guess it's okay, I mean, if you really want." She lifted a shoulder.

Oh yeah. I really want. Which is why he said, "I need to go make a phone call."

GWEN WATCHED BECK WALK AWAY. *What just happened?*

He climbed the stairs, and she jumped when his door slammed. She stood and stared at the ceiling.

What was that all about? Is he upset I asked him why he calls me "honey"? No, that couldn't be it.

Once again, those old suspicions nibbled at the tiny seeds of trust that always tried to take root. *At some point, you're going to have to decide if you trust him or not.*

BECK CROSSED into the bathroom and shut the door. He pulled out his cell and called Caleb.

"Hey, bro. How's our girl today?" Caleb was just being Caleb, but Beck damn sure didn't like him referring to Gwen as "their" girl.

"Gwen"—he emphasized her name—"is hanging in there. She's a lot tougher than she looks." Stubborn was more like it.

Caleb cursed when Beck told him about the bruises he'd seen on her wrists.

"How are *you* doing?" his brother asked.

"Other than being supremely pissed the guy managed to get away, I'm fine." Part of Beck wanted to find the guy, to get some answers. Another, more ruthless part hoped he'd bled out somewhere.

"It's like I told you last night, Beck, that was no burglary gone bad. I'm thinking it was our boy Talbot, and his plan had been to get in, snoop around and get out. I'd imagine he was surprised as hell to find *her* there, let alone someone with your training."

Last night, they'd discussed their plan of action. Beck would stay at the shelter, try to find out the connection between Gwen and Radoslav. Caleb would continue digging into her past and try to find out more about Chadwick and Talbot.

"Yeah, Gwen's the only thing of value in the place right now." Beck leaned back against the edge of the counter. "Any luck on tracking Talbot down?"

"As of about thirty minutes ago, there were two gunshot wounds reported. Nothing suspicious about either of them. We knew it was a long shot." Frustration tinged his voice.

The guy would have to be a complete moron to go to an emergency room or any of the clinics nearby.

"I put in a call to a buddy of mine at the SFPD. A guy I've worked with before." Caleb took a swig of something, then continued. "I asked him to keep an ear to the ground about our boy. He said he'd let me know if anything turns up." He hesitated. "You sure you don't want to bring your old task force in on this yet?"

"I'm sure." It would be nice to have the full resources of the bureau available to him, but they came with strings attached. Beck was done with strings. He refused to go back to having his hands tied because of a bunch of rules and regulations.

"Fine." Caleb sighed. "I'll keep digging. You just take care of Gwen. It sounds like she's special to you."

"Don't be ridiculous. I'm here to do a job. Nothing more." He wasn't sure who needed the reminder, Caleb or himself.

CHAPTER FOURTEEN

Gwen's heart expanded as she wandered from room to room. Over the past week, they'd made amazing progress on the renovations.

Painting, stripping old wallpaper and installing new shelves in the pantry and closets. Pulling up the old carpet and adding it to the pile in the front room. They'd become quite the team. She'd drawn the line at plumbing repairs. *Yuck*.

Gwen smiled at the memories.

Beck possessed infinite patience, always taking time to explain things in the simplest terms. Not once did he talk down to her or get frustrated with her lack of skill.

At the end of each day, they'd prep for the next day's job, and he would put the tools neatly away. The one time she'd tried to help out by putting them away, he'd spent fifteen minutes redoing it before he could relax. After getting cleaned up, they'd make some kind of dinner, nothing fancy, then sit at the old rickety table and talk late into the evening.

It was during these relaxed times Beck had finally begun to open up. A little.

"Yeah, Michaleen and Molly O'Halleran are the best." His eyes softened. "No matter how many times we did something stupid or got into trouble, our folks made sure we knew how much they loved us. Right before they grounded us for a week."

"Did your mom say 'wait until your father gets home'?"

"Hell no." He laughed. "Mom is a tiny force of nature. She is plenty scary all on her own. She handled five rowdy sons and an obstinate daughter with the ease of a drill sergeant."

He tilted his head and looked at her. "You remind me of her."

That had been one of the nicest things anyone had ever said.

She thought back to all the times her only friends had been her books. "It must have been great growing up with so many kids around. Always having someone to talk to."

A home, family, children, things he mentioned so casually were the things she'd never let herself dream of having. Until now.

"Great? I don't know about that." He chuckled. "At one time or another, each one of us ran away from home just to get a little space. And by 'ran away,' I mean we hid in the tree-house in the woods behind our house, and usually for only about an hour or until the next meal. Except Jonathan. He could pack up and be gone for days. Eventually, I learned not to worry about him."

More than once, Gwen had noticed how Beck seemed to take responsibility for his brothers and sister. Maybe it was one of those oldest-child things.

"No matter how competitive we are, or how pissed we get at one another, we always have each other's back. Always."

"Was your sister—"

"Emily."

"Emily. Was she overwhelmed by all you boys?"

"Emily? Overwhelmed?" He scoffed. "She was a pain in the ass. Whatever the boys did, she wanted to do."

In contrast to his words, his voice was rich with affection.

"Dad hated her being on sites with all those construction guys. Tried to make her work in the office. Hell, if he thought he'd get away with it, he would've wrapped her in cotton and bubble wrap."

He scrubbed a hand over the dark stubble along his jaw. "Mom wasn't having it. She told him Emily should have a chance to do any darn thing the boys did. That's as close as she ever came to cussing."

Gwen could only smile. It had all sounded gloriously chaotic and magical and ... perfect. It reignited a fire of longing for something she'd always secretly hoped for. A family of her own.

Beck wasn't the only one who'd opened up. She'd talked about the void left behind by a father she never knew and what it was like being raised by an overly cautious mother. Without meaning to, Gwen had allowed him to finagle his way behind her long-ago-constructed walls.

BECK SET ASIDE the marinating meat and turned to wash his hands. Out the window, tall weeds had taken over the backyard. Once it was cleaned up, a gas grill would be a nice add. They could have neighborhood cookouts during the summer.

What the hell? If things went according to plan, he'd be long gone by then. His mission was his priority. He couldn't afford to get distracted by ridiculous fantasies of backyard barbecues.

Focus, Beck.

He tensed when Gwen walked up behind him, bringing her soft lilac scent with her. Her hip grazed his as she washed her hands. Like it was the most natural thing in the world, she reached up and dried her hands on the towel hanging over his shoulder.

He smiled down at her.

She gave him a mischievous grin and bumped his hip to scooch him over, then set about peeling potatoes.

Out of the corner of his eye, he watched her. Enchanted by the way her nose tipped up just the tiniest bit at the end. Charmed by the way her tongue peeked out between her lips whenever she concentrated on something. The late afternoon sun shone through the window, giving her skin a warm glow. Her long lashes cast shadows over her cheeks.

Not only was Gwen beautiful, something she was completely unaware of, but she was also kind and selfless. Sometimes to her own detriment.

She reached to turn on the water, and her arm brushed along his. Never had the faintest, most innocent touch caused such a visceral reaction.

Not good.

He yanked the towel off his shoulder and tossed it on the counter. “Um, if you’re good here, I’m going to run upstairs for a few minutes.”

Her smile faltered. “Oh, um ... sure.”

Beck turned and walked out of the kitchen. With every step away from her, he reminded himself of his mission. He climbed the stairs, shut the door to his room and called Caleb.

“Hey, man, I was just about to call you.” His brother’s voice held a definite sense of urgency.

“What’s up?” Beck strolled to the window and spread apart the slats of the blinds to view the street below.

“I did some digging on Chadwick and Gwen.”

“What did you find?”

“Okay, Chadwick first.”

Beck settled his shoulder against the window frame.

"Full name, Joseph Allen Chadwick III. Thirty-two years old. Never married. Only child. By all accounts, spoiled by his wealthy parents. Both deceased. They left him an impressive inheritance, which he managed to burn through. He had been moderately successful as a real estate agent. Which, as you know, is how he met Gwen."

"Had been?" There was a *click-clicking* of computer keys in the background.

"Yeah. He runs with a pretty high-end crowd, so I took a peek at his financials. Boy, did it shed some light on a few things."

"I trust this 'peek' can't be traced back to you?" The last thing he wanted was for his brother to get busted for hacking into someone's system.

Caleb made a pained sound. "You wound me." He chuckled. "No worries, big brother. It's like I was never there. During the past eight months"—*click-click*—"he's maxed out his credit cards and taken out two mortgages on his big fancy house in the hills. And, surprise-surprise, he's delinquent on all of them."

"Drugs? Alcohol? Gambling?" Beck asked. Financial problems could almost always be traced back to some combination of the three.

He looked toward the sound of children laughing. *Those damn kids are going to kill someone riding their bikes on the sidewalk.*

"Drugs, mainly. Crack and cocaine. Haven't found anything yet to indicate gambling's an issue. Alcohol doesn't seem to be too big of a problem, other than it's said he acts like an asshole if he's had too much."

More clicking of keys.

"He became a supplier to some of his fancy friends. In the process, he picked up the nasty little habit. Rumor is, he started skimming product off the top and got in deep to Radoslav."

"How much are we talking about?" Chadwick never mentioned a dollar amount during his conversation with Radoslav.

"Over two hundred grand. Not including whatever interest the old man's charging him."

Beck whistled between his teeth. "Still doesn't explain the deal he made with Radoslav. Why not just pick another woman, someone with no ties back to him? Why Gwen?"

"Apparently, he's been putting the full court press on her for a while now. Even after she turned him down, he kept coming on to her pretty aggressively at fundraisers, really embarrassing her." Caleb tsked. "It got so bad, people had to intervene a couple times."

"Wait a minute. You're telling me he was willing to sacrifice her because she rejected him?" Beck resisted the urge to run downstairs to check on her.

"That would be my guess. The guy sounds like a vile maggot. I really hope he goes down hard." Caleb made no attempt to hide his disgust.

"Count on it." A door opened across the street, and a woman stepped onto the stoop to shake out a rug. "Anything else?"

"I've got some info on Gwen."

The woman turned and went back inside.

"Go." He walked over and stretched out on the bed, reclining against the headboard.

Beck justified digging into her past by telling himself he was doing it to protect her. Yet, guilt still nagged at him.

"Her dad's name was Richard Tamberley, right?"

"Yeah, why?"

"I pulled her birth certificate, and there was no father listed."

"What?" Beck slowly sat forward, turned and set his feet on the floor.

"It's not just that. I couldn't find *any* record of Richard Tamberley. *At all*. And before you ask, I tried every possible spelling." He sighed. "It's like the guy never existed."

"Nothing?"

"Nada. And believe me, I dug deep. There is no Richard Tamberley. Not now." Caleb hesitated. "Not ever."

"I don't think Gwen is lying." Beck stared at the floor and rubbed his thumb along his bottom lip. "Which tells me her mother must've lied."

"Yeah, well, that's not the only strange thing she did." Papers rustled in the background. "She kept them pretty damned isolated."

"Isolated?" Beck didn't like the direction of his thoughts.

"The lady who lived next door said she never got more than a glimpse of either one of them. She remembers thinking how strange it was that Gwen's mom wouldn't let her play with the neighbor kids. There were no birthday parties. No sleepovers. No going to church. Nothing. Then one morning they were just ... gone. Left in the middle of the night."

"Assuming she was just being an overprotective mother, why lie about Gwen's father?" Beck's mind raced and halted on one frightening possibility.

"Unless the person she was protecting her from—"

"—was her father," they said in unison.

"Shit," Caleb said under his breath. "Explains a lot."

"What do you mean?" Beck had a very bad feeling.

"Maggie always took jobs that paid in cash, and I couldn't find one single credit card or bank account in her name."

Beck hated Gwen had been lied to by the one person she should have been able to trust. But it sounded like Maggie Tamberley had done it to save her daughter's life.

"Her mom was killed in a hit-and-run in the apartment parking lot about seven months ago." Caleb hesitated. "Gwen was there when it happened."

"Jesus. She told me how her mother died but never mentioned she was there when it happened."

No wonder she was living here. Rather than stay where she'd watched her mother die, she'd chosen to live in a place some would consider barely habitable.

"The cops followed up on a few leads. Nothing panned out, and the file was dumped on the cold case desk." He sounded as pissed as Beck felt.

"Okay." Beck started ticking off with his fingers. "We know she lied about Gwen's father. Kept them isolated. Lived off the grid. Then one day she's the *innocent* victim of a violent hit-and-run?"

"I think we can both agree it was no accident." Caleb echoed Beck's thoughts.

"You're probably right." He walked back over to the window, peeked through the blinds. "Thanks for pulling all that together for me."

Sunlight flashed off a windshield at the far end of the street. Beck squinted, leaned closer. "Shit."

"What is it?" Tension sifted through his brother's voice.

Looks like I'm taking a little walk.

"Not sure yet, but I'll let you know." Beck moved away from the window. "Let me know when Radoslav gets back."

"Roger that, and I'll call you if I find out anything new." Caleb said. "Watch your back, bro."

"Thanks." Beck hung up, stopped at the bottom of the stairs and glanced back toward the kitchen. Gwen sat at the table, flipping through carpet samples.

Without so much as a scrape of sound, Beck drew open the newly repaired door. He stepped outside and quietly pulled it shut behind him. He stood on the stoop and stretched his arms over his head. Using his peripheral vision, he checked out the car at the corner. Only the front end was visible, but Beck recognized it immediately.

Casual as you please, hands in his pockets, he whistled as he jogged down the steps. About two hundred feet from the car, the driver noticed him approaching.

The engine fired up.

Beck started running.

The car slammed into gear, and tires squealed.

He jumped over a pile of garbage.

Dodged around those damn kids on their bikes.

He got to the corner just as the car screeched through a turn at the end of the street. The oily smell of burnt rubber hung in the air.

He leaned over, hands on his knees, to catch his breath.

Son of a bitch. It wouldn't be long before Radoslav knew Beck was connected to Gwen.

CHAPTER FIFTEEN

Gwen was halfway up the stairs when Beck walked in the front door.

"Oh." She turned to him, looked upstairs, then back at him. "I was just coming up to let you know dinner is ready."

She walked down, stopping at the second step from the bottom.

"I didn't know you'd gone outside." She glanced around him. "Is everything all right?"

He locked the door and moved closer, standing eye-to-eye with her.

"I was just helping Mrs. Saulinksi with something." The lie rolled off his tongue too easily.

Mrs. Saulinksi was a frail little eighty-year-old widow who lived in a rowhouse across the street. She'd lived in the neighborhood her whole life. A shameless flirt, she would chat him up anytime he walked down to the barbecue joint or the bakery. Every few days, she ventured out of her home and stopped by to check on their progress. She shared stories and old photos of the family who'd lived here. Her eyes misted up when she'd told him of how the whole family perished in a fire at their summer cabin.

Gwen got this soft look on her face, and her eyes went all warm and gooey.

His brows crunched together and he tucked his chin. "What is that look?"

"You're so *sweeeeeet.*" She looked up at him like he was something special. She couldn't be further from the truth.

He shook his head and grumbled as he walked toward the kitchen.

She followed, chattering at his back the whole way.

"Well, you are. You want everyone to think you're this *big, tough guy.*" She lowered her voice on *big, tough guy*. "But you drop what you're doing to help a little old lady."

Beck turned on the water, pumped some soap into his hands and scrubbed with a bit more vehemence than necessary. "It was no big deal." Christ. He already felt like a big enough piece of shit without her gushing over him for something he didn't do.

"I disagree. I think—"

He scowled down at her. "Can we please drop it?"

He turned off the faucet, shook water from his hands and snatched the towel from the hook.

She opened her mouth, and he cut her off. "Please?"

"Fine. Fine." She held up her hands and stepped into the pantry, where she mumbled, "I still think you're sweet."

Gwen pushed the pantry door shut with her hip and handed Beck a corkscrew and a 2012 bottle of Darby Chaos. When he learned the silky red blend was one of Gwen's favorites, he'd called Darby English directly and asked him to send him a few bottles. Beck and his family had become friends with the winemaker after a visit to his tasting room in Washington State.

It was the perfect choice to accompany the beef stew

Gwen had thrown in a crockpot that morning. Throughout the day, the rich smells from the kitchen had grown and drifted throughout the building. *Good old comfort food.* Every whiff took him back to when they were kids coming inside after a day spent playing in the snow. Back to a simpler time.

Gwen and Beck took their time eating and nursing their one glass of wine each. They had projects to finish tonight, and that wouldn't happen if they drained the bottle. When the kitchen was clean and leftovers stashed away, she went to her office to pay bills. Beck worked in the dining room, getting the new light fixture ready to hang.

He flattened the box and tossed it on top of the pile of stuff to be recycled. A quick look at his watch and he flipped off the light, heading toward the office.

The room was dense with shadows. Her new desk lamp and the standing torchiere lamp in the corner were the only sources of light. Sitting at her big old desk, Gwen looked like a little kid. Though Beck was all too aware she was a full-grown, gorgeous woman.

She's going to ruin her eyes. Not wanting to startle her, he scuffed his boot.

Her head lifted, and her face lit up. "Hi."

Stick a fork in me. I'm done. A smile and one little word and she owned him.

"That's not enough light for when you're working in here." He pointed back and forth between the lamp in the corner and the one on her desk.

"Oh." She looked around as if noticing the darkness for the first time. "You're probably right. I get so involved in what I'm doing, I don't think about it."

Gwen dropped her pen on the desk and rubbed her fingers over her eyes. She yawned, reaching high over her head in a stretch. Beck forced himself not to stare at her chest.

"Come on. That's enough for tonight." He sauntered toward her.

She patted a stack of papers on her desk. "But I still have bills—"

"They're not going anywhere, honey." He loved the way her cheeks pinked whenever he used the endearment.

She clicked off the desk lamp, then walked over and pulled the chain on the torchiere. An intimate light snuck in from the antique wall sconces in the hallway.

Beck extended his arm and, without hesitation, she placed her much smaller hand in his. As had become their ritual over the past few nights, he led her the ten or so feet to the doorway of her adjoining bedroom. Each night, their bodies ended up closer than the night before. Tonight, no more than a whisper of space separated them.

"Well ... good night, Beck." Her low, husky voice shot straight to his crotch. Amazing eyes shimmered up at him, his own yearning reflected back at him from their teal depths.

"Good night." Beck framed her face, rubbing his thumb across the velvety skin of her full lower lip. His hands skimmed down and down until his fingers splayed over the curve between her neck and shoulder.

Gwen gasped, and her heartbeat thundered beneath his thumbs where they brushed against her throat.

Christ almighty. Her instinctual reaction made him want to throw her over his shoulder, haul her upstairs and toss her onto his bed. Like a caveman claiming his woman.

Gwen was guileless. Wasn't into playing games. She had no clue looking at him that way lit a white-hot fire inside him. Every little catch in her breath when he moved closer. The way her pupils dilated, leaving only a thin border of blue-green. Hell, even the way his name sounded on her lips made him wish he could forget all the things he'd been taught about being an honorable man.

Walking away from Gwen each night had become increasingly more difficult. The worst form of torture. Sometimes, it seemed her door and Beck's good intentions were the only things separating them. He'd been tempted to say to hell with Radoslav and this operation. To lose himself in her and let her giving spirit heal the wound festering deep inside. Each time, he'd held back, unwilling to risk destroying her hard-earned trust.

THE LITTLE VOICE in Gwen's mind tapped her on the shoulder. *Step away from him. He's not the man for you.* Overcome by a desperate urge to feel his strong arms around her—and scared to death because of it—she shooed away the pesky reminders and leaned into his touch. Though the thick, sturdy walls she'd constructed and hidden behind her whole life had begun to crumble since meeting Beck, she wasn't sure if she would ever be able to trust him completely. Wasn't sure she knew how.

"You okay, Gwen?" A corner of his mouth lifted. His talented fingers caressed small circles on her shoulders. The devilishly handsome rat fink knew the effect he had on her.

"I'm fine." *As if.* She was this close to jumping into his arms and taking what she wanted.

"Okay then. I'll see you in the morning." His whispered words made her feel all tingly inside.

She'd expected him to back away. Instead, the hands on her shoulders pulled her closer. Gwen's eyes drifted shut. She leaned into him and held her breath, anticipating the feel of his lips on hers. Disappointment speared through her when what she felt instead was a soft, lingering kiss on her forehead.

Beck's fingers dragged across her skin as he stepped back.

He wedged his hands in his pockets, gave her a last long look, then turned and walked away, taking his wonderful scent and big strong arms with him.

Anchored in place, she listened to him take the steps two at a time. Like always. The sound of his door clicking shut snapped her from her reverie.

Gwen frowned. *What the heck just happened?* She walked into her room, shut the door and leaned back against it.

A brotherly kiss to the forehead?

"Well, *that* didn't go the way I thought it would." Her head fell back against the solid wood. "Pretty much squelches any silly romantic notions I might've had."

Disappointed and sadder than she cared to admit, she pushed off the door with a huff and got ready for bed.

CHAPTER SIXTEEN

Beck dragged his eyes open and looked up at the ceiling. Light had barely begun to seep through the blinds, accentuating a thin crack in the plaster overhead as night slowly retreated. He draped his arm over his face just as his phone vibrated on the nightstand. He grabbed the annoying device and saw the number two flashing on the screen. Caleb, the second child.

"Yeah?" His voice sounded like crushed rock.

"They found the guy who went after Gwen. We were right. It was Talbot."

"Where is he?" He tossed back the covers and sat on the edge of the bed.

"The morgue."

"Son of a ... " He scrubbed his hand over his face. *So much for questioning the SOB.*

"A couple beat cops came across the car two days ago when they chased a perp into a parking garage. Found him slumped over in the front seat."

"I know I hit him, but it wasn't a kill shot."

"Not even close. A single bullet to the left temple did the job."

"Why did it take so damn long to find him?" It had been over a week since the attack. Rage crashed through him every time he thought about it.

"The garage was prepped for demolition and didn't have security. Somehow, he managed to get around the barricades without anyone noticing. Except for the guy who shot him, of course. Looks like Talbot pulled in there to patch up the shoulder wound. For all the good it did him."

"Any ballistics on the bullet that took him out?"

"Initial findings say it came from a Tokarev."

No surprise there. It was the same model handgun Radoslav's men carried. They were cheap and, unlike most American-made weapons, extremely difficult to trace.

Beck stood and paced the floor. "I hate that Gwen is in the middle of all of this."

"Can't say as I blame ya."

"What about the car I chased?"

After a short pause and some clicking, Caleb confirmed it belonged to one of Radoslav's men.

"What's next?" his brother asked.

"By now, Radoslav knows I'm here." Beck had known his plan to use Gwen might put her in danger. "I'm sticking close to her."

"She given you anything about him you can use?"

"Nothing. And as far as I know, he hasn't tried to contact her either."

Radoslav's caution was surpassed only by his brutality. He would pull together as much information as possible before making a move.

"Okay. Oh, I'm still digging into Barlow, too." Caleb started investigating him after Beck told him the man was on the take. "Haven't found anything, yet, but I'll keep looking."

The deputy director had been at this game too long to make a mistake. But if he had, Caleb would find it.

"Anything else?" Beck grabbed his jeans from the foot of the bed.

"No, that's it." Caleb's laptop snapped shut in the background. "Take care of our girl."

"Count on it." He hung up, rushed through a shower, then headed downstairs.

Gwen was reaching for a glass in the cabinet when he rounded the doorway. One corner of his mouth lifted. Arms crossed, he relaxed his shoulder against the jamb.

With a tilt of his head, he grinned at her old Converse sneakers. Ankles he could span with the fingers of one hand led to gorgeous, shapely legs. He tilted his head the other way. A pair of denim cutoffs did amazing things to an already stellar backside. She was petite but didn't lack for curves in all the right places. The bottom of her shirt lifted, exposing a sliver of creamy white skin.

His nostrils flared, and an involuntary growl rumbled up from his throat.

She fumbled the glass and caught it against her chest inches from crashing to the counter. She spun around, eyes wide.

"Holy criminy, Beck." Hand to her heart, she exhaled deeply. "What are you doing sneaking up on me like that? You scared the living bejesus out of me."

He pushed off the wall and stalked toward her.

Glass clutched to her chest with both hands, she slowly backed away at his approach. Despite telling himself he needed to be cool, to pull back, he kept closing in until her back pressed against the counter.

Her breath caught, and she swallowed hard when she looked up at him. There was no fear in her deep soulful eyes, only the same yearning propelling him toward her.

He pried the glass from her grip and pressed his body against hers as he reached around to set it on the counter.

"I'm sorry. I didn't mean to scare you." It was the last thing he would ever want to do.

Sunrays sparked off strands of her golden-red hair. He slipped her bandanna off and tucked it in his back pocket. Her hair felt like silk against his palm as he smoothed it back from her face.

The *tick-ticking* of the ridiculous cat clock on the wall seemed unusually loud, its tail swinging back and forth the only movement in the room.

Gwen's breathing accelerated when he skimmed his fingertip along her collarbone, then up and up until he traced over the blush on her cheek.

"Good morning," he whispered into the shell of her ear, need weaving its way through his voice.

She shivered. Her nipples peaked against his chest. She looked up at him, eyelids heavy.

"Good—" She cleared her throat. "Good morning."

Beck enjoyed the feel of her against him and the way her soft scent wrapped around him. *Why do I keep torturing myself this way?*

Last night, he'd gone straight from her to a cold shower. Unfortunately, it had only dulled the rampant thoughts of her in his bed, writhing beneath him. Eventually, they'd morphed into visions of the steak knife sticking out of Jodi's chest. It could just as easily be Gwen.

Protecting her had become his priority. As much as he wanted to stay right where he was, he forced himself to take a step back.

"How 'bout I start some coffee." He grabbed the empty carafe and turned to fill it at the sink. He could feel her eyes on him, confused, wondering why he kept pulling back.

"While it's brewing, I'm going to haul some of the garbage out." He headed to the dining room.

She pushed off the counter. "I can help."

"Not necessary," he called back over his shoulder. "I'm only carrying out a couple bags that are in the way of what I'm going to do today."

He usually waited until just before the scheduled pickup to put stuff out. Too much crap in the bin was a temptation some folks couldn't resist. People rooting around in the adjacent alley were a distraction he couldn't afford.

By the time he came in to wash up, she had a plate loaded with eggs, sausage and toast waiting for him on the table.

What a sweetheart.

"You didn't have to make me breakfast." His mom was the only woman who'd ever cooked for him, and only because she lived for that shit.

She lifted a shoulder. "I was making myself something, so it wasn't a big deal."

They sat down, and he dug in. The egg yolks were perfect for dipping his toast, and the hand-shaped sausage patties were cooked to perfection. He brought a bite to his mouth, glanced over and noticed she'd only pushed her food around her plate.

"Gwen—"

"Beck—"

They spoke at the same time.

He swept his hand in her direction. "Ladies first."

"I'd like to talk about the items on the *To Do* list, if you don't mind."

Okay, so she wasn't going to bring up the frustrated and horny elephant in the middle of the room. *Good.* It was for the best she chose to ignore the sexual tension between them. Didn't mean a part of him wasn't a little bit disappointed.

"Hit me with it."

The view of her backside jogging across the hall made him hard. He shifted in his seat, filled his head with sports scores, wallpaper samples, car parts. Anything to help distract his dick from broadcasting what they both wanted.

List and pen in hand, she sat down, grabbed her toast and took a big bite. She took a gulp of orange juice, ran her pen down the list, stopping halfway.

"Next item is getting the last coat of paint on the walls in the family room."

"Sounds good." He washed his dishes and stood them in the drying rack. "While you finish your breakfast, I'll get the light fixture hung in the dining room."

Gwen caught his arm as he walked past. Her brow arched high as she looked up at him, held out her hand, palm up, and wiggled her fingers.

He smiled and pulled her bandanna from his pocket, disappointed she'd remembered.

She drew her long braid forward. It curved over her left breast. She folded the scarf in a triangle, draped it over her head, and tied it under her hair at the back of her neck.

He couldn't help himself. He ran his hand down the smooth length of her braid.

She gasped, and her chest expanded, causing his knuckles to lightly brush over her breast.

Their eyes met and held.

Static charged the air between them.

His thumb smoothed over her cheek. He loved touching her silky-soft skin.

Before things went too far, he lifted the braid and draped it down the back of her chair, then turned and left the room.

About an hour later, from the corner of his eye, he watched her paint the dark trim around the window. Multiple colors were splattered on her clothes. A splotch covered the end of her nose where she'd scratched it. She was the sexiest little painter he'd ever seen.

"I've been wondering." He ran the paint roller up and down the wall. "How are you able to cover the costs for renovating this old building?" He leaned over, pushed the roller through the paint tray, turned back to the wall. "It has to be a pretty expensive undertaking." Would she finally mention her conversation with Radoslav?

She set the small can of trim color on the tarp and laid the brush across the top.

Beck took a last pass on the wall, put the roller on the edge of the paint tray and laid it on the ground.

They reached for the rag at the same time, and their fingertips touched.

She pulled her hand back and, like so many times before, their eyes locked and the air stilled around them.

Gwen was the first to look away. She squatted down and busied herself with putting the lid back on the paint can.

"We had some savings, and my mom had a life insurance policy. They were enough to cover the cost of the building and some of the renovations. It won't be anything fancy. Just the basics. Which, sadly, is a lot more than a most of the folks around here have ever had. "I can't wait to give them that." Her voice held a well-deserved note of pride. She peeked up at him from under her lashes then stood, wiped her hands across her butt and looked around the big room. "Sorry. I get a little ... enthusiastic whenever I talk about it."

"What you're doing here is amazing." He stepped closer. "Don't ever apologize for being passionate about it. You have every right to be proud."

"Anyway ... " With a wave of her hand, she cast off his compliment. "Donations, endowments and grants will also fund the day-to-day expenses. If they're managed properly, which I can assure you they will be, it'll be enough to keep the shelter operating for a long time." She stretched her neck side to side and dug her fingers into her shoulders. "I'm so excited to get the renovations done. The people in this neighborhood deserve a place like this."

A compact bundle of sunshine, she poured light and warmth into parts of him lost in the dark for so long. Hearing her talk about the people she wanted to help restored some of the faith he'd lost in humanity.

He grabbed the rag off the floor, and her eyes followed him as he approached. Unable to resist touching her any longer, he gently swiped it over her nose to remove the paint, then dropped it on the floor. He turned her around and flipped her braid over her shoulder.

A slight tremor slipped through her. She glanced over her shoulder, a questioning look on her face.

"Be still," he whispered close to her ear. His thumbs slipped beneath her collar and began to massage circles in her tight muscles.

She moaned and her head fell forward. "You must never stop what you are doing."

He chuckled. *Not a problem.* He was in no hurry to take his hands off her.

Kneading and pressing, he could feel the tension leaving her body. She offered no resistance when he pulled her back against him. Sparks seemed to flash under his skin wherever their bodies touched. Being this close to her, his hands on her like this, was playing with fire.

ANOTHER INVOLUNTARY—AND slightly embarrassing—moan escaped Gwen's lips, and her bones seemed to melt. She and Beck had exchanged more heated glances than she could count, and he wasn't shy about touching her. But for some reason, he always pulled away. Until now.

"Do most of your donations come from businesses or private individuals?"

How could she possibly be expected to concentrate enough to answer his questions while his breath warmed her neck and his calloused fingers worked their magic on her shoulders? Her mind was mush, and she blamed him.

"Gwen?" The way he growled her name made her insides quiver.

"Hmm." Her eyes drooped.

"If you keep making those sexy little noises, I can't be held responsible for what might happen."

Had she made a noise? Gosh, I hope I'm not drooling.

She licked her lip, then whispered, "What might happen?"

His hands stilled.

Silence hung in the air.

Relief flooded over her when he pulled her closer, her back flush along his front.

"I might kiss you the way I've wanted to since the first night when I saw how hard you fought against your attacker."

Oh. My. Goodness.

"Or I might kiss you the way I want to every time you talk about how much you want to help this neighborhood."

No way could she stifle the shiver prickling goosebumps down her arms.

His fingers returned to working their magic.

"What did you ask me again?" She really needed to get it together.

"I was asking about your donations. Do most of them come from private individuals?"

She could hear the smile in his voice. Darn man knew exactly the effect he was having on her.

"Oh, right, donations." She tried to step away, yet he seemed unwilling to release her.

Beck was a powerfully built man, yet everything about him always seemed so controlled. Even now, his large hands were incredibly gentle in deference to her size.

Resigned to her wonderful fate, she relaxed into his touch once more. She marshaled every ounce of her restraint to keep from purring like a cat curled up in front of a big log fire.

"We do have a few large, private donors who contribute anonymously, but a majority of the funds come from grants and businesses looking for a tax write-off."

He worked the muscles between her shoulder blades, then up to the nape of her neck.

She turned. "Are you sure you want to hear this?" She scrunched her nose. "It's kind of boring."

"I wouldn't have asked if I didn't want to hear it."

GWEN DIDN'T MENTION individual names. Beck could push, try to get what he needed, but she was a smart woman. He couldn't risk rousing her suspicions.

The trust in her eyes when she turned to face him should've made him happy. Instead, deception's sharp talons dug further into his conscience. When his lies were exposed, he feared she would never look at him the same way again.

He gave himself a quick mental head shake. His selfish concerns were wedged into the same compartment his anger and frustration had occupied since the day Radoslav smirked at him from the other side of that two-way mirror.

"Hey, we've been hard at it all morning." He stepped over the paint pan to create some distance between them. "I'll make you a deal."

"What kind of deal?" Her arms crossed, and she narrowed her eyes at him.

"So suspicious." He took in the mess around them. "I'll clean this up if you'll make us some lunch."

"Oh, well then, *that's* a deal I can handle. Sandwiches okay?"

"Sounds perfect."

With a big smile, she turned and walked away.

He began gathering up the paint, tarps, brushes and other supplies.

Since seeing her illuminated by a streetlamp and glowing like an angel lost in hell, he'd been drawn to her. In spite of the shitty timing and all the crap going on, she'd managed to make him smile again. What worried him was the way she'd made him start to care again, too.

CHAPTER SEVENTEEN

Gwen was just drying her hands when her phone rang in her pocket. She didn't recognize the number.

"This is Gwendolyn Tamberley."

"Gwendolyn, this is Joseph Chadwick."

"What do you want?" Gwen mumbled into her phone as she tossed the towel on the counter and headed into her bedroom.

"I'm calling to see how your meeting went with Mr. Radoslav?"

"It was fine."

"Did he say anything about making a donation?"

"Not that it's any of your business, but he said he would think about it."

"I'm sure he'll realize what a great thing you're doing there."

"Quite frankly, I'm not sure Mr. Radoslav is a good fit for the shelter." She paced across the floor.

"How did you leave it?"

She stopped. "He said he was going to be out of town for

a while. Look, I appreciate you putting in a good word for me and the shelter, *Mr. Chadwick,* but I just don't think it's going to happen."

"What do you mean it's not going to happen?" he shouted.

She gritted her teeth. "I have told you before, I do not appreciate you speaking to me like that." She tamped down her fear and tried to sound unaffected. "And quite frankly, it is no longer your concern. Please do not contact me again."

Gwen tossed her phone on top of her dresser and knocked over the frame holding the picture of her father.

"What a jerk." She righted the photo. "It's like he's completely forgotten what he did to me."

"Everything okay in here?"

She whirled around to face Beck. "What? Oh ... yeah. It was nothing."

He leaned a shoulder against the doorjamb and waited.

She chewed her bottom lip and headed into her office. "Just someone who won't take no for an answer," she mumbled to herself.

"*Who* won't take no for an answer?"

Shoot. She should've known he could hear her. The man never missed a thing. Unwilling to show how unnerved she was, Gwen forced a smile, turned and ran into Beck's chest.

"Oh—" She stumbled back, and quick as a flash, his hand reached out to steady her. "It's nothing."

Time to change the subject.

"How about I get to those sandwiches?" She turned and brushed past him on her way to the kitchen.

"Nice try." Beck followed. "Come on. Spill it."

She yanked lunchmeat, cheese, pickles and condiments from the fridge and plunked them on the counter. She grabbed four slices of bread, remembered she was feeding Beck and grabbed two more. With a bit more vigor than necessary, the innocent bread was slapped with mustard and mayo.

"It was Joseph Chadwick, the real estate agent who sold me this building." She banged the knife down on the counter. "He was friendly enough ... at first."

Slap. Slap. Slap. Lunchmeat assaulted the bread.

"Then he got a little *too* friendly."

Slap. Slap. Slap. Slices of cheese joined in the attack.

"I made it clear I wasn't interested in anything more than friendship."

She picked up the knife and prepared to saw through the towering sandwiches. "That's all. The end."

"The end, huh?" Beck's arms reached around her.

She jumped. "You have *got* to stop doing that."

"Doing what?"

His hands covered hers, and he lifted them away from the sandwiches. He took the knife from her and set it on the counter. Hands on her shoulders, he guided her to the table, pulled out a chair and settled her in it. Any other time, she would have loved the feel of his hands on her.

"Sit. Otherwise, I'm afraid our lunch won't survive."

"Ha. Ha." She rolled her eyes.

Beck went back to the counter and finished building the sandwiches and poured them some tea.

"Come on, Gwen. Don't you know by now you can trust me?" His voice took on a strange quality whenever they ventured close to the territory of trust. An intangible thing she'd begun to notice the more time they spent together. For a gal with her own history of trust issues, it troubled her.

You're being silly, Gwen. She was just keyed up after talking to Chadwick.

"Of course I trust you, Beck." She picked at her sandwich. Ran her thumb over the condensation on her glass.

She could feel his gaze boring into her. Curse him. Sometimes his ridiculous patience was super annoying.

Gwen threw up her hands. "Okay, fine. If you *must* know. He got a little bit ... aggressive one time and—"

"What do you mean by 'aggressive'?" Anger saturated his words. Big shoulders drew back, and he slowly set his sandwich on his plate.

Okay. Wow. He looks really mad.

"It was nothing, really. I handled it," Gwen reassured him. "It's just kind of embarrassing, is all."

Beck pushed his plate away, crossed his forearms on the table and settled in.

"Fine," she growled. "But you have to promise not to laugh."

"I promise." He crossed his heart and held up three fingers. At six-foot-four, with dark hair begging to be stroked, eyes so blue they defied description, not to mention a body fit to be climbed, he looked like the world's studliest Boy Scout.

"Now quit stalling and spill it." He picked up his sandwich and took a huge bite.

"One day he showed up here high on something. He waltzed into my office and asked me out. Again." She tapped the pickle spear against the edge of her plate. Took a gulp of tea. "After I told him I wasn't interested—again—he got a little rough and kissed me."

"What the hell?" Beck shoved up out of his chair and loomed over her across the table. His chest expanded, and a look she'd never seen before darkened his face. She knew his anger wasn't directed at her, but it didn't make it any less terrifying.

She held her hands out in front of her. "It's okay. I managed to shove him away. Told him to get out and not come back." Gwen flicked her wrist. "It was nothing. Just a stupid kiss." She'd tried to convince herself of that many times. Then she'd get a flashback of Chadwick's eyes when he'd grabbed her and knew there was something more sinister involved. "He called the next day and apologized. Said he'd made arrangements for me to meet with an important man named Nikolai Radoslav."

AT THE MENTION of Radoslav's name, Beck lowered himself to the chair.

"He told me Mr. Radoslav was looking for a place to donate money."

Manipulative bastard. Chadwick knew Gwen would never turn her back on an opportunity to help the shelter.

"Did you take the meeting?" Of course, he already knew the answer but wanted to see what she'd say.

"Yes, I met him at a restaurant in Little Russia. The only thing is ... " She hesitated, pushing away her uneaten sandwich.

He remained silent.

Brows drawn together, her eyes troubled, she turned to stare out the window.

"Mr. Radoslav ... He ... Well, he kind of gave me the creeps." She gnawed on her thumbnail.

Good instincts. "What do you mean?"

"I'm probably being ridiculous, but he kept looking at me in the strangest way."

Beck laid his hand over hers. "It's not ridiculous at all. Listen." He waited until she looked at him. "I'm a firm believer in following your gut. If you weren't comfortable with this Radoslav guy, you shouldn't let him get involved with the shelter."

She shifted in her seat.

"You said your meeting was in Little Russia?"

She nodded. "At the Mt. Elbrus Restaurant. He seemed very ... *at home* there."

"That's a seriously sketchy part of town. If this guy is a regular there, I would recommend you stay as far away from him as possible." Beck couldn't stomach the thought of her being anywhere near the psychopath again. "And anyway, you don't need his money. Once word gets out about all the great things you're doing here, you'll have donors lining up to throw money at you."

"From your lips to God's ears." She chuckled.

Beck looked at their hands. His big and scarred, hers delicate and fragile-looking.

It was becoming near impossible to be noble.

CHAPTER EIGHTEEN

Beck's cell phone vibrated next to him. He was sure he'd just fallen asleep after another restless night being tormented by images of Gwen lying beneath him, all her beautiful hair tangled out across his pillow. Her amazing eyes luminous with desire as he enjoyed the warmth of her welcoming body.

He cracked his eyes open. His hand scrubbed over his face, and he grabbed his phone. He saw the number two and swiped his finger over the screen.

"What?" He hoped his voice conveyed his displeasure. Not that his brother gave a shit.

"And a fine good morning to you, too, brother dear." After everything Caleb had been through, it was hard to understand how he maintained his cheerfulness. "Gosh, I hope I haven't interrupted something." Caleb paused. "I haven't, have I? You can tell me, ya know."

His brother tweaked him about his relationship with Gwen any chance he got.

Relationship? Whatever this *thing* was between them, it wasn't a relationship. Not as long as he was lying to her.

"It's ... " Beck pulled the phone from his ear and looked at it. "Six o'clock in the morning. I hope you didn't call just to give me a hard time."

"Geez, who stole your lollipop?" Caleb chuckled, not the least bit contrite.

"You know what you can do with your lollipop."

The jerk just laughed harder.

"Okay, okay." Caleb's laughter faded. "Man, I don't know what's going on over there, but dude, you're as surly as an old bear with a toothache."

Beck's hand scraped across his whiskered jaw. "Nothing's going on."

"Well, why the hell not?"

Beck opened his mouth to respond, but Caleb kept talking. "Hear me out on this. You like this girl, right?"

After a moment, Beck decided, *what the hell.*

"Yeah, I like her." *I like her too damn much.* He threw his arm over his eyes. "But she deserves better than what I can give her."

"What the hell does *that* mean?" Caleb almost sounded angry. "You're a good man, Beck. You deserve to have something, some*one,* good in your life."

Why should I get a "happily ever after" when Jodi will never have the chance for one? His brother couldn't understand. He'd never let anyone down.

Once Radoslav's organization was destroyed and Gwen was safe, he would force himself to walk away from her. Assuming she hadn't already walked away from him.

"Tell her who you are." Caleb released an uncharacteristic sigh. "Tell her the truth. She'll understand why you had to lie to her."

"I appreciate all that, but I know what I'm doing, okay?" He sat up. "Just let it go."

"We're not done talking about this. You know this, right?"

"If you say so." His brother was like a dog with a bone, and Beck couldn't deal with it right now. "Now tell me what you really called about."

"First, Talbot. The only lead they have is a guy who stumbled out of a nearby bar. He may or may not remember seeing a dark car pull into the parking garage."

"Makes sense." Beck threw back the covers and got out of bed. "Radoslav has a thing for big, black cars." He made all his people drive them.

"Speaking of the old wackjob," Caleb said, "he arrived back in town around three o'clock this morning."

"Can't say I'm surprised." Finding out Beck was hanging out at the shelter would cause the old man serious heartburn. "We had a development here yesterday. Chadwick called Gwen." Knowing Chadwick had put his hands, his mouth on her had pricked every possessive cell in his body. He couldn't stand the thought of another man touching her. Hell, he didn't even want another man's *eyes* on her.

Like you have any right to feel that way.

"She's not easily intimidated," Beck continued, "and she tried to hide it, but she was pretty freaked out just hearing the guy's voice on the phone."

Caleb cursed. "Well, confirms our theory he was pissed at her for being shut down."

"Keep digging on this guy. I want to find something, *anything* we can use to put him away."

"You got it. Listen, Beck, I ... " He hesitated.

"What is it?"

"I know I've said it before, but I think you need to pull the plug on this whole thing. Bring Simmons in on it and let your old team handle it."

"I'm not walking away from months of work until I have what I need to bring Radoslav down. I'll keep doing what I'm doing and stick close to Gwen. He's not going to make a move on her while I'm here."

"You sure about that? Because I'm not. She might be safer if she knew the truth."

"I disagree." If she learned the truth, she would reject him and the protection he offered.

"But—"

"Drop it, Caleb."

"If you say so. Just ... be safe. Love you, man."

"You, too." Beck set his phone on the table and went into the bathroom. He showered, dressed, and headed downstairs to his girl. He stopped.

Mine? It seemed so natural to think of her that way.

Could his brother be right? Was it okay to let himself live again? Was it time to let go of the past?

The idea pinged around in his conscience and wrestled to overpower the denial and self-recrimination, the anger and hate rooted there.

Anxious to see her, he hurried his steps. He rounded the corner to the kitchen just as she was reaching for the coffee maker. "Stop. Right. There."

She jumped, let out a little *ack* and turned to look at him. "Why do you insist on doing that?"

He felt bad about startling her, but the way her chest went up and down with each heavy breath kind of turned him on.

"You have *got* to start clearing your throat or shuffling your feet or ... *something.*"

Miss I Hate Mornings turned back to her task, muttering something about how she ought to put a bell on him.

Even giving him hell, she was the sweetest, most gorgeous creature.

His smile slipped. Like a frying pan to the back of the

head, it hit him. *Shit. I'm a goner.* He'd been fooling himself to think he could deny or ignore his feelings for her.

What had tipped the scales? The way her tiny body was swallowed up by her ridiculous old T-shirt? Or was it all that irresistible hair, mussed from sleep? Maybe it was how the golden light of morning streaming through the old window seemed to seek her out. Like *it* was drawn to *her* warmth.

There was no one thing about her. It was everything about her. The way a beautiful blush warmed her makeup-free face whenever he looked at her. How her laugh chipped away at the ice around his heart and her smile chased away some of the darkness. It was in the way she treated people with such compassion.

Gwen was the only person who gave him hope.

"I thought we had a deal you weren't *ever* going to make coffee again." He crossed his arms and leaned his shoulder against the door frame.

"I apologize. Let me start again. Good morning, Beck." She peeked up at him through long lashes, and one side of her mouth lifted in a sexy little smile.

His noble intentions vaporized. The way she looked at him together with the way his name sounded on her lips unlocked a long-starving need, and his craving for vengeance was overshadowed by his longing for this woman.

As if caught in a current too strong to resist, his long legs ate up the space between them until he forced himself to stop. No more than a foot separated them, and her lilac scent wrapped around him like a delicate caress.

Brows furrowed, she stared up at him.

He cradled her face in his hands.

Her delicate fingers curled around his wrist. As if to keep him from letting go.

I never want to let go.

He forced himself to take a deep breath. To slow down.

Her eyes drifted shut, and she pressed her cheek into his touch.

He skimmed his free hand from her jaw, combed his fingers through her hair.

"Let me see your eyes, honey." Longing tinged his whispered words.

Heavy lids lifted, and her eyes followed him as he closed the space between them. Giving her time to stop him, if she wanted.

Close enough their rapid breaths mingled, Beck hesitated.

Her eyes dropped to his mouth. Her pink tongue swiped across her bottom lip, leaving it shiny.

"Good morning yourself." He leaned down and stroked his mouth delicately back and forth over her lips.

On a small sigh, she relaxed into him.

A storm raged within, but he held himself back. His tongue dragged slowly across her soft bottom lip.

She whimpered, and a small moan burbled up from the back of her throat. All hopes of being nice and gentle were obliterated by those small sounds.

His restraint snapped.

Beck crushed his mouth to hers, and a surge of lust fired through him like fine whiskey on a cold night. He grabbed her waist and set her on the counter.

An adorable giggle escaped her as she wrapped her arms around his neck and held on tight.

He draped a hand over each knee and slid them apart. He wedged himself between them.

She gasped when her center came in contact with him.

He twisted her braid around his fist, pulled her head back, elongating her neck, and dropped his mouth to hers. His tongue plunged, explored, as if his salvation existed in the corners of her mouth. He wanted to take, to consume, to *own* her.

The intensity of the kiss seemed to surprise her. She was slightly awkward at first but was a quick study. He loved knowing he was the first to spark this level of passion in her. *I want to be the last.*

GWEN HAD BEEN KISSED BEFORE. Or so she'd thought. What Beck was doing? Not even in the same galaxy. With each sweep of his tongue against hers, a surge of heat pulsed through to every one of her millions of nerve endings. It seriously messed with the firing of her brain synapses.

He consumed her. Couldn't seem to get enough of her. He nibbled on her lower lip. Skimmed his mouth across her cheeks. Kissed her eyelids, then her jaw.

Her hum of pleasure surprised her.

"I shouldn't be doing this." His lips whispered over the shell of her ear and sent a riot of shivers swarming over her.

Shouldn't be doing this?

Before she could dwell on his words, his tongue traced around the edge of her ear and trailed down. He stopped at a spot just below her ear, where his teeth gently nipped and his tongue darted out to soothe the spot.

She dropped her head to the side, giving him better access. Far be it from her to make it more difficult for him to continue doing what he was doing.

Long fingers speared through her hair, grabbed up her braid, then drew her head back.

Her breath caught. The slight sting heightened her awareness. Gwen gripped his biceps, held on tight as he scattered open-mouth kisses along her neck, his tongue circling the spot where her pulse beat frantically.

She stifled a whimper when he lifted his mouth from her skin.

His fingers opened, and her braid fell against her back.

Her eyes dragged open, connected with his. She was sure she glimpsed a kind of internal conflict steal through their blue depths, but he blinked, and it was gone.

Stop thinking so much, Gwen.

The roughened tip of his middle finger leisurely grazed her collarbone, then dipped briefly into the hollow at the base of her throat. Down and down it continued until it skimmed ever so lightly over the slope of her breast.

Her involuntary moans and whimpers seemed to encourage him to explore further. Her breasts tightened when his fingertips teased a circle around them, just shy of where she wanted them.

She arched, pressed herself into his touch, an unspoken signal of what she wanted. What she needed.

Beck cupped her breasts, and her head fell back on a sigh.

Hallelujah.

His large hands opened and spanned her entire chest. Her heart pounded beneath them. He caressed his palm over a taut nipple, lightly plucked it between his finger and thumb.

Her senses kicked into overdrive, and she became a panting, whimpering mass of sexual need. Her fingers tightened around his arm as if to keep from falling off the edge of the world.

Beck reached behind her and pulled her snug against him.

She wrapped her legs around his waist and crossed her ankles behind his back. His erection pressed against her, intensifying the aching throb between her legs.

He groaned, and his mouth smashed down on hers. He cupped the back of her head, held her where he wanted her. Took what he wanted.

Gwen couldn't get close enough. Wanted him inside her more than her next breath.

Just when she thought their first time would be right

there on the kitchen counter, which would've been fine by her, he wedged his hands under her butt and lifted.

She *squealed* and tightened her legs around him. "What are you doing?"

"Moving this to a more suitable venue." His mouth took possession of hers, and he started out of the kitchen.

She forced herself to pull away from his lips. Between heavy breaths, she managed to say, "Shouldn't you watch where you're going?"

He didn't respond, just turned into the hallway and headed toward the stairs.

She pointed at her room as they passed by. "I have a bed right in there, ya know."

"For what I want to do to you, we're going to need my bigger bed."

Well, alrighty then.

She nuzzled against the crook of his neck and inhaled his masculine scent. The tip of her tongue stroked the outer rim of his ear.

He sucked in a breath and tightened his grip, setting off a tingling pressure between her legs.

Empowered by his response, Gwen speared her fingers through his hair and crushed her mouth to his. Not wanting to risk scaring him off with the words, she channeled her "I love you" into her kiss.

Loving Beck was the most beautiful thing she had ever experienced in her life. Which is also why she was afraid it could end up being the most painful.

CHAPTER NINETEEN

Beck stopped halfway up the stairs. He pulled his mouth free, rested his forehead against hers. His chest heaved with each breath.

"Christ, Gwen, you're killing me."

He felt her smile against his throat just before she took a quick nibble, then kissed and sucked at the underside of his jaw. He'd been hard since the second their lips had touched, but when her warm breath blew across the shell of his ear, he was sure he'd explode right then and there. He took the rest of the stairs in two long strides, worried he would suffer permanent damage if he didn't ditch his jeans—and soon.

He kicked the door shut behind them, the best he could do to keep the world and all its ugly truths at bay. He crossed the room, lowered her to the bed and lay down between her legs. He dragged the tie from her braid and spread her hair across his pillow. *Better than any fantasy.*

She was like a delicately sculpted piece of art. Curves and nuances, colors and light, purity and serenity. Simply put, she was flawless.

Her head fell back, exposing the creamy white surface of

her neck, a temptation he couldn't resist. He tasted her soft skin with open-mouth kisses, then trailed his lips to where the curve of her shoulder met her neck. His teeth nipped, then his tongue darted out to soothe.

He worked his way up and up until he sucked her earlobe between his lips.

She gasped, and the sound vibrating from the back of her throat flew miles past sexy.

Beck did his best to ignore the part of his anatomy standing up and taking notice.

This moment mattered too much. *She matters too much.*

GWEN'S HEART raced and butterflies swarmed at the feel of Beck's mouth against her skin. And, boy, did she love the way his touch lit up all her nerve endings.

He took hold of the bottom of her T-shirt, dragged his fingertips up her body and tickled along her ribcage.

She squirmed, then lifted her arms without hesitation.

He pulled it over her head, tossed it over his shoulder, then sat back.

Unnerved by his silent perusal, she moved to cover herself.

"No." His voice was rough as sandpaper. "Do you trust me, Gwen?"

She nodded. Loved his deep voice, the way it swept over her ... through her.

"Can you give me the words, honey?"

Seriously? Remembering how to breathe was challenging enough. Now he expected her to form words, too?

"Yes, I trust you." And it was the truth. Her body tight with anticipation, she could only manage a whisper.

"Good." He unrolled her fingers, kissed the center of each

palm and extended her arms above her head. He curled her fingers around the rails of the headboard. "I want you to keep these right here."

Gwen swallowed and nodded.

Goosebumps charged across her chest. Her nipples beaded, and her breasts felt full.

She ducked her chin and watched his hands on her as he dragged her panties off and set them aside.

Nearly panting, mouth slightly open, she let her head fall back on a sigh.

He continued his tactile journey by smoothing his hands up her shins, over her knees, slowing as he trailed them over her thighs, before tickling them along her ribs.

She trembled.

"Are you cold?" He started to reach for the blanket.

"No." She cleared her throat. "Not even close."

"You are so damn beautiful," he whispered.

She looked at him through hooded eyes.

He smiled, then his mouth resumed its journey across her hypersensitive skin. First stop, her right hip, where he took a soft bite before stroking his tongue over it, then he moved over to her left and did the same. Giving her no time to process the sensations bombarding her, he pressed a tender kiss just above the patch of hair between her legs.

She squeezed her knees together. "Beck? I ... "

"It's okay, Gwen. I've got you."

Did he ever. Her pulse raced. Her mind whirled. She writhed beneath his touch, and a moan escaped.

"Jesus." His thumb stroked over her bottom lip. "It makes me crazy when you do that."

"What?"

"Chew on this succulent bottom lip of yours. It makes me want to do all sorts of things."

"Like what?" She really did want to know. Gwen wasn't a

virgin, but she didn't have a lot of experience, either.

"Open your legs for me, honey." Beck looked up at her, a devious spark in his eyes. "And remember, keep those hands where I told you." He wedged her legs farther apart with his broad shoulders. "Beautiful." Without warning, he lowered his mouth and dragged his tongue the length of her intimate folds.

Gwen's back arched, her hips shot up off the bed and her heels dug into the mattress. His big arm pressed her back to the mattress. His low groan vibrated against her most sensitive area and shot a low buzz of current through her. Sparks crackled and flashed beneath her skin. She struggled to catch her breath as her heart tried desperately to beat from her chest.

Like a lightning strike, sensations blasted through her. Her inner muscles contracted and slickened. "Beck—"

"Relax." Lowering his head, he worked her with his tongue, his lips, then added his finger, sliding it up and down her folds.

Thoughts scattered. She whimpered, "Oh, God. I can't ... It's ... "

"Yes, you can." He inserted his finger, gliding it in, then out, crooking it until he hit what had to have been her elusive G-spot.

Her head rocked side to side on the pillow.

"Come for me, Gwen." Adding his tongue to the intimate assault, he circled her clitoris then pulled the bud between his lips and tugged.

She thrust her hips against his mouth as he worked the tight bundle of nerves. Her sex squeezed his finger. Gwen gripped the pillow. Her heels battled for leverage. She held on tight, helpless against an unseen force lifting her up and up, to the top of a cresting wave. Her climax burst outward, and she shouted Beck's name. Stars exploded behind her eyes, and the wave crashed. She tumbled, turned, caught in a churning wash of emotions and sensations.

Her chest heaved with the effort to catch her breath. After soaring in the clouds, she felt suddenly heavy. Gwen swallowed back the intense emotions pouring through her and tried to gather herself.

She wasn't sure how long she languished in her thoughts when she heard the rustle of clothing then felt the bed shift.

Gwen managed to drag her eyes open and found Beck, all broad shoulders and looking amazing in his muscled, naked glory, standing at the foot of the bed. His dark hair was a mess from where she'd grabbed hold of it. Feet apart, hands at his sides, his erect penis had already been encased in a condom.

She stuck out her bottom lip. When had he done that?

"What?" he asked.

"I didn't get to watch you undress." She lifted to her elbows as her eyes strayed to his crotch. "Or put that on."

His penis twitched as if she'd touched him.

"Next time, honey. I wouldn't have survived having your hands on me right now. I need to be inside you too much."

"You're very ... um ... big." She couldn't stop staring at him.

"Trust me, we're going to fit together perfectly." Uttered in a deep voice, oozing with confidence, his words rolled over her like warm caramel.

"Prove it." She lifted one brow.

At her challenge, his fingers circled her ankles, smoothing up her legs, over her calves, and his chest pressed against her hips. He kissed the valley between her breasts, directly over her heart. With his forearms on either side of her head, he lowered his hips and settled his hard length in the apex of her legs. One corner of his mouth lifted, then he ground himself against her.

Her eyes rolled back, and an involuntary hum vibrated deep in the back of her throat.

Eyes never leaving hers, as if seeking an answer to some unspoken question, he reached between them, took himself in hand and teased the head of his penis up and down her intimate folds. Without delay, inch by amazing inch, he pressed into her. A bead of sweat traveled down the side of his face.

Arms wrapped around him, she pulled him close, feeling the ripple and bunch of muscles across his taut back. Her fingertips crept down the valley formed by the muscles on either side of his spine. Inquisitive hands that had wanted to touch him for weeks continued their trek until they curved and stroked over his rock-hard butt cheeks.

"Beck, please." She hovered in the gray area between pleasure and pain.

Her plea, combined with her provocative touch, must've been enough for him. In one deep thrust, he seated himself fully inside her. He groaned long and low. His big body quivered with restraint as he held himself in place.

Gwen gasped.

Worried eyes stared down at her. "You okay?"

"I am so much more than okay." She purred, smiled up at him, then wrapped her legs around his waist, drawing him deeper into her. Now she was the one groaning.

Close to his ear, she whispered, "I'm not made of glass. I won't break."

It was all the encouragement he needed. His hips began to move. With each stroke in and out, he ground himself against her clitoris. His hard length dragged along her inner walls, stoking to life fires long dormant within her.

Her stomach tightened, and her breaths came in pants. The world narrowed to this room, to the two of them.

"Eyes ... honey." His voice, strained, rough, filtered through the sexual fog clouding her senses.

She opened them halfway—hadn't even realized they'd closed.

Beck slipped one hand beneath her butt and hauled her closer still. At this angle, he touched a part of her that made her body sing. His pace quickened. Body damp with sweat, he pounded into her.

Gwen did her best to match him stroke for stroke, to give as much as she received. The slickness of her inner walls increased, and she began to quiver around him.

No longer holding back, he was relentless, dominating, driving into her again and again, pushing her beyond all perceived limits. With each surge, a shockwave of sensations plowed through her, stealing her breath.

"Come for me again, Gwen." His jaw tightened, and his eyes drilled into hers, commanding her, forcing her to confront what they shared.

His words, like magic, pushed her over the edge, and she cried out his name as she flew into an infinite number of tiny particles scattered across the universe. Her remaining defenses shattered. Lingering whispers of concern were obliterated. She bit the inside of her cheek to stop herself from screaming out an untimely proclamation of love for him.

Beck's thrusts quickened. One, two, three pumps later, he ground his teeth and threw back his head on a roar. His hips twitched a few more times as he found his final release. Then he buried his damp forehead against the side of her neck and dropped down onto her with a burst of breath.

She held him as his breathing slowed.

His mouth charted a lazy course along her neck and collarbone to her shoulder. When he started to lift his weight, she tightened her legs around him and held on, unwilling to break their connection.

"I don't want to crush you." His words tickled against the side of her neck.

She giggled and squeezed him tighter. "But I like the feel of your weight on me."

Her legs still tight around him, he levered up on one elbow. His hand smoothed over her hip, up across her thigh.

"Are you okay?"

"Yes, why?" He couldn't possibly know.

"For a second there, I thought I saw something in your eyes."

"Like what?" She didn't want to do this now.

"Worry."

Crap.

His tone suddenly serious, he caressed the space between her brows. His fingertips drifted down her temple, settling on her cheek.

"I want to kiss away whatever is causing it. To take you in my arms until you know you're safe. You're not alone." He spread his hand over her heart. "And never will be again."

Gwen squirmed, uncomfortable with his insight. Had he sensed the loneliness that had held her emotionally hostage for so long? Unshed tears burned behind her eyes, and she gave herself a swift, internal kick. *Knock it off, Gwen. Don't drag your childhood hangups into this beautiful moment.*

"Because I'm here."

But for how long?

As if to back up his pledge, he leaned down and placed the most tender, lingering kiss on her chest.

Perhaps if she shared her concerns, he would finally share the secrets she'd seen lurking deep within his eyes. They'd been there whenever she caught him looking at her. If he wouldn't, she wasn't sure how any relationship between them could survive.

CHAPTER TWENTY

Beck had just finished prepping the floor when Gwen shuffled up behind him, wrapped her arms around his middle, laid her head on his back and gave him a squeeze.

He stifled a groan when her perfect little breasts pressed against him.

"Why didn't you wake me?" She yawned. "I would've helped."

He turned, wedged his hands in her armpits and lifted. Her smooth legs automatically hugged around his middle, her arms draped loosely around his neck.

"You looked so comfy lying in my bed, I didn't want to wake you." He drank in a deep kiss.

She hummed as she pulled slowly back, a contented smile on her face.

Beck growled. He would love to take her back to bed, but the rest of the trim pieces for the bedroom were being delivered sometime today. He planted another quick smacking kiss on her lips before setting her back down on her feet, keeping her at arm's length.

"I don't think either one of us wants to be caught with our pants down when the delivery guy shows up." He turned her around, gave her a gentle nudge. "Besides, don't you have your own project to get to?"

"Fine. I should probably change first." She plucked at the front of her oversize shirt, turned with an extra little wiggle of her butt, and headed downstairs.

He smiled, adjusted himself in his jeans, then put on his earmuffs and started the sander.

GWEN STOOD IN HER BEDROOM. The sander droned steadily overhead. Her mind wandered back to when she'd awakened, alone. For several minutes, she'd laid there, confused. Her sexual experience consisted of a couple of times with a guy she'd met in college. It had ended quickly and been anticlimactic. Literally. Since then, she'd been too busy with her job and dealing with her mother's death, and then there was all the work at the shelter.

What was the proper etiquette here, anyway? Hop up out of bed with a "thank you, that was fantastic" and go about her day? Or was she expected to throw out declarations of love and assume all would be right with the world?

Their situation was unique, what with them already living under the same roof. Would they sleep together from now on? Or had it been a one-time thing?

I hope not.

She trusted Beck enough to reveal the pain of her loneliness and to share her body with him. He'd awakened a part of her she hadn't known existed, and she experienced sensations and a level of emotion not even the most eloquent poets could describe.

Did it mean something deeper that he cared enough to ensure our first time was nothing short of spectacular?

Frustrated with her thoughts, she'd climbed out of bed, thrown on her T-shirt, and went looking for him. The instant she saw him, all her worries fell away. There was no awkwardness, no embarrassment, only their natural attraction pulling them together. It seemed the most comfortable thing in the world to go to him.

Gwen loved him, was pretty sure she had since the night he'd barreled into her life. It was as simple—and as complicated—as that, because Beck was still holding back. She could *feel* it.

Could there be someone else? For a fleeting moment, she was rendered motionless.

No. He was an honorable man. Not the type to sleep with a woman if he was already involved with someone else.

She shook her head. Decided to stop over-analyzing what had happened between them and let herself enjoy whatever time they had left together. Later, she would deal with any heartache she might suffer.

Gwen poured more paint in the pan and carefully climbed the tall ladder. The pan secured in place, she started applying the last coat to the crown molding. Just as she was about to dip the brush, she heard the front door open. She'd gotten a call from the lumberyard letting her know their truck was only a few minutes away and, worried about not hearing the buzzer over the sander, she'd left the door unlocked.

"Hello?" she called out over her shoulder as footsteps approached from the foyer. "In here—" Her smile fell.

Joseph Chadwick leered up at her.

"From the look on your face, I take it you're surprised to see me." He quietly pushed the bedroom door shut behind him, then reached behind his back. The distinctive click of the lock reached all the way to where she was trapped at the top of the ladder.

A black eye and a split lip marred his features, and still he managed to smirk at her. One shoulder of his expensive suit gaped open at the seam. A bloody knee peeked through a jagged hole in his pants. Like a gruesome work of abstract art, blood dotted the front of his untucked dress shirt and was smeared along one cuff.

Aside from his alarming appearance, what really worried her was the look of lustful rage in his eyes. The way they scanned up and down her length made her feel dirty. She suddenly wished she'd worn something besides cutoff shorts and a tank top.

Her options were slim. With the sander running, Beck would have on hearing protection. Calling out to him would be futile.

Gwen was on her own.

She decided it was safer to be on solid ground, instead of perched atop a ten-foot ladder. Her eyes never left him as she cautiously made her way to the floor.

She drew back her shoulders, refusing to show him any weakness.

"What are you doing here?"

"You'd be wise to watch your tone with me, Gwendolyn." His right eye twitched. "I've been watching you. Bet you didn't know that, did ya?" He glanced up at the ceiling. "Saw the ape you have working here, too. Looks like you two are pretty chummy." The anger seeping through his voice betrayed his false smile.

"Beck and I are friends. And he won't be happy when he finds you here." She raised her chin, belying the fear racing through her.

"Friends." He scoffed. "We both know you haven't got any friends."

His callous remarks couldn't touch her. You had to care about someone's opinion for it to hurt you.

"Not that I'm concerned, but if he should try to play hero, it *would* be a shame." He wrestled a small black gun from his suit pocket. "Because if he were to come charging in here, I'd have no choice but to kill him."

Gwen's heart skipped a beat. Her eyes widened, unable to look away from the gun. He meant it. It was there in his crazed eyes. In the matter-of-fact way he spoke. Beck would destroy him in a fight, but a loaded gun made up for Chadwick's inadequacies.

"Now—" He rolled his shoulders and cricked his neck. "I see we understand each other."

"Just tell me what you want." She was proud of how strong she sounded, considering her insides were rattling like a snake's tail.

"I want to hear exactly what you said to Radoslav."

What I said to ... ?

She frowned. "Why do you want to know about that?"

Like a bull after a red cape, Chadwick charged across the room until she was jammed against the wooden table she used as a nightstand. Her mother's picture tipped over, breaking the glass inside. The lamp teetered back and forth, then settled into place.

A sense of déjà vu slithered through her.

"What did you tell him about me to make him do *this?*" He pointed at his battered face.

"Mr. Radoslav beat you up?" Her back dug into the table as she leaned away from him. Her hand settled on cold metal.

Scissors.

"Don't play innocent. You said something to him, and now he wants to back out of our deal." As he ground out the accusation, his face tightened and turned red.

She turned her head as the sour scent of his body odor assaulted her nose, and spittle hit her cheek.

"What deal, Joseph?" Gwen used his name for the first time. Kept her voice level, calm. "Please, help me understand."

"I made a deal with the old man." His eyes rolled toward the ceiling. "Then your boyfriend shows up, and all of a sudden, Radoslav's sending his goons after me."

"First off, I have no idea what *deal* you're talking about." She raised her nose in the air defiantly. For whatever reason, Chadwick had decided Beck was to blame for all his problems. She had to deflect him from that line of thinking. "Secondly, he doesn't even know Mr. Radoslav."

He searched her face then his mouth curled in disgust. "You're doing this guy, aren't you?" He shook the gun in her face. His finger was much too close to the trigger.

Her fingers closed tight around the scissors.

"You turned *me* down for that filthy piece of white trash? For a construction worker?"

Her hand shook and her heart pounded as she whipped the scissors around and pointed them at him.

Quick as a snake strike, he bashed the gun handle against the side of her head.

She whirled, the scissors clattered to the floor just as she knocked into the ladder and fell to her hands and knees. Paint splattered over her legs.

Vision blurring, head pounding, Gwen wavered back and forth. She shook her head to clear the fuzziness, but it only intensified her dizziness. The strong taste of blood at the back of her throat nearly gagged her, and a loud ringing had taken up residence in her ears.

"I like seeing you on your knees at my feet." A mocking smile on his face, Chadwick looked down his nose at her. The gun hung at his side, his knuckles white from his tight grip.

As her vision darkened at the edges, her rattled mind tried desperately to focus on the fading sound of the sander. She was terrified what would happen to Beck if he came downstairs.

"Don't ... do ... this." Her words rasped through her foggy mind, past her constricted throat.

"Don't do this." His taunting sing-song filtered through the haziness of her mind. "You had your chance, bitch."

As if in slow motion, she watched his foot pull back. Her body tightened and she turned turn away, but not before foot connected with her ribs.

She cried out as breath exploded from her lungs.

Her head smacked hard against the table leg as she collapsed to the floor.

Before she could gather enough breath to call for help, Chadwick flipped her onto her back.

He sat on her, his butt on her thighs, trapping her arms at her sides with his knees.

There was no doubt in her mind he intended to rape her. She could not let that happen.

Come on, Gwen. Fight.

She struggled against him. Arched her back. Bucked her hips, twisted, squirmed. Anything to shake him loose.

He fumbled briefly, cursed, then regained his position. His hand tightened around her throat, kept her fighting for air. He leaned to set the gun out of reach. The nails of his newly liberated hand raked up her ribcage as he pulled up her shirt. He pinched her breast through her bra.

Gwen choked out a sob, tried to free her arms.

Strung-out and angry, he was just too strong.

His brutal hand traveled over her, groped between her legs. He leaned down and licked her ear and spewed the most hateful, vile things, then whispered what he was going to do to her.

The only thing keeping her from throwing up was his hand around her throat.

Her eyes raced around, looking for something, anything she could use against him. Sweat or blood, she wasn't sure which, trickled toward the corner of her eye. She managed to wipe it on her shoulder and spied the cord hanging from the table.

Gwen spread her fingers and stretched them as far as possible. The damn cord was just out of reach.

Chadwick relaxed slightly and leaned over to run his tongue up her neck.

Underestimating her resolve was a huge mistake. She took advantage, rallied every ounce of energy within her and thrashed about, stretching her fingers along the rug until she touched the cord. She wrapped her fingers around it. With each twist of her wrist, the lamp inched closer and closer, until the base hovered over the edge. *Come on.* With one last tug, it teetered, then tipped over and crashed to the floor. The bulb exploded and scattered everywhere.

Chadwick drew back his arm and slammed a fist into her jaw.

Pain exploded through her head, and she lost her battle with the darkness.

CHAPTER TWENTY-ONE

Beck switched off the sander, pulled the earmuffs down around his neck and grabbed his water bottle. The sudden silence held a certain malevolence, and a prickling sensation crawled up his spine.

After a moment or two, he shook his head. He was about to slip his earmuffs on when he heard a crash. He tossed them aside and bolted from the room.

Light poured in from the open front door.

His work gloves hit the floor as he ran to his room. He slid the quick-access biometric handgun safe from underneath the bed and placed his fingertips over the keypad. The top popped open, and he yanked out his weapon. He made for the stairs, threw his legs over the banister and landed in a crouch in the foyer.

He rushed down the hall and jiggled the bedroom doorknob. It was locked.

"Gwen!" Another crash. "Gwen!"

He tucked the gun in the back of his waistband, raised his size fourteen boot and kicked. The frame splintered. The door exploded inward and hung by one hinge.

Chadwick was on top of Gwen, his hands around her throat.

Savage rage surged through Beck.

The defeat eclipsing her beautiful eyes, just as they closed, cut through him like a band saw.

"NOOO!" he roared.

Chadwick had no time to react before Beck grabbed the back of his waistband and collar and wrenched him off of her. Beck sent him plowing headfirst into the wall nearby and turned back to Gwen.

Obscene, angry marks on her neck glared up at him, and the room became awash in red fury. Glass crunched behind him. He turned to find the asshole, his eyes like a rabid dog's, coming at him.

Beck cocked back his arm, focused every ounce of anger in his fist and bashed it into Chadwick's face. Bone crunched, and his head spun sideways. Blood flew from his mouth. Beck unleashed a brutal left hook, then another right.

Chadwick's body twisted from side to side, arms swinging back and forth like a ragdoll's with each vicious blow from his bloodied fists.

Beck hammered at Chadwick's midsection until he heard a gratifying *crack*.

The guy's head lolled, his eyes rolled back, and he collapsed to the floor in a motionless heap.

Beck towered over him. Adrenaline coursed through his system with each powerful beat of his heart. He grabbed the gun from his waistband and pointed it at Chadwick.

Come on, you piece of shit. Make a move. Give me a reason.

He poked him with the toe of his boot. Nothing. He was denied his need for retribution.

His eyes scanned the room until they landed on an extension cord. He tucked away his gun and yanked the cord from the wall. He grabbed the back of Chadwick's collar, dragged him as far away from Gwen as possible and wrapped the cord around his wrists, then ankles.

Beck turned back to Gwen and cursed. He dropped to his knees next to her. His hand shook as he gently placed a finger against her abused throat. Eyes closed, he waited.

A faint pulse beat beneath his fingertips. A gasp of relief exploded from his lungs and his head sagged forward.

He pulled his phone from his pocket and called 9-1-1. Assured the ambulance was on its way, he slipped his phone in his back pocket and took his first good look at her.

Paint was splattered on her, but most was on the tarps. The ladder was on its side. *Had she fallen, too?*

Carefully, he searched her body for signs of trauma.

Dark red marks marred her upper arms.

A small amount of blood glistened beneath her nose and at the corner of her mouth.

Her neck was inflamed and bore clear marks from Chadwick's fingers.

What concerned him most was the growing lump bleeding near her left temple.

Beck's anger threatened to overpower him.

Pull it together. Gwen needs you. He closed his eyes. Took a few deep breaths until he reached a state of relative calm.

He settled down carefully next to her head, his back against the foot of her bed. From the corner of his eye, he spotted the nose of a revolver sticking out from beneath the bed. He flipped open the cylinder and was relieved to see no rounds had been fired. All six cartridges were dumped onto the floor and he set the gun down next to him.

He lifted his hip, pulled his phone from his pocket and called Caleb.

"Gwen's been hurt." He cleared his throat to ease the tightness of his voice. "I need you here."

"On my way," Caleb responded without question.

No matter how hard he tried to isolate himself, his family would always be there for him. No questions asked. His brother's steadfast support was a strong reminder.

He set his phone on the floor next to him and took a deep breath.

His eyes focused on Chadwick.

His skin tingled with a killing urge, and the gun pressed against his back presented a near-irresistible temptation.

Gwen moaned, and he looked down at the injuries marring her beautiful face.

The son of a bitch isn't worth it. Maybe if he kept telling himself that, he'd start to believe it.

Beck gently lifted a few strands of hair away from her face. The crimson color and darkening bruises were harsh against her porcelain skin. He laid the pads of his index and middle finger at her wrist. *It's getting stronger. Thank God.* A breath huffed out, and his head cluncked back against the oak desk.

Knowing how close he'd come to losing her made it difficult to dampen the adrenaline burning through him.

"Come on, honey." He leaned over and placed a featherlight kiss to Gwen's forehead, then searched her face for any signs of movement. "Let me see those beautiful eyes."

Long lashes twitched and fluttered until a sliver of teal peeked through. Her eyes widened and frantically looked around, and her entire body tensed. Her breathing accelerated.

She tried to sit up, but Beck stopped her.

Eyes wild, she struggled against him.

"It's okay." He kept his voice low. "Shhhh. I've got you."

Her eyes connected with his, and she relaxed. Gwen broke into quiet sobs and Beck's heart, which he'd long thought dead, was torn apart by her tears.

GWEN DRAGGED HER EYES OPEN, then quickly squeezed them shut. Light through the windows felt like twin daggers through her temples.

"What ha—" Fire tore through her throat, and she grimaced.

"Hey, hey, take it easy." Beck's voice wound its way through the muzziness. "Don't try to talk."

Her head felt trapped in a vice and, like leaves on a breeze, her thoughts were scattered. Flashes bombarded her confused mind.

Chadwick jumping her.

Hitting her.

Grabbing her.

Pinching her and choking her.

Oh God. He tried to ... to rape me.

"Did he ... ? Was I ... ?"

"No, baby." His thumb smoothed her brow. "And he's never getting near you again."

Gwen shuddered. Had it not been for her own six-foot-plus avenging angel, he would have raped her. Possibly killed her.

"He never should've gotten to you again." Beck's warm lips brushed her forehead as he spoke, chased away some of the coldness within her. "That's on me."

Before she could set him straight, a sound came from the foyer.

Beck called out, "Back here."

An older officer with a familiar face peeked his head around the doorway. She beetled her brows. His name was trapped in the miasma clouding her mind.

He looked at them. "Status?"

"It's all clear, Marden," Beck said.

Officer Marden. Of course.

Marden yelled over his shoulder. "All clear." He stepped in, took in the mess and whistled low.

Beck tilted his head toward the other side of the room. "Name's Joseph Chadwick."

Gwen tried to turn her head, but two paramedics rushed in and knelt beside her, blocking her view. They opened their big black cases and snapped on latex gloves.

"He's part of my undercover investigation. I'd prefer as few people know about it as possible."

Gwen looked up at Beck to find him watching her. *Undercover investigation?*

"Okay, let me get things started here. Then you and I will have a little chat, Agent O'Halleran." The veteran officer moved away. Voice muffled, he began reading Chadwick his rights.

Agent O'Halleran? What in the hell was going on?

"Sir, I'm going to need you to give us some room so we can take a look at her."

Gwen looked back and forth between Beck and the female EMT. The short, heavy-set woman didn't appear to be the least bit intimidated by the fierce look he flashed her.

Beck hesitated.

"I promise, we'll take good care of her," the EMT reassured him.

Finally, he relented, carefully pressed a kiss to her forehead, then shuffled back a foot or so on his knees.

A voice screamed in her head, *He lied to you. He's not the man you thought he was.*

"Gwen,—" The loud *rip* of the Velcro on the blood pressure cuff interrupted whatever he'd intended to say.

She turned away from the pleading look in his eyes.

The paramedic shared a look with her partner, then looked at her. "Ma'am, can you tell me your name?"

"Gwendolyn ... Tamberley." Her voice was unrecognizable.

"Okay, Ms. Tamberley, my name is Laura. I'm going to check you over. I'll be as careful as I can, okay?"

She gave a small nod.

Laura slid a penlight from her shirt pocket and clicked it on. Gwen grimaced with each flash across her pupils.

Nothing like having a hot poker impaled through your head.

"Sorry about that. I know it hurts." She kept her voice quiet. "Can I get you to move your fingers and toes for me?"

She did and whimpered. It was like flipping a switch that turned on the pain of every grope, every smack and every punch she'd suffered.

The paramedic gave her a sympathetic smile. "I know you might not believe this, but the pain is actually a good sign."

Not so sure I agree. But it certainly beat the alternative.

"Do you have any allergies?"

"No," she rasped.

Laura jotted something on her clipboard.

Beck leaned in to smooth his hand over Gwen's hair.

She ignored him as she cursed his ability to tune in to her distress.

There were a few more of the usual questions. Blood type, family medical history, insurance, etc.

"Do you remember how you got this?" The EMT nodded to the cut she was treating at Gwen's hairline.

"He had a gun. I think—" She closed her eyes to concentrate. "I think he might've hit me with it."

Beck's hand stilled, and she could've sworn she heard him growl.

The EMT pressed a stethoscope to her chest. "Okay, this is going to hurt, but I need you to take a deep breath."

Boy, was she right. Gwen's breath caught as pain sliced through her ribs and across her back. Without thinking, she grabbed Beck's hand and squeezed. Too late, she realized what she'd done and tried to pull away. He held on. *Whatever.* She didn't have the energy to out-stubborn him right now.

What did it say about her that she instinctively reached for him?

The EMT gave them a surreptitious look from under her lashes, then looped the stethoscope over her neck and made some more notes.

Broken glass crunched under footsteps just before Marden stepped into view. "O'Halleran, a word."

Beck brushed his thumb lightly across her cheek. "I'll be right back."

Gwen turned away from his touch.

He stepped around her and joined the officer a few feet away.

Marden leaned into him. "Your boy's ready for transport." His voice was low, conspiratorial. "I'm assuming you'll want to have a little chat with him at some point?"

"Yeah, but I want to take care of things here first." He looked down at her.

Marden cleared his throat. "Yeah, I sorta figured."

Chadwick moaned.

Gwen could see the bastard on a stretcher from the corner of her eye. Relief and a huge dose of satisfaction barreled through her to see him handcuffed to the side rail.

Miserable excuse for a human being.

"You did a pretty good job on him." The officer smirked. "When he's done at the hospital, I'll take him to the lockup myself." He clicked his pen and slipped it and a small note-book into his chest pocket.

"Appreciate it." They watched the stretcher roll away. "I've got a friend at the jail who will take good care of him."

Marden looked around. "Well, we're about finished up here."

They shook hands. Marden tapped a finger to the visor of

his hat, then left.

Beck rubbed the back of his neck, then turned to Gwen. His eyes held the same regret she'd seen there before.

At least now I know what caused it.

Gwen wanted to kick herself for breaking her mother's cardinal rule. She'd opened herself up to trust and let someone get too close. What a fool she'd been, freely giving her body, her *heart* to a man who was now a stranger to her. Ravaged by the truth, she felt her world cave in beneath her. She was overcome by an urgent need to escape. To find a dark place where she could curl into a ball and deny what she'd learned.

A wave of nausea crashed through her and dizziness assailed her.

Can't ... breathe. The room spun, grew darker by the second.

"Gwendolyn, I need you to relax and take a few nice breaths for me." The EMT's voice remained calm as she slipped an oxygen mask over Gwen's face.

She *felt* more than saw Beck rush over and kneel beside her. There had been a time when she cherished her intuitive awareness of him. Now it seemed to mock her.

"In, then out. In, then out." The paramedic spoke close to her ear, yet it sounded as if it came from a distance.

Beck's fingers felt warm wrapped around hers, and she chided herself for gaining comfort from them and tried, without success, to tug free.

"That's right, nice deep breaths. Good girl." The woman turned to her partner. "Let's get her on the stretcher and get her transported."

"No." Her voice muffled, she rolled her head side to side, then dragged the mask away from her mouth. "No"—deep breath—"hospital."

The paramedic looked at Beck.

"Don't ... look at him. It's ... my ... decision. Not his." She tried to sound forceful, in charge, but her voice had other ideas and was no more than a pitiful, raspy whisper. "And I don't ... want ... to go."

He leaned over, searching her eyes. "Gwen, you might have a concussion. I'd feel better if you would go with them."

"I don't really care ... how you ... feel *or* what you ... want." Gwen hated hospitals, ever since she was seven and spent four horrible days in one with a case of pneumonia. "I'm not. Going. Anywhere."

The EMTs turned away and busied themselves picking up their instruments, jotting notes, organizing their kits. Anything to give the impression they couldn't hear every single word.

She could give two craps if they thought she was being difficult.

"Stubborn woman," Beck grumbled. "If you're done here, I'll put her in bed."

"Since she's refusing transport, there's not much else we can do." They bagged up medical waste, tossed it in their kits and snapped them shut.

Careful of her sore ribs, he slowly put one arm under Gwen's knees, the other under her shoulders, and held her to him as he stood and headed toward the foyer.

"Why are you taking me upstairs?" she grouched at him, even as her head drooped to his shoulder.

"Your room is a bit of a mess right now." His rumbly voice vibrated through her, and he rested his cheek atop her head.

It was aggravating how it still consoled her.

He carried her up the stairs as if she weighed nothing, then turned into his room.

Gwen looked at the still-tousled bed and stiffened. Her face heated, and she averted her eyes.

"Don't." His voice was like granite.

She flinched, gave him a furtive glance.

His jaw twitched, and his eyes sparked like sapphires.

"I know what you're thinking, and you're wrong." He stalked around the bed and gently laid her down. His hands settled on either side of her hips, and he leaned close. "It meant something, dammit."

She turned away.

He straightened, stepped back and crossed his arms over his chest. Like a six-foot-four thundercloud, he hovered over her while the paramedics did a last check of her vitals.

She had the first signs of some pretty dramatic bruising, her ribs were tender, and her throat would likely bother her for a few days. The impressive lump on her head had spawned a ferocious headache, but there were no broken bones. *Thank God.*

The male paramedic, who hadn't said much to this point, told Beck to watch for signs of a concussion.

"I'm not going anywhere," he replied as he stared down at her.

A few hours ago, she might've let herself believe there was more to that statement.

At least I didn't make an even bigger fool of myself by telling him I love him.

Anxious to be alone, Gwen scribbled her name on the release form then Beck accompanied the paramedics from the room. She rolled over, and pain slashed through her ribs. She hissed out a breath and tried to lay perfectly still. Once the pain dulled, she drew her knees up, closed her eyes and turned into the pillow. His scent permeated the fabric. Visions of them making love began to sneak through her mind. Her hand pressed against her chest as if to soothe away the heartache. She squeezed her eyes tight, and silent tears dampened the pillow. The most beautiful experience of her life had all been a part of Beck's deception.

CHAPTER TWENTY-TWO

Beck shook the EMTs' hands and thanked them. They lugged their equipment outside, and he closed the door and flipped the deadbolt. His eyes traveled to the top of the stairs. Dim light escaped through the partially open door, spilling into the landing.

He wanted to smash something when he thought of Gwen lying up there abused, angry and hurt. He hated being responsible for some of it.

The knot in his gut and the hairs standing out on the back of his neck told him this was only the beginning of the oncoming shit storm that *was* Nikolai Radoslav.

Moving from room to room, he secured windows and turned off lights. After all the activity of the past few hours, the old building was hauntingly quiet. Gwen's positive energy and light were stark in their absence.

Caleb was bringing one of his high-tech security systems to install. Even so, from now on, Beck's weapon would be his constant companion.

He left the small light on over the stove and dimmed the overhead light in the foyer. On his way up the stairs, he rolled his shoulders and cricked his head side to side. The last thing she needed right now was to deal with the fury still raging through him.

The *squeak* of the old hinges on the door broke through the weighted silence. An unintentional artist, the streetlight snuck through the blinds and painted muted strips of glowing amber across the floor. It reminded him of the way the sun shone through those same blinds as they'd made love earlier.

He leaned his shoulder against the jamb and took in his first real breath. Cast in shadows from the small lamp on the bedside table, Gwen lay with her back to him, her body protectively curled into itself. He drank in the sight of her.

She was always such a powerful force of nature, it broke his heart to see her looking so defeated. He wanted to scoop her into his arms and feel the beat of her heart against his chest as the heat of her body seeped into him, absolved him.

Throughout his time in the military and during his career with the bureau, he'd been in more dangerous situations than he could count. Not once in all those years had he come close to experiencing the gut-slamming fear that hit him when he'd found Chadwick on top of her. It had been bone-deep and life-altering.

Beck stepped into the room. He tugged his phone from his pocket, set it on the bedside table, then sat behind her on the bed.

She tensed.

"I don't blame you for feeling angry and hurt." His head fell forward on a sigh. "Betrayed."

She didn't turn her head or acknowledge his presence in any way. She'd already begun pulling away from him.

He wasn't going anywhere until he knew she was safe. If he had his way, not even then. Hopefully, she'd find a way to forgive him once he explained the reasons behind his deceit.

Beck gripped the sheets to keep from reaching for her. She looked like she might shatter if he touched her.

Time to tell her everything.

"I've been investigating Nikolai Radoslav for a few years. When he killed one of my agents, I vowed to destroy him and his entire organization by any means necessary."

He told her about Jodi being undercover. How Radoslav had killed her when he found out. Beck left out the brutal details of her murder.

"He was brought in for questioning, but they couldn't hold him." Thanks to a crooked deputy director. "That's when I walked away. I couldn't stand by any longer and watch bastards like him twist the system in their favor."

Everyone knew the alibi was total bullshit, but endless red tape and bureaucracy made it impossible to do anything about it.

"I heard the conversation between Chadwick and Radoslav, when they talked about you. I knew the meeting had nothing to do with donating to the shelter, honey."

Gwen whipped her head around to glare at him. Her hand flew to either side of her head. She sucked a breath between her teeth. Closed her eyes.

"You have no right to call me that."

Beck stood, careful not to jostle her. Personal experience had taught him how painful a concussion could be, even a minor one. He went into the bathroom, grabbed the bottle of ibuprofen from his bag and dumped a couple of pills into his palm. Glass of water in hand, he turned back to the room and caught her wiping her eyes.

With her past, he figured, Gwen had years of practice burying her feelings, hiding them behind a façade of forced happiness. It killed him to see her doing it with him.

"Here, take these."

She narrowed her eyes at the pills in his palm, as if worried they might be poisonous.

He sighed. “They’re ibuprofen.”

“No, thank you. I’m fine.” Oh-so-proper. And stubborn as hell.

She started to sit up.

Beck set the glass and pills on the table, then leaned over to gently slide his arm under her shoulders.

Her body tensed.

“Relax, hon—”

She gave him a ferocious side-eye.

He sighed. “Relax, *Gwen*. Let me help you.”

She had no choice but to accept his offer, and he could tell it really ticked her off. She hinged up at the hips, and he leaned her against his chest.

He held her there as he gathered up the pillows with his free hand and wedged them behind her. It might’ve taken him a bit longer than necessary to ensure they were *just right*. Eyes closed, he filled his nose with her scent, and a wave of calm flowed through him. Hell, he would’ve kept her right there in his arms, forever, had he not sensed her brewing protest. Satisfied with the pillow placement, he gingerly settled her back.

“What do you mean, it had nothing to do with donating to the shelter?”

She pulled the blanket up to her waist and carefully adjusted her position. Her discomfort was clear in the tight set of her jaw and the pallor of her skin.

Beck locked down his reaction to her discomfort, afraid of pissing her off further. “Radoslav has his fingers in a lot of illegal activities, including human trafficking.”

“What does any of it have to do with—” Her eyes widened, and her mouth dropped open. “Wait. You mean ...

that snake was *giving* me to Radoslav? Why? Why would he do that to me?"

She seemed to search inward, trying to understand.

Beck waited.

"Oh my God," she whispered, giving him a questioning look. "Is this because I turned him down? Because I wouldn't go out with him?"

"That's what we're guessing." He sat next to her on the edge of the bed. "He was using you to pay off a debt to Radoslav." His hand curved over her knee. "Did he say anything that might explain why he showed up here?"

She shifted from under his touch. "When the policeman questioned me before, the details were all so fuzzy." The blanket twisted in her grip. "I've started getting flashes of memory."

"Take your time."

"I was painting the crown molding." Her fingers trembled as they grazed her forehead. "I heard someone come through the front door."

She coughed. Her hand went to her throat, and she wrapped an arm around her middle.

Beck grabbed the glass of water and held it out to her.

One perfect eyebrow shot up. She looked at the cup, at him, back at the cup.

He could see her wrestling with the idea of rejecting his offer.

She finally accepted. Whether it was due to the pain or her good manners, he couldn't say for sure.

"We can do this later, if you'd rather."

Eyes closed, she took a few tentative sips, then handed it back to him. "I'm fine."

Of course she is. Not like she'd admit otherwise.

"You were painting the crown molding." He kept hold of the glass, ready to hand it to her should she need it.

The sooner this was done, the sooner she could take a short rest. She was not going to be happy when he started waking her every thirty minutes or so. He doubted she'd give a shit that it was the only way the paramedics would agree to leave her.

"When I turned around, he was standing in the room. He locked the door and ... " Eyes closed, brows scrunched, she tilted her head to the side. "He asked about my meeting with Radoslav. Pointed at his face and wanted to know what I'd said to him 'to make him do this.'"

She tried to clear her throat.

Beck handed her the glass, and she took a few careful sips. This time, she kept hold of it.

"He pointed at his face?"

Gwen nodded, took another sip. "I had no clue what he was talking about. There was blood on his shirt." She laid her hand on the center of her chest. "And he had a fat lip, right here." She touched the center of her bottom lip.

"His suit was pretty messed up, too."

Sounded like Radoslav was cleaning house. Chadwick had no idea how lucky he was. He could've ended up like Talbot. Not to say it still wouldn't happen. If the Russian wanted to get to him, a little thing like the asshole being in jail wouldn't stop him.

"Did he say anything else?" Beck stood, pacing back and forth at the foot of the bed.

"He said something about 'making a deal with the old man,' and then my—" She glanced away then scooched farther down into the pillows.

"What is it?" Beck rushed to sit on the edge of the bed next to her.

She held the glass out to him and he set it on the table.

"He kept calling you my boyfriend," she groused, waved

the idea away as if it were a ridiculous notion, "but I told him you weren't."

"We'll discuss that later." She opened her mouth, no doubt to protest, but he cut her off. "Right now, I want you to tell me what else you remember."

She harrumphed and crossed her arms over her chest with a grimace. "For some reason, he blames you for what happened to him. How you showed up and suddenly Radoslav's goons came after him."

"Just his bullshit excuse. It pissed him off I was staying here, especially after you rejected him." The guy's ego couldn't handle it. "I was there the night you met with Radoslav." He braced for her reaction, her outrage, and was surprised when none came.

"What?" she scoffed. "Did you think I hadn't already figured that out? If you were eavesdropping when Radoslav talked to Chadwick, it makes sense you would've been listening to our conversation as well." Her tone held a hint of accusation.

He wasn't keen on her use of the word *eavesdrop* either.

Technically, she was right, but he would never apologize for it. Beck had made peace with doing whatever was necessary to destroy the Russian long before he'd laid his shield and credentials on his commander's desk.

"Radoslav's reaction when he first saw you and the way he acted during your meeting, set off all kinds of alarms for me," Beck said. The old man had been beyond agitated. Troubling behavior for a man who never exhibited anything but iron-hard control. "Asking about your parents and your past? About things having nothing to do with the shelter?" Beck shook his head. "It just didn't fit his pattern of known behavior."

"I remember thinking how odd his questions were. How

personal." She finally looked at him. "The whole meeting was just very—"

"Unsettling?"

She nodded.

"I have been watching that sadistic bastard a long time. I've never seen him behave that way with *anyone*. Ever."

Eyes down, she said, "Still doesn't explain why you followed me?" Her fingers tortured the edge of the sheet.

"When I saw how interested he was in you ... " Beck cleared his throat. No sense delaying the inevitable. "When I saw how he responded to you, I thought I might be able to use his interest in you to get closer to him."

She speared him with a look, a torturous combination of anger, mistrust, hurt and unshed tears in her eyes.

He wanted to wrap his arms around her and tell her everything would be okay. But he had to finish this first.

"The more time I spent with you, the more I cared about you. The thought of you being anywhere near a man like Radoslav slayed me. You can't begin to imagine the kinds of things he's capable of, Gwen."

Without warning, he found himself back in that derelict warehouse, staring down at Jodi's battered and lifeless body, her final plea captured in her wide, bloodshot eyes. The metallic smell of blood mingled with the stench of mold, garbage and decay. Subdued voices blended together around him, fellow task force members and cops angry and hurting from losing one of their own. Plastic and paper crinkled from crime scene technicians bagging up anything and everything in hopes of catching the animals responsible. Water pooled in patches across the large open space, and there was a steady *drip* coming from somewhere in the dark. Shoes quietly splashed through random puddles. He'd found it strange that, even in the midst of so much horror, there was a morbid sort of beauty in the way the camera flash caught on the ripples.

Beck scrubbed his hand over his face in a useless attempt to brush away the sounds, smells, and images that would never fade. He dropped his hand to his lap and discovered Gwen watching him. The unabashed concern she probably had no idea was showing in her eyes heartened him.

"The old man had one of his people, a guy named Talbot, digging into your past. He's the man who first attacked you."

"If he wanted to know about my past, why attack me?" She asked.

"We think he might've come here hoping to find something that would prove useful. Our thought is, he never expected you to be here."

Fresh regret over not subduing Talbot swamped Beck. If he'd had the opportunity to question the guy, he might've been able to end this thing. Chadwick never would've gotten his hands on her.

"You keep saying 'we.' Who else is in on this deception of yours?" She white-knuckled her hands together in her lap.

"My brother has been helping me out while he's on medical leave." She would be meeting his too-charming-for-his-own-good younger brother soon enough. "Gwen, I know I hurt you, and I know you don't trust me right now, but I will *never* regret following you that night. If I hadn't, I wouldn't have been here when Talbot climbed through the window."

On this, he was firm.

"If you believe nothing else, believe when I came in here that night, my one and only thought was to get to you. To protect you. My investigation of Radoslav never even entered my mind." He looked at her, willing her to understand how he felt about her. How much she meant to him.

I love you.

CHAPTER TWENTY-THREE

Gwen easily dismissed the conviction of Beck's words. After all, he'd proven to be a proficient liar. Harder to deny was the pain lacing his voice when he spoke of his partner and the torment shadowing his eyes. Whatever caused the desolation there still haunted him.

He'd lied to her, yet she still hurt for him. She wanted to soothe him and to take away his pain. *How messed up is that?*

She shifted, lay down and turned her back to him, then whispered, "Why didn't you just tell me why you were really here?" *Why did you lie to me?*

"I needed to be near you—"

"Why?" God, she wanted desperately to sound strong. As if her trust hadn't been trampled underfoot on his ruthless march toward breaking her heart. Instead, she sounded small and defeated.

He hesitated.

"The truth. You owe me that much." Another lie from him might break her.

"I was drawn to you from the moment you stepped out of

your ridiculous little car in front of the restaurant." His voice held a smile.

She rolled to her back. Her eyes squeezed tight, and she huffed a few breaths in and out. *Note to self, no more sudden moves.* It felt like an elephant was sitting on her chest.

Her sluggish eyes opened. *Maybe if I look him in the eye, I'll be able to tell if he's being straight with me or not.*

Who was she kidding? Thanks to him, she no longer trusted her instincts and judgment.

His thumb massaged between her brows, then smoothed across her forehead to tuck hair away from her face. He leaned over her, a big hand on either side of her head, and his eyes strayed to the bump near her hairline. His jaw ticked.

She pressed her head into the pillow. A few hours ago, she would've given anything to have him this close.

"Beck, really, I'm fine." The minute the words left her mouth, she wanted to retrieve them. Why was she comforting him?

Never-ending stupid, that's why.

"You told Radoslav you were ready to find a contractor. My plan was to approach you the next day," he said, his voice deep and low. His thumbs smoothed over the curve of her cheeks.

Gwen's eyelids grew heavy.

"I wanted to find out why he seemed so interested in you." As if seeking redemption, cobalt eyes with flecks of silver sparkling in their depths searched hers. "Everything changed when Talbot attacked you. Not only did I want to destroy Radoslav, but I wanted to protect you." With a sigh, he sat up and rubbed the back of his neck then released a hard breath. "Remember when I said I was helping Mrs. Saulinski?"

She gave a small nod.

"From the upstairs window, I spotted a suspicious vehicle

parked down the street. I went outside and, as I got closer, the driver took off. He was one of Radoslav's men."

She didn't protest as his fingertips feathered over her furrowed brow. Blamed it on being overwhelmed by all his revelations or on the drugs kicking in. It certainly had nothing to do with her enjoying it. *Now who's lying?*

"If he really does have an interest in me beyond the shelter, then I guess it would make sense." Gwen shivered at the thought of Radoslav's men watching her.

"He knows who I am. When I was with the bureau, our paths crossed more times than I care to remember. My being here is going to be a big problem for him."

She thought back to the night of the attack. "That first night, you lied to the police when you told them you were an agent, didn't you?"

He nodded.

"After Radoslav killed Jodi, I knew I'd be taken off the case and shuffled to another task force. That wasn't going to work for me." He lifted one big shoulder. "So I walked away."

"How long were you with the FBI?"

"Little over six years." He cleared his throat and sat up. "But I've wanted to be an agent since I was about twelve."

His voice held a hint of loss tinged by regret.

"I'll never forget the day I found out I'd gotten into the Academy. It had been a while since I applied and I hadn't heard anything, so I was this close"—he held his thumb and forefinger about an inch apart—"to re-upping with the Army when I got the call." A smile ghosted across his face as he spoke of his time at the Academy. "My folks and every one of my brothers and sister managed to make it to my graduation."

Hearing him admit he'd given up his dream to go after Radoslav was a stark reminder he would do whatever was necessary to accomplish his goal, including using her.

"The night the guy ... " She hesitated, her brows furrowed.

"Talbot."

"The night he broke in here, if they'd known you were no longer an agent, the police would've taken you in for questioning." She flicked her wrist. "Or whatever it is they do after someone beats someone else to a pulp."

"Yes, they would have. No way could that happen. I had no intention of leaving you alone." He shook his head. "When you insisted I leave, I asked Marden and Packard to keep watch over the building until I returned the next morning."

"It's not their job to babysit me." How was all of this going on around her without her knowing it?

"The only reason I left was because you didn't trust me, and I didn't want to force the issue. But let me make something crystal clear, Gwen. That is *not* going to happen tonight."

"It's hard to use me if you're not here, right?" Bitterness coated every word. "Seems to me, now the truth is out—that you were just using me—there's no reason for you to stick around. Unless ... " She tipped her head and narrowed her eyes at him. "Oh no. No way." Her back stiffened, and she shook her head, then instantly regretted it. "You're sticking around because you blame yourself for me being in danger."

It was humiliating enough to know he'd slept with her for no other reason than to gain her trust. Now he was going to stick around out of some misplaced sense of responsibility?

Not only no, but *hell*, no.

Like a naïve idiot, she'd allowed herself to believe he cared about her, then she'd compounded her foolishness by conjuring up fantasies of a shared happily ever after. Well, no more.

She gathered up her battered pride and looked him straight in the eye.

"Well, guess what. I've been taking care of myself for as long as I can remember. I don't need you or anyone else taking over the job now."

She rolled over, then closed her eyes. "Just ... go away."

CHAPTER TWENTY-FOUR

The spark in Gwen's eyes, the one that served as Beck's north star, his compass point to keep him from falling back into the dark, soulless place he'd been before her, blinked out, replaced by sadness and resignation.

Why couldn't she yell at him? Throw things or hit him? Anything would be better than the damnable silence of her withdrawal. He didn't deserve it, but he would give anything to hear her laughter again. To have her look at him the way she did before learning the truth.

"Sorry, Gwen," Beck said. "I know you're pissed, and you have every right to be."

"I'm so glad you approve," she mumbled into the pillow.

With great difficulty, he held himself back from touching her, from trying to reestablish their connection.

"Until we figure out why Radoslav is so interested in your past, I'm not letting you out of my sight." Her safety was paramount. His investigation be damned.

Gwen glared over her shoulder. Beautiful lips pinched into a straight line. Oh yeah, she was about to let him have it.

What did it say about him that he couldn't wait, that he welcomed her anger? Hell, anything was better than her silent indifference.

"I don't need your pity and, as I believe I mentioned before, I certainly don't need you to take care of me." Her haughty tone as she gave him her back did little to mask the pain she tried to hide.

"Sorry, no can do." He'd meant what he said about protecting her. "I know you're upset but ... "

She blew out a resigned sigh.

"I'm ... I'm tired, and I just want to rest." Her raspy voice held little emotion. "Please. Just leave me alone."

Beck stood and circled around to the other side of the bed and gazed down at her. The bruise on her temple had already darkened to a deep purple in the center, filtering out to garnet around the edge. His ire rose at the sight of the inflamed marks from Chadwick's hands around her delicate neck and upper arms.

He sat on the edge of the bed. His weight on the mattress shifted her toward him. A desperate need to hold her, shelter her, lashed at him, like a caged beast banging against the bars of his self-control. Unable to hold it back any longer, he rolled back the covers.

"What are you—?" She tried to pull the blanket back over herself.

"Shush." Mindful of her injuries, and over her stubborn protests, he slipped one arm under her knees, the other under her back, then settled her on his lap.

Her body tightened, but she offered only cursory resistance as he cradled her against his chest. Probably due to the pain meds the paramedics had given her.

"Gwen, please," Beck said. "Just let me hold you."

Little by little, she allowed herself to relax into his embrace.

Beck's hand gently curved over her head, and he tucked her beneath his chin. He held her there. His hand trembled as it smoothed over her silken hair. His eyes drifted shut, and he took the opportunity to breathe her in, letting her sweet scent calm him. His cheek atop her head, he enjoyed the feel of her in his arms. His insides gradually began to uncoil.

I'm not going anywhere, and I am not giving her up.

Arms limp in her lap, she made no effort to reciprocate, nor did she try to move away. Hurt and angry, she would be reluctant to risk trusting him again. But, for now, she was back in his arms where she belonged.

Beck felt the tension steadily drain from her body. Deep, even breaths of sleep whispered against the skin just above his collar. He held her close a bit longer before laying her down.

She rolled to her side, then tucked one hand beneath the pillow, the other curled against her chest. Even in sleep, her eyebrows furrowed in pain, and a small whimper escaped until she settled into a more restful slumber.

Beck crouched down next to the bed. He pulled the blanket over her and rubbed his hand down her arm until it came to rest on her hip.

Heavy eyes peeked open to look at him.

"What happened between us wasn't part of the rest." He leaned close and whispered. "It meant something to me, Gwen."

You mean everything to me.

Her eyes closed. Full, pink lips parted slightly, and she drifted back to sleep.

Beck watched her for a few more minutes, pressed a kiss to her cheek, then stood. Worried she might wake up and be disoriented, he left the small lamp next to the bed on. After a last lingering look, he scooped his phone from the table, then headed downstairs to wait for Caleb.

He leaned back against the kitchen counter, legs crossed at the ankles. His head fell forward on a sigh, and he tried to rub the binding tension from his neck. His body was beginning to feel the effects of the adrenaline crash. And the final *gurgles* and *sputters* of the coffee pot were music to his ears. Caffeine was critical if he had any hope of making it through the next several hours.

His phone vibrated on the counter with a text from Caleb letting Beck know he was there. On his way to the door, he cast a quick glance at the mess in Gwen's bedroom. He would get it squared away before she awakened. After everything she suffered, she shouldn't have to deal with that, too.

He looked through the peephole, Caleb had ducked down so his face could be seen. Laughable really. He would've recognized his brother by the relaxed set of his broad shoulders and the wavy hair curling up at his collar. Not exactly regulation, but he was on medical leave and probably didn't give a shit.

Beck flipped the deadbolt and swung the door open.

His brother stepped in, tugged a large duffle off his shoulder and placed it on the floor as if it contained explosives. Knowing Caleb, it was very possible.

Beck locked the door and turned to his younger brother, who immediately wrapped his arms around him and held on tight. Damned if it wasn't exactly what Beck needed after a day like today. He returned the hug and, after the requisite thumps and slaps on the back, they released each other and put some space between them.

"You look like shit." Caleb never was one to hold back.

"Yeah, well, I can still kick your sorry ass." He wasn't so sure anymore and hoped his brother didn't take him up on the challenge.

The guy put off a laid-back surfer-dude vibe, but he was one tough son of a bitch. These days, the O'Halleran boys were all pretty closely matched. Well, except for Jonathan. None of them was stupid enough to go up against their stoic Navy SEAL brother. He was proof of the old saying—it's the quiet ones you have to watch out for.

Caleb took a couple of steps into the foyer and turned full circle, his eyes taking in the space. "Wow, this place is pretty awesome."

Beck looked around and had to agree. Thanks to Gwen's boundless energy, they'd gotten a lot done in a relatively short time. At the end of each day, he'd practically had to sit on her to get her to stop working. Come hell or high water—or her own physical collapse—she was determined to meet her self-imposed deadline for opening the shelter. Maybe soon he would find out the real reason behind her obsessive drive.

"Coffee?" Beck headed toward the kitchen.

"Sounds good." Caleb grabbed his duffle and followed. "Where can I set this?"

"Just put it in here for now." He pointed to Gwen's bedroom as he headed toward the kitchen.

His brother took a quick glance at the destruction and whistled between his teeth. "How is she?"

"Pretty banged up. Sore ribs, swollen lip, a nasty lump on her head. In pain but too stubborn to admit it." He could feel the tension seeping back into his muscles.

Caleb set his bag on the bed and joined him in the kitchen.

"She's still trying to wrap her head around the idea Chadwick basically sold her to Radoslav." He tugged on his earlobe. "Mostly, she's hurt and angry. At me."

He raised a hand to stall his brother's *I told you so*.

"I know. I know." Beck picked up the mug he'd set on the counter. "You were right. I should've told her the truth from the beginning. But, damn it, I did what I thought was best."

"Oh, please," Caleb scoffed. "Best for whom?" He

snatched the mug from Beck's hand, grabbed the pot and helped himself to a cup of coffee. "At least be honest with yourself. The minute you saw her, you were hooked, and you chose not to tell her because you were afraid she'd toss you out of here on your ass."

Caleb blew across the top of his mug, then took a tentative sip.

"How did you know?" Beck reached into the cabinet for another cup and held it out.

"What? That you had a thing for her?" His annoyingly accurate brother filled the cup, then slid the pot back on the burner.

Beck nodded.

Caleb shrugged. "Every time you talked about her, there was this sort of gentleness in your voice. You didn't have your typical *cut-to-the-chase* approach when it came to her."

They dragged back chairs from the table and settled across from each other.

"I love her, but I haven't even had the chance to tell her yet. She's shut down, determined to close herself off from me." If Beck wasn't so frustrated, he could almost laugh at the stunned look on his brother's face.

"What?"

Beck balled up a napkin and tossed it at him. Caleb caught it when it bounced off his chest. "Is it so hard to believe I could be in love with someone?"

"I guess ... well, I never thought about it, is all." Visibly uncomfortable treading across such emotional terrain, his brother scratched the back of his head.

"Relax, Caleb." Beck lifted a hand and shook his head. "It's not like I'm planning to share any gory details about all my feelings or anything so heinous."

Just because their parents never hesitated to show their affection for anyone close to them didn't mean the brothers were in the habit of talking about stuff like this with each other. Or anyone, for that matter.

"Whew." Caleb relaxed into his chair. "Thank you, Jesus."

"You're an ass, you know that?" Beck shook his head as a low chuckle rumbled in his chest.

Caleb lifted his mug in a mock toast, then tipped it to his lips.

Beck glanced at his watch.

"I need to get Gwen's room straightened up before I have to wake her."

They grabbed some garbage bags, moved across the hall and got to work. Twenty minutes later, her room was back in some semblance of order.

Beck's watch beeped, and he pressed a button to silence it. "I'm going to run up and check on her."

Caleb held up the full bags. "I'll take these out to the garbage, then I'll take a look around the building."

"Thanks. There's a flashlight hanging in the kitchen pantry." He headed upstairs, knowing his brother would have a security plan worked out by the time he came back inside.

The bedroom door squeaked open. He cursed himself for not fixing it before.

He moved into the room, sat on the bed and watched her sleep. The small lamp cast shadows over her face. He stroked the back of his fingers across the silky skin of her cheek.

Gwen turned into his touch, her anger and distrust forgotten when she was cradled in the arms of sleep.

Beck leaned close, brushed a kiss over her forehead and whispered, "Time to wake up, honey."

She stirred, and a contented little hum sighed through her. Eyes he intended to look into for the rest of his life fluttered open. Her face scrunched up and turned into the pillow with an adorable, grouchy little grumble.

He hovered his hand over her face to block the hall light.

She peeked up at him.

"Beck?" Her body tensed, and she struggled to sit up. "What is it? What's the matter?" The abuse to her vocal cords had roughened her voice.

"Sh-sh-sh, nothing's the matter. I just need you to wake up for me."

She shot daggers at him, growled, then rolled over and fell back to sleep.

He couldn't hold back his grin. His girl liked her sleep.

"Uh-uh-uh." He stood and pushed back the covers and lifted her from the bed.

God, she felt good in his arms.

"Sorry, but I'm under strict orders from the paramedics to wake you."

After he checked her injuries, he wanted her to take one of the pain pills Caleb picked up on his way over. He was hoping to convince her to eat something, too.

"What in the world? Put me down." She shot him a surly look. The pillow had left a crease on her cheek, and her long hair was a wild mess. Still, she was the most stunning woman he'd ever seen.

"What is it with you and carrying me around?" She groused and grumbled a bit more, even as she rested her head on his chest. "Where are you taking me now?"

It was kinda cute the way she kept growling at him. Such a departure from the woman who would normally do anything *not* to hurt someone's feelings.

"You need to try to eat something." He hid a satisfied grin and carried her downstairs.

They rounded the corner to the kitchen. Caleb turned and straightened from where he'd been digging through the refrigerator.

Gwen's head lifted and she blinked a few times, as if trying to determine if he was real or imagined.

His brother's mouth dropped open, and he stared at her like a gobsmacked moron.

Beck rolled his eyes and cleared his throat—loudly—to break the lengthy and borderline awkward silence.

Caleb snapped out of his stupor and looked at him.

"I told you." Beck smirked.

Caleb glanced at her again and could only nod his head in agreement. Clearly, he'd fallen under the spell of Gwendolyn Tamberley.

Been there, done that, bro.

His brother managed to pull his shit together and flashed her one of his trademark smiles. "Hey, you must be Gwen. I'm Caleb." He moved closer. "The much more handsome brother of the doofus holding you. It's nice to finally meet you."

She made a point to cross her arms, refusing his outstretched hand. "I wish I could say the same, but I'm not sure it would be true. After all, you *did* help him lie to me, right?"

Beck grinned, thankful she had a new target for her ire. He gained a certain sadistic delight watching his playboy brother twist in the wind.

Caleb held up his hands. "Hey, I told him to tell you the truth."

Beck shot him a look.

"Well, I did." His chicken-shit brother returned to the fridge and grabbed a bottle of water.

So much for the Bro Code.

"Go easy on him, Gwen, he's a wounded man." Beck chuckled at the mutinous look on his brother's face.

Caleb didn't want people knowing about his injury. Hated the thought of anyone feeling sorry for him.

"Put me down, you ... you big gorilla." She squirmed in Beck's arms.

"Settle down, honey. You're going to hurt yourself." He set her on her feet.

The color bled from her face, and she began to sway. He made a move to help her, and she thrust her hand forward. He stopped, ready to catch her if she went down. Hell, if he didn't think she'd brain him, he'd scoop her up and set her in his lap.

Drawing upon her well-honed stubbornness, she flattened her palm on the table, closed her eyes and took a few steadying breaths.

Caleb set his water down and rushed to pull a chair out for her. He held it until Gwen carefully lowered herself into it with a sigh. She took another bracing breath, then drew back her shoulders, determined to hide her discomfort from them.

CHAPTER TWENTY-FIVE

Gwen sat quietly as the O'Halleran brothers buzzed around her. Caleb was only about an inch shorter than Beck. His shaggy hair teased his collar. Lighter shades of caramel streaked throughout the rich brown mane, as if kissed by the sun. It just didn't seem fair women the world over were paying a lot a money for the very same look.

He was built like his older brother. Big shoulders, narrow hips, sculpted arms. She noticed he maneuvered around the kitchen with the same fluidity she'd witnessed from Beck over the past few weeks.

One of the biggest differences between them was their eyes. Not the color—they were the same deep, dark blue. It was what lingered in their depths that set them apart. Caleb's contained a mischievous twinkle, like he had either a funny or dirty little secret he was holding back. Beck's, on the other hand, harbored the captivating intensity of a man who thrived on being in control.

If these two brothers were any indication, the O'Hallerans had won the genetic lottery.

Her mind segued to thoughts of their family. Oh, how she'd loved listening to all the wonderful stories. Like a stupid, lovesick fool, she'd begun to imagine what it would be like to be part of such a big, loving family. Pain having nothing to do with her injuries settled deep in her chest.

Beck's deep voice pulled her from her dark thoughts.

"While I'm at the jail, he's going to stay with you," he tipped his head toward Caleb, "then I'm—"

She was slowly shaking her head before he finished. "Absolutely not."

"Honey, I need to—"

"I don't care what you—"

Beck held up his hand.

"It's that, or I'll have you taken into protective custody." He watched and waited, daring her to argue with him.

Nails digging into her fists, she wanted to scream. Knowing it would only hurt her throat, she settled for glaring at him instead. How was she supposed to lick her wounds and begin figuring out how to move forward without him if they were hanging around?

He grabbed a chair, sat next to her and wrapped his fingers over her hands on the table.

"I have to question Chadwick before my old team at the bureau takes him into federal custody."

"Knowing how much I still have left to do here, you would really make me leave?" Angered by the zing she felt at his touch, she slid her hands from under his and crossed them in her lap.

He nodded.

"It seems you're not giving me any choice." She crossed her arms in a huff and instantly regretted it. *I really must stop doing that.*

"You're right, honey, I'm not. Where your life is

concerned, I'm not taking any more chances." He leaned back in his chair and crossed his arms over his chest.

Their eyes held for a moment. Two tenacious people locked in a battle of wills. His threat loomed like a dark cloud in the air around them.

He raised a questioning eyebrow.

She lifted a shoulder and said, "Fine," as she hid her physical and emotional pain behind a cloak of disinterest. "But I want it on record I agreed under duress." She looked away from him and mumbled, "And quit calling me *honey.*"

Her next target was Caleb. She pointed at him and said, "Just make sure you don't get in my way."

The poor guy must've felt like he'd been thrust into hostile territory by agreeing to keep watch over her. A part of her felt bad for him. Albeit a very *tiny* part.

She'd accepted her life might be in danger so, of course, he had to stay. After all, she wasn't stupid. Didn't mean she had to be happy about having a babysitter forced on her. If acting like a bitch was the only way she could regain some smattering of control, then so be it.

"I'm willing to deal with any fallout from this unpopular decision in order to protect you." Beck's tone was adamant. "And don't let her size fool you. She may be tiny, but she's a beautiful handful of stubborn." His words were directed at his brother, but he never took his eyes from her.

Gwen pretended it didn't tick her off that he talked about her like she wasn't sitting two friggin' feet from him.

"Hey, stop with the control-freak stuff, man. Can't you see you're just pissing her off more?" Caleb winked at her and drained his bottle of water. He walked over and tossed it in the recycling bin in the corner.

She fought to contain her smile.

Beck had said his brother was quite the ladies' man.

Might explain his keen insight into her current mood. His outward demeanor might say *I'm just another chill dude,* but underneath all his relaxed charm was an alertness and an innate awareness of his surroundings.

"I'm sorry you have to be inconvenienced by babysitting for me, but your brother hasn't given me any choice." She rose from her chair with great deliberation.

Beck jumped up. Caleb turned to help her.

They spoke at once.

"What do you need, honey?"

"Can I get you something, Gwen?"

Caleb ignored the way Beck scowled at him.

"Oh, for the love of ... " She looked back and forth between them. "I'm just getting a glass of milk." If it wouldn't hurt so much, she would've rolled her eyes at how ridiculous they were being.

"Here." Beck cradled her elbows and guided her back to her chair. He didn't let go until she was seated. "Sit down and let me, then I'll get him settled in my room upstairs."

He turned to grab a glass.

Gwen stuck her tongue out at him. Childish? Sure. Did she care? Not. One. Bit. She also tried not to care about the warm tingles flaring out from where his rough fingertips had brushed her sensitive skin.

Caleb snickered, and she glowered at him. He pointed at her then repeatedly swept one index finger over the other. A sort of *naughty-naughty, tsk-tsk*.

She stuck her tongue out at him, too.

Caleb bowed his head and rubbed his hand over his mouth to smother a chuckle.

"He's staying in your room?" She was disappointed, which made her a fool.

"As much as I'd prefer you be in my bed, I would worry about you on those stairs."

Well, that was kinda nice to hear. Oh, wait ... No, no it wasn't!

Beck dug into a small white paper bag with a logo from a local pharmacy, twisted off the cap and shook a pill into his palm.

"You might as well take him up there now then. I need to clean up the mess in my room anyway." A shiver rippled through her. She dreaded what she would see.

"We already took care of it." Beck grabbed the milk from the fridge and filled the glass. He set it and a little white tablet in front of her.

"Oh, well, thank you," She mumbled as she glared down at the pill. "What's this?"

"You're welcome, and it's a pain pill. The paramedics had the doc at the ER call in a prescription. I made sure Caleb could pick it up for you on his way here."

She set it on the table and pushed it away. "I'm fine."

"Hey." Caleb squatted next to her. "Why don't you take it. If for no other reason than to make me feel better. As sketchy as your voice sounds, I know you have to be super uncomfortable."

He rose and looked down at her.

She looked back and forth between the two giants looming over her, their arms crossed, feet braced apart, waiting for her to acquiesce.

Whatever.

Gwen heaved a sigh and picked up the pill. She looked Beck straight in the eye as she dropped it on her tongue. She tipped back the glass, and the cool liquid forced the pill down her battered throat. She stifled a wince. *Crap. That was dumb.*

She set the glass on the table with a loud *thud*, pinned Beck with a look, then opened her mouth and stuck her tongue out.

"Satisfied?"

Beck stared at her mouth for a beat, then heated eyes

flipped up to hers. "Babe, I am far from satisfied. But I'm a patient man. I can wait."

Her mouth opened and closed like a fish on the deck of a boat. Unable to think of a snappy retort, she flattened her hands on the table and carefully stood, then pushed the chair under the table.

"I've got a few things I need to do in my office." She turned on a huff and retreated, albeit it slower than she would've like. Clearly, she had no business trying to verbally spar with Beckett O'Halleran.

BECK SHOOK his head as she walked away.

"Come on." He brushed past Caleb. "I'll show you where you can crash."

While his brother grabbed his duffle, Beck stopped at the partially open door to her office. She sat at her desk shuffling through stacks of papers. He wanted to go in there and reassure her everything would be okay. Unfortunately, it was an empty promise until Radoslav was brought down.

Caleb whistled low. "Boy, you've really got it bad," he whispered.

She's my everything.

Beck turned, and they headed up to his bedroom.

"Bathroom's through there." He pointed toward the door as he stripped the bed. "If there's anything in your bag of tricks needing to be secured"—he nodded toward the large duffle—"you can lock it in the closet."

Beck grabbed his keys from the nightstand, found the ones he wanted, then twisted them off and handed them to Caleb.

"Come on. The sooner I settle this shit, the sooner Gwen

will be safe." And the sooner he could start busting his ass to earn her trust again.

Beck left his brother in the kitchen. He walked across to her office and stopped short.

She sat in the near-dark, her forehead resting on her crossed arms on the desk.

He pushed the door open and stepped into the room.

Her head shot up off the desk. She winced, then swiveled her chair around and started fumbling with something on the shelf behind her.

He circled the desk, crouched down and turned her to him. A lone tear tracked down the center of her cheek.

"Ah, honey." A dagger straight to his heart. "Please don't cry."

She swiped away the wetness with the back of her hand, then made a move to stand.

A hand on each armrest, he caged her in.

"When I saw what Chadwick had done to you, the way he'd hurt you, I wanted to tear his arms off and beat him with them." His hand scrubbed over his face. "But what's worse is, I hurt you, too."

He looked up. Her eyes slid to his.

"All I can hope is, eventually, you'll find a way to forgive me."

Her eyes telegraphed an instinctual urge to protect herself, to retreat back to her customary solitude.

Not going to happen.

What they had together was worth fighting for. He refused to let her give up on them.

Beck stood and took a step back. "Come on." He held out a hand to her. "We need to talk about what's next. And you need to try to eat something."

Gwen stood. Denying his outstretched hand, she

squeezed past him and left him standing in the darkened room without so much as a backward glance.

CHAPTER TWENTY-SIX

Needing to put some space between herself and Beck, Gwen walked across the hall to the kitchen just as Caleb was setting things on the table.

"Hey, there you are." He smiled and pulled out her chair.

Beck came in a moment later, glanced at his brother, then sat down across from her.

She settled carefully into her chair and scrutinized the covered pot in the center.

"Don't worry." Caleb chuckled as he pulled the lid off the pot. "All I did was heat up some of the soup you made and threw together some sandwiches. Even *I* can't screw that up."

His attempt to lighten the mood crashed and burned. No surprise. The tension in the room was thick enough to walk across.

"Your soup smells awesome, by the way." Caleb opened the cabinet and reached in for some bowls, set them on the counter, then grabbed three spoons from the drawer.

"Thank you. It was my mother's favorite." Her good manners kept her from ignoring him. After all, he was stuck with her, as much as she was with him. No sense punishing the poor man further. *He's not the one who slept with me and made a fool out of me.*

Most insane part of this whole mess? She still felt so much love for Beck, it was nearly tangible. He'd scaled her walls and forced his way into her heart. Without knowing it, he'd kept her from becoming a scared, lonely woman who was afraid to let anyone in. What would happen when he was gone? Would she return to her solitary existence?

Not since losing her mother had she felt this adrift.

She was pulled from her thoughts by the sound of Caleb ladling soup into her bowl.

Gwen touched her throat as she looked down at the sandwich on the plate in front of her like a torture device threatening to tear her already battered throat to pieces. Not willing to risk the discomfort, she cut it in half and put a section on each of their plates.

Caleb cursed. "Sorry. I should've thought of that."

"It was sweet of you to think of me." She reached across the table and patted his hand. "I'll just stick with the soup for now."

She dipped the spoon in the broth and felt Beck's eyes on her as she brought it to her mouth.

Apparently satisfied she'd managed to swallow the warm liquid, he dug into his own meal.

The sound of the clock, a scrape of a spoon against a bowl, or the occasional *slurp*, followed by compliments about her cooking, broke up the relative silence.

"Holy crap." Caleb, having polished off three servings of soup and a second sandwich, dropped his spoon in his bowl, sat back and put his hands on his flat belly. "I'm stuffed."

"Since you cooked, I'll clean." Gwen started to stand.

"Stay put." Beck waved her back down and shoved back his chair. "I'll take care of it."

He grabbed the spoons, stacked the bowls and carried them to the sink.

"I need to go check my voicemail." His brother stood. "You want to make some coffee?"

"Sure, I'll take care of it." Beck tossed the words over his shoulder.

Caleb held up his phone and waggled it. "Fingers crossed." He smiled and left the room.

Beck rinsed the bowls and spoons, put them in the new dishwasher and started making coffee. His T-shirt pulled tight across his broad shoulders, and the muscles along his back flexed when he leaned over the sink to fill the carafe with water. Biceps bulged when he tipped it to fill the reservoir. He twisted to reach into another cabinet for mugs, emphasizing his tight abs and fine butt. Who would have thought an ordinary task could be so extraordinarily sexy?

Gwen gulped—audibly. Her fingers locked together against the urge to run her hands over him like she'd done when they were in bed together. She cursed Beck for awakening a sensuality she hadn't known she possessed.

He started the coffee, then moved to squat next to her, "Can I get you anything else?"

She shook her head.

Beck lingered. He was too close. Too warm. Too concerned. He was just too ... *too*.

"What did Caleb mean by 'fingers crossed'?" She hated the idea of putting him out. "If his being here is creating issues for him, I can check in to a hotel and he can get back to his life. There's no need for him to babysit me."

"Nice try." He ignored her glower. "Caleb's on leave from the team right now, so there is no place he'd rather be than here, making sure you're safe."

"But—"

"There is not a hotel in town where Radoslav won't find

you." He stood. "My brother is the only person I trust to take care of you."

Gwen crossed her arms with a *harrumph*.

A smug grin lit his face as he turned and wiped down the counter.

The reality of him not being in her life struck her with a crushing sense of despair. Made her question her resolve. *Am I being petty?* Could she overlook his lies and just enjoy being with him for as long as possible? Would memories of their time together be enough to help her survive the inevitable pain of his departure?

BECK LOVED GWEN. Even if she was too angry to admit it, he was pretty sure she loved him, too. No matter how hard she tried to disguise it, it was in her eyes whenever he caught her watching him. He knew it by the way her body responded to his touch. The way her breathing changed whenever they were close.

He turned to her, and she looked away.

For shit's sake. This is ridiculous. It was past time he told her how he felt about her.

She tensed as he drew closer.

Cognizant of her injuries, he cupped his hands under her elbows and maneuvered her up from the chair. Brows drawn together, she looked up at him as he cocooned her in his arms. A sense of warmth, of homecoming poured over him. He tucked her head against his chest, and muscles he hadn't known were clenched relaxed with her in his arms.

"Gwen, you have to know I would never intentionally hurt you." He pulled back just enough to lift her chin. Willed her to see the truth in his eyes. "You are a *part* of me. We're connected, you and I. You can't deny you feel it, too." His thumb smoothed over her jawline.

He kissed one cheek, the other. When he drew back, his eyes searched her face.

"Ten," he whispered.

"What?"

"Ten is the number of freckles across the bridge of your nose."

"I—"

"Five. The number of paint samples you always pick to choose from before deciding on 'the perfect one.'"

"I need to see them in the room first." She watched her fingers as they fussed with the front of his shirt.

"Three. The number of times you dunk your teabag before you pull it from your cup."

"Beck, I don't see what—"

"Perfection. What I see every time I look at you." One side of his mouth quirked up. "And magic is what we have between us. The time we've spent together has meant more to me than you can know." Both hands cradled her head. "*You* mean more to me than you can know."

Her mouth opened, then closed.

Tell her, you idiot. Tell her how you feel.

"Gwen, I—"

"Got a message from my team leader." Caleb came to an abrupt halt and looked back and forth between them.

"Uh ... sorry." He held up his hands. "My bad. Go on with what you were doing. Just pretend like I was never here."

Caleb backed away, then turned and hustled from the room.

As if just noticing their closeness, Gwen lifted Beck's hands away from her and stepped back, her guards firmly back in place. Loving her and knowing she was doing all she could to create distance between them was a special kind of torture.

Beck's moment of disclosure was lost, but the feel of her soft hands seared his flesh long after his arms fell to his sides.

He called out to Caleb, "Come on back."

His brother returned, a look of apology on his face.

She gave Beck a last look, wrapped her arms around her middle and moved to the other side of the table.

He stifled a snarl and turned to the sink. Arms spread, elbows locked, his hands gripped tight over the edge of the counter as he stared into the darkness of the backyard.

"Okey-dokey then." Caleb poured himself a cup of coffee. He pulled out a chair, turned it around and straddled it.

"My commander called to say they've selected a new dog for me. A Czech shepherd named Jake. As soon as the doc gives me the all-clear, we start training together. The sooner it happens, the sooner I can get back to my team."

His younger brother was pretty good at hiding his feelings. Always trying to make like things were great. But working with another dog would be tough for him. He and Power started with the team five years ago. They'd worked and lived together every single day. Just because the dog was gone didn't mean the deep bond between them ceased to exist.

"You work with dogs?" Gwen asked.

Caleb gave her a quick description of what he did, even shared how he'd lost Power.

"Oh, Caleb." From the reflection in the window, Beck watched her reach out and squeezed his brother's hand. That was his girl, always offering comfort. "I am so sorry. It must have been horrible for you."

"Yeah, it was." Caleb cleared his throat. "Why don't you join us, bro."

Beck pushed off the counter, turned and stalked back to the table. His body bristled with tension.

Gwen sat down, avoiding his gaze. She gathered her long hair and pulled it forward over one shoulder, exposing the darkening bruises on the side of her face and neck.

He wanted to kiss them, replace pain with pleasure. The harsh reminder helped renew his focus. Radoslav must be destroyed.

"Tell us about your relationship with Chadwick. Don't leave anything out, no matter how unimportant you think it might be." Of course, Beck knew the story, but it was necessary for his brother to hear it in her own words.

This did not make her happy. Her shoulders stiffened at the severity in his voice, and she directed her response to Caleb.

"As your brother already knows, there was no *relationship* with him. He was the real estate agent for the sale of this building." She glared at Beck. "Nothing. More." Then she turned back to his brother. "He tried several times to be more than friends, but I wasn't interested."

"Several times?" Caleb asked.

She sighed. "He would show up at the same fundraisers. Always made a point to ask me out in front of people. After a while, it became pretty embarrassing. Even though I kept turning him down, he came by here and he ... " She trailed off. Her fingers flexed and unflexed in her lap.

Beck wanted to soothe her, comfort her. Not reaching for her went against every instinct he had.

"Tell him what happened before." Like a bastard of the first order, Beck pushed when she didn't respond. "Gwen?"

She lifted her chin, straightened her spine and scowled at him across the table. If looks could kill, he'd be six feet under.

"Like I told you before, Chadwick strolled into my office one day and asked me out, *again*."

She turned her attention back to his brother. "And again, I told him I wasn't interested in anything more than friendship. Well, he ... " She cleared her throat. "He grabbed me and kissed me. I managed to push him away from me, told him to leave, and he did."

She shrugged one shoulder and smoothed her hands back and forth over her napkin on the table. "In hindsight, it's really not that big of a deal."

Caleb remained quiet, but the tension in his body and the way his jaw jumped indicated his disagreement.

"I knew he was drunk. I could smell it on him." She shivered. "I'm pretty sure he was amped up on cocaine, too." She reached up and put her hand to her throat. "Like an idiot, I underestimated how dangerous he was."

Her hand dropped, and she returned her attention to the napkin.

"It wasn't your fault, Gwen." Beck wanted to rage at what had happened to her, but it wasn't what she needed or wanted.

One small shoulder lifted, and she continued. "The next day he called me. Wanted to apologize for what he'd done. He said he'd talked to Radoslav about donating to the shelter. His way of asking for forgiveness." She shook her head and muttered to herself, "Some apology."

For the next several minutes, she recounted her meeting with the Russian.

Beck and Caleb exchanged a look.

"What?" She glanced at one, then the other. "What are you not telling me?"

Beck hesitated.

"The truth." She glared at him in challenge. "You promised me the truth."

Beck nodded once, then continued. "There's more you need to know about Radoslav."

"You already told me the real reason he wanted to meet with me. I get it, he's a very bad guy, but—"

"No," Beck exploded, no longer able to contain months of pent-up guilt and frustration, "you *don't* get it!"

Gwen jumped.

He cursed under his breath, slashed his fingers through his hair. Frightening her was the last thing he wanted to do, but it was important she understood the kind of animal they were dealing with.

He took a deep breath and forced a calm he didn't feel. "A guy who steals cars is a bad guy. A guy who beats his wife or kids is a *really* bad guy. Radoslav? He is pure evil."

Beck hesitated.

"She has a right to know," Caleb said.

Damn it.

At the risk of losing her forever, she had a right to know the entire horrid truth. The most powerful way to make his point was to tell her how he'd failed Jodi, to drag her further into his dark and ugly world. Once she heard all of it, he hoped she'd have a better understanding of why he'd been compelled to lie to her. How there'd been no choice but to keep her in the dark.

"Radoslav likes his women young and, well ... let's just say *inexperienced."* Disgust dripped from his voice.

Beck sagged back in his chair, putting a bit of space between them. As if by doing so, he could keep the ugliness he was about to share from spreading to her.

"Jodi was a member of my team. She was very street-savvy and, even though she was twenty-seven, she looked a lot younger. All of those things made her the perfect person to infiltrate his organization. It was her first field assignment."

He leaned his elbows on the table, laced his fingers together and swallowed past the hard lump his throat.

"In a very short time, she was making some real progress.

Even managed to gain the old man's confidence. As much as anyone can, anyway." It was a well-known fact the evil bastard didn't trust anyone completely.

"We were so close to getting him when—" Beck shifted in his chair and lowered his clasped hands to the table, one thumb rubbing back and forth over the other.

Sam Simmons, Caleb and the five members of the review board investigating Jodi's murder were the only people who knew the details of what had happened. Beck hadn't even spoken to his parents about it. He'd felt it was his cross to bear and it wouldn't be right to burden them with such horrendous memories. For months, he'd avoided them, despite the fact he knew they were worried about their oldest son. It was out of character to isolate himself from the family, but they'd been trying to respect his need for time and space.

Guilt, anger and hatred—his constant companions for months—burned in his guts. They'd taken root so effectively, he could no longer remember his life without them. Telling Gwen would be like letting them go, which felt like a betrayal to Jodi's memory.

Her hand curled over his forearm. Its warmth burrowed through the dark, murky memories holding him captive.

"Tell me what happened? Please?" she pleaded softly.

"We were real close to having enough to pull him in. Then we found her."

He coughed to loosen the tightness gripping his throat.

"They'd dragged her to some filthy, abandoned warehouse. By the time we found her, she was already dead. Radoslav had killed her, but not until after he let his men rape and torture her." Each word ground out past his clenched jaw.

Gwen's gasp wrenched him fully from his nightmare.

He blinked a few times, scrubbed his hand over his face.

"Jodi was my responsibility." He jabbed his finger to his chest. "Mine. And now she's dead."

CHAPTER TWENTY-SEVEN

Gwen blinked, and a tear rolled down her cheek. She turned her face and rubbed the dampness away with her shoulder. Beck didn't need to deal with her emotions right now. She tightened her grip on his arm, as if to keep him from being dragged under by his own pain.

His jaw jumped.

"Those animals left her there. Naked. Alone." His body might be in the kitchen with them, but his mind was stuck back in that warehouse. "The sick fuck had used an old steak knife to attach a note to her."

Her hand flew to her mouth to smother a sob.

Beck looked at her, his eyes red-rimmed and desolate. "Want to know what it said?"

She remained silent. He didn't expect an answer.

"In very neat, capital letters, it said, 'NICE TRY.'" He shook his head. "Nice. Try." He spit out each word as if it was too bitter to contain. "When he made her for an undercover, he knew she was a threat to him and his organization."

Beck turned to Gwen. For the first time in several tense

moments, he really seemed to *see* her. "Now do you understand why I couldn't tell you about all of this?"

His big hand enveloped hers where it clutched his forearm.

"I've spent my life working in the dank bowels of hell. The thought of you being touched by any of it killed me. Now, thanks to me, you're at risk, too. It was my fault Jodi died, and I will not let the same thing happen to you." Desperation edged his voice and his grip tightened around her fingers.

Caleb's fist slammed down on the table. "God*damn it*, Beck!"

Gwen jumped.

Coffee sloshed over the edge of a mug. The salt and pepper shakers toppled over and sprinkled across the table.

Caleb erupted from his chair and sent it crashing to the floor. A breath burst from him, and he clasped his neck as he looked up at the ceiling. A moment later, he leaned on the table with one hand, pointed in Beck's face with the other. "That is so much bullshit. We all know our job is dangerous before we ever take the oath and sign on the dotted line. Jodi was a well-trained agent who knew the danger involved when she volunteered to go undercover."

Caleb straightened, turned and took a step away, paused, then turned back.

"Jesus, Beck. You had no way of knowing her cover had been blown. And you sure as hell had no way of knowing about that damn warehouse."

"I *should've* known." Beck bolted up from his chair. It slid across the floor. Bounced off the cabinet. Nose-to-nose with Caleb, he roared, "We all knew what that animal was capable of, and I let her go in there anyway!"

"Give me a break." Unintimidated, his brother didn't budge, just rolled his eyes and shook his head. He pointed at

Beck's chest. "Contrary to what you might think, you are not all-knowing or all-seeing. And what the hell? You 'let' her go in there?"

Caleb cursed under his breath.

"She *vo-lun-teered.*" He enunciated each syllable. "You couldn't have stopped her. Besides, you had too much respect for her as an agent to even try." Shoulders tight, he stared at his older brother, dared him to disagree.

Chest heaving, hands fisted at his sides, Beck shook his head, as if denying what he was hearing.

"Beck." Caleb relaxed his stance. "You are doing her a disservice by minimizing her role in accepting the assignment. She deserves better from you. Hell, she deserves better from all of us."

Caleb counted off with his fingers. "She knew the risks when she went through all those weeks of undercover training. She knew the risks when she signed on to the task force. And she sure as *hell* knew the risks when she volunteered to get closer to that sick pile of steaming dog shit."

Gwen sat, speechless, while two of the strongest people she'd ever met went toe to toe. Caleb refusing to back down. Beck refusing to accept absolution.

"I am done standing back, doing nothing, while my big brother dies inside one little piece at a time." Caleb's voice was stilted, each word seeming to choke its way out. "Jodi was a damn fine agent." He clamped his hand around the back of Beck's neck. "What happened to her was not your fault. You've got to move past it. You've got to."

He gave a quick squeeze, his hand dropped to his side, and he eased away.

Intense emotion rolled off both men, permeated the room. Beck righted his chair and dropped into it with a resigned sigh. Elbows propped on his knees, he ground the heels of his hands into his eyes.

Caleb shoulders rose and fell on a breath, he gave her a solemn nod then slipped quietly from the room.

Within the brittle silence, Gwen found clarity. She finally understood what drove him.

For years, he'd been living in a world with no black and white. No right or wrong. A world where trust was not easily given, if at all, because giving it to the wrong person could get someone killed. Sadly, to a lesser degree, she could relate to the part about not trusting easily. Yet even after he had misrepresented himself and lied to her, there was no denying she trusted him with her life.

Her feelings swamped her as she watched him struggle to accept the truth of his brother's words. His torment was too much for her to bear. She moved to stand between his knees, cupped his face in her hands and tilted his head back.

Eyes plagued by loss looked up at her.

The sight of his unshed tears caused a physical pain in her chest. She cradled his strong jaw with one hand and skimmed her fingers through his hair with the other.

Like a drowning man desperately reaching for a lifeline, Beck bunched the fabric at her hips in his hands and tugged her into him. His forehead dipped forward and came to rest against the center of her chest.

Heat surrounded her, drove away the cold she'd felt since learning of his deceit. They held each other, absorbed each other's anguish, and everything else fell away.

She would fight to the death to rid his soul of its shadows, because that's what you did when you loved someone.

BECK WRAPPED his arms around Gwen and dragged her in close. Each silent tear she shed for him seemed to wash away the frustration and anger, the guilt he'd been shouldering for so long. Her healing light shone through the darkness in his soul, chasing away the nightmare of Jodi's lifeless eyes and her unanswered cries for help. It began to strip away the memory of the young agent's mother collapsing into the arms of her husband upon hearing of their only child's death. Perhaps now, they would no longer play on an endless loop in his mind.

Neither of them spoke. Words were unnecessary. Her holding him tight was enough to purge the ugliness from his soul.

He basked in the simple joy of the way her cheek felt atop his head. The way her hands soothed up and down his back. Gwen anchored him in the present. Shielded him from the nightmares of the past.

He lifted his head, and she looked down at him with a small smile. There was no contempt, nor was there pity in her eyes. There appeared to be acceptance. Trust.

Beck gently circled his arms under her butt and rose from the chair.

She sniffled and giggled and wrapped her arms around his neck. A shy smile lit the face of the most beautiful, fierce, amazing woman he'd ever known.

One hand cupped the back of her head as his thumb grazed over her cheekbone to wipe away a tear. He placed a soft kiss to the center of her forehead.

He lowered her feet to the floor, rubbing her body against his in a slow, torturous journey. The slight curve of her hips made the perfect resting spot for his hands, and Beck drew her closer.

She locked her arms around his waist and nuzzled her cheek against his chest. Her hands spread over his back, and she squeezed so tight he worried about her injuries. When he tried to ease away, she held on tighter.

A sigh whispered from him, and he secured his hold on

her. *Far be it from me to argue with her*. Eyes closed, Beck settled his cheek atop her head. He ran his fingers through her silky hair to where it ended at the top of her butt. Hearts beating against each other, an unspoken communication seemed to pass between them, binding each to the other. Only then did he allow contentment to wash over him.

A moment later, he leaned back.

Her eyes dropped to his mouth, and her tongue snuck out to taste her bottom lip. The shine of moisture was more than he could ignore. He tilted his head and gently pressed his mouth to hers, keeping the kiss gentle across her full lips. Beck poured every ounce of love he felt for her into his touch.

Like a match to dry tinder, Gwen's passion sparked. He felt it in the way she transformed the kiss from a tentative reintroduction to a hunger-driven five-alarm scorcher.

He pulled back. "Your lip—"

"Is fine." She raised up on her tiptoes, pulled his head down, then wrapped her arms around his neck.

Cradling her face in his hands, he started slowly devouring her mouth the way he'd been wanting to all day. He loved this stubborn, strong, passionate woman. Never again would she have cause to doubt his feelings for her.

Before Caleb could come in and screw things up for him again, Beck broke their kiss, reached around and scooped her up. He plopped down in a chair with her in his lap.

She let out a surprised squeak, and her arms looped around his neck. "What on earth are you doing? I was rather enjoying kissing you."

"We'll get back to that in a minute, hon—" He cut himself off. "Oops, sorry. You told me not to call you 'honey', didn't you."

She blushed, ducked her chin. "Hm, did I? Well, forget I said that."

"Gladly." He gave her a quick smacking kiss. "There's something important I need to tell you." His thumb caressed her cheek. "I knew you were special the first time I saw you muster up your courage before walking into that damn restaurant."

"I will admit, I was a nervous wreck before I ever got out of my car." Proving once again what great instincts she had.

"Speaking of, we are going to do something about that piece of junk." Beck said.

"Hey, I'll have you know that 'piece of junk' has served me well for years. When it starts." She mumbled.

Beck wrapped his arms around her and, carefully, pulled her close. "May I please continue?"

"Please proceed." She swirled her hand in the air with a sort of "go on" motion.

His eyes scanned her delicate features then followed his fingers as they traveled and held at the side of her neck. He loved touching her, would never tire of it.

"There was no way you could see me, but—and this is going to sound strange—when you looked in my direction, I'll be damned if it didn't feel like you were looking right at me." He shook his head. "I have to admit, it really knocked me for a loop. Nothing like that's ever happened to me before."

"That's so odd, because ... " Gwen laid her hand on the side of his face. "I *felt* like someone was looking at me. Is that weird?"

"After what I just told you? I don't think so." He tugged on his ear. "I hope you'll get to a point where you can understand why I did what I did. And you'll—"

Beck cursed when his phone vibrated across the table. Would he never get the chance to tell this woman he loved her?

"I'm sorry." He snatched up his phone. Looked at the screen. "I really should take this. It's my buddy at the jail."

"Oh, yes, of course." She released him and started to stand.

"Oh, no, you don't." He pulled her back down and dropped a kiss to her lips. He answered the call. "What have you got for me, Abe?"

Gwen snuggled into his arms. Her perfect ass wiggled and settled into place on his lap.

Beck stifled a groan.

She cast a coy glance up at him just before she threw in an extra little wiggle. The little temptress.

Only through sheer iron will did he manage to control the part of his anatomy always wanting to sit up and take notice whenever she so much as looked at him.

"Great. I'll be there within the hour. Thanks for the heads-up." He hung up and set his phone on the table. Chadwick was being transported to the federal holding facility in a few hours. Beck needed to get to him before that happened.

Shit. His declaration of love was going to have to wait. No way could he drop something that heavy on Gwen as he was charging out the door.

"I'm sorry, but we need my brother back in here." Again, she tried to climb out of his lap and, again, he held her close.

He framed her face with his hands and looked into her eyes. "Until I have to leave, I want you right here. With me. Okay?"

She gave a quick nod and curled back into him as he called out to his brother.

Caleb cleared his throat, peeked around the doorway, then sauntered into the kitchen with a big shit-eatin' grin on his face.

"Everything okay in here?" Eyebrows raised, he looked back and forth between them as he pulled out a chair and joined them at the table.

"Everything's great." The words left their mouths simultaneously, and they shared a smile.

"Just got a call from my buddy at the jail. A couple guys from my old task force are picking Chadwick up in the morning. I need to get down there to question him before they do." Beck kissed Gwen's temple and rubbed his hand slowly up and down her thigh. "Gwen, I need you to stay here with Caleb."

As if he'd goosed her, she jumped up out of his lap and jammed her hands on her hips. Even with him sitting, she was still only eye level with him. Which made it easier for her to lean in close enough you couldn't shine a light between their noses.

"Oh no you don't, Beckett O'Halleran." The most adorable scowl creased her forehead. "You are *not* leaving me here with Caleb!" She turned to his brother. "No offense."

"None taken." Caleb shrugged, lounged back in his chair and grinned, gaining pleasure from seeing Beck in the hot seat.

"Gwen, we already talked about this." Beck said gently.

"Yes, but that was before I knew everything about that snake, Chadwick, and his buddy, Radoslav. I have a right to be there when you question him. After all"—she tapped her finger to her chest—"I'm the one he attacked. No way I'm going to sit around twiddling my thumbs like some ... some ... " She fluttered her hands in the air and nearly sputtered, "damsel in distress."

She was fucking magnificent when she was fired up. Like an adorable little Tasmanian devil. The raspy quality of her injured voice had very little impact on the passion of her statement. But she still wasn't getting anywhere near the asshole ever again.

GWEN SHOOK HER HEAD, then looked back and forth between them.

Caleb's shoulders shook with silent laughter.

Beck's hand rubbed over his mouth, but he couldn't hide the spark of laughter in his eyes.

She pointed at him and said, "Don't you dare laugh."

Then she turned to Caleb. "This is *not* funny."

They both began to chuckle.

She threw her hands up. "What is *wrong* with the two of you? I'm being serious!" She huffed and crossed her arms over her chest.

"Okay, okay, take it easy. I don't want you to hurt yourself any more than you already are." He reached out and dragged his hands down her arms, then laced his fingers with hers.

Caleb snickered.

She turned and narrowed her eyes at him.

He started whistling and looked up, suddenly fascinated by something on the ceiling.

"You're right. It's not funny." Beck's thumb smoothed over her knuckles. "You just look so damn cute standing there spitting fire."

She didn't resist when he drew her back onto his lap. Why would she? She loved him, and it was exactly where she wanted to be.

"Look, first of all, a jail interrogation room is the last place you need to be tonight."

She opened her mouth, and Beck held up his hand, stalling her protest.

"Secondly, you wouldn't be allowed in anyway. The only reason I'm being given access is because I have a connection there who's willing to stick his neck out for me." He gently curled a strand of her hair around his finger. "Now, if that makes you angry, I'm sorry, but that's the way it has to be. You're just going to have to trust me."

Gwen *did* trust him. Hadn't it been there in her heart all along? Hadn't he proved it in everything he did during their time together? Yes, he had misrepresented himself, but everything he'd done had been with her safety, her best interests in mind.

An involuntary shiver rippled through her at the thought of him leaving. Silly, really. He was only going to question Chadwick, and they would be at the jail. Nothing bad could happen. Right?

Then why can't I shake this prickling sense of dread?

"I know it sounds incredibly naïve, but I just wish this whole thing would go away." She opted not to bother him with her groundless apprehensions.

"And I wish you'd never been exposed to this world in the first place." Beck said. "I intend to squeeze him for every last bit of information he has on Radoslav. Maybe he can give me a clue as to why the old man is so interested in you."

He released her hair, wrapped his long fingers around her hand, and went back to massaging his thumb over her knuckles. He seemed to enjoy touching her, almost as much as she enjoyed being touched by him.

"What could he possibly want with me, if not as some sort of trade?" Gwen didn't even know the man. It made no sense.

"I don't know, honey, but I will stop at nothing to find out." Beck vowed.

CHAPTER TWENTY-EIGHT

The first step on Beck's journey back to *normal*—whatever the hell that meant—was to honor Jodi's sacrifice. He started by placing the blame for her death firmly and fully where it belonged, on Nikolai Radoslav. The next step was bringing the murdering son of a bitch down for good. His desire to attain justice for his former teammate was intensified by his urgent need to protect Gwen.

"You sure you don't want me to question the guy?" Caleb leaned his shoulder against the doorjamb. "I'd enjoy having a few words with the asshole."

Tempted as Beck was to cocoon himself away with Gwen, it would be more effective if he questioned Chadwick.

"The guy knows this is personal for me. I plan to use that to my advantage." Beck was counting on him being scared shitless to the point of talkative.

He slipped his weapon from the holster at his hip and popped out the magazine. After counting the rounds to make sure it was full, he slammed it back into the gun with his palm. He jacked back the slide to put a round in the chamber, released it with a metallic *ca-clack,* then returned it to the holster like a child coming home to its momma.

"What about Radoslav?" Caleb asked.

"If I have to go after him myself, I will." Beck performed a quick inventory of the other paraphernalia in his bag. The full-size black KA-BAR knife with the serrated edge his parents had given him for Christmas on his eighteenth birthday was secured in its sheath. His trusty binocs were nestled among a climbing rope, duct tape, a dark balaclava, gloves and a few critical tools. His protective vest was on the floor, propped against the foot of the bed.

"What do you mean, 'go after him'?" Gwen stepped around Caleb. "I thought you were just going to the jail to question Chadwick. Has something changed since I went downstairs to clean the kitchen?"

Beck shared a glance with his brother then said, "Nothing's changed. It's just smart to have a plan in place in the event we have to make a move against Radoslav."

"Is that what all this is for?" Her eyes widened as she looked from his duffle to the vest on the floor. "Can't you just get the answers you need and let the FBI handle it? Why does it have to be you?"

"It's not that easy." Beck rounded the bed then bent his knees to look in her eyes. He rubbed his hands up and down her arms. "Before they can make a move against him, the bureau requires irrefutable proof, evidence linking him to Jodi's murder. Rules, laws and a certain high-ranking official have made it impossible to get that proof. These are just a few of the reasons why I left."

After achieving his dream of becoming an agent, the long fall from childhood expectations to adult reality had been a crushing blow. Then he reminded himself he never would've met the beautiful woman standing in front of him, doing her best not to look scared.

She heaved a sigh. "You'll come back here as soon as you're done at the jail though, right?"

"I can't promise anything until I hear what information Chadwick can give me." Beck smoothed one hand over her shoulder and lightly curved his fingers around the back of her neck.

She closed her eyes and he pulled her to him.

He pressed a gentle kiss to her bruised temple, leaving his lips there as he whispered, "I'll call you as soon as I possibly can. Okay?"

He levered back to look down at her. "Will that work?"

Gwen gnawed on her bottom lip, looking back and forth between him and Caleb.

"Fine." She pointed at Beck. "But you call me the minute you're free."

"It's going to be all right, I promise." Beck smoothed his thumb along her jaw and planted a quick kiss on her lips.

He slung his duffle over his shoulder, picked up his vest, then looped his free arm around her and headed downstairs.

At the front door, he turned her and splayed his hands across her butt and pulled her tight to him.

She wrapped her arms around him and flattened her hands over his shoulder blades.

"Please listen to Caleb, and do whatever he tells you, no questions asked." Beck kissed the top of her head. "Even if it doesn't seem to make sense, okay?"

"I'll be fine." Her hands stroked up and down his back, as if to reassure him.

"Ahem. Sorry to break this up, lovebirds, but"—Caleb pointed at Beck—you've got a bad guy to interrogate." Then he pointed at Gwen. "And you've got a shelter to finish."

Beck's hands framed her face and his eyes traveled over her features. He leaned down and pressed a lingering kiss on her forehead then stepped back.

He turned and gripped Caleb's shoulder, giving him a little shake.

His brother's jaw bulged, but he gave a terse nod and stepped back.

Beck scooped up his duffle bag and vest then, after a last look at Gwen, he turned and walked into the night.

CHAPTER TWENTY-NINE

The large metal door ground open in front of Beck, then came to a stop. The ominous *bang* caromed off the metal and concrete of the large open space. He followed Abraham Bradley, the Head Corrections Officer, or CO, down the long walkway.

There were no catcalls or whistles like in prison movies. No other voices or sounds of people moving around. This block of the jail was empty in preparation for a new paint job. All the prisoners had been moved—temporarily wedged into cells with others. Except for one. Joseph Chadwick was being kept in the only cell with its bars locked tight.

Abe was keeping him isolated as a favor to him for helping get the veteran CO's kid into the Academy. Hell, the kid had worked his ass off. All Beck had done was guide him through the process.

They stepped in front of the bars.

Slouched on an old cot with his head in his hands, Chadwick turned to look at them. Red, puffy eyes met Beck's, and Chadwick bolted off the cot, backing away until he bumped the far wall of the cell.

Fucker ought to be scared.

"You've got a visitor." Abe's deep voice was raspy and rough from a life spent barking orders.

"Officer"—the shithead leaned forward and squinted at his nametag—"Bradley, I don't want to see this man."

I'll just bet *you don't.*

Abe's bushy graying eyebrows rose high, contrasting with his dark skin.

"What the hell makes you think I give a crap *what* you want? Hell, if I had my way, I'd leave you in here to rot." Abe sneered as he looked over his prisoner. "What the hell kind of pussy beats up on a woman anyway? And I hear tell from my big, angry friend here she's just a little bitty thing."

Beck's entire body tensed. He folded his arms over his chest and nodded to Abe.

His friend reached up and put his hand on the mouthpiece clipped to his shoulder. With the press of a button, it crackled to life, and he turned his head to speak into it.

"Open up number four."

There was a harsh *clank,* and Chadwick jumped. The heavy steel bars slowly scraped to one side, then shuddered to a stop.

Beck waited outside the cell while Abe secured shackles around Chadwick's wrists and ankles. When he was done, the CO looked over his shoulder and gave a succinct nod.

Beck ducked his head as he stepped into the cell. His hand clamped hard on the worm's shoulder, and he could feel him trembling. A rough jerk and he turned him around.

The prisoner cowered back a step, stumbled on the chain at his ankles and bumped into Abe's big chest.

The big guard locked his hand around Chadwick's upper arm and lifted, forcing him to walk on his tiptoes. He yanked him from the cell, then tugged him down the walkway.

Loose shower sandals, dragging pant legs and the chain

between his ankles continually tripped him up. He peeked at Beck over his shoulder, then quickly turned his head front.

Beck smirked. Right about now the POS was probably wishing he'd never gotten involved with his buddy Radoslav.

At first, Chadwick had only been connected to the mob's drug operation. Everything changed when he'd offered Gwen as a trade for his debt. No way was he getting out of this unscathed, and he knew it.

They reached the end of the walkway, and Abe signaled to his guy on the other side of the thick window. A few buttons were pressed, then the large steel door slowly scraped open. A guard with a shotgun stepped back. Abe pressed a hand between his prisoner's shoulder blades and shoved him into the processing room. Water from showerheads in the open stalls dripped onto the concrete. A long stainless-steel table was secured to the floor on the right.

Chadwick turned his head. Guards glowered at him from the other side of the thick glass. He lowered his chin and his shoulders rolled forward, as if he were trying to disappear.

That's right, dick. They all know what you did.

"Move." Abe shoved him forward.

Other than the occasional sideways glance, Chadwick kept his head down as he shuffled along the corridor.

A long way from your big house and trust fund days, huh, buddy.

Stark, gray, concrete-block walls surrounded them. The scent of body odor leached through the strong industrial cleaner they used to try to cover it. The fluorescents buzzed overhead just enough to get on a prisoner's nerves. Hell, if Beck didn't know better, he'd almost think they were rigged to do that.

Abe squeezed Chadwick's shoulder to stop him. He unclipped a ring of keys from his wide leather belt. When he found the one he wanted, he opened a door with a small square window covered by a metal grate.

He shoved his prisoner into what had to be the most cramped interrogation room they had. He pointed at a table with two stools attached to the floor.

"Sit."

The guard with the shotgun stood in the doorway while Abe pushed Chadwick down onto the stool and attached his wrist shackles to a ring welded into the top of the metal table.

The guy at the door stepped aside.

Beck entered and lowered himself onto the stool across from Chadwick.

Chadwick's lip was split, and his hair stuck up all over the place. He looked away and spotted his reflection in the two-way mirror. The vain SOB reached up to straighten it, came up short when the chain pulled tight. He wiped his bloody nose against his shoulder.

Beck gave a quick tip of his head, and Abe and his guard left them alone in the room. The door slammed shut, and locks were engaged from the other side. His friend assured him they wouldn't be interrupted.

Chadwick's eyes roamed over the room. They widened and his throat moved up and down when he noticed the drain in the floor.

The heavy silence must've become unsettling, and he blurted, "What do you want? You have no right—"

Before he could finish his tirade, Beck crushed Chadwick's cheek against the metal table. The prisoner squirmed and panted. His eyes watered, and his nose started bleeding again.

"I have *every* right, you son of a bitch." Beck leaned close. His words ground through clenched teeth.

He gave a last hard push to Chadwick's head, straightened, then moved across the room. Feet braced apart, arms crossed, Beck stood with his back to the mirror.

His concern for Abe's job was the only thing keeping him

from beating the holy hell out of the bureau's soon-to-be star witness. He didn't want his buddy taking the fall if anything happened to the little pissant whimpering in front of him.

"You and I are going to have a little chat about Nikolai Radoslav."

Every stitch of color drained from Chadwick's face. He tried to disguise his shaking hands by folding them together on the table. The clinking of the chains against metal gave him away. His eyes flashed to the mirror, no doubt hoping someone would come in and intervene.

Not happenin', dickhead. You got off on Gwen's fear; now let's see how you like it.

Beck turned to face the mirror, looking at Chadwick in the reflection. Who knew it could be so satisfying to see a guy who draped himself in thousand-dollar suits and custom-made Italian loafers wearing prison orange with blood smears on it.

Chadwick looked up, and their eyes connected.

Beck nodded to the mirror, then drew his thumb across his neck, as if instructing someone on the other side to stop recording. Classic psychological tool—make a prisoner think you'd be willing to do anything to get answers.

The guy chewed his thumbnail, and his knee bobbed up and down under the table. His eyes followed Beck until he came to a stop behind him. Then Chadwick whipped around as far as the chains would allow.

"Turn. Around." Beck leaned into his face. "I don't remember giving you permission to move." Beck clamped onto Chadwick's shoulders and growled close to his ear. "I know the real reason you sent Ms. Tamberley to see Radoslav."

When Chadwick's shoulders drew up and he opened his mouth, Beck squeezed hard enough to bruise.

You bruise Gwen, I bruise you.

"I have to warn you. I hate liars. So if you're about to feed me some bullshit about a donation to the shelter ..." He let the threat dangle. "Remember the night you met with him at the restaurant? The night you traded her for your debt?"

Chadwick tried to squirm from his grip, and Beck squeezed harder.

"I was there, you miserable piece of shit."

The guy looked back at him. Shock and fear widened his eyes.

Beck thought of each mark, each bruise, every drop of Gwen's blood shed at the hands of this bastard, and his hold tightened.

Chadwick whimpered, and his face contorted in pain.

Beck shoved him away and moved back to the other side of the room.

"You're not allowed to put your hands on me." Chadwick sniveled like the little coward he was as he rolled his shoulders.

"Is that right?" Beck crossed his arms again and leaned his shoulder against the mirror. "I'm curious. Who do you think is going to stop me?"

Chadwick cast a furtive glance toward the door.

"Oh, you think one of the guards will come to your rescue?" Beck slid his thumb back and forth across his bottom lip as if pondering the feasibility of the idea. "Maybe Officer Bradley? You know, the big guy you've been treating like shit since you got here? The one with a daughter close to Ms. Tamberley's age?"

Beck snapped his fingers. "No, I've got it. Maybe it'll be the guy with the shotgun who has a pregnant wife a year younger than Ms. Tamberley." Beck shoved off the mirror and leaned his hands on the table. "See where I'm going with this?"

Chadwick's shoulders slumped, and he puffed out a defeated breath.

Good, now maybe we can actually get somewhere.

"Talk." Beck straddled the stool across from Chadwick.

Over the course of the next couple of hours, the guy verbally vomited everything he knew about Radoslav.

Apparently, the Russian had proof Chadwick had played fast and loose with some escrow funds, dipping into them for his own personal use. And that he'd cut a few corners and bent a few laws when he closed on a couple of high-dollar real estate deals. Radoslav used it as leverage to get him to work for him.

Initially, the old man had him pushing drugs to his uppity, jet-set crowd. The money was good and, after Chadwick proved his loyalty, his responsibilities expanded to include *acquiring* women for the old perv. Then he'd rattled off a list of names of the women he'd sent to Radoslav. Those he could remember, anyway.

Radoslav was brutal, and very few ever survived their time with him. Those who did were sold off in some foreign auction to the highest bidder, never to be seen again. Though the chances were slim of finding all of them, Beck would do everything he could to locate everyone on the list. He forcibly shut down any thoughts of what would've happened to Gwen had he not been in that alley.

At one point, he'd asked about Radoslav's unusual interest in Gwen.

"After Gwen's meeting with him, Radoslav lost his shit and ordered someone to dig into her past." Beck crossed his forearms on the table and got in Chadwick's face. "Why do you suppose he's so interested in her?"

"What? Digging into her ..." Confusion contorted Chadwick's brow and he shook his head. "Hey, I didn't know anything about that. I swear! I have no idea what he wants with her. After that one meeting, he never mentioned her. Not until he sent his goons after me to find out about you."

By then, Chadwick was too damn scared and desperate to lie.

He'd provided tons of useful information about the Russian's drug operation, prostitution and human-trafficking trade. Beck now had multiple addresses for where girls were held before the auctions. Locations for the auctions themselves, along with names of buyers and sellers. Chadwick had surprised him when he'd coughed up information regarding girls being shipped into the states in cargo containers.

Beck waited until the end to slide a copy of Deputy Director Barlow's and Jodi's government IDs across the table.

The guy's entire body stiffened. "I've never seen them before." He'd spit the words out then shoved the IDs across the table like he was afraid they'd jump out and bite him.

"Chadwick, I'm done fucking around with you." Beck moved toward the door and raised his hand, poised to knock. "Either you be straight with me or I'll cut you loose right now. And you can bet your ass I'll make sure your old pal, Radoslav, knows you're back on the streets before you've stepped one foot outside this building."

The color drained from Chadwick's face, bringing his injuries into stark contrast. He hesitated a moment, as if weighing his options. Realizing he had none, he finally spoke.

"I saw this guy," he tapped his finger on Barlow's badge, "twice at one of the old man's private sex parties. Radoslav's man, Gregor, introduced him to a couple of girls, then they slipped into one of the back rooms."

"And her?" Beck picked up Jodi's ID and held it close to Chadwick's face. "Did you ever see her with Radoslav?

Chadwick nodded. "Five times."

"Five times? You're sure?" Beck asked.

"Yeah. She was really good looking and I thought, maybe we could hook up sometime."

Disgusting pig.

By the end of the interview, with nothing left to say, his head hung in defeat, his cocky attitude a thing of the past. How ironic a loser like this would end up providing the final nail for Nikolai Radoslav's coffin.

Beck stood, walked to the door and rapped his knuckles against it.

"Chadwick, I'm going to leave you with a little piece of information I hope will make your day."

Chadwick turned his head and looked at him with glazed-over, bloodshot eyes.

"All the shit Radoslav said he had on you to get you to peddle his poison wouldn't have been enough to send you to prison." Beck lifted a disinterested shoulder. "If you'd refused and taken your chances, you probably would've only had to pay restitution and ended up with probation."

Officer Bradley's face appeared in the small window. He unlocked the door and pushed it open.

Beck took a step, stopped and looked back over his shoulder. "Looks like you ruined your life for nothing."

CHAPTER THIRTY

Gwen yawned but gave up on a good morning stretch when her ribs protested. After a deep, tentative breath, she sat up with a groan. All night she'd tossed and turned, unable to get comfortable, unable to stop thinking about Beck. Her eyes felt like they were coated with wool, and her body was feeling the full impact of Chadwick's attack.

She snatched her cell phone from the nightstand. Tamped down her disappointment when there were no missed calls. *Duh. It's not like you were ever more than a foot away from the darn thing since he left.*

Pain shot through her from head to toe when she turned and dragged her legs over the edge of the bed.

She gasped.

Eyes closed, she tried to remember what she'd learned about breathing in the one and only yoga class she'd attended. A minute later, feeling more centered, or whatever, she carefully slid off the bed. Her feet touched the floor, and she steadied herself.

Happy she hadn't fallen on her face, she moved to the

window and peeked through the blinds. A soft pinkish-orange glow from the early morning sun funneled through the surrounding buildings, burning off the last of the stubborn fog lingering in the patchy shadows.

She turned and marched ... well, shuffled into the bathroom and dragged open the shower curtain. The rings clicked together as they screeched across the metal bar. She turned on the water.

As she waited for it to heat up, she risked a look in the mirror. She turned her head slightly to see the marks on her throat and side of her face. They'd morphed into a potpourri of colors—none of them the least bit flattering. An uncontrolled tremor ran through her at the memory of Chadwick's hands around her throat. She shook it off and replaced it with one of Beck gently kissing each of her bruises.

His huge T-shirt fell to her knees, and she wrestled it over her head. Eyes closed, she lifted it to her face and inhaled a deep breath. His scent lingered in the soft fabric. Then she hung it over the hook on the back of the door.

After performing a cursory inventory of her other injuries, she turned and fluttered her fingers in the water. *Perfect.*

One hand on the wall, the other on the edge of the tub, she stepped in and pulled the curtain closed. The warm water and the massaging showerhead soothed her muscles, easing some of her discomfort.

About fifteen minutes later, she'd managed to shower, get dressed and pulled her hair back in a single, crooked braid. She winced as she lifted her arms to tie a bandanna over it. Mission accomplished, she smiled. Beck had told her this one made her eyes sparkle. It had instantly become her favorite.

She threw open the door between her bedroom and office and nearly tripped when her foot came in contact with a hard body. Her hand flew to her heart, and she stepped back to avoid falling on Caleb.

He lay on the floor in a tangled mess of sleeping bag, blankets and pillows. His hair stuck out all over the place, and morning whiskers shadowed his jaw.

"Caleb, please tell me you didn't sleep there all night."

He yawned and stretched, then scratched his head, which messed his hair up even more. "I'm too big for the desk or the chair. Only thing left was the floor."

She frowned. "I thought you were going to sleep upstairs."

"Too far away." He shrugged his big shoulders. "Besides, I've slept in much worse spots, believe me."

"Well, that may be, but is it really necessary, especially now that we've got the fancy-shmancy alarm you installed after Beck left?"

Last night she hadn't been in any condition to learn how to use it, so he was going to walk her through it this morning. Gwen was thankful for the high-tech system, even if it looked like something NASA would use to launch a shuttle.

"We haven't really had a chance to test it out fully. Until we do"—he pointed at her—"I'm sticking close."

Grateful tears threatened.

He was recuperating from a gunshot wound and the shattering loss of his partner, yet he slept on a hard floor and talked about her safety like it was the most important thing in his world right now. For whatever reason, the O'Halleran men had decided she was worth caring for. She vowed never to take them for granted.

She shook her head, cleared her throat and sniffed back unshed tears.

"Well then, let me show my appreciation by making you pancakes." It seemed the least she could do.

"It's really no big deal, but I would never turn down an offer of pancakes." Caleb put his arms straight out to the side and stretched them back like a giant bird spreading his wings.

"I *am* a growing boy, after all." He bobbed his eyebrows up and down.

She rolled her eyes.

He gathered up his bedding, wedged it under his arm and stood.

"After we eat, I'd like to get started on my list." She grabbed her phone charger from her desk and headed to the kitchen.

He groaned, then quickly shouted across the hall, "I'll make the coffee."

Gwen shook her head and smiled. Beck had obviously shared his thoughts on her coffee-making ability. Or lack thereof.

She opened the door to the large pantry and flipped on the light. Before grabbing the stepstool, she poked her head out to make sure Caleb wasn't nearby. He'd probably have a hissy fit if he caught her using it. He and his brother had protective streaks a mile wide and tended to treat her like she was a delicate piece of crystal.

She snorted at the ridiculous notion. *Yeah, right.*

Pancake mix in hand, Gwen turned off the light, closed the pantry door and set the container next to a big bowl on the counter. She plugged in her electric griddle to heat up while she stirred together milk, eggs, cinnamon, a couple of scoops of pancake mix, and applesauce.

She flicked a drop of water on the griddle, watched it dance across the hot surface, then poured six large pancakes. While they cooked, she pulled open the oven door and slid a cookie sheet covered with bacon strips onto the top shelf. Baking it was easier and a lot less messy than frying it on the stovetop. She closed the door and set the timer. Air bubbles had begun forming in the pancakes, her cue to flip them.

Gwen breathed in the wonderful aroma of bacon cooking. The comforting smell took her back to all those times she and her mom had worked side by side making breakfast in their tiny little kitchen. As in a choreographed dance, they'd gotten good at moving around the small space together.

She fortified herself, expecting to be hit by the ache of loss that usually accompanied memories of her mother. It didn't happen. She felt happy, settled.

The timer *dinged,* and she loaded plates with food. She'd just put Caleb's in the oven to keep warm when her phone rang. She yanked it from her pocket, swiped her finger across the screen.

"Beck!"

BECK SMILED. *God, it's good to hear her voice.* "Hey, beautiful, I didn't wake you, did I?"

"Wake me? Of course not. How are you? Where are you? What happened? Is everything okay? Will you be back soon?"

He leaned his shoulder against the wall outside the dingy interrogation room as his girl peppered him with questions. If anyone caught him smiling like a lovesick fool, so be it.

"Slow down, honey." He chuckled. "Take a deep breath."

"Sorry." He heard her breathe in, then out. "I've just been so worried about you."

Exhaustion laced through her voice, and he kicked himself for not calling earlier.

"Don't apologize. I should've figured out a way to call you." He grabbed the back of his neck and squeezed the tense muscles. "Once Chadwick started talking, I didn't want to risk breaking the flow of information."

He'd kept expecting the guy to wise up and ask for a lawyer. Fortunately, the scared-shitless idiot had been so desperate to save his own ass, he never even thought of it. Beck sure as hell hadn't felt inclined to suggest it.

"Did you ... find out anything helpful?" She hesitated, as if unsure whether she had a right to ask or not.

"Yeah, he gave me some pretty decent information." A lot more than Beck had expected, which led him to question Chadwick about how he knew so much.

"Information is power. I made a point to listen and pay attention whenever I was around Radoslav." The idiot had actually gloated. Like spying on a brutal Russian mob boss made him some paragon of virtue, even as he ignored the atrocities he'd witnessed.

"He swore he doesn't know why Radoslav's fixated on you, and I believe him." Beck rolled his head and dug his fingers into the back of his neck.

"About that." She cleared her throat as if preparing to make a big announcement. "Not being able to sleep last night gave me time to think. I want to do something to make sure no one else becomes a victim the way I almost did."

Her voice held grit, determination. In typical Gwen fashion, instead of worrying about herself, she was already thinking of ways to help people she didn't know.

"I think that's a great idea. When this is over, we'll make it happen." For some time, he'd been planning to start a company that would take down the people who victimized the innocent.

"You sound tired, Beck. Are you sure you're okay?"

"Nah, honey, I'm fine," he reassured her. "Just damn happy to hear your voice."

"I don't think your brother feels the same." She laughed. "At one point last night, he actually pulled out his wallet and offered to pay me to stop asking him questions about you and your family."

Beck chuckled low. Sounded like something Caleb would do. "Do I even want to know what kinds of things he told you?" Beck was pretty sure he didn't.

"He told me about your parents and how they started their construction business right after they were married. How all you kids worked for them during the summer."

Now she knew how he was able to help with the renovations.

"I heard about the time you boys took care of a kid who was picking on your little sister."

"The kid was a bully. We found out he'd been picking on Emily." She was a small nine-year-old at the time.

"She was so stubborn, she told us to let her handle him. All bets were off the day she came home crying with two bloody knees." That shit didn't fly with him and his brothers. They'd seen red and took matters into their own hands.

"All of us boys snuck out one night and followed the asshole around town. We got pictures of him slashing people's tires, dumping garbage in people's yards, soaping windows, just stupid shit. Our dad had the photos processed and gave them to the sheriff, who then dragged the kid in for questioning."

The kid never knew how lucky he was his parents shipped him off to military school. Otherwise, he'd have had to face off with all five of the O'Halleran brothers.

"Awwww, you guys stuck up for your little sister." Gwen's voice went soft. "That is so sweet."

"What can I say? No one messes with an O'Halleran." If he had his way, Gwen would soon fall under the same protective umbrella. "Where is my overly chatty brother anyway? I tried his cell but got his voicemail."

"He went upstairs to shower. I expect he'll be down soon." She lowered her voice to a whisper. "He slept on the floor outside my bedroom door. I almost tripped over him this morning."

"Sounds about right. Caleb knows you're important to me,

honey. You've become important to him, too. Besides, he's slept in far worse spots."

"Maybe so, but I'm making him breakfast this morning to thank him." In the background, he could hear her rummaging through a drawer.

"You're not getting ready to make coffee, are you?" Her coffee could be used to torture prisoners. Come to think of it, he could've used it when he questioned Chadwick.

"No." Though she didn't say it, he could hear the *duh* in her voice. She mumbled, "Caleb told me not to."

Beck smiled. He'd been doing a lot more of that since meeting Gwen.

"You do what you need to do there. I'll be fine. I'm finally going to go through the boxes with my mom's stuff in them."

"If you want to wait until I get back, we can do it together." It worried him to think of her going through them alone.

"I love that you're offering, but I think this is something I need to do by myself."

There was that word, *love.* He should've found the time to tell her he loved her. It would be the first order of business as soon as he saw her again.

"Well, if you change your mind, I should be back soon." He wanted to give his former commander a heads-up about what he'd learned. It was the least he could do, since Sam had given him space to run his unofficial *investigation*.

His phone vibrated against his ear.

"Hang on a sec, Gwen. I'm getting a call." He pulled it away and looked at the screen. "Caleb just left me a message. I should call him back."

"Oh, okay. When you talk to him, tell him his breakfast is getting cold." She laughed, and it set him at ease.

"Will do. As soon as I'm done at the federal building, I'll head home." He stopped, rolled the idea around in his head. Yeah, Gwen had become his home—his safe harbor.

"In the meantime, do me a favor and stay at the shelter until I get there, okay? No running errands or anything." Beck was uneasy about the fact Radoslav had dropped off the radar the past few days.

"I'm not going anywhere. After I get through the boxes, there are a couple other projects on my list to keep me busy." She snickered like she had a secret. "Caleb doesn't know it yet, but I'm going to put him to work on the plumbing in the other bathroom upstairs."

"Good. Means I won't have to do it." A small part of him almost felt sorry for his brother. A larger part wished he could see his face when she told him about the disgusting job.

"No, you won't. I guess that means you owe me one, Mr. O'Halleran." The sudden huskiness in her voice motivated him to finish up his business and get back to her.

"Is that right?" Beck glanced around to ensure he was alone. "Well, I'll see what I can come up with to clear my debt to you, Ms. Tamberley."

Thinking about all the things he'd like to do with her, to her, he had to shift his stance to relieve the sudden discomfort of his jeans.

"Hurry back to me, Beck." Her voice washed over him.

"I will, honey. See you soon." They said their goodbyes and hung up.

After he'd been in the company of scum like Chadwick, Gwen reminded him of everything good in the world.

Beck returned Caleb's call as he made his way through the city jail's maze of hallways.

"Sorry I missed your call. I was on the phone with Gwen. What's up?"

"Then you already know all's quiet here." Which in no way meant Caleb would let down his guard.

"Yeah, she sounded better than when I left last night. Said

you slept on the floor outside her room. Thanks, man. I appreciate you keeping such a close eye on her."

"Nah, it was no biggie." He blew it off. "Besides, she's special."

Beck smiled. "She is, isn't she? Probably why I'm in love with her." The words came so easily to him now.

"Have you told *her* that?" Typical Caleb, right to the point.

"I tried last night, but *someone* interrupted me." Not that it was really his brother's fault.

"Yeah, well, sorry, but you should've found the time to tell her before you left. Women like to hear these things."

For a guy who didn't believe in getting serious with any one woman, he sure had a lot of opinions about Beck's love life.

"Did you get what you needed?" Caleb changed topics, obviously worried they were headed down another touchy-feely path.

"And then some." He told him about Chadwick's bombshell.

His brother whistled low. "Holy shit. You know what that means, right?"

Hell yeah, he knew what it meant. They now had a witness who put Radoslav with Barlow and Jodi.

"I'm headed over to Sam Simmons's office right now. He's going to want to get Chadwick into witness protection with the marshals ASAP."

"Now things are winding down with Radoslav, what are your plans?"

"You've heard of Jeffrey Burke, right?" Beck had been working on something since before leaving the bureau.

"Of course." Anyone who worked for the government knew the man's name. "He's conducting his own side investigation into what happened when I was shot." Burke had been involved peripherally, providing communications and remote visibility for the team.

"Good." Beck was glad to know Burke was involved. The man was relentless in his pursuit of the truth. "Anyway, I had literally just walked out of Simmons's office and my phone rang. It was Burke. He wanted to discuss a professional opportunity with me."

Beck still couldn't decide if the timing of the call had been pure coincidence or a result of the man's legendary connections. The guy always seemed to be at least two steps ahead of everyone. Rumor had it he held dossiers on some of the most important and influential people from all levels of government, all over the world. He was a very powerful ally and even more dangerous enemy. Beck liked the idea of having a man like Jeffrey Burke interested in working *with* him, rather than *against* him.

"Are you fuckin' shitting me?" Caleb's surprise matched the way he'd felt when he'd received the man's call.

"I shit you not. The strangest part of the whole thing is, I had never discussed starting my own company with anyone." He'd wanted to talk it over with his family first. "He wants to send me jobs that are too hot for the government to handle." Meaning way off the books, black-ops type stuff. With what he was going to pay, Beck would be able to hire the best of the best. "I'll be able to do things my way, with my people." Autonomy is what had sealed the deal for him. No more red tape and bureaucracy. Only justice.

Beck shared his business plan, and they briefly talked about the company's structure. How it would be founded on the tenets of family, honor and loyalty. He hoped, one day, all his brothers would be working with him. "I know you're happy being on the team, but if that ever changes, there will be a spot for you." No pressure. He just wanted his brother to know how he felt.

Since Jonathan was currently an active duty Navy SEAL, the same conversation and offer to him would have to wait. Beck would talk to the twins, Mathias and Killian, the next time he went back home to visit his parents.

"Thanks, man. I'll keep it in mind." The distinctive *beeps* from Caleb's new alarm system could be heard in the background.

"Everything good with the new system?" A rhetorical question. His brother's systems were legendary.

"Thanks to the old wiring in this place, it's taking a bit longer than expected." Another series of *beeps,* then he said, "I should have it up and fully-functional by this evening."

"Excellent." Beck rounded the corner to the elevator, pushed the button and waited. "Okay, I'll be back there as soon as I'm done with Simmons."

"Well, hurry the hell up and get back here before Gwen makes me paint another room." Caleb grumbled, "I swear, for someone so little she sure is bossy."

"Yeah, that she is." He smiled at the thought of petite Gwen bossing around his much larger brother. "Watch her, Caleb. I'll be there soon."

CHAPTER THIRTY-ONE

Gwen looked up from where she sat at the kitchen table. "Good morning, again."

Caleb walked in, hair wet, his face freshly shaved.

She stood, snagged the hot pad, then opened the oven and grabbed his plate.

"Have a seat." She set it on the table and reached in the fridge for the orange juice. "Be careful. The plate's kinda warm.

"Is this for me?" He pointed at the plate laden with food, then looked at her. "Please tell me this is for me."

"Of course it's for you, silly." She shook her head. "I could never eat that much food."

"Holy sh— er, crap." He stared in awe at the eggs, pancakes and bacon like they were the ark of the covenant. "You did all this while I was taking a shower?"

"Mm-hm. It's the least I can do, since you slept on the floor and, well ... " She chewed the inside of her cheek.

"What?" Caleb didn't look at her, just plopped down, laid

three strips of bacon over the stack of pancakes and saturated the whole thing with syrup.

"Hm? What, *what*?" she asked innocently as she reached across and poured juice in his glass.

He carefully set his fork down on the edge of the plate, pushed it away and crossed his arms on the table.

"Well ... um ... " She poured herself some juice. "If you're still willing to help, I do have a little teensy-tiny project I could use your help with." She held her finger and thumb about an inch apart.

"Name it." He pulled his plate closer, picked up his fork and knife and sliced through the mountain of food.

"See, here's the thing ... "

A forkful of pancakes stopped halfway to his mouth. One dark brow shot up and he lifted his eyes to her.

Gwen fortified herself with a sip of orange juice, then said, "I was hoping you might be able to work on the plumbing in the upstairs hall bathroom."

She situated her napkin perfectly across her lap, adjusted her knife and fork on the table, turned her plate, and gave the salt shaker a little jiggle next to her ear, as if to see if it was empty. Generally avoided eye contact any way possible.

Back down went his fork.

She started talking really fast.

"I'm not sure what's wrong. There is some sort of strange-colored ... substance coming from the faucet in the tub, and it looks *nothing* like water." She scrunched her nose. "I know it's a lot to ask, but I really think we need to do something about it before ..."

Caleb raised his hand.

Her mouth snapped shut.

"No problem," he said past what had to be a fake smile. "I'll take a look at it when I'm done eating."

"You will?" Her shoulders relaxed. She clapped her hands like a kid. "Thank you. Thank you. Thank you."

"Just remember"—he pointed a forkful of pancakes at her—"the doors stay locked. If someone shows up, I'll answer it. Got it?"

"Got it. Doors locked. Don't open them for anyone. Get you if someone shows up." She crossed her heart. "I promise. I'll be careful."

"Okay. Good." He started lifting the fork to his mouth, stopped and looked at her. "Any more surprises for me?"

"No." She laughed. "That's the worst of it."

He nodded once, then, finally, took his first bite of pancakes.

He moaned. "Oh. My. God." His eyes drooped shut. "These are awesome."

She blushed at his praise. "The secret is the applesauce. It's a little trick my mother taught me."

"Well, whatever it is, it's magical. You'll need to tell my mom about this when you meet her."

Her own fork stalled on its way to her mouth, and she stared at him as he dug into his food.

When I meet their mother.

He said it like it was a foregone conclusion. Oh, how much Gwen hoped to meet the rest of the O'Halleran family.

NIKOLAI WAS PULLED from a sound sleep by the annoying chime of his cell. The faintest hint of daylight had only just begun to sneak between the panels of the thick drapes over his large windows.

"What?" he growled. There was only one man who had the balls to wake him.

"O'Halleran has been questioning Chadwick for hours." Gregor spoke without preamble.

Nikolai sat up. "Wait a minute."

He rubbed his sleep-filled eyes as he lumbered into the bathroom and set his phone on the custom quartz countertop. Gregor could wait while he took a piss.

He flushed the toilet, then wedged the phone between his shoulder and ear while he washed his hands.

"Where you are now?"

"Across from the jail." Gregor had been tasked with watching the fed after the last guy fucked up.

"Well?" Nikolai yanked the towel from the rack, dried his hands, then tossed it on the floor.

"He walked out about five minutes ago."

Gregor was a man of few words. At times, Nikolai found it to be quite tedious.

"And?"

"He got in his car and left."

"Then why in hell are you still sitting there? Follow him." Did he really have to tell him that?

"I was about to pull away, and I saw Chadwick being escorted out a side door by a couple feds. They shoved him in a van and took off."

Nikolai cursed. The man knew things, dangerous things.

Before he could ask, Gregor said, "They had three decoy vans, or I would've followed."

Nikolai snatched a bottle of cologne from the glass shelf and hurled it against the wall. The strong-smelling liquid splattered across the expensive marble tiles, reminding him of the Jackson Pollock hanging in his foyer.

"It will be difficult to get to him while he is in federal custody," his most trusted employee said.

Difficult, but not impossible. Everyone had a price, even a U.S. marshal. And a deputy director with a sex addiction.

Nikolai's slippers scuffed over the carpet as he moved to the window. He pulled the cord to draw back the heavy fabric, then gazed at the ornate gardens below as he listened to Gregor.

"My contact was assigned to a different wing and could not get to him. The head of the guards seemed to make it his personal responsibility to ensure no one had access to him other than O'Halleran."

Like many other weak men, Gregor's *contact* had a lot of dirty little secrets he did not want his pretty little wife, or his boss, to know about.

"Chadwick has become a liability. See to it he is taken care of."

The man didn't know much, but he'd seen things he shouldn't have. Things that could bring added and unwelcome scrutiny to his organization. Unfortunate, since his foreign and domestic partners had already expressed concern about the FBI's increased interest.

"What are your instructions for Ms. Tamberley?"

"You are to pick her up before O'Halleran returns to the shelter. Then bring her to the compound." The property was secured, and the feds knew nothing about it. "Do this quietly. We do not want to draw attention."

If Gwendolyn Tamberley turned out to be who he thought she was, there would be hell to pay.

"And Gregor, there is not to be a mark on her. Do you understand this?" That was a privilege reserved only for him.

"Yes, Mr. Radoslav." Gregor had never failed him. Once given an order, it was followed.

Nikolai hung up and dropped his cell on the table in front of the window. He picked up the house phone and rang the housekeeper.

"This morning, I think young Brigitte should bring up my coffee and breakfast."

She should be ready for me by now. Not that it mattered to him.

"Just a minute." He pulled the phone from his ear and tapped on the window.

The gardener looked up from where he pulled weeds and scanned the house. The fear on the old man's face when he noticed him in the window filled Nikolai with joy. He pointed at the dying bush in front of the solarium. The man nodded once, grabbed a shovel, then dashed over and began digging it up.

He put the phone back to his ear. "Make sure my private wing is clear. I do not want to be disturbed."

Nikolai hung up and turned from the window. He stripped off his silk pajamas and dropped them on the floor as he moved to his bed.

CHAPTER THIRTY-TWO

Gwen scooped the last of the construction garbage into a large plastic bag and sealed it tight. Legs burning, arms shaking, she dragged it across the room. With a grunt, she laid it next to the four bags she'd filled earlier. Someone bigger and stronger would have to take them out to the dumpster in the alley. Even if she could lift them, Caleb would flip out if she went outside by herself.

Determined to finish at least one room, she swiped her forearm across her brow, pulled off her work gloves and headed upstairs. He was working on the plumbing and, if his language was any indication, it hadn't been going well. Even though many of the words he'd used were spoken in something other than English, she'd be willing to bet her last dollar they weren't appropriate for all ears.

"Caleb." She knocked on the doorjamb to get his attention. "I really hate to bother you, especially since it looks like you're having so much fun."

He glared over his shoulder at her. A black smudge ran across his forehead.

"I was hoping you could take a quick break to help me

carry out some bags of garbage. They're the only thing keeping me from marking the front room off my list." She flashed him her biggest smile and batted her eyelashes at him. "Please, please, pretty please." She put her palms together like she was praying.

"Absolutely! I'd be happy to." Quick as a cat, he bounded up from the floor, pulled a rag from his back pocket and wiped his hands. His scowl replaced by a big toothy smile, he blew past her and headed downstairs.

Gwen rolled her eyes. The man wasn't fooling her for a second. His excitement had nothing to do with taking out garbage and everything to do with having an excuse to step away from the fouled-up plumbing.

She followed him down the stairs.

He rounded the corner into the room, stopped short.

Gwen bounced off his back.

"Holy crap. Look how much you got done." Hands on his hips, he took in the mini-mountain of garbage bags.

She peeked around him, then moved to his side. "All I did was gather up the last of the garbage and stack it together."

"Well, it looks amazing." He stomped across the room, swung a bag over each shoulder like a muscle-bound Santa, and tromped out the back door.

I will not resent him for making that look so easy.

As much as Gwen wanted the garbage collected and gone, she was self-aware enough to recognize the task for what it was—a stall tactic.

Earlier, she'd had Caleb pull the boxes of her mother's things from the closet, fully prepared to go through them. She'd plopped down next to one on the floor and, when she'd started to pull back the flap, a strong sense of foreboding stopped her. Like shards of ice, it had prickled along her spine. Gwen had jumped up and backed away, opting to bury herself in a task with zero emotional risk.

She did a quick scan of the large space and was forced to accept she could no longer put off the inevitable.

Gwen took a deep breath and headed to her room. She stood at the threshold and stared at the boxes. When she'd decided to move to the shelter, she hadn't been strong enough to go through her mother's things. She'd merely tossed them in these few boxes and shoved them to the back of the dark closet. Like not seeing them meant she could deny the reality of her new existence. Having had time to heal, she now gained comfort knowing her mother would always be with her.

She walked over and sat cross-legged on the floor.

A few minutes later, the first box was empty. Gwen tossed it aside, proud of how she'd managed to get through it with only a few sniffles. She pulled the second one closer and reached inside. Her fingers brushed over the plush imitation angora of her mom's favorite old sweater.

She lifted it to her nose. Her mom's comforting smell clung to the soft garment. Tears tracked down her cheeks, the sadness and loss of never seeing her mother again liberated with each one. Purged from her heart was the anger over how she died and how the person responsible had gone unpunished.

Like a scar left by a healed wound, there would always be regret for the things her mother would never experience. Seeing their shared dream for the shelter become a reality. Meeting Beck. Getting to experience the joys of being a grandmother someday.

Moments later, a weight lifted. The last of her tears shed, she lovingly placed the soft sweater atop the *keep* pile and continued with her efforts.

Caleb poked his head in the door. "Hey there. All the garbage is out, and I swept up the front room. Need me to do anything else?"

"Yeah, I need you to get back upstairs and fix that plumbing." She laughed.

"Oh, man. You are so mean."

Gwen pointed toward the stairs.

"I'm goin', I'm goin'." Caleb shuffled away.

An hour passed, and Gwen took a second to stand and stretch, shake out her legs. The last box contained books. Gwen smiled. Her mother loved to curl up in the corner of the couch, a book in her hand, a cup of tea forgotten and growing cold next to her.

She pulled out a large picture book about exotic birds, flipped through it, then turned to set it on the floor. Out of the corner of her eye, she glimpsed a baby book.

I remember hearing about a baby book, but ...

Baby book ... Baby book... Safety deposit box ... Ledgers ... FBI ...

Her mother's incoherent last words whispered in her memory.

Heart pounding, hands shaking, she reached for the book.

She hesitated.

Her fingernails bit into her palms.

It's only a book. It's only a book, she chanted to herself.

Before she could change her mind, Gwen snatched it up and turned it over in her hands. Her finger traced over one of the faded cherubs in the center of the worn pink cover.

"Now I know why you always called me Angel."

She shoved her bizarre uneasiness aside and slowly opened it. A small book fell out and landed in her lap. Gwen set it on the floor next to her and carefully turned the pages of her baby book.

Other than a few photos and her mother's handwritten notations about some of the milestones throughout Gwen's childhood—a lock of hair from her first haircut, her first lost tooth, when she took her first steps, first word, things of that nature—there was nothing earth-shattering in its pages. Certainly, nothing about a safety deposit box or anything worthy of the FBI's attention.

Maybe you're remembering something that never happened?

Confused, she closed the book, rubbed her hand over the cover, set it with the sweater, then reached for the smaller one. It appeared to be a journal of some sort. Upon closer inspection, Gwen felt the stirrings of a faint memory. When she was about five or six years old, she'd snuck out of bed and spied her mother writing in this book late one night. It was the only time she'd ever seen it. From the tattered condition of the cover, her mom must've written in it for years.

The old binding crackled as she carefully opened the book. Her mother's flowing script looked up at her from the very first page. Gwen closed her eyes, reverently smoothing her hand over the text. She opened her eyes and read the first page. Instead of her mother's name, Margaret Tamberley, it said "Property of Alice Madison."

Gwen's brows scrunched together. *Alice Madison?*

She turned the book over in her hands, looking at it more closely. It was older and a bit more haggard, but she was certain it was the same book she'd seen her mother scribbling in. Her distinctive handwriting confirmed it.

Confusion and disquiet grew as she turned the page to read the first entry, dated seven and a half months before Gwen was born.

Well, I'm pregnant. I took two separate pee tests and they both came back positive. I cried when I told Feodor, but he said it doesn't matter that he's not the father. He loves me and he knows it wasn't my choice to sleep with Nikolai. Feodor and I were already planning to runaway together, but we'll have to leave sooner than we thought. I'm terrified of what Nikolai will do if he finds out about the baby.

Gwen looked at the entry date again. She re-read the words, and her world as she knew it was ripped from her grasp.

No, this can't be possible. Her vision narrowed. She slowly shook her head.

Richard Tamberley wasn't her father? Gwen looked up at the picture on her dresser. *Who are you?* She'd been told her father died before she was born. In her mind, he'd been brave and strong and had loved her mother like no man had ever loved a woman before.

Why would her mother lie about such a thing?

With instant and frightening clarity, she understood why.

Gwen's father was Nikolai Radoslav.

The book slipped from her numb fingers.

Her new reality was a heavy weight on her chest, suffocating her. Every stitch of air was sucked from the room. She blindly crawled her way to the window, sunlight and the promise of fresh air her only guide.

Whimpering, she clawed at the windowsill. She flattened her hand against the glass pane.

A brutal wave of nausea slammed into her, and dizziness threatened to snatch her down into darkness.

A last panicked shove, and the window scraped up.

She plunged her upper body out, drawing in deep, gulping breaths.

Gwen didn't register the bite of the sill digging into her belly as she leaned out. Couldn't smell the rotting garbage on the other side of the alley. She had no idea how long she stayed there, hanging out the window, gasping for air. It wasn't until the spots began to clear from her eyes that she dared pull back into the room where her new reality loomed.

Bolstering her nerves, she swallowed past the knot in her throat, then slowly turned back to where the journal lay on the floor, like a serpent coiled to strike. How could something so innocuous-looking have such a cataclysmic impact?

Gwen wanted to toss the book in the box and shove it back into the closet. Pretend she'd never found it. If she'd had a match, she might've been tempted to burn it. Even as the thought entered her mind, she knew she could never destroy it. It wouldn't change what she'd learned. More importantly, it was the only way to find out who her mother really was.

It's the only way to learn who I *really am.*

Had the one person Gwen trusted without question been the first one to lie to her, too?

She thought back over her life, and certain things began to make sense. The way they'd lived—always isolated and afraid. The real reason her mother rarely spoke of her father. More recently, Radoslav's unnerving reaction to her when he saw her and why he'd hired someone to dig into her past.

Oh, God. Could such a terrible man really be my father? She swallowed back the bile the sickening thought triggered.

Heart racing, her insides trembling, she stumbled back to the book. Gwen dropped to her knees and reached for the journal.

She snatched her hand back.

Swiped her palm down the back of her shorts.

Gave her hand a good shake, then picked up the book.

I was in the hall outside Nikolai's office when I overheard him talking to a man who was complaining because his wife was pregnant again. Nikolai laughed and told him what he would do if "some whore" he slept with ever got pregnant. I can't even bring myself to write the awful things he said. He is a monster, and we have to get away. After he left with the man, I snuck in his office and stole some money and a couple ledgers from his safe. I knew the combination because I watched him open it a few times. He never seemed to notice.

Probably because he was so sure I would never leave him. I'm not proud of stealing, but Feodor and I need money to run away. We'll use some of it to change our names. I saw that in a movie once. I have no idea how to do that, but we have to figure it out. Alice Madison and Feodor Kuznetsov have to disappear forever. The ledgers will be our insurance in case Nikolai ever does find us. He has a lot of secrets in those books he'll want to protect. He's going to be out of town tonight. That will be our only chance to sneak away.

Her mother's deadly secret was the reason she took cash-only jobs and why they never stayed in one place very long. It was why Gwen was never allowed to have any real friends. The fewer people in their lives, the less risk of them being discovered. Alice had made huge sacrifices to protect their anonymity and keep them safe. Yet, when Gwen was awarded a scholarship to attend the prestigious Presidio Graduate School, her mother risked everything by moving back to San Francisco—the very place her nightmare had begun.

With each word, Gwen's deep love and respect for her mother returned. And her hatred of Nikolai Radoslav grew.

She flipped to a page with a key taped to it. A folded piece of paper slid out. The entry scribbled below the key was dated five years ago. It provided details for a safety deposit box her mother had secured at a small local bank.

Gwen hesitated before opening the piece of paper. What secret was hidden within those folds? She exhaled, relieved to discover it was the lease document for the box. Her name was listed as the sole heir. On the opposite page of the journal, Alice had listed the contents.

Birth Certificate of Gwendolyn Tamberley, Father "Unknown"

Two green ledgers taken from Nikolai Radoslav's safe

$2,736.00 in cash. This is what's left of the $5,000.00 I took from Nikolai's safe. The other $2,264.00 I used to pay for a new identity and a fake birth certificate. I wanted nothing to do with the rest of his blood money.

It was weird learning the document she'd used her whole life was a forgery. Over the course of a few pages, Richard Tamberley had been obliterated, replaced by the shocking truth of the man who was her biological father. Gwen was gripped by a profound sense of loss for a man who never even existed.

She continued reading, anxious to learn more about Feodor Kuznetsov. The man who'd loved her mother enough to risk his life and raise another man's child as his own. Turns out, he was the handsome young man in the picture frame that Gwen had spent her life believing was her father. He'd worked for Radoslav and had been tasked with watching over her mother. The more time they spent together, the closer they became and they fell in love. What Gwen read next, broke her heart ...

Zoya, Nikolai's mean housekeeper just came in my room with one of Nikolai's men. She said he would be keeping me company from now on. What she meant was, he was my guard now. I asked where Feodor was and she said he left, that he went back to Russian. It's a lie—Feodor would never leave me here alone. He wouldn't! I k`now this in my heart, in my very soul. Nikolai must've found out about us and killed the only man I will ever love. It's only a matter of time before he kills me and my baby, too. I will never let that happen. I've been locked in my room and my new guard is right outside my door. I'll have to go out the window. They *would never expect that, since I'm on the third floor. I'll climb down the big tree outside. I have to at least try, because I have to leave tonight. No matter what.*

Young, pregnant, terrified, heartbroken and alone, her mother still had the internal strength to do whatever was necessary to protect herself and her unborn baby.

Gwen quietly closed the book, wiped the tears from her eyes and held her mother's words close to her chest. She had no concept of time, but the ache in her back told her she'd been there a while. She straightened her legs in front of her and stretched to touch her toes. She glanced at her watch. Had it really only been two hours since her world collapsed in on her?

She should call Beck. *What if his feelings for me change when he finds out my father is the evil man he's devoted his life to destroying?*

"No, I'll wait until he gets back." He could look through the journal himself and decide how to proceed. After all, these secrets had been hidden for twenty-five years. A few more hours certainly wouldn't make a difference.

With a groan, she rolled to her hands and knees and pressed herself up from the floor. She stood for a minute until the lingering ache in her ribs subsided. When she turned, she bumped into the chest of a very large human. She stumbled back a step. The journal fell from her grasp and bounced on the floor. Her head tilted up, and she recognized the man from the restaurant where she'd met Radoslav.

Gwen opened her mouth to scream and a very large, very rough hand covered the bottom half of her face. Her mouth and nose were covered, making it difficult to breathe. As panic set in, she felt a sharp pinch in the side of her neck. Her thoughts began to jumble together, and she realized her mistake. She'd forgotten to close the window.

Her legs went numb, and she waited for her body to hit the floor. Unable to focus, her fuzzy mind meandered from thought to thought. *Shouldn't I be falling? How come I'm not falling? Can Caleb hear me screaming?* I am *screaming, aren't I?*

The world spun, and Gwen found herself draped over a huge shoulder like a sack of potatoes. She heard a groan, realized it had come from her. The pattern in the old secondhand rug swirled and blurred beneath her as he circled and moved to her dresser. Before she could figure out what he was after, they swung around again. Her head bumped against his back and it was becoming impossible to slog through the muddiness in her mind. As the world went dark, she thought of Beck and the future they'd never share.

CHAPTER THIRTY-THREE

Beck sat across from his friend and former boss. He'd just finished telling Simmons everything and was waiting to see if his head would pop off.

"Sam, look, I know you're pissed—"

"Pissed? You think I'm pissed." He laughed. Not a *ha-ha, that's really funny* kind of laugh, but more of a *you have GOT to be fucking kidding me* kind of laugh.

Beck opened his mouth to plead his case further, and his phone vibrated. Seeing the vein bulging in the center of Sam's forehead, he opted to let it roll to voicemail. A second later, it vibrated again.

He yanked it from his pocket, saw it was Caleb, and a sliver of concern pierced him. "What's up?"

"She's gone!" Caleb shouted, his voice uncharacteristically frantic.

"What the hell do you mean she's gone?" Beck sprang from his chair.

Sam slowly stood. Elbows locked, he leaned his knuckles against the desk.

"She's gone, Beck!" Caleb cursed. "I was upstairs working

on the plumbing. When I came to get her to eat some lunch, she was gone."

Beck had never heard Caleb panicked before.

"I looked everywhere for her, then I noticed the window in her bedroom was open. Wide fucking open," he yelled.

"What was she doing when you last saw her?" Beck tried to exude calm. On the inside, he wanted to tear the world apart.

"She was going through those boxes of her mom's things. Since I couldn't finish setting up the alarm system until the power company came out to install a new meter, I went upstairs to work on the plumbing and to give her some privacy. I swear to you, Beck, I verified that all the doors and windows were closed and locked."

Normally, when the system is fully-functional, an alarm would sound throughout the building if any threshold—door or window—was breeched.

"Damn it! I should've been more aggressive about getting Pacific Gas and Electric out here." His voice dripped with self-blame.

"Not your fault." Beck had instructed him to put in the best system he had. Unfortunately, the old building wasn't built to handle the demands of such high-tech electronics.

"Hang on, Beck. I might've found something."

Beck heard what sounded like pages flipping.

"What is it?" He was going crazy thinking of what might have happened.

"It's some kind of journal. I didn't notice it until now, because it was almost completely under her bed. Looks like she might've dropped it when—" *She was grabbed*, were the words his brother wasn't saying.

"Caleb, I don't think an old journal is going to—"

"Oh shit." His brother's tone was way too fucking ominous.

"What did you find?" Beck looked at Sam.

"According to one of the entries, Gwen's mother's real name is Alice Madison, and Richard Tamberley isn't her father ... " Caleb hesitated. "Nikolai Radoslav is."

Beck's heart fucking stopped. *"That's* why he's been so fixated on her. Gwen once told me she's a carbon copy of her mom. He must've seen the resemblance."

More pages flipped in the background.

"I think I know why he grabbed her." Caleb's voice was flat. "Gwen's mom snagged a couple of Radoslav's ledgers before she ran from him. They're in a safety deposit box at a bank here in town."

Christ. He thinks Gwen knows about the ledgers.

"He has to know I'll come after her, so he's going to take her someplace he thinks I don't know about."

"Jesus, Beck. I fucked up. I am so sorry. You know I'd give my life to keep her safe, right?" Caleb's guilt was another thing Beck could lay at Radoslav's feet.

"I know you would. This is on Radoslav, no one else. You hear me?" Caleb, and the rest of his family, were the only people he would trust to keep watch over Gwen. No way was he letting his brother shoulder the blame.

"Yeah." A sigh exploded from Caleb. "I hear ya."

"Listen, get on that magic computer of yours and—" Beck stalled, looking up at his old boss looming across the desk.

Their eyes met and held. A long moment later, Sam nodded.

"Beck?" Caleb said.

"Yeah, I'm here. I need you to find where he might've taken her."

"I'm on it. I'll call you when I find something." Caleb hung up.

Gwen's life depended on Beck's ability to focus on finding her and getting her back. In order to do that, he had to compartmentalize. He couldn't allow himself to think about how scared she must be or what she might be enduring.

He shared this new information with Simmons.

"If you want what's in that safety deposit box, you'd better send someone over to the shelter to grab the key."

"I'll send someone over now."

With a quiet tip of the head and a solid handshake, his old boss let Beck know he had his back.

Beck turned out of Sam's office and ran. He ignored the *hey, mans* and *how the hell are yous* from his former colleagues as he passed through on his way to the stairwell. The door banged against the wall when he shoved it open, and he took the stairs two at a time. When he reached the door to the garage, he slammed his hand against the metal bar and dashed across the lot to his SUV.

Beck clipped his seatbelt just as his phone rang. He cranked the engine and answered Caleb's call on the car's hands-free.

"Please tell me you found something." He put on his sunglasses, backed out of the spot and slammed it into drive. Tires squawked when he jammed his foot on the gas pedal and tore out of the lot.

"She's in Cambria. She *has* to be. Radoslav has a property there. I've already gained access to the blueprints and am working on a breach plan." Caleb had shaken off his self-recrimination and was now the well-trained, disciplined hostage rescue specialist Beck knew him to be.

He looked at his watch. Radoslav was already an hour ahead of them. "Can you get in touch with Mason?"

"I'll give him a call. If he's around, he'll help."

Mason Croft was Caleb's best friend. He was a good old Texas boy who just happened to be able to fly anything with wings or rotors. He used to fly Spec Ops for the Navy. Now he had a couple helos and small jets and flew charters for big-shot businessmen.

"Tell him we'll meet him at his airfield in twenty minutes." Beck screeched to a halt, drumming his fingers on the wheel while he waited for the exit bar to lift.

"Roger, that. If he can't help us, I know someone else we can call."

The bar lifted and, the second it cleared the top of his rig, Beck drove through the gate. He turned right and sped toward the airfield.

"Beck, we *will* get her back," Caleb reassured him.

"She's my life, Caleb. We *have* to."

NIKOLAI HUNG UP THE PHONE. He smiled and leaned back. The *creak* of the rich leather of his large chair was the only sound in his office sanctuary. He held up a glass of scotch in his right hand. The sun shone through the cut crystal, casting prisms of color over the top of his desk. Ice cubes shifted with a *clink-clink*. His relaxed posture belied the anticipation zinging through him.

Gregor would be arriving with Gwendolyn Tamberley soon.

Alice Madison entered his thoughts. Sixteen years old, hungry and desperate, she'd had nothing when he first spotted her huddled in the doorway of one of his vacant properties. Concealed beneath layers of filth and distrust, her beauty called to him like a temptress's song. She'd looked up at him and bedeviled him with her hypnotic eyes.

Nikolai had taken her in, giving her his protection and a place in his home. And his bed. He'd thought to destroy the discomfiting pull she had on him by using her like he did so many others. It hadn't worked.

The moment he'd realized she was gone was as clear to him today as it was twenty-five-plus years ago. As soon as he had discovered her ... dalliance, he'd had her confined to her room and assigned one of his men to keep an eye on her. Later that evening, after he'd taken care of Feodor, Nikolai himself went to retrieve her for dinner. He'd unlocked the door and, the second he entered her room, he knew he'd made the mistake of underestimating her. A strange stillness was all that remained. As if some unseen energy had disappeared along with her. She was gone.

When questioned, a member of the household staff recalled seeing her outside Nikolai's office a few days earlier. At that point, there'd been no reason for suspicion. He'd searched his office and discovered cash missing from his safe. An insignificant amount, Nikolai dismissed it as unimportant. What enraged and worried him then—and every day since—were the ledgers she'd stolen. They contained enough information to destroy everything he'd worked to build his entire life.

Nikolai finished his drink, set the glass on the desk and hefted his girth from the chair.

A thick Persian rug silenced his footfalls as he moved to the large wooden door. He flipped the deadbolt, ensuring his privacy, and returned to his place behind the desk. As he sat down, he reached in his breast pocket and pulled out a small, brass key. His thumb rubbed across the shiny, worn surface. A habit ingrained over years of carrying it. The edges dug into his palm as he tightened his grip around it, as if doing so would further protect the secrets it kept locked away.

The bottom right-hand drawer rolled open. He grabbed the handle to a cheap metal lockbox and lifted it out. He set it on the leather desk blotter with a muffled *thump* and turned it to face him. Nikolai inserted the key and jiggled it. Years of repeated access had taught him a certain *finesse* was needed in order to disengage the lock. With a quiet *snick*, the catch released, and he lifted the lid to expose the secrets within.

A cursory glance would lead one to believe the contents seemed like nothing more than an innocent stack of old notes and a lone photograph. To Nikolai, they were a reminder of his one protracted weakness. An obsession with a woman whose death wasn't enough to slake his fixation or exorcise the enduring craving she provoked.

Nikolai picked up his reading glasses and slipped them on. He sifted through the stack and pulled out the old photo of a smiling teenage girl. Even years later, the edges frayed, the colors faded, there was no dulling the shine of adoration in Alice's large blue-green eyes.

His jaw tightened.

The smiles she'd given him had never reached her eyes. No, the happiness and unveiled joy that taunted him every time he looked at this picture had been directed at Feodor Kuznetsov. One of his men had become concerned and taken a series of photos of them with their heads together, as if conspiring, and given them to Nikolai. The next day, he'd sent Feodor back to his family in Russia. In three separate containers.

No one betrays me and lives.

Alice had vanished that very same evening.

This was the only remaining photograph he had of her. The rest he'd burned in an effort to cleanse her from his system. Setting it aside, he grabbed the worn envelope and tugged out the single sheet of notebook paper inside. Unfolded and folded so often, the seams were splitting, and it was beginning to fall apart. Nikolai re-read the words of love Feodor had written to her. Alice probably hadn't meant to leave one of her precious love letters behind. His housekeeper found it at the back of a drawer in her room after she'd run away.

Nikolai settled his head back against the chair. He gazed up at the ceiling, remembering his initial reaction to the young Tamberley woman.

He'd always been very careful to use protection whenever he was with any of the girls. Dealing with an unwanted pregnancy could be such a bother. That left Feodor—the only other person with one-on-one access to her. Nikolai would bet his empire that Feodor was Gwendolyn Tamberley's father. The only consolation for Nikolai was knowing he'd crushed Alice's heart by destroying the man who'd dared to touch what belonged to him.

He reached for the photo, stroking his thumb over her face. "Did you give your daughter my ledgers, sweet Alice?"

Made sense. Who else would she have trusted with their safekeeping? *If that is so, why has she not already turned them over to the FBI?* Perhaps she was waiting for the right time to blackmail him.

Alice's face smiled up at him, mocked him with unanswered questions.

Gregor seemed to think Gwendolyn Tamberley was very important to Special Agent O'Halleran. Good. Nikolai looked forward to taking care of her the same way he had the pretty fed. He had enjoyed every strike of his fist, every swipe of his blade across her flesh. Watching his men take turns with her had given him a sense of power eclipsed only by the moment he'd held the gun to her head and pulled the trigger.

Nikolai sneered. He would take away another person close to O'Halleran and solve his problems with the Tamberley woman all at once.

He carefully re-folded the note, tucked it in the envelope and dropped it in the box. After a last look, he pressed the photo on top of the stack and flipped the lid shut with a metallic *clank*. He locked away his torment before setting the box back in the bottom drawer. Once he was done with

Gwendolyn Tamberley, the box and all its contents, along with the curse that had plagued Nikolai for years, would be buried with whatever was left of her.

Nikolai secured the key in his pocket, picked up the empty glass and strode to the fully-stocked bar he kept in his office. Pouring himself another two fingers of scotch, he turned and took a sip as he looked out the floor-to-ceiling window. Perched on a cliff high above the Pacific Ocean, the property's remoteness offered the privacy and concealment he demanded.

He stared out over the water. A cool, salt-tinged breeze spilled through the nearby open window. The rhythmic *tink-tink-tink* of his ruby ring tapping against the fine cut glass sounded delicate compared with the unrelenting crash of the dark waves slamming into the rugged rocks below. Several kinds of birds dived and swooped, fighting the gusts of wind swirling around the cliff face.

Nikolai's blood sizzled in anticipation of the fun he would have with Gwendolyn Tamberley.

CHAPTER THIRTY-FOUR

Beck turned onto the dirt road leading to Mason Croft's private airfield. Dust kicked up behind him as he sped toward the large metal hangar. Up ahead, he saw Caleb just beginning to unload his stuff from his truck next to the big building. Beck pulled in next to him, jumped out and grabbed his own gear.

On the tarmac about two hundred feet away, Mason was performing his pre-flight check on a sleek, black Bell 412. He smoothed his hand over the helicopter's fuselage like a lover. He popped open a small compartment on the side, looked in, then closed it and turned the small metal latch to secure it. He glanced over, noticed them approaching and jogged toward them.

"Hey, Caleb." He extended his hand.

Caleb set down his gear bags with a *tsk*, grabbed Mason's hand and dragged him in for a back-slapping hug. "Mason, it's damn good to see you, bud."

They broke apart, and Beck stepped in for his own quick hug.

"I really appreciate you helping us out with this, Mase." Beck stepped back.

"No prob." Mason turned and started walking toward the helicopter. "So what's the plan?"

Beck and Caleb slung duffels over their shoulders, then hefted a large bag in each hand and followed. From the corner of his eye, Beck watched Caleb, relieved when he didn't see any signs of discomfort at carrying his heavy gear.

Last thing I want is to be responsible for him getting reinjured.

"If it's no problem, I'd like to fill you in on the rest of what's happening while we're in the air." Beck was concerned about how much time had passed since Gwen was taken.

Mason turned a lever and dragged open the side door.

"Not a problem at all." His Texas drawl colored his words as he jogged around and opened the door on the other side. "I figured that might be the case."

Once all their gear was loaded and their harnesses locked, Mason flipped some switches and pressed some buttons, and the bird fired up. The high-pitched whine of the big engine and sound of the blades cutting through the air reverberated throughout the helicopter.

Mason twisted around in his seat, pointed at his ears and waited for them to put on their headsets before saying, "Thumbs up if you can hear me."

After getting two thumbs up, he opened a map and handed it to Beck.

"This is the best spot for us to land." He pointed at a green circle. "And this"—he dragged his finger to a smaller red circle—"is where you said she's being held."

Beck looked at Caleb for confirmation.

Caleb nodded. "The property was bought by a shell corporation seven years ago, and there's only one owner listed. The cousin of the guy who owns Mt. Elbrus Restaurant, where Radoslav hangs out. Problem is, the guy died *fifteen* years ago."

Kinda hard for a dead man to purchase anything.

"Okay, the landing area is about three klicks out from the house. We'll have to hump it the rest of the way, but that'll give us the element of surprise." Mason looked at Beck. "We'll get her out of there."

He faced forward and wrapped his left hand around a lever. He steadily pulled back, and the sleek bird lifted smoothly from the tarmac. At the same time, his right hand inched another lever forward, and their airspeed increased.

Beck watched the small airstrip drop away beneath them.

Wait a minute. We?

"Mason, I don't want you messed up in this. You just get us there, and we'll take care of the rest." Beck already regretted Caleb's involvement. He didn't want to drag Mason into this nightmare as well. What they were about to do wasn't exactly legal.

"I can't stand a bully." Mason looked back at him in the small cockpit mirror, his reflective sunglasses hiding his eyes. "I'm in."

"Thanks, man." Beck was humbled by the guy's unselfishness.

"Good." Perfect teeth smiled back at Beck. "Now let's go kick some ass."

With the ease of years of experience, Mason's hands manipulated the levers while his feet worked pedals on the floor. They did a smooth roll to the right and sped through the early afternoon sky.

The first half of their flight was spent strategizing, then going back over every detail of the plan multiple times. They'd not only come up with a plan A, but they had a plan B, C, and even a plan D. In the beat of a heart, things could go sideways on an unsanctioned op like this, and they needed to be prepared.

Beck closed his eyes and wondered what Gwen might be going through. The core of stubborn strength in her petite frame would be no match for the brutality of a man like Radoslav.

A quick shake of his head, and he slammed the door on the encroaching doubts. He began a mental run-through of every single breach scenario they'd come up with. Every angle, every move, every course of action should things go south.

Emotions locked down tight, his mind firmly in the game, he was ready to take down Radoslav.

"Gentlemen, time to saddle up." Mason's voice filtered through their headsets, breaking the pensive silence. He pointed to a spot below where tall brown grass undulated in the breeze.

Caleb and Beck looked down and did a double-take at the tiny clear patch surrounded by trees.

Mason chuckled. "I've landed in much smaller spaces and under much worse conditions."

Beck could only imagine the kind of hot spots he'd flown into and out of.

"Besides," Mason continued, "those trees provide excellent cover for our arrival."

He pointed at the tall evergreens surrounding the clearing. Their tops rustled and swayed hypnotically in the strong breeze. The setting sun cast their long shadows over the field. *Perfect. It'll be dark soon.*

Beck checked the magazine in his gun. Tension coiled in his gut as they began their descent.

The long fiberglass blades churned up tall grass and other debris as Mason brought the helicopter softly down on the dry ground. The second the skids touched, he began flipping switches and powering down.

Caleb and Beck wasted no time unhooking their harnesses and pulling off their headsets. They replaced them with smaller earpieces. They would provide a reliable two-way form of communication and were invaluable during stealth missions like this.

Mason adjusted his own earpiece, swung open the front door and climbed out.

Beck and Caleb hopped out the side doors. Beck grabbed the Kevlar vests and handed one to each of them. He tugged his on over his head and tightened the Velcro straps along his sides.

In addition to gear loaded in their duffels, they each brought an H&K 416 rifle with nifty holographic sights and ATPIAL targeting lasers attached. Caleb had contacted the Hostage Rescue Team's weapons officer and told him what was happening. With one phone call, he'd arranged for them to borrow what they needed from one of the bureau's field training office nearby. Apparently, he'd said, "Anything for Beck," then he'd not-so-gently reminded him he was sticking his neck out and would personally end Caleb's life if he didn't return them in one piece.

Each was loaded with a thirty-round magazine, but extras were securely attached to their vests, as well as a few other helpful pieces of equipment like C4 with detonators, a small med kit, extra magazines for the sidearm they carried on their hips and a small folding knife. Strapped to their thigh, they each had a twelve-inch black knife with a serrated edge. He'd seen grown men piss themselves just seeing one of the big knives being unsheathed.

With the special sights and lasers, not to mention a healthy supply of explosives, they were prepared for any contingency, especially a nighttime breach. After all—thanks to the element of surprise—most successful operations are carried out under the cover of darkness without a shot being fired.

Out of the corner of his eye, Beck watched Mason check his own weapon before holstering it. He shoved extra magazines into the pouches on his belt and vest. Since he was no longer an operator, he didn't routinely carry the big firepower. It wouldn't matter. Mason was widely known for being an expert marksman no matter what the weapon, not to mention his legendary hand-to-hand combat skills and use of a KA-BAR.

He looked up and noticed Beck watching him.

"Good old Glock 41 Gen4." The corner of his mouth lifted, and he patted the gun at his hip. "This bad boy has served me well. Never saw any reason to switch."

Beck shrugged. "What's the old saying, '*If it ain't broke, don't fix it*'?"

"I like the way you think, partner." Mason laid on the good ol' boy Texas accent real thick, then swung an RD706 tranquilizer gun over his back.

In spite of the seriousness of what they were about to do, Beck chuckled. It felt good and helped relieve some of the battle-ready tension gripping his shoulders.

Finally, the rotors slowed to a stop, and they locked everything up tight.

The ensuing silence heightened his senses. Beck inhaled the crisp, piney scent of the giant evergreens as their branches rubbed and scraped, could hear the *swish* of the tall blades of grass brushing together in the wind. Grasshoppers *crick-cricked* as they jumped from one stalk to another. The buzz of cicadas hiding against the bark of the nearby trees created a droning backdrop. Under different circumstances, the happy chirps and whistles of birds swooping up and down in search of grasshoppers would be peaceful.

Beck pulled up the map in his mind, looking around to assess their location. His eyes met those of the two skilled warriors ready to risk their lives alongside him. Without a word, they nodded, turned and moved out quickly and silently toward the surrounding woods.

CHAPTER THIRTY-FIVE

Gwen felt trapped deep in the bowels of an endless tunnel. A barely discernible sliver of light and sound teased from the opposite end. The promise they radiated seemed hopelessly out of reach.

A far-off sound captured her attention, kept her from sinking back into the contentment found only in sleep.

She waited. *Did I imagine it?*

No, there it was again, eking its way through the murkiness of her mind, past what sounded like someone using her head as a bass drum. She battled through the painful cacophony hampering her thoughts to identify the sound. Was it voices or merely her addled brain teasing her with the promise of consciousness?

Gwen wanted to open her eyes. Instinct forced her to remain still. Moments passed with no sound, and she'd almost convinced herself she'd imagined the voices. Until she heard them again.

The unmistakable accent and guttural speech sent goosebumps racing across her skin. Her heart began beating with such force, it intensified the ceaseless pounding in her ears.

Certain it could be heard outside her head, she took in a furtive breath through her nose, then silently released it. Harsh clarity struck her and, like a rapid-fire slideshow, images assaulted her mind.

A journal.

An open window. *Gwen, you idiot.*

A burning sting in her neck.

Then nothing.

She dredged deeper, mining for any tidbit of memory she could find.

Dread crawled over her like the legs of a thousand spiders. A violent wave of nausea blindsided her. *Don't throw up. Don't throw up. Don't throw up.*

A tingling sensation began tickling up and down her arms and legs, then an intense burning pain stabbed through her shoulders. Gwen stifled a whimper and tamped down the panic trying to sabotage her safety. Willed herself to remain still, though the adrenaline flooding her body urged her to flee.

The side effects of the injection were beginning to fade. Even though her brain felt like a box of rocks, she was cognizant enough not to let on she was recovering.

I need to give Beck time to find me. With certainty born of her trust in him, she knew he would never stop looking for her.

Gwen mentally cataloged all of her aches and pains as she lay on what she assumed was a cold floor. The dull discomfort in her cheek was a remnant of Chadwick's attack. Her hands were bound behind her, causing the pain in her shoulders and wrists. That was definitely going to make it harder to do anything. *One problem at a time.* Right now, her biggest concerns were the screaming headache and persistent high-pitched whine in her ears.

She risked sneaking a peek through the veil of her lashes. Did everything possible to remain still and not draw unwanted attention as she scanned the room. Being able to carry out this simple act made her want to pump her fist in the air, a sign of how desperate her situation was.

A shiny metal table was pushed against the wall. She couldn't see what was on top, but a row of boxes labeled "Syringes" lined the shelf below. Next to it stood two glass-fronted cabinets full of bottles and vials of various shapes, sizes and colors.

What is this place? Her imagination conjured up several horrific possibilities, and a chill shivered through her from the weight of the malevolence and soulful despair haunting this space.

Columns of sunlight stabbed down into the room.

"Did anyone see you take her?"

"No. My men went in through an open window in the alley. No one saw them enter or leave the building."

Gwen risked opening her eyes a fraction more.

Facing her, about ten feet away, in a patch of yellow light like Satan lit by the fires of hell, stood Nikolai Radoslav.

Facing him was a man she guessed to be about five or six inches shorter than Beck. The sun bounced off his bald head. Tattoos peeked out between the folds of fat at the back of his head and neck. As wide as he was tall, he seemed more fat than fit. He glanced over his shoulder at her. He was one of the men who'd been sitting at a nearby table when she met with Radoslav.

"Move her to the chair." Radoslav had the voice of a lifelong smoker. "And make sure she is secured."

Gwen closed her eyes.

The sound of pants brushing together and the muffled *squeak* of rubber-soled shoes drew closer.

She dug deep, forced herself to relax.

Hard hands squeezed her upper arms in an iron grip and lifted.

She yelped.

Her feet dangled in the air, and her head flopped forward against his chest. He dropped her onto a hard chair. Pain rocketed up her spine and rattled her teeth. She mewled softly as her previous injuries reared their ugly heads.

"Ah, Gregor. It appears our guest is awake." Satisfaction oozed from Radoslav's words.

With what felt like a Herculean effort, Gwen strained to lift her bleary head. She opened her eyes and instantly regretted it. Light from a window high above the table assaulted them, and pain bombarded her head.

After a deep breath, she blinked a few times, then squinted before prying them open a little at a time. The pain had lessened to a mild roar, which made it easier to focus on her surroundings.

Radoslav stood directly across from her. One hand was tucked in his front pocket. The other rolled a big cigar between two fat fingers. He brought it to his mouth and took a few puffs. The tip went from gray to a bright reddish-orange glow. Smoke poured from his nose and mouth and circled his head. Through the haze, a smug smile split his porcine face. The wicked glint in his deep-set, black eyes pierced through the dense haze.

Staring into his dead eyes, she thought of her mother as a young girl falling prey to this man's evil. Scared and alone, she'd been forced to run and hide. To live a solitary existence in order to protect her daughter from a deadly secret.

How could this demon be my father?

The man called Gregor flattened his broad hand between her shoulder blades and bent her forward, her chest pressed against her thighs. Gwen closed her eyes against an onslaught of nausea as he held her in place. When she opened them, he had a small pocketknife in his other hand. For the first time, she noticed he was wearing rubber gloves.

Before she could obsess over that little detail, there was a *fwip,* and the knife snapped open close to her cheek.

Her body tensed. She tried to lean away from the sharp edge.

The corner of his mouth lifted as he lowered it and cut through the plastic zip ties digging into her bleeding wrists. Gwen's lifeless arms dropped like overcooked noodles.

He removed his hand from the middle of her back, grabbed her tortured wrists and jerked her arms forward.

Gwen cried out. Fire burned from her shoulders to her fingertips.

Though it was futile, she struggled against his grip as he strapped her to the arms of the chair. The rough leather tightened and scraped her already battered flesh. Tears threatened, but she held them back. Instead, her eyes bored holes through Radoslav.

He chuckled. "Ah, so you are a tough one, eh? We shall see about this."

Gregor squatted in front of her. The overhead light flashed off the blade of his knife as his wrist swiped down.

Gwen held her breath. Waited to feel the sharp edge slicing through her. It didn't happen. The plastic bindings at her ankles loosened and dropped away. Her shoulders sagged as a breath exploded from her.

Gregor's tattooed hands jerked her knees apart, and he moved in between them. The heat from his body poured over her legs. The corner of his mouth lifted, and his tongue dragged across his bottom lip.

Gwen pressed herself to the back of the chair, trying to put as much space between them as possible. Before she could gather her wits enough to take action—like kick him in the crotch—he wrapped a big hand around her ankle. As if he'd heard her thoughts, he turned slightly and squeezed hard enough she feared she would hear the crack of bone.

It's not like I can control my legs yet anyway.

Gwen couldn't stand to see the vileness in his eyes as he bound one ankle, then the other, to the legs of the chair. Instead, she focused over his shoulder, her eyes on Radoslav.

Gregor tightened the shackles to the point of nearly cutting off circulation to her feet. He leered at her once more, stood and moved to her left. Like a good, obedient henchman, he stood there with his feet planted apart, arms hanging in front of him, his hands loosely crossed. The man might look like he was "at ease," but he wasn't fooling her. If Gwen so much as twitched, he would be on her in a second.

Her eyes shifted back to Radoslav. She infused her glare with every bit of anger, contempt and disgust she felt over what he'd done to her mother.

I'm not a scared teenager. You will not do to me what you did to her.

Radoslav smirked.

"It is nice to see you again, Ms. Tamberley." He lumbered closer, dragging the rancid smell of cigar with him like an old friend.

As a little girl, Gwen dreamed of knowing her father and wondered what their relationship would be like. She would pretend to have conversations with him from heaven. He was warm, kind, generous. A real hero. Never in her wildest imaginings was he a psychopathic killer like the one standing a foot in front of her.

She was beginning to think he had no knowledge of his paternity. Her best bet was to play dumb until she knew for sure.

"Mr. Radoslav, I don't understa—"

Pain exploded across her left cheek. Stars burst behind her eyes, and her head lurched sideways. Long hair hung in strands around her face. The intensified ringing in her ears hinted at a ruptured eardrum. She could taste the metallic tang of blood as it dripped from her mouth.

Gwen moaned, gave her head a little shake. *Must ... not ... black out.*

"Do not presume to play games with me." Radoslav's foul breath whispered across her ear.

His fingers tangled in her hair, and he jerked her head back. His mouth was an inch from hers when he said, "You will not like the outcome."

The stench of alcohol, stale cigars and evil hung off him like a second skin.

Gwen gagged, and her stomach revolted. By some miracle, she managed to keep from vomiting, even as she smiled internally at the thought of throwing up all over Radoslav's shoes.

"Now—" He untwisted his fingers from her hair. "Do we understand each other?"

Her head fell forward. *Think, Gwen, think!* Tears pricked her eyes. The left one was beginning to swell shut, making it difficult to focus.

Alert. That's what she needed to be. As alert as she could get, anyway, considering the bells clanging around in her brain. She took a deep breath and fought for clarity.

What do I know about Radoslav? He was a narcissistic lunatic with a huge ego who loved to expound on his greatness. He couldn't help himself; it was like it was a part of his DNA.

Gwen bobbed her head once. Let him think she was cooperating.

"Good. Now. You will tell me why you *really* came to me." He pinched her chin hard and tilted her face up to him. "And do not tell me it has to do with your shelter. Not when you are playing house with an FBI agent."

"I'm not ... " She coughed a few times. "I'm not sure what you're asking me, Mr. Radoslav."

He clamped her jaw in his hand and forced her head back.

She swallowed past the dryness. Tasted blood trickling down the back of her throat. "Mr. Chadwick told me you were interested in making a donation for tax purposes. I'd never heard of you until then."

Gwen was a horrible liar. The smart thing to do was keep her responses as close to the truth as possible. "The man working at the shelter told me he was a contractor. I swear. You have to believe me, Mr. Radoslav." Her desperation would feed his ego, and she didn't have to fake it.

"Tell me again about your father." His hold prevented her from turning away. He was so close, she could see the utter lack of humanity in his eyes, the tiny red veins marking his bulbous nose. The onions he must've eaten earlier seeped from his pores and fouled the air between them.

She frowned, hesitated. "I—I don't ... I don't really know much about him."

Which was the truth. She *didn't* know much about the man she'd thought was her father.

"His name was Richard Tamberley. He died before I was born." Gwen's life depended upon him believing her.

He squinted, searching for any hint of weakness or deception he could capitalize on.

Don't flinch. Not even the slightest twitch. And for God's sake, don't break eye contact with him.

"What did he look like, this ... Richard Tamberley?" He released her with a jerk and moved away from her.

Gwen hinged her jaw side-to-side, relieved to have some space between them. She thought about the framed black and white picture of Feodor, the young man she'd spent her life adoring.

As a little girl, Gwen had been awakened more than once by her mother's muffled sobs. Each time it happened, she'd snuck out of bed and found her mother sitting in the dark, a tissue in one hand, his picture in the other.

Even as a young child hiding in the shadows, she'd recognized sadness and loss, could see the longing in her mother's eyes. Her mother had loved the smiling young man in the picture frame. Because of that, Gwen felt a sense of loyalty to him.

"He was a *very* handsome young man." She couldn't resist needling the animal who'd kept them apart.

A muscle in Radoslav's jaw twitched, and his shoulders stiffened.

Every muscle in Gwen's body tightened, preparing for the next blow. When it didn't come, she willed her aching muscles to relax.

"My mom told me the picture was taken just before his twenty-second birthday."

In the picture, he was outside at a park or something. His hair was really dark and kind of messy, like the wind had tousled it around. Her mom had told Gwen he had warm, brown eyes.

Radoslav lumbered back and forth. His features becoming more agitated with each step.

"I remember one time she said to me, 'Gwendolyn, his warm brown eyes glowed with love whenever he looked at me.'" It was one of the few things her mother ever said about him. As a little girl without a daddy, that was like something out of a fairy tale. Only seven years old, yet she remembered those words to this day. Whenever she felt sad or missed having him around, she'd wrap them around her like a security blanket.

Gwen cleared her throat, choking down the sadness caused by memories of a young man whose life was cut short by evil.

Radoslav stopped pacing. He stomped over and snatched

something off the table. It scraped across the stainless steel like nails on a chalkboard. In his hand was the familiar frame she'd stared at more times than she could count.

"Is this the man you speak so highly of?" He moved toward her, held it in front of her face.

She leaned away, nodded.

"This man right here." His fingernail tapped the glass. "You are telling me he is your father?"

"Yes." She frowned. "Mr. Radoslav, I don't understand. Why are you asking about him? Why are you doing this?"

Hostility bounced from him like a living thing as he commenced pacing. Only faster and more ... agitated.

"This"—*tap tap tap tap tap tap*—"is Feodor Kuznetsov. He worked for me a very long time ago and he betrayed me!"

He turned and hurled the frame across the room. It shattered against the far wall, and broken glass rained down. The fading sunlight bounced off the shards scattered across the floor.

Gwen couldn't help it; she flinched.

"This man dared to touch something that belonged to me." His shoulders lifted with each heaving breath. "It cost him his life."

Belonged to him. The words tore through her like claws. Gwen's anger grew, as did her hatred for the monster who treated her mother like chattel and ripped her great love away from her.

Thank God, momma had known love once. The thought gave Gwen a small amount of peace. It also strengthened her resolve to survive, to make sure he was punished.

Radoslav gazed down at all the broken pieces of glass.

Silenced saturated the room.

Gwen took in her surroundings, hoping for a clue to their location.

From the corner of her eye, she looked up at the window. *Ground level. Must be in some kind of subfloor or basement.*

There was a quiet hum from air conditioning being pumped into the room.

She'd caught a glimpse of the only door—behind her—right before Radoslav's stooge dropped her into the chair.

Have to assume it's locked and there's some kind of security system.

A grunt and the cracking of knees captured Gwen's attention.

Nikolai had lowered his sizeable girth to sift through the glass. He grabbed a large piece and held it up, turned it back and forth, then looked over his shoulder at her. A sinister smile slithered across his face.

Knowing the heartless bastard's blood ran through her body sickened her.

He stood, dug in his back pocket and pulled out a handkerchief. With a flick of his wrist, he shook it out and wrapped it around the widest end of the sharp piece of glass. His sneer grew more malevolent with each step closer.

"You look just like her, you know." He looked down his nose at her. The heels of his dress shoes clicked as he circled her chair.

He stopped in front of her.

"For twenty-five long years, eyes so much like your own have haunted my every nightmare." He leaned forward and lightly dragged the tip of the homemade dagger across her cheek. Not hard enough to break the skin, but his message was clear.

The impulse to beg him to stop was overpowered by her unwillingness to show this man any weakness.

"Even her death did not end my torment."

Gwen's eyes widened. "What—"

"When your mother left, she took something of mine."

He spoke between clenched teeth but lowered the glass from her face.

Gwen exhaled, not realizing she'd been holding her breath.

"I spent years tracking her down. When I finally found her"—he leaned close and whispered across her ear—"I made sure she was no longer a threat to me."

"Oh my God." She whispered, drew back her head and looked at him. "It ... it was you." Not some random hit-and-run. "You son of a bitch!" Gwen bucked and pulled against the restraints. Months of pent-up anger, loneliness and overpowering loss burst forth. "You killed her! You killed my mother!"

"Now, unless you want to end up like her"—he slid the sharp glass gently up the inside of her thigh—"you will tell me where you are keeping my ledgers."

"What ledgers?" she shouted. "I don't know what you're talking about."

Like a pressure cooker past its limit, his fury exploded. The sharp glass dug into her thigh, tearing through her flesh.

Gwen screamed. Her head fell forward, and her quiet sobs filled the desolate corners of the room.

Radoslav laughed. A man like him thrived on others' weakness and fear.

Giving up was *not* an option. She sucked air in through her teeth and, as she wiped her tears on her shoulder, snuck a quick glance at her leg. Blood seeped from the laceration, but it wasn't deep enough to cause any permanent damage.

Nostrils flaring, she closed her eyes and breathed in and out a few times. She defiantly lifted her head and stared into the eyes of the beast. If he thought for one minute she was going to play the fragile, helpless victim, he was dumber than he was ugly. Her mother had sacrificed her entire life to keep those ledgers hidden. Gwen's body might be battered, abused and torn, but she would die before she told him where they were.

His smug grin faltered as her silent revolt pricked his overgrown ego. Determined to reassert his power as her captor, he moved his makeshift weapon to her other thigh.

"I will ask you again. Where are my ledgers?"

Gwen leaned close to him and ground out, "Go. To. Hell."

She was done pretending.

Radoslav watched his hand as it zigzagged the jagged glass down her other thigh. He looked up, expecting to see defeat.

Gwen, her eyes on his, squeezed her jaw tight, bit the inside of her cheek. She would *not* give him the satisfaction of crying out. Unfortunately, nothing could be done about the tears streaming from the corners of her eyes.

Radoslav's animalistic shout roared through the room. He tossed aside the glass then plowed his fist into the side of her head. The force of the blow sent her and the chair crashing to the floor. Her head struck the hard surface. There was a loud *crack,* and pain lanced up Gwen's arm.

"You think you are tough." Panting, he swiped the back of his hand across his mouth. "We will see how you feel when I am through with you."

"Pick her up!" He bellowed at his man.

Gregor grunted as he wrestled the chair, with her strapped to it, back in place.

Gwen's head sagged forward. Had she not been bound to the chair, she would've crumpled to the floor. Her vision faded in and out. Blood dripped from her mouth and head, dotted the front of her shirt. Cold fear was replaced by the warmth of her memories of Beck.

She managed a last sideways peek at the window. As the last of the sunlight ebbed, she closed her eyes, and the relentless arms of unconsciousness dragged her to its depths.

CHAPTER THIRTY-SIX

Beck looked up and watched a bank of clouds cover the moon.

Go time.

"Mason, wait till the guards are in those camera blind spots, then drop 'em." Mason's tranquilizer gun was capable of taking down a large wolf at seventy meters. He'd have no problem knocking out a few overweight guards. Especially since the dumbasses left themselves exposed, instead of sticking close to the wall.

Beck and Caleb would then be able to breach the perimeter and make their way to the house without alerting anyone.

"Everyone good to go?"

Caleb and Mason both answered in the affirmative.

"Mason, whenever you're ready."

"Aye-aye, Skipper." Beck shook his head. Navy guys.

Heart rate slow and steady, Beck listened in his earpiece for the distinctive *thwip thwip* with each shot from the suppressor on Mason's rifle.

Seconds ticked by, giving the darts time to do their job.

"Bogies down," Mason confirmed.

Confident Caleb would do the same, Beck bolted from his place behind the trees and headed straight for the high wall. He vaulted himself up and grabbed the top. His toes gained purchase and he lifted himself up until he could swing his legs over. With a low grunt, he landed in a crouch on the other side of the wall and froze. He checked his surroundings, then ducked behind a nearby shrub.

"I'm over," Caleb confirmed, just above a whisper. He wasn't even winded.

"You know what to do." Beck located the nearest sleeping guard and dragged him out of sight. He covered the guy's mouth with duct tape and zip-tied his hands and legs, then moved in a crouch toward the back of the house.

Mason's voice interrupted. "Freeze, Caleb."

Beck pressed his back against the bricks near the main power box.

"Our TV-watching friend at the gate just stepped out for a smoke. Give me a sec."

"Caleb, can you get to him and stash him in the guard shack without being made?" Beck whispered. Last thing they needed was to have a body lying where it might be seen.

"Yep."

Another *thwip,* then Mason said, "He's down."

A minute later Caleb confirmed, "Guard's secured. Moving to the house."

On a hunch, Simmons questioned Chadwick about the property and, jackpot, it had paid off. Beck's old boss had contacted him en route with what he'd learned. There were usually only four people there whenever Radoslav was in residence: his faithful lap dog, Gregor Yolkov; a butler and a housekeeper-slash-cook who'd been with him for years; and, of course, Radoslav. Girls being prepared for sale were brought here for a doctor to check out. Because he'd brought

Gwen here, they were assuming no other girls would be inside. They'd prepared a plan for either likelihood.

Yolkov would be sticking close to Radoslav, who would be sticking close to Gwen. The Russian wouldn't give a second thought to killing her. If he hadn't already. Beck wouldn't let his mind go there. *I would've felt the loss in my heart.*

His eyes lasered in on the dot glowing at the tip of the clicking second hand. Wire cutters in hand, his grip firm and steady, he held the tool over the bundle of cables in the power box.

Tick-tick-tick ...

The second hand clicked straight up to twelve.

Snip-snip. Beck worked his way through the wires. The house plunged into darkness from the top floor down. The corner of his mouth lifted.

He sprang into action. In less than a minute, he'd pried open the window and climbed into the utility room.

"I'm in." He waited for confirmation from Caleb.

A low buzz came through his earpiece just before Caleb said, "I'm in."

Beck flipped his night-vision-goggles, NVG's, down. The room slipped into a monochrome of greens. He glanced around the door and picked up a single, bright image to his right. Shape and size matched the description of the housekeeper. She was rummaging through a drawer, mumbling something in Russian about a flashlight.

The racket created the perfect cover for him to move silently across the smooth marble floor. Beck came up behind her and wrapped his left arm around her thick middle. His gloved right hand covered her mouth just as she was about to scream. He lifted her so her feet no longer touched the floor.

"Don't make a sound," he whispered in Russian.

Eyes wide, her nostrils flared as her panicked breaths fought to escape.

"Nod if you understand."

She began to cry.

Shit. He felt a twinge of guilt, then reminded himself she willingly worked for a killer.

Beck asked again.

She tipped her head down once.

He tightened his hold around her and carried her into the utility room. He lowered her feet to the floor in front of the door to a storage closet and pressed the nose of his gun into her ribcage.

"Open it," he instructed in Russian.

She grabbed a ring of keys from her apron, reached out a shaky hand and unlocked the door.

Beck guided her into the space, turned her around and lowered her onto a stool.

The housekeeper watched him with big eyes as she crossed herself and started to mumble what sounded like Hail Marys. Beck brought a finger to his lips, and she quieted. He was sure the only thing that kept her from yelling for help was the threat of him using one of the many weapons strapped to his body.

He grabbed the duct tape hanging from his vest, took one look at her wrinkled old face, and hesitated. For thirty-plus years, while she'd worked for Radoslav, this woman had turned a blind eye to the suffering of thousands of young women. Including Gwen. *Screw her,* he thought, and ripped off a long strip and pressed it over her mouth.

Beck pulled her arms behind her back and secured her wrists to a pipe running up the wall. Then he connected a few zip ties together and wrapped them around her puffy ankles.

She whimpered and her nostrils flared in an effort to breathe through her sobs.

Your tears mean nothing to me. Beck felt zero sympathy.

"Don't do anything stupid, and you just might live

through this." He turned and left her stashed in the cramped space.

"Housekeeper's secured." Beck glanced at his watch.

"Butler's down," Caleb confirmed. "Heading your way."

Beck moved silently through the large kitchen into the formal dining room. From there, he used a large hutch in the hallway for cover.

"Approaching." Caleb's bright signature appeared in Beck's goggles as he rounded the corner a few feet behind him.

His brother's ability to move so quietly never ceased to impress him. Had he not given him a heads up, he was pretty sure he wouldn't have known Caleb was there.

Using the same hand signals they'd made up when they played war as kids, they moved together down the hallway. Their destination—Radoslav's office. The only access to the basement was hidden in this room. Chadwick hadn't been able to tell them exactly where it was.

They approached the large wooden door, took up positions on either side.

"Registrirovat'sya." Gregor Yolkov's voice came from inside the office.

Your boys won't be "checking in" anytime soon.

Yolkov cursed. "Son of bitch." Some words required no translation.

A small beam of light cut a swath through the darkness.

Beck peeked around the doorway.

Yolkov lifted his gun and fired.

Wood exploded near Beck's head. Splintered fragments embedded in his cheek just below his goggles.

Pop pop. Caleb returned fire.

The hollow points pierced Yolkov's midsection and thigh, dropped him where he stood. His flashlight fell from his hand and spun on the floor. The beam spiraled around the room and slowed to a stop, where it pointed at the side of Yolkov's head.

They charged into the room.

Beck dropped to his knees next to him and flipped up his NVG's. "Where is she?"

Gregor's face split in a ghoulish smile. Blood had settled in the spaces between his teeth and ran from the corner of his mouth.

"Tell me where she is!" Beck gave a quick squeeze to the wound in his thigh.

Yolkov's agonized scream filled the air.

Beck ignored the blood seeping through his gloved fingers.

"I do not know what you are talking about!" Yolkov shouted in English. He huffed and puffed. Color drained from his face. Sweat poured into his eyes.

Caleb quietly communicated an update to Mason then kept watch for any threats. Radoslav was around somewhere.

A hand over both wounds, Beck pressed down hard.

Yolkov threw back his head, his body bowed off the floor, and he growled between his gritted teeth.

"This can go one of two ways." Beck leaned close to his ear. "You either tell me what I want to know and live. Or you continue to fuck with me and you die. I don't give a shit either way. Now ... " Beck lifted his hands. "Where is she?"

Yolkov's body relaxed. He looked from Caleb to Beck, then smiled. "Poshel ty."

Fluent in Spanish, Arabic and Farsi, Caleb looked at Beck.

"Our Russian friend here said, 'Screw you,'" Beck informed him.

Caleb shrugged. "Guess he needs a little more encouragement."

"Guess you're right." Beck flexed his fingers, laid them on the wounds and leaned his full weight against them.

A scream tore from Yolkov and blood gurgled in the back of his throat. His back arched, and his legs stiffened.

"Okay." Racking coughs ravaged his body, and he began to spit up blood. "Okay. There is a door ... " His cheeks puffed in and out, sucking in air. Blood oozed from his mouth and nose. "Behind bar ... stairs ... to the examination room." His chest heaved, and he coughed.

Beck grabbed the front of his shirt and pulled him close.

"Where's the key?" he growled.

"Coat ... pocket."

Beck patted down his pockets until he felt a lump, then reached in and yanked out a ring of keys.

"Which one is it?" He held the keys in front of his face.

Yolkov wheezed. "You're too late." He smiled, then his eyes rolled back in his head and his lids drooped shut. His body relaxed, and his head sagged to the side.

Beck cursed, then shoved up and away from him.

Caleb laid two fingers to the side of the Russian's tattoo-covered neck. He shook his head.

They stood and passed the beam of their flashlights around the room.

"Here," Caleb said.

They ran toward the bar in the corner.

Crystal glasses of varying shapes and sizes crashed to the floor as they tore the bar apart. A revolting blend of odors filled the room as one crystal decanter of liquor after the other shattered at their feet.

Hidden at the back of the bottom shelf, they found a small button. Beck slapped his hand against it and stepped back. The wall swung toward them, dragging over the floor, grinding broken glass into the carpet. The few pieces of glassware and bottles that were still in one piece clinked against one another.

A nondescript steel door with two deadbolt locks

loomed before them. Beck worked through the keys, one after the other, until they heard a solid *clunk*. He tried the same key in the other lock with no success and began the process all over again. Two keys later, the mechanism turned.

Caleb grabbed his arm before he could jerk the door open.

"I know you want to get to her," he whispered, "but you can't just go charging in there. By now, he knows we're here. You're no good to her if you're dead."

Beck jerked his arm from Caleb's grasp. *Damn it!* His brother was right.

Beck took a deep breath and nodded. "You go low and right, I'll go high and left."

"Let's go get your girl." Caleb squeezed Beck's shoulder, gave it a little shake.

A quick bob of the head, and they took their positions against the wall on either side of the doorway.

Beck raised three fingers, then counted down silently.

On "one," he turned the nob. The fingertips of his right hand slid against the door, and it swung open without a sound.

Dim light poured through the doorway. Radoslav must have a generator that backed up the power to this room. So much for their strategic advantage.

They tossed off their NVGs.

Caleb tossed in a flash bang explosive.

They put their hands over their ears and turned away as it detonated. There was a blinding flash at the same time a loud *bang* shook the room.

Adrenaline fired through Beck's system.

They exploded into the room. Their weapons swept toward the sound of coughing.

Beck sighted down the barrel of his gun, and his chest

constricted. He would be haunted forever by what he saw as the smoke cleared.

Radoslav crouched behind an up-ended bed in the far corner, coughing and sputtering, snot running from his nose. He dragged Gwen up from behind the bed and held her in front of him with his left arm. The finger of his right hand was curled around the trigger of a gun pressed against her temple.

The bed must have shielded the fucking coward from the worst effects of the flash. It wouldn't have helped protect against the concussion from the *bang*. Most likely, both their eardrums were blown, muffling their hearing for a while.

Beck's eyes roamed over Gwen, who hung limp in Radoslav's grasp. The left side of her face was coated with a mixture of drying blood and dust. Blood was smeared all over her legs and trickled from wounds on her thighs. The odd angle of her right wrist had to be excruciatingly painful, yet she made not a sound. What little he could see of her beautiful face through her tangled hair was dark purple and puffy. One eye was swollen shut, the other only open a sliver.

The peaceful light in Gwen's eyes, the one that had broken through to his damaged soul, was fading.

She coughed, sputtered, managed to lift her head enough to look at him. Recognition and relief shined from her face, and he felt like the most powerful man in the world.

"Beck." Her voice was decimated. No more than a labored whisper.

Agony and rage shot through to Beck's core. The urge to kill for what she must've endured at the hands of this animal was near uncontrollable.

"I'm here, honey." His gun never wavered.

She struggled to stand upright.

Radoslav pressed the gun harder into her temple.

She whimpered.

Beck's entire body tensed, and he willed her to be still.

"Do. Not. Move," Radoslav ground out between his teeth.

Gwen raised that proud, stubborn chin of hers in the air. "I'm ... okay, Beck."

Beaten and tortured and still she exhibited such amazing strength.

"DO NOT COME CLOSER OR SHE DIES!" Knowing his situation was hopeless, Radoslav's rabid desperation meant he wouldn't hesitate to kill.

"Look around." Beck hitched his head to indicate Caleb pointing a gun at Radoslav from the other side of the room. "There are two of us and only one of you."

"Yes." A grin slithered across Radoslav's face. "but I have something you want, O'Halleran."

The Russian shifted. Gwen's wrist bumped against the exposed bed frame, and she cried out.

"Okay, okay." Beck raised his free hand. "Just tell me what you want, and I'll see what I can do to make it happen."

"No! Beck, listen to me." Gwen's speech was slurred, but she seemed determined to speak through her pain.

"Gwen, please, stop—"

"Do you trust me?" Her good eye zeroed in on him.

"Yes." Beck frowned. *What are you doing, honey?*

"Radoslav," she said, "I know something you don't know."

Beck's heart nearly stopped. He figured out what she was doing and gave her a nearly imperceptible shake of his head, a silent plea to stop.

"I trust you, too, Beck." One side of her mouth lifted in an attempt at a small smile.

"Enough talking!" Radoslav yelled in her ear as he shook her.

"You've spent years being obsessed with a woman you thought betrayed you with another man." Gwen would not be dissuaded.

"Gwen ... " Beck shook his head.

Stop, honey. Please, stop.

Radoslav was beyond unhinged. Beck had no idea what he would do once Gwen shared what she'd learned.

She forged ahead. Kept hammering away at the madman holding a gun on her.

"Well, guess what, you dumb, ignorant animal. You were wrong."

"Gwen, honey, please." Beck hated this sense of helplessness.

She tried to smile again, only this time it held a sort of melancholy, and resignation had settled in her features.

Oh hell no! He was *not* letting her give up, not after everything they had been through.

Radoslav's shout interrupted him before he could reassure her they were both leaving here alive. He swung his gun around to Beck, prepared to shoot.

"Shut up! Shut up or I will kill him!"

"Feodor isn't my father, you sick bastard. *YOU* are!" Gwen's loud, clear proclamation crushed the psychopath's tirade.

Radoslav faltered.

"No, you ... you are lying." He shook his head. The hand holding the gun lowered slightly. For a moment, he seemed to consider the validity of her claim. "You think that will save you?" Radoslav dismissed the idea with a shake of his head. "She wanted to destroy me."

The gun began to rise.

"Now you are here haunting me with her same witch's eyes!"

What happened next played out in slow motion.

Before he could press the gun to her head, Gwen went lax in Radoslav's arms.

He lost his balance and was forced to shift his weight.

She had given Beck the opening he needed. In a split second, years of training took over, and he squeezed the trigger.

Bang!

He watched in horror as Radoslav and Gwen collapsed to the floor behind the bed.

Guns ready, Beck and Caleb rushed across the room. Destruction caused by the explosive was all around them. Cabinets were toppled and broken, their contents spread across the floor. Their boots crunched over chunks of acoustic ceiling tiles and glass from fluorescent light fixtures dangling from wires overhead. Beck ground out a curse when he moved past an overturned chair, the bindings still dark with blood.

"Fuck." Caleb saw it as well.

Beck looked over, saw the anger and concern in his brother's eyes.

Tension mounted as they made their way to the other side of the bed.

Beck rounded the end of it the same time Caleb pointed his gun over the top.

Nikolai Radoslav was sprawled out on the floor. Eyes wide with shock, he had a perfectly round bullet hole in the middle of his forehead. A pool of blood oozed and expanded into the dust and debris beneath his fat head.

Caleb picked up Radoslav's semi-automatic, popped the magazine free, pulled back the slide to remove the round in the chamber, then tucked it in one vest pocket, the weapon in another.

Beck holstered his own weapon and knelt next to Gwen. He yanked off his gloves and dropped them at his sides, then reached out and placed two trembling fingers—fingers now covered with her blood—to the side of her throat. His shoulders relaxed, his head fell forward, and he released his breath. Her pulse was weak, but thank God it was there.

In the background, he heard Caleb updating Mason, who was making his way to the house from his perch high above.

"Caleb," he called over his shoulder.

His brother rushed over and looked down at Gwen.

"Jesus," he said under his breath.

Gwen's eyes were closed. The upper part of her body was on the floor, but her legs were tangled with Radoslav's. Long snarled hanks of hair were matted in the blood on her face. Even with the piss-poor light in this corner of the room, they could see she'd suffered terribly.

"Caleb, shine your flashlight down here." He didn't want to risk hurting her while he fumbled around in the sparse light. One strand at a time, he carefully lifted her hair away from her face. "Move it over here." Beck pointed at the side of her face.

His brother squatted down and cast a beam of light over her cheek. He cursed and looked away.

"Christ, honey, what did they do to you?" Beck swallowed past the jagged rock lodged in his throat.

The gash on her hairline from Chadwick's attack was deeper and wider than before. Her lips were cracked and puffy. A trail of dried blood from a smaller cut in her eyebrow trailed down her cheek, past her badly swollen eye. Gone was the glow of her usual peaches and cream complexion. The freckles he loved so much were stark against her pasty-white skin.

"Move it down." Beck's eyes followed the beam from her face down across her body, then her legs, all the way to her feet. A muscle in his jaw twitched. Her wrists and ankles were mangled and ringed with dried blood.

He carefully untangled Radoslav's legs from hers, shoved them away. Gouges on her thighs seeped bright red blood.

He heard Caleb's swift intake of breath. "How the hell could anyone do this to her?"

"Radoslav is ... was a feral animal." Beck cupped his hand gently over the top of Gwen's head and looked up at his brother.

"Looks like her wrist is broken." Caleb swept the light to her arm.

"I'm most concerned about this." Beck pointed at the deep cut on her head. "And these." He nodded toward the cuts on her legs.

Beck put his mouth close to her ear and whispered, "I'm here, honey. You're going to be okay. You are the strongest person I know. Fight your way back to me."

"I'm heading in, so don't shoot me." Mason's low voice echoed through their earpieces.

A few minutes later, a sound came from the hallway. Gun raised, Caleb positioned himself between Gwen and the doorway.

"It's just me," Mason called out before entering.

Caleb lowered his weapon.

Mason whistled low as he took in the damage. "Ambulance is on the way." He moved closer, saw Gwen's condition and added, "They should be here any minute."

Caleb grabbed a blanket from the floor, shook it out a few times, then carefully draped it over her.

Beck stayed with her. Mason and Caleb moved to the door to stand watch, lethal sentinels prepared to defend if necessary.

"Please don't leave me, baby," Beck continued to whisper in her ear. "My world is nothing without you in it."

A siren approached in the distance.

"I'll go flag 'em down." Mason took off at a run to meet the ambulance.

Less than five minutes later, paramedics appeared in the

doorway and hesitated. They took in the physical chaos before starting into the room. Their stretcher bounced and rattled as they navigated their way through the rubble.

Caleb and Mason lifted the bed and tossed it out of the way.

A young paramedic came up behind Beck, placed a hand on his shoulder.

"Sir, I'm going to have to ask you to let her go now." He pulled a large black case from the stretcher and set it down next to her.

"She is my life." Unshed tears in his eyes, Beck looked at the EMT, then back to Gwen.

"I promise, we'll take really good care of her, sir."

Beck was surprised to see the depth of understanding in the eyes of someone so young. The kid had obviously seen a lot in his job.

Beck placed a soft kiss to her forehead, stood, but moved back only enough to give them room to work. As he stared down while they worked on her, he felt Caleb and Mason move to stand on either side of him. They each curved a hand over his shoulder. Beck had to gut it out so as not to break down.

Gwen was hooked up to an IV, and an oxygen mask was placed over her mouth and nose. Blood was already soaking through the glaring white gauze wrapped around her thighs. More gauze wrapped around her head, holding a patch in place over her left eye. An AirCast stabilized her right arm.

Seeing her this way tore Beck's heart out. He wanted to kill Radoslav all over again.

The paramedics gently loaded her on the stretcher. One held the IV bag high while the other covered her with a clean blanket. They secured her in place with one strap across her chest, another across her lower legs.

Mason and Caleb cleared a path through the debris as she

was rolled out of the room. They acted as escorts as the stretcher made its way through the house.

Cops had arrived and taken the butler and housekeeper into custody. Crime scene techs were already processing the scene. They all stopped what they were doing to get a glimpse of the woman who'd been tortured by an animal. One guy stopped taking pictures, raced forward and swung open the large front door and held it open.

The cool night air brushed over them. Beck reached down and tucked the covers more closely around her.

The ranking EMT said, "On three, we all lift."

Getting a nod from everyone, he counted, "One—two—three."

They carefully lifted the stretcher and carried it down the wide stone steps, not setting it down until Gwen was tucked safely inside the back of the ambulance with Beck.

Caleb and Mason stood and watched the ambulance pull away—siren blaring—carrying a warrior who refused to let go of his angel's hand.

CHAPTER THIRTY-SEVEN

Gwen was stuck in that strange place between sleep and wakefulness.

"Come on, honey. Time to wake up."

Beck? No, it's a trick.

She was terrified to open her eyes for fear she'd still be trapped in that horrible room. Afraid her tormented mind was imagining things. But if there was even the slightest possibility it was him, she had to know.

Her eyelid dragged open a millifraction at a time. Soft light peeked through her lashes. Gwen braced herself against the potential discomfort, blinked slowly, then opened her right eye.

"That's right, honey." Beck's face hovered inches above her.

He came into focus, and the most glorious smile she'd ever seen beamed down at her.

"Beck?" She didn't recognize her own voice, it was so scratchy and weak.

"It's me, honey." He leaned his forearms alongside her head. His thumb gently stroked across her right cheek.

"You're here?" She tried to reach up to touch him, but her arm was trapped. "You're really here?"

"Careful, honey. They casted your arm and put it in a sling."

Gwen's eyes dropped to the bright pink cast from her right elbow to her hand.

"I'm so sorry, honey." Beck's jaw rippled. His body tensed.

She rocked her head back and forth on the pillow. She scrunched her eyes closed. *Okay, that was a mistake.*

"Careful, careful." He kept his voice low. "You have a concussion, so you need to take it easy."

Gwen took a deep breath and waited for the pain to pass. "Radoslav is responsible for all of it. Not you." A dry cough rattled through her. "Radoslav."

No way would she let him take any of the blame for what happened to her.

Beck twisted and grabbed a plastic cup off the side table. He held the bent straw to her lips.

Parched, her throat dry, Gwen was tempted to gulp the cool liquid.

"Just a little at first, honey."

She risked a tentative sip, then another slightly longer one.

"What happened?" She relaxed into the pillow.

"He's dead." Beck set the cup on the table. "The bastard can never hurt you again." His thumb returned to stroking her cheek.

Gwen waited for some latent sense of loss to hit her. After all, she shared DNA with the man. There was none. She thought of the young man in the picture frame—Feodor. He hadn't been her real father, but he'd loved her mother and, for that, he would forever have a place in her heart.

"So ... it's over?" *Please let it be over.*

"Yeah, honey. It's all over." His eyes searched her face and brushed a sweet kiss to her forehead.

"I knew you'd come," she whispered. The dream of spending her life with him had given her the courage to fight so damned hard to stay alive. "I knew you'd find me."

"I love you, Gwen." He blessed her with one of those soft smiles reserved just for her. "I never would've stopped looking for you. Never."

"Wait. Did you just say ... you love me?" Her good eye widened, and one side of her mouth managed to lift in a partial smile.

"I love you so much it hurts. When I thought I'd lost you ... " He hesitated, looked away. His throat moved up and down, then he turned back to her. "It nearly destroyed me."

"I love you, too. So much." It felt amazing, liberating, to finally say the words she'd been holding back.

"You can't ever leave me again." His lips brushed a soft kiss to her right cheek, the tip of her nose. "That's all there is to it."

Her happiness bubbled up in the form of a giggle.

"I want us to get married." Beck smiled down at her, and in his eyes she saw their future. He rushed to say, "When you're better. I mean, if you want to."

If I want to? Is this man not paying attention?

"Yes, yes, of course I want to."

He heaved a sigh, and his shoulders seemed to relax.

Did he really think she would say "no"?

"Why don't you try to get some sleep." Beck tucked the covers around her.

Gwen thought she might've heard the shuffle of footsteps and the whisper of voices around her. Comforted by the knowledge Beck loved her and was there to watch over her, she fell into a peaceful sleep.

"Oh, did she wake up?" Beck's mom whispered as she looked over at Gwen.

"Yeah, just for a few minutes." At least one member of his family had been sitting with him while he waited for Gwen to regain consciousness. He'd finally insisted they all step out to grab something to eat. "She just fell back asleep."

Gwen stirred behind him.

He turned to find her staring at the wall of O'Hallerans lined up at the foot of her bed.

"Why don't you guys come back in a little bit. Let her sleep." Beck started herding them from the room.

"No." Gwen cleared her throat. "Beck, it's okay."

Gwen's uninjured eye tracked down the row and stopped on Caleb's familiar face. "Please, stay."

Beck grabbed her water and gave her a drink.

"Gwen, this is my family. *Your* family now, too." He set the cup on the table and made the introductions. "You already know this guy."

Caleb walked over and leaned close, one of his devil-may-care smiles shining down at her. "Hey, you. Glad you're back."

"Thank you," she whispered. "For everything."

"Think nothin' of it, pretty lady." Typical Caleb, laying down his bullshit charm.

The FBI had already started weeding through the information found on Radoslav's computer about The Farm. Caleb should be there, but he'd refused to head back to Quantico until he knew Gwen was okay. "Family comes first," he'd said.

Beck would never be able to thank him and Mason enough for what they'd done for them.

The task force also found incriminating evidence against Deputy Director Barlow. The piece of shit. When Mrs. Barlow was presented with photos of her husband in compromising positions with underage girls, she couldn't confess fast enough to lying for him. She admitted to being pressured into saying the Russian was at their house the night Jodi was killed.

Barlow was partially responsible for what happened to Gwen. Beck would gain a great deal of satisfaction knowing the traitorous bastard would spend the balance of his years isolated behind the walls of a federal penitentiary.

"Okay, okay, enough." Beck curled his hand over Caleb's shoulder and tugged the Irish Romeo away from his fiancé. Yeah, *fiancé*—he loved the sound of that. But he would like the sound of *wife* even more.

"This is Killian and Mathias." He pointed toward the twins.

They smiled and dipped their chins in unison.

"Which is which?" Gwen whispered.

"I'm Killian." He took a small step forward, puffed out his chest and smirked at his twin. "I'm the good-looking one."

"Actually," Mathias clarified, "the best way to tell us apart is this." He pointed at a scar cutting through his left eyebrow.

Beck pointed his thumb at them over his shoulder. "These two knuckleheads were farting around in the basement, tossing a musical teddy bear around. Mathias decided it would be a good idea to douse the lights at the exact moment Killian chucked it at him. The metal wind-up key caught him in the face."

"He bled like a stuck pig." Killian laughed.

Mathias laughed and shoved him.

Beck just shook his head. *Idiots. Mathias was lucky he didn't lose a friggin' eye.*

"The only one who's not here is Jonathan. He's deployed overseas." Beck tried not to worry about the fact they hadn't heard from him in months. After all, he was a Navy SEAL and could take care of himself. *Right?*

"Me next." Emily didn't wait for Beck's introduction. In her typical *I-rule-the-world, it-doesn't-rule-me* kind of way, she shoved past her much bigger brothers and walked over to the side of the bed.

In the softest voice he'd ever heard from his baby sister, she bent over the bed so Gwen didn't have to strain to see her, and said, "Hi, I'm Emily, 'the girl.'" She did the air quotes thing. "I'm so glad to meet the woman responsible for taking down big, bad Beckett O'Halleran. I'm also glad to have some female reinforcement."

Beck stepped up behind her, wrapped an arm around her shoulders and gave a quick squeeze. "Watch yourself, kid."

Emily wriggled out of his grasp. She leaned over and whispered in Gwen's ear. Gwen blushed, peeked up at him, and they both giggled. His sister gave him a sly glance before she sauntered back to stand next to Killian.

Beck could practically feel his mother vibrating with anticipation behind him.

"Gwen." He walked over and curled his arm over his mom's shoulder and led her to the bed. "This is my mom, Molly O'Halleran."

His mother leaned over Gwen and gently laid her hand over the right side of her face.

"It's so nice to meet you, Gwen. Beck has told us so many wonderful things about you."

A quiet sob broke free from Gwen, and Beck freaked. He shot forward, but his mother stopped him with a subtle shake of her head and he stepped back. It killed him to see Gwen cry, but he trusted his mom knew what she was doing.

She hiked her hip up onto the edge of the bed, bent down and put her face close to Gwen's.

"That's right, sweetie. You just let go of all that bad stuff." Without looking away, she extended her arm, snapped her fingers and pointed at the box of tissues on the table.

Beck popped a couple free and handed them to her.

"Everything's going to be just fine." She dabbed the tears from Gwen's eyes.

As a child, Beck had heard the same soothing voice many times.

"She's right, ya know." His father stepped forward, smoothed his hand across his mom's back and left it resting on her shoulder. "You're one of us now, and no one will ever hurt you again. You can take that to the bank." The harnessed power in his father's voice spoke to the truth of his words.

"Gwen." His mom reached up and patted his dad's hand. "This is my husband, Beck's daddy, Michaleen O'Halleran."

Gwen looked way up at him. "Hi," she squeaked out between sniffles.

"It's good to see you awake, Little Bit. You had us scared there for a while."

Her brows beetled, and she looked at Beck.

"It's your new nickname." He smiled. *Better get used to it.* "Once you've been given a Michaleen O'Halleran nickname, it's yours forever."

"Yeah, forever." Emily tsked and rolled her eyes.

"Speaking of *forever* ... we get to keep her, don't we?" his sister asked as she shot him a threatening scowl.

"Yes, we're keeping her." He smiled and looked down at Gwen. "I asked her to marry me, and she said 'yes.'"

Gwen smiled up at him amid a chorus of approvals.

"Oh, Beck, honey ... " His mom stood, smiled up at him and pulled him into a tight hug. "I'm so happy for you."

When she tried to pull back, Beck held on a little longer. And she let him.

"Okay." His mother gave Beck a last squeeze, stood on tiptoes to kiss his cheek, then stepped back. "Let's give these two some privacy."

She shooed everyone from the room.

Mathias and Killian both tossed up their right hands and said in unison, "Congrats, you guys. Welcome to the family, Gwen." Then shuffled past the bed and out the door.

They did freaky *twin stuff* like that all the damn time.

"See ya later, sis." Emily stopped mid-step, tilted her head. "Sis ... yeah." She nodded. "I like the sound of that."

She blew Gwen a kiss and hustled out to catch up with the twins. The energy level in the room seemed to drop after her departure. His baby sister had that effect wherever she went.

"My new partner, Jake, arrives in the states next week." Caleb walked over to Gwen. "Now I know you're okay, I'm going to head back to Quantico tomorrow to start training with him."

She crooked her finger at him. He bent down, and she wrapped her good arm around his neck.

"Thank you, again, Caleb," she whispered, then lowered her hand to her side.

He straightened, winked at her, then gave their folks and Beck a hug and walked out whistling some random tune.

"Welcome to the family, sweetie. We're so glad you and Beck found each other," his mom said, then she and his dad gave her a gentle kiss on the cheek.

Beck's dad stepped in to give him a back-slapping hug. "You done good, son." He held him at arm's length, patted him once on the upper arm and walked out, his arm wrapped around his wife.

"They're wonderful." Gwen looked up at him the same way she had when she thought he'd helped Mrs. Saulinski.

"Yeah." He looked toward the door. "They're pretty great."

He was happy to have them back in his life after his self-proclaimed exile.

Beck sat next to Gwen on the bed and stroked the fingers peeking out from her cast.

"The doc says you can leave in a couple days, and I'd prefer if you didn't go back to live at the shelter."

She opened her mouth, but he forged ahead. "Instead, I'd love it if you'd come live with me. My place isn't fancy, but when you're well enough, we'll find something we both like."

He waited, hoping he hadn't read her wrong.

She yawned. "I would love that." And her eyes dragged shut.

"I love you, Gwen." His lips feathered over her forehead.

"I love you, too." Her voice was a mere whisper as she dropped into a peaceful sleep.

Beck reached up and clicked off the light over her bed. All the hospital noises faded. The only sound was the deep, even breaths of the woman he'd almost lost. The woman he would love forever.

EPILOGUE

Beck stopped in the doorway to his back porch and smiled.

His dad guided Gwen down the wide wooden steps and across their big backyard. After getting her settled in a comfortable lounge chair, he sat next to Beck's mom.

Killian grabbed an ottoman to set it in front of her, then Mathias propped her feet up on it.

Gwen laughed. Relaxed and smiling, his wife loved her new family with an unrivaled fierceness. She was like a lioness, devoted to and protective of every single one of them.

Emily tromped over to her. "She's not an invalid, ya know." She shooed the guys away.

Beck chuckled as his brother's headed over to resume their game of bocce.

No, Gwen wasn't an invalid, but she *was* almost six months pregnant, and everyone treated her like spun glass. She didn't seem to have the heart to tell them to knock it off.

It had taken a few months, but she'd finally fully recovered. Her nightmares had lessened, and she insisted the faint scars she carried didn't bother her.

For a while, Beck couldn't look at them without getting angry, until his dad told him they were a lasting reminder of her strength and courage. The man was beyond wise.

His sister handed her a glass of lemonade, then plopped down on the ottoman next to her feet. The two of them had become thick as thieves. Talking on the phone all the time. Planning ways they could meet. Since Emily went to graduate school in Washington State, and he and Gwen lived in California, the two women didn't see each other as much as they'd like.

He and Gwen had been married in a private ceremony with only family in attendance. Around the same time, they'd gotten lucky and found this old farmhouse. It needed updates and there was always something in need of repair. For him, the most important aspect of their home was its location. In the middle of several hundred acres, it included a large private lake at the back of the property and dense woods bordering the rest. Along with the state-of-the-art security system Caleb installed, it provided them with the privacy and security Beck required.

His bride had stubbornly insisted on continuing to oversee the remaining renovations to the shelter.

He'd hired a contractor, hoping to keep her home, where he knew she was safe. Which wasn't realistic. Though he had insisted they put a halt to the remaining work until after she recovered.

Gwen had acquiesced, *thank God*, and the renovations were almost complete.

Beck's company, O'Halleran Security International, or OSI, was up and operational. He was in the process of putting together teams that would specialize in close protection, private security, national and international hostage retrieval, tracking, and cyber security. Pretty much anything Jeffrey Burke decided to throw his way, OSI would be ready to handle.

Eventually, Beck would expand the operation to Washington State. His plan was to have his brother Jonathan run it. He just had to convince him to leave the Navy and agree to come work with him. Which might be easier to do now that his wife, Marilyn, had expressed a desire to start their own family soon.

Owning the company made it possible for Beck to sleep in the same bed with his wife every night. On those rare occasions he was required to travel, she'd come with him. When she reached the point in her pregnancy she could no longer travel safely, he would suspend his travel.

Needing to touch his wife, Beck walked down the steps and made his way across the yard, the grass soft and warm under his bare feet.

She sensed his approach and turned to him.

They shared a private smile, and he squatted down next to her. He glided her hair back over her shoulder and grazed his fingertip over the thin scar at her hairline. He gave her a soft kiss.

"What can I get for you?"

She rubbed her belly as she looked at the activity swirling around them, then back at him with a warm smile. "I have everything I need right here."

"Me, too." Beck flattened his hand over hers and their daughter gave a little kick underneath.

They chuckled then she kissed him softly and cradled his jaw in her hand. "I love you, Beck."

"I love you too, honey." Then he leaned in and kissed his wife, his life.

DON'T MISS OUT!

Sign up to receive the "COVERT DETAILS" newsletter. You'll receive advance notice of release dates, get the first look at book covers, have access to exclusive content, and be eligible for fun giveaways.

You can also find TJ on ...
Facebook: https://www.facebook.com/authortjlogan
Twitter: https://twitter.com/TJLoganAuthor
Instagram: https://www.instagram.com/tjloganauthor/
Website: https://www.tjloganauthor.com/

SNEAK PEEK AT DEADLY DISCIPLE

Watch for DEADLY DISCIPLE and DEADLY DECEPTION,
Books 2 and 3 in TJ Logan's
O'Halleran Security International series

DEADLY DISCIPLE

It felt like someone had thrown a fistful of sand in each of Caleb O'Halleran's eyes. The rigorous tactical training he'd been taking part in with his K9 partner, Jake, and the rest of the FBI's Hostage Rescue Team had kicked his ass. The still-healing gunshot wound to his shoulder ached like a bitch, and he had bruises in places bruises had no business being. All he wanted was to take his dog home, crack open a cold one, and watch Jake run around and play in the backyard. After that, the only thing on his wish list was a little one-on-one time with his king-size bed.

Instead, he'd rushed to this swanky soiree straight from their training segment on Alcatraz Island. His 5.11 tactical pants and HRT T-shirt were a stark contrast to the fancy dresses and tailored suits mingling about the room. They didn't know it, but everyone here should appreciate that he'd managed to sneak in a quick camp shower. Thank God for rainwater. An awful lot of unique smells started coming off a guy's body after twenty days of strenuous work, outdoors, without running water.

As he took in the crowded room, he swelled with pride for his sister-in-law. The party was a celebration of the official opening of Maggie's Embrace. The community center and homeless shelter was her dream realized. She'd not only survived a nightmare; she thrived in spite of it. After the nightmare she'd endured, Caleb sure as hell wasn't going to complain about a few aches and pains or being tired.

He rocked his head side to side, rolled his shoulders. Maybe a beer would help ease the strained muscles at the base of his neck.

He flagged the bartender. "Can I get an IPA, please?"

The bartender dug into a large cooler, popped the top on a bottle and set the beer in front of Caleb.

"Here ya go." He turned and started restocking the liquor.

"Thanks, man." Caleb dropped a five-spot in the jar and leaned back against the bar. He took a swallow of his favorite brew, enjoyed the bitterness of the hops as it flowed over his tongue. *Damn*. After the past few weeks, that was just what the doctor ordered.

He scanned the crowd for his partner and finally spotted him across the room, sitting at his sister-in-law's feet. If Gwen was in the vicinity, Jake found his way to her side. It was as if the dog knew she'd been through hell and wanted to provide whatever comfort he could. Eyes closed, tongue hanging out, a big slobbery grin on his dark face, Jake was the picture of four-legged contentment.

Caleb tsked and shook his head. Anyone who didn't know better would think Jake was a pussycat, not a badass tactical K9. His dog could take down a man twice his size, rappel from helicopters, and ignore explosives going off all around him, yet he was putty in Gwen's small hands.

Gwen's hand moved away from scratching behind his dog's ears only to be replaced by another woman's long, slender fingers. Caleb's eyes made a leisurely trip up the lean arm to a bare shoulder. He slowly lowered his beer and tilted his head to the side, shamelessly enjoying the view of a neck created for open-mouth kisses.

The dangling of an earring drew his gaze upward, away from the elegant neck, and Caleb was thunderstruck when he got his first look at her face. Whoever she was, she was ... *exquisite*. Yep, hokey as it sounded, exquisite was the perfect word to describe her. And to think he'd almost begged off coming tonight. Maybe he wasn't so tired after all.

Her warm olive skin seemed to glow from within. If he had to guess, he'd say she was of Mediterranean descent—Greek, Italian maybe.

She crouched down next to his dog. How she managed it in those sexy high heels of hers, he had no idea. They had these thin strappy things tied around each of her delicate ankles, and Caleb wanted to undo them with his teeth.

Jake, the lady-killer—and unabashed opportunist—licked her on the chin. She giggled, and Caleb saw the sparkle in her huge, almond-shaped eyes from across the room. He squinted but couldn't make out the color from so far away. His dog, the lucky mutt, drew his sloppy tongue across her tempting neck, the very same one Caleb had just been fantasizing about, and she threw her head back and laughed with unrestrained joy. It was a husky, deep, from-her-toes kind of laugh.

Caleb put his hand to his chest. *Holy shit. Be still my heart.*

He looked around. He wasn't the only one affected by her. The woman was totally unaware of the attention she got from every man in the room. He stifled a growl, wanting to tell every single one of them to back the hell off. Which was stupid since he had no more of a claim to her than any one of *those* assholes. Hell, for all he knew, one of them could be her boyfriend or husband. His eyes flew to her left hand, and he tried not to think too much about why he was relieved not to see a ring. Thoughts of her with some other guy really bugged the shit out of him. And wasn't that moronic.

She wasn't even his usual type. His tastes steered more toward stacked, blond-haired, blue-eyed gals who were in it for a good time. Caleb had no time for and certainly no interest in anything more. One or two nights of fun and stress release in the form of some good old-fashioned sheet wrestling, then they would part friends. Everyone got what they wanted, and no one got hurt. His siblings gave him grief about being a man-whore, but, at this stage of his life, it worked for him.

This woman seemed to be the antithesis of *all* those things. She exuded sophistication and elegance, but not in a stuck-up, cold kind of way. She wrapped her arms around Jake and rested her cheek on top of his head. Dark, shiny hair slid over her shoulder and draped over his dog's back. Caleb reflexively rubbed his fingertips together, itching to feel its silkiness. The deep, rich color reminded him of expensive dark chocolate. She looked up and said something to Gwen. Just watching her full lips move sent his mind in a decidedly sinful direction. Oh, the places he'd love to see ... and feel those lips.

He shifted his stance to gain some relief, since a certain part of his anatomy didn't seem to give a shit that every vibe she put off indicated she was a one-man woman, not the kind to go for casual ... well ... *anything.*

What got to Caleb the most was the way she didn't seem at all concerned about getting dog hair all over her. Most women wouldn't go anywhere near a dog as fierce-looking as

Jake, let alone frolic with him on the floor wearing a fancy dress.

She bestowed upon his partner another big hug and a few scratches behind his ears.

"Lucky son of a bitch," Caleb muttered against the edge of his bottle before taking another long swallow. For the first time ever, he was jealous of his damn dog.

In one smooth motion, she rose and stood next to his diminutive sister-in-law. Even without her boner-inducing sky-high heels, she had to be at least five nine. Unlike a lot of statuesque women, she *owned* her height. No slouching or shying away from it. She commanded it. And sweet merciful heaven, her little black dress showed off smooth shoulders and hugged subtle curves, stopping a few inches above her knees, granting him an unfettered view of the longest, shapeliest pair of legs he'd ever seen.

She smiled and thanked the waiter when she accepted a glass of champagne.

When she turned back to Gwen, the waiter surreptitiously checked out her ass.

Caleb scowled and straightened from the bar. He would react the same way no matter what woman the guy gawked at. At least that's what he told himself.

A nudge to his shoulder and he turned to find his older brother, Beck, chuckling at him.

"What's so funny?" Caleb grumbled.

"You." Beck smirked. "I'm laughing at the way you're looking at Dawn. It's an awful lot like the way people say I look at Gwen." A sappy look hung on his brother's face as he stared at his wife across the room.

Oh, hell no!

Beck was full of shit. Ever since marrying Gwen, he seemed to think everyone should get tied down. *Noooo, thank you!*

"I have no idea what you're talking about. Who is Dawn?" Caleb took a long swallow of beer.

"Uh-huh, sure you don't. Dawn is the woman standing next to my wife, and you're looking at her like you want to throw her over your shoulder and cart her out of here. And you're looking at that poor guy"—Beck tipped his head in the direction of the server working his way around the room —"like you want to take him outside and beat the shit out of him."

Caleb turned his back to the room and leaned his elbows on the bar. No way would he let his brother know how much he was getting on his nerves. Or how right he was.

"You're full of shit." Caleb shrugged. "I don't even know her, and I could give two shits about some server checking her out."

"Ah, so you *did* notice." Beck reclined on his elbows against the bar, all smug in his marital bliss.

If Caleb didn't think Gwen would kill them both, he'd knock that grin off his brother's stupid face. It wouldn't be the first time they'd thrown down. Growing up in a family with five aggressively rambunctious boys, tussles were a common occurrence.

"Give it a rest, will ya?" Caleb picked at the label on his bottle.

"So, you guys ready?" Thanks to Beck's powerful connections, he knew the purpose behind their current training.

"Yeah, we're beyond ready." They'd been busting their asses running through every possible scenario until things happened instinctively.

Not that it bothered him. Caleb loved everything about being part of the FBI's elite Hostage Rescue Team. Only the best of the best were selected and made it through the demanding training. He would argue it was even tougher for the K9 handlers.

He and Jake were assigned to Gray team, referred to as the support team. It included the other K9 operators and their partners, mobility, medical, and breachers—the guys who got them through the door, wall, roof or whatever else stood in their way. Blue, Gold and Silver teams were all tactical operators. Members of Gray team supported the other teams, based on where they were in the rotation. For this mission, he and his partner would be backing up Gold team. Not that it mattered. Every single member of every single team was highly skilled, and Caleb trusted them to have his and Jake's backs during any operation.

"But, as you know all too well, we can't make a move until we get the *all clear* from higher up," Caleb added, knowing his brother understood his frustration. Waiting around for the bureaucrats to get their heads out of their asses had been one of the reasons Beck bailed on the Bureau.

They had reliable intel that children were being exposed to some pretty dangerous shit at an isolated religious community hidden away up in the mountains of northwest Montana. *Religious community.* What a fuckin' joke. It was a cult, plain and simple.

Two men ran the place. John Proctor, their self-professed religious leader, was, by all accounts, a depraved sociopath with a taste for young girls. His partner, Grady Teague, was a disgraced cop hell-bent on retribution for something that happened to his brother.

"Still no word on the missing girl?" Beck kept his voice low as he glanced surreptitiously around.

"Not a damn thing." They suspected Proctor was connected to her disappearance, but all they had were a few somewhat reliable and chilling rumors. They couldn't do a damn thing without proof.

"Shit," Beck muttered.

"Yeah. Shit." Caleb would never forget how devastated her

mother looked when he'd watched the playback of her interview with a local news station. Her desperate plea for information about her teenage daughter would shatter the hardest of hearts. How awful it must be not knowing where your only child was or if she was even alive.

The parameters of this mission were alarmingly similar to the whole mess with the Branch Davidians. There were a lot of lessons learned as a result of that nightmare. Still, Caleb prayed for a better outcome for this operation.

Beck glanced over and caught Caleb sneaking a look at Dawn.

"Geez, dude. You are pitiful. Come on." He tilted his head. "I'll introduce you to her."

Yes! Caleb did a mental fist pump.

"Nah, I'm good." He stayed where he was and took his sweet time draining his beer.

Beck pointed at Caleb's empty bottle and held up two fingers to the bartender. "Come on, just admit it. You know you're jonesing to meet her."

Hell, yeah, he was, but he wasn't going to let his brother know that.

"Eh, she's not really my type." Which made him sound like the world's biggest dumbass, because seriously, what normal heterosexual male wouldn't want to meet the most beautiful woman in the world?

Beck handed Caleb a beer and shook his head as they clinked the bottoms together. "You really are an idiot, aren't you?" He started ticking off with his fingers. "Number one, she's crazy smart, a doctor. She was working the ER the night we found Gwen. Number two, she's tough as hell. Had to be, since she pretty much raised her kid sister by herself. Three, she provides free medical exams to people here at the shelter. Shall I continue?"

Hold up. Did his brother just say Dawn was at the hospital that horrible night? How the hell had he missed her? And why the hell hadn't his brother introduced him? *Asshole.*

"I get it. I get it." He held up his hand. "She's a brilliant doctor, a freakin' saint, a real goody two-shoes." The hottest thing he'd ever seen on two legs and, sadly, totally wrong for him. "No, thanks. Like I said, not my type."

Just then, a throat cleared behind him.

Caleb closed his eyes on a sigh and his head fell forward. *Crap.* Ready to pay the piper, he straightened from the bar, pasted on a smile before he turned around and came face to face—well, face to top of head, really—with his sister-in-law. Gwen tilted her head way back, like she had to do with most everyone. From the scowl on her cute pixie face and the way she stood with her arms crossed atop her baby bump, he could tell she wasn't pleased. He understood why as soon as he saw his very own Mediterranean mystery woman, the one he'd just mocked, standing next to her.

Crap.

Jake gave an excited yip, as if to brag, *look what I found.* His dog looked much too damn happy and content leaning against her leg.

"Zrádce." Jake's head cocked to the side when Caleb mumbled the Czech word for "traitor."

Looking down at him was the perfect excuse to get a nice, long look at her spectacular legs. Yep, they would be featuring prominently in Caleb's future dreams. Hell, he was already imagining them wrapped around his waist as he ... *Hold the phone!* Now was definitely *not* the time to be having thoughts like that.

He gave Beck a *thanks-for-the-heads-up* kind of look, and his brother just shrugged and tipped back his beer to hide his grin.

"Hey there, Little Bit." Caleb leaned over, gave his sister-in-law a peck on the cheek and wrapped his arms around her.

He hoped using the beloved nickname their father gave her would butter her up. "Congratulations. Everything looks great."

When she didn't immediately return his embrace, Caleb knew he was in trouble. He leaned away and looked down.

Her eyebrow arched up high.

Nope, his masterful strategy of using her nickname failed. If he could see past her tummy, he'd bet she was tapping her foot, too. She wasn't going to make this easy for him. Not like he deserved *easy*—what he'd said *was* pretty jackassy.

He could easily blame it on being tired and beat up, which would be partially true. Mostly, it was because the woman standing next to Gwen, trying unsuccessfully to hide her disdain, managed to do something in a matter of minutes no other woman had ever done. She'd burrowed under Caleb's skin, and he didn't know how to handle it. So he'd acted like an immature jerk instead.

Great fallback, dumbass.

Why would just looking at this woman from across a room make him want to possess her, to keep any other man from having her? Her beauty captivated him, and being this close to her wasn't making it any easier to deny.

"Nice try, dipshit," Beck muttered loud enough for Caleb's ears only.

Then, like a rat fleeing a sinking ship, Beck set his beer on the bar and moved to stand behind his pregnant wife. Arms around her, he leaned her back against his front and kissed the top of her head.

"Now honey, give Caleb a break," Beck said as his big hands massaged her swollen belly.

What is it with these two? Seemed like whenever they were in the same room, they had to have their hands on each other.

"He drove here straight from some serious hardcore training. He can't help it if he's a little tired and cranky."

Tired and cranky?

Caleb glared at Beck. Christ, he made him sound like a toddler who'd missed nap time. Whatever. He would take any help he could get if it meant surviving this encounter unscathed.

"Oh, shoot, Caleb. I am so sorry."

Gwen slipped out of Beck's arms and wrapped hers around Caleb's middle. As much as she could with her tummy wedged between them, anyway.

"When Beck told me you were at training, I guess I didn't realize how difficult it would be." She stepped away, both of her small hands enfolding one of his. Patting. Rubbing. Soothing away hurt feelings. The forlorn look of apology on her face made Caleb feel like an even bigger schmuck.

"Nah, that's no excuse, Gwen." Caleb brushed his finger down her nose, tapped the end.

This petite dynamo slipped into his heart the first time he heard his tough, older brother gush about her. Caleb loved her as much as he did his own brothers and sister. He couldn't let her go on feeling bad just because he'd behaved like a first-class douche.

He snuck a glance at Dawn standing quietly. Listening. Taking it all in. *What is going on in that beautiful head of hers?* Hell, at this point he'd pay cash money just to hear the sound of her voice.

As if she'd heard his thoughts, she spoke for the first time.

"Gwen ... " She flicked a dismissive glance his way, then turned to face his sister-in-law. "You're busy with your family. I'm just going to go upstairs and make a quick house call."

Caleb's heart skipped a beat. God almighty, her voice. Deep and smoky, it stroked across his entire body like warm liquid velvet. Christ, he'd be perfectly happy to stand here and listen to her recite the alphabet.

Wait? What? *Where the fuck did* that *come from?*

He loved women, liked to do a lot of things with them. Talking wasn't generally one of them. And it was messing with his head how badly he wanted to hear his name on her lips.

"Don't be silly." Gwen laid a hand on Dawn's arm. "You're a guest tonight. I never expected you to treat patients. Besides, I want you to meet Caleb."

Finally! He'd been worried she would get away before he had a chance to meet her. And to apologize.

"Dawn." She patted his upper arm. "I'd like to introduce you to Beck's younger brother, Caleb O'Halleran." She smiled from her to him. "Caleb, this is my very good friend Dawn Pannikos."

Nose in the air, Dawn drew her shoulders back as if heading into battle, then turned to Caleb.

He felt like a dick knowing he was responsible for the tension in her gorgeous shoulders and for making her look like she wanted to escape.

He also felt cheated, because the forced smile she gave him didn't sparkle like the one she'd lavished on Jake or even the polite one she'd directed at the asshat server.

She took a deep breath and extended her hand. But only because it was the polite thing to do, and they had a rapt audience. "Nice to meet you."

Did she just roll her eyes? Interesting. One side of his mouth hitched up. Seeing that little bit of sass sneak out from behind that veneer of control only served to pique his interest further.

Thrilled to have an excuse to touch her, he flashed his most charming smile.

"It's nice to meet you, too, Dawn." He enveloped her long,

delicate fingers, their palms met, and a surge of heat scorched up his arm.

Her eyes widened in surprise. Intelligence danced in their mossy green depths, partnered with a kind of wisdom that seemed far beyond her years. A shadowy weariness hovered there as well, and his smile faltered at the sight.

He resisted the unfamiliar urge to pick her up and cradle her in his arms. To take care of her and whisper words of reassurance. Against what, he had no clue. He was pretty sure she wouldn't be receptive to the idea anyway. Instead, he stroked his thumb across her knuckles, doing the only thing he could to let her know she wasn't alone. Which made zero sense.

She cleared her throat, tugged her hand free and turned to Gwen. "If you'll excuse me."

Caleb missed the warmth of her skin and envied Gwen and Beck the affectionate hugs she bestowed upon them.

"I'm just going to grab some supplies from the pantry and take a quick peek in on Mr. Seiler to make sure he's taking care of that foot of his."

Before Gwen could protest further or Caleb could apologize, Dawn walked away without a backward glance.

ABOUT THE AUTHOR

TJ Logan is an award-winning author of romantic suspense anchored by strong themes of Family, Honor, and Loyalty. Her writing journey began one day, back in 2012, when a bunch of strange voices popped into her head. Hoping to exorcise the craziness, she started typing, which simply ushered in more—as if she'd cracked open some sort of portal for fictional characters to charge through.

Those random voices morphed into the O'Halleran family. The family grew with the addition of lovers, friends, neighbors, and co-workers. Voila, the first six books of the O'Halleran Security International (OSI) series was born.

TJ grew up in a military family, lived all over the country and was surrounded by five brothers ... and, amazingly, lived to tell about it. She was also a key member of a team who managed a Secret program for one of the world's top defense companies. All of these things have given TJ an interesting perspective on life. And every bit of it goes into her writing!

Family, Honor and Loyalty aren't just words in a tagline to TJ, they are everything.